WHEN WE TOUCH

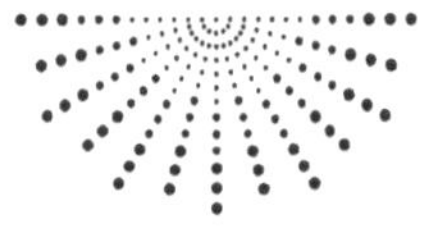

CARRIE ELKS

If there was one thing Becca Hartson hated, it was saying goodbye. One way or another, she'd been saying it for most of her life. First to her mom – who'd died when Becca was only four. She could barely remember that goodbye, but her four older brothers had filled in the painful blanks.

And then one by one they'd left her, too. The eldest – Gray – to become a rockstar, then the twins, Cam and Logan, who went to college and settled down in Boston. And finally Tanner. Her playmate when she was a child and her bête noir as an adult. With only a few years between them, they'd spent most of their lives fighting like cats and dogs.

But she loved him anyway. And saying goodbye to him had been the hardest of all, because it meant she was alone in her childhood home with only her taciturn father and Aunt Gina, her mother's sister who brought up the five Hartson siblings after their mother died, for company.

Yet one by one all her brothers had come back to live in town, making her beyond happy. Especially Tanner.

Even if right now he was driving her crazy.

"Move your hand away from the frosting before I chop it off." She yanked the cake she'd spent two hours decorating out of his grasp. "Why are you here anyway? I have to leave for the distillery in twenty minutes."

Her brother glanced at the Rolex Submariner on his wrist. Sure, he was aggravating, but Tanner Hartson was also rich as heck, thanks to selling his financial tech business a few years earlier. Nowadays he invested in property – it felt like he owned half of their small home town of Hartson's Creek.

"Why are you going to work now? It's nearly seven. You don't work night shifts."

Becca sighed. "It's Nathan's leaving party." Her chest tightened all over again. Yep, she still hated goodbyes. "And this cake is for him. So I'll repeat myself. Why are *you* here?"

"Well, first of all, because I'm the only one of us who's free to check on you tonight." Tanner looked around Becca's small condo. "Is everything okay? Your neighbors been quiet? Anybody causing you problems?"

"Everything's fine." She shook her head, because *seriously*, her brothers drove her crazy. She'd moved out of her childhood home a few months earlier, into a condo she'd saved for all by herself. And it hadn't gone over well with her family.

But she loved the little home she'd made here. With the cost of buying it, she hadn't had much money available to decorate the rooms to her taste. Instead she'd scoured the local markets and thrift shops for furniture and paintings for the walls, draping the sofa with jewel colored embroidered throws and cushions she'd made from soft cashmere sweaters.

The only room she'd furnished from new was the kitchen. It was her baby. The place where she worked out all of her problems and stress. She loved her job at the local whiskey distillery, but it could be overwhelming at times.

Baking sweet, flaky creations was her way of pushing away the anxiety of being an adult.

"I don't like the guy in number eight," Tanner told her. "He's shifty."

"He's almost eighty." Becca shook her head. "You guys have to let go. I'm happy here. I'm safe, my neighbors are friendly and there's no crime here at all. I even let you install those damn locks on the door. Now if that's all you wanted, I need to get out of here."

Tanner leaned on her breakfast bar, showing no intention of leaving. "Actually, there's something else I wanted to ask you."

Becca glanced at the clock on her oven. She was definitely going to be late. "Can you make it quick?"

Tanner pouted. She'd always been jealous of his lips. Full, pink, and perfectly pouty. "I have a favor to ask," he said, lowering his voice as if they were being monitored. "This goes no further, okay?"

Becca tried not to grin. "I could have so much fun with this, but I don't have time. Okay, shoot. What's the favor?"

"Van's pregnant."

"Oh my god!!" Becca squealed and hugged her brother tightly. "Congratulations. That's amazing."

Tanner rubbed her back with his flat palm. "Thanks. She's suffering from morning sickness. Says the only thing she wants to eat is carrot cake. I bought some from the diner, but she just turned her nose up at it. So I… ah… wondered if you could make a cake for her tomorrow."

"Poor Van." Becca frowned with sympathy. "And of course I'll make something. I can have it ready by mid morning." Sure, she'd have to get up early, after a night partying with her workmates. But that was okay, right? "Has she tried anything else to curb the nausea?" she asked. "Maybe you should talk to Gray, remember how sick Maddie got when she was pregnant with the twins."

Tanner paled. "We're not having twins."

Biting down a smile, Becca gently released herself from his embrace. "I know," she reassured, even though twins ran through their family. "But Gray could probably suggest some remedies."

"I'm not telling Gray. If I tell him, all of Hartson Creek will know within a day. And Van will kill me, because I promised to keep it a secret until the second trimester." Tanner sighed heavily. "This being a father thing is hard."

She rubbed his shoulder affectionately. "You're going to be a great father. And I'd love to reassure you, but I have ten minutes before I need to leave and I still have to shower and change."

His hand reached out to touch the cake again.

"Tanner!" She gave him the stink eye. "Go now. Or your baby's going to start life with a one-handed father."

He put both hands up in surrender. "Okay, okay. I'll see you tomorrow, right?"

"Yes, you will. I'll call when the cake is ready."

Tanner kissed her cheek. "You're the best."

She beamed. "Thank you." There was nothing she loved more than seeing her brothers happy, even when they knew how to hit every single one of her buttons. "Now get out of here."

"I'm leaving, I'm leaving. Love you, frog face." Tanner blew her a kiss.

Ugh. She loved him, too. But right now she had a party to get ready for.

———

EVERYBODY WAS GATHERED in the main function room of the distillery when Becca got there thirty minutes later. She shuffled in, the oversized cake box precariously balanced in her arms, her bag slung over her shoulder bumping rhythmically against her hip.

By the time she got to the table and put the box down she was exhausted. Maybe she needed to hit the gym. She'd forgotten to go for at least the last two years.

"Oh wow," the distillery's receptionist, Sandy, breathed, looking over Becca's shoulder as she unclipped the box and gently pulled the cake out. She was such a mother hen, she reminded Becca of her Aunt Gina. "What's inside it?" Sandy asked.

"A triple layer Belgian chocolate sponge," Becca told her. "Nathan's favorite." It was iced with a white chocolate ganache, and topped with dipped chocolate strawberries and chocolate swirls. "I figure if we kill him with sugar he might stay."

Sandy squeezed her shoulder. "We're going to miss him."

Becca swallowed hard. She wasn't going to cry tonight. Not even if her favorite boss was leaving for Tokyo in the morning. Nathan had been the first person to see potential in her when she'd started at the G. Scott Carter distillery straight after college. And over the past five years he'd promoted her several times, until she was one of the senior distillers, and the lead on their latest venture – the International Blend.

"It's good that he has this opportunity, though," Becca said, her voice thick. "He's so excited about going to Japan." He hadn't stopped talking about it for months. The Okamoto Distillery was part-owned by Nathan's family, and had provided a third of the whiskey for their latest International Blend. It was a coup – Japanese distilleries rarely let other businesses share in their products.

"Yeah. And he's been working like a Trojan here for years," Sandy agreed. "He deserves the break. It's about time Daniel came home to take on some of the load."

That was the other thing making Becca's stomach feel like it was taking part in an Olympic gymnastic event. She'd never met Daniel Carter, but from the moment she'd started working here she'd heard of his reputation. He'd worked at the distillery for years, but had left for Scotland a few months before Becca had been recruited. People talked about his impeccable nose for whiskey, his perfectionism, and his no-nonsense attitude. His name was uttered in revered tones in the still rooms of G. Scott Carter. It made Becca nervous as heck, because he sounded the complete opposite to his brother, the lovely, laid-back Nathan.

She smiled at Sandy, who was staring at her expectantly. "It'll be interesting to meet him."

"I expect things will change around here." Sandy nodded.

"Is that for me?" a warm voice asked, tickling her ear. Becca turned to see Nathan standing there, his warm face beaming at her.

"Yep. Freshly made today."

"When did you get the time? You worked until five." He was still smiling. Because that's what Nathan did.

"I made the sponge this morning before work. Then iced it as soon as I got home."

"You shouldn't have put yourself to so much effort. Not that I don't appreciate it, because I do. I'm going to miss your baking." Nathan elbowed her gently.

"I can send treats to you in Tokyo. A little taste of home."

"I'd like that." He tipped his head to the side. "Are you sure I can't persuade you to come work over there with me?"

Becca shook her head. "I can't. I'm needed here." Not at the distillery. But at home. If she wasn't making cakes for somebody in the family, she was babysitting one of her nephews or helping one of her brothers out with an emergency. "But it's tempting, I have to tell you."

His eyes crinkled. "Liar."

She laughed. "I'm not lying." Okay, so maybe she was. Just a little. But she'd made him smile, so that was a win.

Over the years, her friends had asked her if there was more going on between her and Nathan than a boss-employee relationship. But the fact was, the friendship between them was purely platonic. She was used to having older brothers, and he was like an honorary sibling to her. They messed around, teased, and then when they had work to do, they knuckled down to it.

He knew her skills. Encouraged her when she lacked confidence in herself, and made her push herself forward when her natural instincts told her to hang back. It was Nathan who'd suggested her as one of the lead distillers on the International Blend, and it's success had instilled her with a new level of self-assurance.

And now he was leaving.

Her throat tightened. She blinked to stop the tears but they formed anyway. She couldn't cry this early in the evening. The party would go on for hours, and if she started now, she was going to sob all night. Inhaling a ragged breath, she picked up the cake box and put it to the side, swallowing hard to push away the sadness.

"You okay?" Nathan asked her.

"I just need a minute." Another breath in. "I'm going to head to the bathroom, check my makeup."

He patted her shoulder. "It's going to be okay. Daniel's a good guy, he'll see your talent."

She nodded wordlessly. She knew it was going to be fine. It always was. By tomorrow she'd be over this. The goodbyes would be forgotten and she could spend the weekend baking and seeing her family.

But first, she needed to get through tonight.

———

IT FELT like nothing had changed in the six years he'd been gone. The distillery looked exactly the same – the sprawling double high wooden clad exterior fronted by a glass reception, the familiar logo of G. Scott Carter emblazoned in large green lettering.

The evening sky had darkened, but the building was illuminated by downlights, a contrast to the gloom of the mountains rising in the distance.

Daniel Carter touched his credit card to the reader before climbing out of the cab, being sure to add a hefty tip for the driver. Tomorrow he'd pick up the car he'd ordered weeks ago.

But tonight, it was time to reintroduce himself to his distillery.

There was nobody at reception, even though the door was unlocked. He raised an eyebrow, making a note to himself to check the security protocols. Leaving his suitcases behind the desk, he pushed open the door that led to the oversized vaulted room that housed the distillery itself, inhaling sharply to take in the low undertones of mashed barley and yeast that dominated the air.

The equipment was off – the mash tuns that mixed the corn grists and water lay silent. He still stopped by them, checking for any rust or smells that didn't seem quite right. Then he made his way into the next oversized room that housed the wash and spirit stills, their huge copper forms topped by a thick pipe that distillers called the swan neck.

In here he could hear the faintest rumble of conversation and a low thump of music. He'd thought he wouldn't make it to his brother's farewell party, but his flight had landed thirty minutes early, and the baggage handlers had been mercifully fast. So here he was, standing in the distillery he'd left without looking back six years ago, his body exhausted from eight hours travel and more than twenty-four hours without sleep.

Pushing the door open to the office area, the thumping of the bass and the sound of voices got louder. But there was something else there, too. Something lower and softer that made him frown.

Stuttered breaths. Broken gasps.

Somebody was crying.

If he'd have thought it through, he would have walked away from the sound. He didn't do emotions – not if he could help it – and he was certainly the last person who knew what to do when somebody was crying. Nathan was so much better at that. The empathetic brother to his strong, silent type.

But still, his curiosity got the better of him. He walked into the executive corridor that housed the directors' suite. His mother's office door was closed, no light spilling through the frosted window. So was the boardroom, and the office that used to be his own.

Nathan's door was ajar. Daniel's brows pinched together as he reached it, blinking at the sudden rush of light to his eyes.

His gaze clashed with a pair of almond shaped green eyes that seemed to see right through him. They were rimmed red, shiny with tears, thick lashes sweeping down as they blinked at their sudden connection.

It felt as though all the air had left his body. He inhaled sharply to replace it, his gaze dipping to take in the woman's red, swollen lips. Her cheek was pressed against his brother's chest, as Nathan softly stroked her hair.

For a moment none of them moved. Daniel pulled his

eyes from hers, dropping his gaze to her cream diaphanous blouse, the neck low enough to give him a glimpse of the swell of her breasts as they pressed against his brother's shirt. She was wearing jeans, the denim clinging to the curve of her behind like a damn limpet. Her dark hair flowed over her shoulders, shining beneath the strip light in Nathan's office.

And he wanted to laugh, because his brother had somehow landed himself a scorching girlfriend.

The woman pulled away from Nathan's arms, and he looked across the room to the door, Nathan's lips lifting into a grin when he saw Daniel standing there.

"You're early," Nathan said, striding across the room, holding his hand out for Daniel to shake. Daniel slid his palm against his brothers, and then pulled him in for a hug, because even if his brother was a damn dirty dog, he was still so happy to see him.

Even if he was leaving tomorrow.

"My flight landed early," Daniel told him. "I thought I'd come straight here and join the party." He looked over Nathan's shoulder at the pretty woman. She'd turned so her denim-clad behind was resting against Nathan's desk, her hands clasped together as she stared at them both. "I didn't realize you had company. I'll catch up with you later."

He went to back out of the doorway, holding his hands up in a mea culpa sign.

"What do you mean, company?" Nathan asked. The woman hadn't moved an inch. She had a smear of mascara across her cheek, which somehow added to her attractiveness.

She's your brother's girl. Some of us don't go there.

"I interrupted something private. I should leave." Daniel's voice was terse.

The woman smiled at him, her lips trembling. He didn't return it. His unmoving face made her brows pinch together.

"Wait, you think…" Nathan looked back at the woman. "No, you've got it all wrong. There's nothing going on. This is Becca Hartson. One of our distillers. You've seen her before on our video conferences."

Daniel frowned, looking again at the crying woman. She looked nothing like the Becca Hartson he'd seen on his computer screen. That Becca always had her hair in a tight ponytail, and wore the usual G. Scott Carter green polo and loose chinos.

But this Becca? She was damn gorgeous. The kind of woman that would catch his eye no matter where he was.

Yeah, and she's an employee. We don't go there, either.

He looked at Nathan and shook his head. "You're messing with the staff now?" he asked, his voice a low accusing drawl. "Jesus, man, what kind of idiot are you?"

CHAPTER TWO

Three things struck Becca as Daniel Carter stared over his brother's shoulder at her.

The first was that he was a bit of an asshole.

The second? He had a strange Scottish twang to his American accent.

And the final was that he was incredibly good looking, if you liked assholes with weird accents. Which she didn't. Especially when they were staring at her as though she was a piece of chewed up gum they'd scraped off their shoe.

Standing to her full height, a fourth thought struck her. One that made her skin want to shrink back off her bones.

He was her new boss. Dear god, could this get any worse? On the plus side, the tears had dried up from her cheeks. On the minus, she was now being accused of sleeping with the management. And everybody knew that's how rumors started.

"I should go," she muttered, walking across Nathan's office. "People will be wondering where I am."

Her arm brushed against Daniel's as she walked past him,

and he practically jumped to get away from her. "I'll see you back at the party?" she asked Nathan. He grinned and nodded, completely unperturbed by his brother's accusation.

Her cheeks flamed as she walked down the corridor. Reaching for the door, she heard Nathan's voice echo in a low murmur.

"It's not what you're thinking. Seriously."

"I hope not. Because she's a lawsuit waiting to happen. You know better than to mess with staff. No matter how hot they are."

Yep, definitely an asshole. She gritted her teeth and walked away, not wanting to hear any more. Nathan wasn't lying. It *had* been completely innocent on both of their parts. He'd found her sobbing outside the staff bathroom and led her to his office to give her a chance to get control of herself. And sure, he'd given her a hug. Everybody knew Nathan gave the best hugs. He was like a teddy bear, but bigger and with a better smell.

But she also knew how it looked. And she should have thought about that before it happened. Anybody could have walked in on them. She'd worked way too hard to get a negative reputation in the distillery.

On the plus side, she wasn't crying anymore. And as she walked into the function room, she heard dance music pumping out of the speakers on the wall, and saw that her co-workers had moved the tables out of the way and were dancing in the center, shaking their booties like there was no tomorrow.

Painting a smile on her face, she walked over to join them, letting the music fill her mind and chase away the stupid thoughts.

She'd worry about the beautifully angry Daniel Carter on Monday morning. Right now? She just wanted to dance.

———

NATHAN TOOK two cut glass whiskey tumblers from the cabinet in his office and poured a fingerful of G. Scott Carter twenty-one year old malt into each, passing a glass to Daniel.

"Cheers." He held up his glass, and Daniel touched his own against it. "And welcome back."

Daniel's smile was wry. "And bon voyage to you. Do you think we'll ever be in the same country for more than a few days?"

Nathan laughed. "Don't take it personally. Anyway, you were the one that left first." He took a slow sip of the aged whiskey. "And I'm grateful that you've come back. I wouldn't be able to leave if you hadn't."

It was the truth. Nathan was the only reason Daniel had made himself get on that airplane and leave his quiet, easy life in Scotland behind. The reality of being back was just starting to hit him.

"I figure it's your turn. I appreciate you holding the fort down while I was in Scotland." Daniel lifted his glass to his mouth, closing his eyes as the deep, earthy liquor slid down his throat. "Damn, this is good. So what did I miss, apart from your inappropriate relationships with the staff?"

Nathan grinned. He was impossible to rile. "There's nothing going on with me and Becca. I already told you that."

"I notice that you don't call her Miss Hartson."

"That's because she's not sixty years old. And we've been working closely together on the International Blend. Her brother's the face of it, after all."

"I'd forgotten that," Daniel murmured, taking another sip of whiskey. The truth was, he hadn't paid much attention to the International Blend, or anything going on at the US distillery. Partly by choice – the distillery was well established and his mom and brother were easily able to run it –

and partly because Scotland wasn't only two thousand miles away, but a whole different time zone. He knew about the big changes – the new blend, any major investments – from their biannual shareholder meetings. But the minutiae of running the distillery had passed him by. And he let it.

Until now. Because this building and everything that happened in it was all his again.

"So why isn't there anything going on between you?" Daniel asked him. "She's a good looking woman, you're a single guy, and you obviously get along well." He blinked, remembering her moss green eyes. The way they'd shone as she'd stared at him.

The way his body had reacted.

Damn, he needed to get some sleep. Jet lag was messing with his mind.

"Because she's our employee." Nathan shrugged. "And anyway, it isn't like that between us. We're friends. Colleagues. She's good at what she does and I appreciate that. She's the little sister I never had."

"Well at least one of us has managed not to mess up the family business by falling for the wrong person." Daniel ran his finger around the rim of his glass.

"Nina hasn't either," Nathan pointed out, referring to their half-sister. "It's just you and Lawrence that like to complicate things." He tried not to show his distaste as they talked about their older half-brother. Like Nina, he was their late father's child from his first marriage.

"How is Lawrence anyway? You heard from him recently?" Daniel kept his voice steady.

Nathan looked at him carefully. "You really want to know about Lawrence?"

"I want to know if he's going to be a problem now that I'm back and running GSC."

Nathan poured them both another splash of whiskey.

"The last time I spoke to Lawrence was when we were finalizing the marketing spend for the International Blend. He's settled in Charleston. He's not interested in coming to Hartsons Creek or interfering with the business. As long as he gets his profit sharing, he's happy." Nathan lifted his eyebrows. "Or he was. I can't guarantee what he'll do now that you're back. You two seem to enjoy driving each other crazy."

"He's always been jealous of me. Wanted what I have." Daniel lifted an eyebrow. "It's not my fault."

"So you're not the one who pushed yourself until Dad had no choice but to promote you ahead of Lawrence? Or the one who played every sport that Lawrence played, but better?" Nathan shook his head. "You guys have always been deadly rivals. And I know it was encouraged by Dad, but he's gone now. Isn't it time you two made up?"

"There's nothing to make up. We've got nothing in common except half our blood. I'll be civil to him, I always am, but there won't be any picture perfect reunions or Sunday barbecues for us. And I know that disappoints you because you're a romantic at heart, and you wish life was a Hallmark movie." Daniel smiled at his brother, ruffling his hair affectionately. "Sorry, bro. But at least if there are any major explosions, you'll be safely shielded from them in Tokyo."

"Why do you think I'm going?" Nathan muttered, though he couldn't help but grin back at his older brother. "Seriously, just try to get along. For Nina's sake. You know how she hates us bickering."

Daniel lifted his glass. "To complicated families. And spending time with those that don't make you want to carve your balls off with a rusty spoon."

"To us." Nathan raised his own glass. "And to having my

big brother home, even if we're only together for a few hours." His eyes crinkled as he smiled. "It's good to see you, man."

Daniel clinked his glass against Nathan's. "Right back at you."

———

"Okay, it would be really good if you stopped laughing now," Becca said, as Mia spluttered out her coffee, putting her mug on the kitchen island so she didn't spill any more.

"I'm sorry." Mia's eyes were watering, both from choking on her coffee and from the subsequent laughing fit she suffered after Becca told her about meeting Daniel the previous evening. "It's just that I can picture it perfectly. Only you could meet our new boss when you're canoodling with his brother."

"I wasn't canoodling. I was crying and Nathan was giving me a hug."

Mia lifted her eyebrows.

"A completely platonic, non-sexual, friendship hug," Becca added, giving her almost-sister-in-law what she hoped was a withering glare. But it only made Mia laugh harder.

Okay, so maybe it was a bit funny. Or it would be, when Becca got over the embarrassment some time in the next thirty years. She sighed loudly, leaning on the counter as she stared out of the huge glass doors leading to the backyard.

Her brother, Cam, was throwing a football out there with Mia's two boys. The three of them were laughing as Mia's youngest son, Josh, threw the ball as hard as he could at Cam, trying to knock him over.

"Is there no pee wee training today?" Becca asked.

"They just finished. Then came straight back here to play

some more football." Mia smiled softly as she watched her boys play. "If I ever get pregnant, I'm praying for a girl. There's way too much testosterone in this house."

"If you need any pointers on being the only girl in a houseful of boys, I'm your woman." Becca shot her a sympathetic look.

"I don't know how you did it. Four older brothers." Mia's eyes widened. "And all of them so…"

"Alpha?" Becca grimaced.

Mia laughed. "I was going to say forceful. But alpha works. Anyway, enough about our families, I want to know all about our new boss. What's he like?"

Mia and her two sons – Michael and Josh – had moved to Hartson's Creek the previous year. She was the marketing manager at the G. Scott Carter distillery, and had quickly become one of Becca's closest friends.

"It's hard to say," Becca said honestly. "He kept to himself all night." And she had to admit, she wasn't in any hurry to talk to him while the music was pumping and he was leaning on the bar next to Nathan. "He's kind of aloof. Not like Nathan at all. You know how Nathan's always laughing and cracking jokes? I'm not sure I saw Daniel smile once."

Not that she was looking.

Okay, so maybe she looked a little. It wasn't her fault he was a handsome son-of-a-bitch.

"Ah, you'll charm him around to your way of thinking," Mia told her. "The same way you do with everybody."

"You think?" Becca's stomach was still twisting at the thought of having to go into work on Monday and face her new boss. Even if Nathan had emailed her this morning to tell her that he'd explained the situation to his brother and that everything was fine, it had been a terrible first impression to make.

The truth was, she wanted Daniel Carter to like her. Not

just because he was her boss and it was important for her career. But because she *liked* being liked. It made life so much easier.

"Yep." Mia nodded. "I predict you'll have him eating out of your hand by Monday afternoon. By Friday he'll probably be your new BFF. So stop frowning and tell me about last night's party. I'm still bummed I couldn't go. Damn football fundraisers. They spoil everything."

"What spoils everything?" Cam asked, walking through the glass doors. "Hey, Becca." He leaned down to kiss her cheek, then grabbed Mia and pressed his lips against hers. Grabbing a bottle of water from the refrigerator, he half-emptied it with one glug.

"Football does." Mia smiled at him.

"Not true. Football makes everything better." He raised an eyebrow. "Everything okay? You two look deep in conversation."

"Becca was caught in a tryst last night," Mia said, ignoring Becca's annoyed stare. "With her boss. In his office."

Cam's smile melted from his face. "What?" He turned to Becca, his expression full of concern. "Is something going on with you and your boss? Has he been harassing you? Should I go have a word with him?"

"Thanks." Becca rolled her eyes at Mia, before turning back to Cam. "No, there's nothing going on between me and my boss. Or my ex-boss now, if we're being specific. There's no romance, no harassment, and I definitely don't want you knocking on his door to beat him up, okay?"

Cam shrugged. "You're my sister. It's my job to look after you."

"And Gray's job and Logan's job. Not to mention Tanner's," Mia said, still smirking.

Becca rolled her eyes. "And this is why I don't talk to any of you about my love life. I swear when we were younger I only had to mention a boy's name and one of you would scare him off. Do you know how hard it is to date when you have four overprotective older brothers? I'm going to end up an old maid. How do you feel about that?"

"Pretty damn good," Cam said, leaning his elbows on the counter as he finished his water. "I think I'm speaking for all four of us when I say we'd be very happy if you never look at a guy again."

"Stop teasing," Mia said, swatting his arm playfully. "Of course you want Becca to find somebody. You want her to be happy, don't you?"

"Would she be happy if one of us was in jail for beating up a guy who'd hurt her?" Cam asked. Becca and Mia stared at him, their mouths gaping. "I thought so," he said smugly. "So it's better all around if you stay single forever."

Mia shook her head. "Are you being serious right now?"

Cam shrugged nonchalantly. "Kinda."

"Then go back outside and play football. Leave us to our girl talk. The last thing Becca needs is you cramping her style any more."

Cam grinned and crushed the bottle, throwing it into the recycling can. "Whatever," he said, lifting Mia's hand to kiss her palm. "I'll make us some lunch in an hour." He glanced at Becca. "You staying?"

She shook her head. "I gotta babysit for Logan and Courtney this afternoon." And she'd already delivered Van's carrot cake on her way over here for crisis talks with Mia. Just another busy family Saturday.

"Okay, sis." He kissed the top of her head. "You sure you don't want me to have a chat with this guy?"

"I'm sure. Anyway, he'll be on a plane to Tokyo in approximately..." she glanced at her watch, "two hours. So there goes your opportunity to ruin my life."

"I wouldn't bank on it," Mia muttered. "Cam has a lot of frequent flyer miles."

He laughed and headed back out of the door, shouting to Josh for the ball.

Becca let out a sigh, resting her chin in her hands. "Sometimes I hate having big brothers."

CHAPTER THREE

*B*ecca arrived at work on Monday morning all bright and breezy. She'd even made an apple and pecan cake to cheer everybody's day up. And then she'd spotted her new boss walking across the still room floor and she'd smiled and waved at him.

And he'd ignored her. Completely

Giving him the benefit of the doubt – because maybe he was short sighted or something – she'd walked out from behind the spirit still and tried again, calling out his name.

"Hi! It's Becca. We met on Friday." She'd twisted her lips into what she hoped was an awkward-yet-endearing grimace. "Have you managed to get over the jet lag yet?"

And he'd given her a nod. *A nod!* Then he'd stalked across the still room to the far door that led to the offices, leaving her standing there, her nose wrinkled up, her lips all mashed together, and a hopeful puppy-dog look in her eyes.

Yup. He hated her. Okay, so maybe hate was a strong word. He obviously disliked her, despite Nathan's attempts to smooth things over. Even worse, she'd watched one by one as each distiller, then each head of department was called in to see him in his office.

But her name hadn't been called at all.

"He's going to fire me," she whispered to Mia as they stood in the staff kitchen that afternoon, sipping their coffee and eating the cake she'd made. All the women working at GSC were part of a coffee club, and Becca had negotiated a discount from a local café that delivered twice a day.

"You're not going to get fired," Mia said, shaking her head at Becca's dramatics. "He'll call you in at some point. If not today then tomorrow. He's busy, that's all. And as you said, he's jet lagged. That explains him not noticing you this morning. He seemed all right when I met with him. Less overtly enthusiastic than Nathan, but he knows his stuff. He asked some really pertinent questions. So stop panicking that he hates you."

"I practically jumped in front of him and waved my arms. And all I got was a nod. That wasn't jet lag, it was scorn."

"Maybe he takes a while to warm up to people. We're so used to Nathan, and Daniel's bound to be different. Give him a few days."

Becca picked up another piece of cake, then put it back down again. She was jittery enough, she didn't need any more sugar. "Was he cold with you?"

Mia wrinkled her nose, as though she was trying to think. "I don't know. He's professional. And there was no real small talk. But he smiled and shook my hand when I introduced myself."

"He actually smiled?" Becca asked. "Because I was starting to wonder if it was a physical impossibility."

Mia laughed. "You're being paranoid. He's fine. A change from Nathan, but fine. Now go back to work and stop eating cake before you get a sugar high."

"Too late." Becca picked up the chunk she'd abandoned

and stuffed it into her mouth, crumbs sticking to her lipstick. "The only way to deal with my paranoia is to eat my feelings."

When they'd finished their break, Mia walked back to her office in the administration corridor, and Becca turned right to head back to the distillery rooms.

"Becca?" a low voice called out. She looked up, breathing a sigh of relief when she saw who it was.

"Hi, Joe."

He was one of GSC's three engineers. If something went wrong with a still or a mash tun, he was always the guy she called.

"I just had a piece of your cake. It was delicious." He grinned at her. "I was wondering, would you take a commission? It's my wife's sixtieth birthday next month, and I'd love to surprise her with a cake. I'd pay, of course."

"You don't have to pay me. I'd love to make her a cake. Did you say she was sixty?" She smiled at him. "What are you, her boy toy?"

Joe gave a low chuckle. "This is why I like you. Even though you came to my sixtieth birthday party last year and know full well I'm older than her."

"I thought it was your fortieth," she said, her eyes twinkling at him. "Did I even get you the right card?"

Someone cleared their throat. One glance at Joe, whose cheeks had pinked up at her compliment, told Becca it wasn't him. Joe looked over her shoulder and smiled, and a shiver wracked down Becca's spine.

"Mr. Carter," Joe said. "It's good to have you back. Was it me you wanted to talk to?"

Becca froze. She couldn't have turned to look if she wanted. Her spine would have cracked or something.

"Thanks, Joe. No, it's Miss Hartson I was looking for. That's if she can spare me a couple of minutes."

Joe didn't notice the undertone in Daniel's voice at all. Instead, he smiled again. "Of course." He patted Becca's arm. "She's the best. As gorgeous on the inside as she is on the out. Take care of her." He winked at Becca. "I'll email you the details for the cake later."

Becca nodded. "Fine," she managed to squeak. "Thanks."

Inhaling a ragged breath, she forced her feet to move because her spine still wasn't playing ball, and turned to look at Daniel.

He was only inches behind her. Close enough that she had to lift her head to look him in the eye. He was staring down at her with dark eyes, his brows pulling together. Becca breathed in and immediately regretted it because he smelled way too good. Warm and spicy, like a pine forest on a hot day. She smiled at him, and was completely unsurprised when he didn't smile back, because, *ha*, she'd anticipated that.

He could play the moody Heathcliff-esque card if he wanted to. Sure, he was good looking if you liked guys who filled out their expensive blue cotton shirts perfectly, unbuttoned at the collar to reveal a strong neck.

But his defined Adam's apple and sprinkling of dark hair at the top of his chest didn't affect her. Not one little bit. She judged people on personality, not looks, and so far Daniel Carter hadn't indicated he even had one.

"You're very friendly with the staff," he said as they walked toward the executive corridor.

Why was it that everything he said felt like a criticism? Becca kept her voice steady. "You say that as if it's a bad thing." She glanced up at him from the corner of her eyes. He was facing straight ahead, his broad shoulders pushed back.

"I find it's better to keep a distance," he told her. "The higher you climb, the more important it is to define the difference between you and the people who work for you.

You can't be everybody's best friend and their manager, too."
He opened the door to his office, stepping aside to let her
walk in first.

"Maybe there's a middle ground," Becca said. Because
there was no way she wanted to be like Daniel.

His expression was unreadable. "Take a seat," he said,
pointing at the chair in front of his desk. His office was
completely different to Nathan's. No mass of papers strewn
across the desk, no photos of his family and friends on every
surface. Just a laptop and a phone on his desk, along with a
glass of water.

Becca sat in the chair he'd indicated and reached up to
check that her hair was perfectly pulled into her bun. She
found it so much easier if she kept her thick locks tied back
while she was at work. Spending half your day with your
head bent over a still or a mash tun meant you got hot and
bothered. And it was so much easier to tuck into a plastic
cap.

Daniel walked over to a cabinet on the wall and pulled
out a bottle of the International Blend Becca had been
working on for the past year and a half, along with two small
tasting glasses. Without saying a word, he poured a glug of
whiskey into each, passing one to her.

"Taste it."

Becca blinked. "I've just had a cup of coffee," she told him.
"I'm not sure my tongue's ready for it."

"I know. I saw the coffee being delivered. How many cups
do you drink a day?"

"That's a personal question."

He shook his head. "It's a professional question. You're
one of my distillers. The quality of your taste is my business."

"I drink two, maybe three a day."

"And you eat a lot of cake, too. Do you have a sweet
tooth?" His voice was low.

Becca pressed her teeth together. The way he looked at her was unnerving. It felt like being pulled into the principal's office when she hadn't done anything wrong. "I don't eat a lot of cake, I *make* cakes," she said, refusing to pull her gaze from his. He couldn't know she'd just stuffed a huge slice down her throat. "There's a difference."

He pushed the glass toward her. "Taste it."

She lifted the tumbler to her lips and let the whiskey cover her tongue. Daniel did the same, his gaze set on hers as the dark amber fluid passed over his full lips. She felt like she was in some kind of battle, but she had no idea for what.

"Tell me how it tastes." His voice was low.

"It's sweet. A little hint of vanilla. I can taste the warmth of the scotch and the honeyed notes from the Japanese whisky." She looked up, her brows raised. She and Nathan had worked on the International Blend for over a year. It had taken all of his diplomacy to get their sister distillery in Tokyo to agree to the blend. And of course, Daniel's distillery in Scotland had provided the Scotch. Both of those, along with the whiskey produced here at GSC formed the body of the new product.

"Do you like it?"

She nodded. "Of course I do. I worked on the blend with Nathan."

"And you think it's the best blend it could possibly be?"

Her chest tightened. "I... I think so." She hated the way she felt uncertain. They'd all been so proud of the International Blend. Becca's eldest brother, Gray, led the marketing campaign, and she'd even featured in the long form adverts they'd run in the movie theaters.

"It's not."

"Okay." The air wooshed out of her. *Asshole.*

"It's too smokey. You needed to have less of the Scotch in there. It overpowers the softer notes in the blend. There's no nuance to it, and it's too sweet. That's why I asked you about your sweet tooth."

"Nathan approved it," Becca pointed out. "And your mother did, too."

"They both have good taste. But as the lead on the blend, it was your job to make sure it was perfect. Not theirs."

Becca pressed her teeth into the soft skin inside her cheek. She'd been so proud of the blend, and so excited that she was the lead distiller. "Yes." She nodded. "It was my job. I thought I'd done my best."

"Your best isn't good enough if it isn't perfect. There's no half assing this, Miss Hartson."

She felt her hackles rise. "I'm not half-assing anything. I love my job. I'm good at it. You can check my last review if you want to see all the commendations I've received for my work."

"From my brother," he murmured. Her chest tightened even more.

What the hell was he insinuating? "Yes. He was my boss."

"And now I am." He raised a brow. "And I'm not Nathan."

Yeah, well that was perfectly clear. Nathan was a warm, funny guy who made working here enjoyable. His older brother? He was…

Ugh. He wasn't Nathan. That was for sure.

"How old are you?" he asked, leaning back on his chair as though he didn't have a care in the world.

"Twenty-six." Her neck was aching from keeping her head so upright.

"You're very young to be the lead on any product. It takes years to train your taste. To understand how a tiny change in the type of water or grain can make a massive change in how the whiskey matures."

"Nathan thought I was capable enough."

Daniel gave a half-nod. "Yes. He did." Pulling her glass

back toward him, he stood and took them over to the wet bar on the far side of his office. "Okay, you can go."

Becca bit her lip. "Don't you want to hear what I'm working on at the moment?"

"I know what you're working on." His back was still to her. Beneath the blue cotton of his shirt, she could see the ripple of his shoulder blades as he ran the glasses beneath the faucet.

She stood, waiting for him to turn around so she could say goodbye, but he picked up a towel to dry his hands, then placed the bottle of GSC International Blend back into the cupboard, never once turning to look at her.

"I'll head back to the stills then," she said. Finally, he turned, and he gave her the slightest of nods. She flashed him a smile that she wasn't sure even registered, as his own lips remained pressed together.

"Bye." She left his office, and immediately screwed her face up, letting out a silent scream as she walked back toward the administration offices. When she closed the door to the executive corridor behind her, she banged her head against the glass center.

He definitely hated her. But on the plus side, the feeling was fast becoming mutual.

Daniel Carter was the most annoying, aggravating, rude man she'd ever met.

It was just her luck to have him as her new boss.

CHAPTER FOUR

"*O*ur finances are a mess."

Daniel's mother looked up from her desk, her lips curling into a smile when she saw him standing in the doorway to her office. At sixty years old, Eliana Scott Carter was still a striking woman. She'd let her hair grow naturally white, and always wore it in a low chignon, the color striking against her uniform of black dresses and jackets.

Since the death of her husband – Daniel's father – seven years earlier, she'd been the head of GSC Distilleries, though over the years both Nathan and Daniel had taken on more of the operations.

"They're not a mess," she said, the smile still playing at her lips. "They're just not up to your standards."

"Or yours."

She lifted an eyebrow. "There are things that could be improved, certainly, but we're not in dire straits."

"Cashflow is down."

"That's because we've spent a lot of money in creating and marketing the International Blend. Things will improve now that it's on the market." She nodded at the dark leather chair opposite her desk. "Sit down, darling. Tell me about your day. Are you jet lagged?"

"I've been back since Friday. I'm fine." He sat down anyway. Truth was he felt exhausted. Not just from the time difference –it was sometime around midnight in Scotland – but from spending the whole day talking to employees, going through the finances, and trying to work out exactly what the situation was with the distillery. And with each new piece of information he found, the situation only looked worse. They'd overextended themselves on a new blend that was far below the standards GSC was known for.

He blamed himself. He was the one who'd left Nathan to run things, when his brother was too young.

"You look tired," his mom said softly. "It must be strange to be back."

He gave her a half-nod. "It's strange but weirdly familiar. Like nothing's really changed."

A smile flashed across her lips. "But *you* have."

He tipped his head to the side. "Have I?"

"You're less…" She sighed. "I don't know. Less agitated, I guess. It was understandable, after everything that happened. But I'm glad to see you happier."

Daniel nodded, his jaw tight. "We need to talk about the future of this place."

"Isn't that something we should save for our next board meeting?" She closed her laptop, her red-painted lips curling into a smile. "Any decisions need to be agreed to by Lawrence and Nina, after all."

Daniel's throat dried at the thought of his half-siblings. When their father died, he left each of the siblings a quarter of his shares in the business. His mother owned the other half – inherited from her own father. Technically, if Nathan and Daniel teamed up with their mother, they could outvote their half siblings. But Eliana preferred consensus to division.

"Do they really?" The thought of talking to his half siblings made him want to head right back to Scotland. Not that Nina ever did anything to hurt him. She was just a reminder of Lawrence.

His mom sighed. "I know you and Lawrence don't see eye-to-eye. I blame myself for that. And your father. But he's still your brother, and he has a big interest in this business."

"He's too busy playing golf to care what's going on here."

Eliana clicked her tongue. "If you want to make changes, you're going to need to persuade him. And Nina. Not to mention Nathan. I know you don't agree with everything he's done here, but he's kept the business going. If you go in head first you're going to hurt him."

"I know." Daniel leaned back in his chair and ran his fingers through his hair. The last thing he wanted to do was make his younger brother feel bad. Of all his siblings, Nathan was the one he cared for the most. The one he'd grown up protecting from their father's incessant demands. "But something needs to be done. We need to think about the future. I understand the International Blend was part of that." And the least he said about that, the better. "But we also need to look at our super premium brands. Anything we do now won't mature for at least seven years. This is a long term business, it needs constant planning."

"And that's why I'm glad you're back. We need you, darling." She stood and smoothed the wrinkles from her dress. "Now, how about we stop talking about business and you take your mother out for dinner? We have a lot to catch up on."

———

"TELL me you're making another carrot cake right now," Van said with a plea in her voice, squinting her eyes on the tablet screen, and leaning in until her nose was almost touching the camera. Becca was FaceTiming with her sister-in-law from her tiny kitchen. On days like these, even though she'd moved into her condo months ago, she still hadn't gotten used to being alone.

Sure, most of the time having her family constantly checking up on her drove her crazy, but right now she needed some company. Anything to stop her from thinking about her meeting with Daniel Carter.

"It's not carrot cake. I'm making cheese scones," she told Van, giving her an apologetic look.

"Cheese what?"

"Scones. They're like a cross between a muffin and a biscuit. I found the recipe online." Sure, she'd happened to Google sugar-free baking and Scottish recipes. But it had nothing to do with her moody-as-hell boss with a hatred of sugar.

Pure coincidence.

"There's no chocolate in them?" Van asked.

"Nope. No sugar, either."

"What the hell? Are you ill? Have you undergone a personality transplant?" Van laughed. "I don't think you've ever made something without sugar before."

"I've made bread."

"Yeast needs sugar," Van pointed out.

"You know a lot about baking for somebody who hates going near an oven," Becca said, shaking the flour from her hands. "And I thought food made you feel sick."

"Your food doesn't." Van smiled sweetly at her. "Your cakes always make me feel better."

"Have you already finished the carrot cake I made you?" Becca knew when she was being flattered for a reason.

"I might have. It's the only thing I can keep down, so I've been eating it for lunch and dinner. I figure it's got grains and vegetables in it, so it has to be good for me, right?"

Van was sitting on an easy chair on her porch. The setting sun was tinting her face with an orange hue, her golden hair glistening beneath its dying rays.

"How are you feeling?" Becca asked softly, running her hands under the tap.

"Tired. Sick as a dog. And I hate your brother."

Becca laughed. "Which one?"

"All of them. But especially Tanner. If it wasn't for his killer sperm I wouldn't be in this situation."

"Can we avoid any talk of how you got into this situation, please?" Becca wrinkled her nose. "I don't want to have nightmares tonight." Her face softened as she looked at her tablet screen. "And it'll be worth it in the end. You should talk to Maddie or Courtney; they both have experience with pregnancy after all."

"I will. I just want to wait a few more weeks. Tanner and I agreed not to tell anybody until the second trimester."

"He told *me*," Becca pointed out.

"Ah, but we always let you into our secrets," Van said warmly. "Remember when we used to drag you along on our adventures?"

Van and Tanner had been best friends as kids. The two of them had been known in Hartson's Creek for being practical jokers, always pulling off antics that drove the townsfolk crazy. Sometimes they'd let Becca tag along, her tiny stick legs struggling to keep up with them as they ran away from the scenes of their crimes.

"I remember. And I was always the first to be caught."

"Yeah, but you used to charm whoever caught you. One little cheeky Becca smile and all was forgiven. You could talk yourself out of anything."

Becca let out a lungful of air. "I wish I still could." The memory of Daniel Carter's stupidly pretty mouth twisted into a scowl flashed through her mind. She'd spent the afternoon ruminating on their meeting. And as soon as she'd gotten home she'd poured herself another glass of the GSC International Blend and let the earthy liquid swill around her tongue. It still tasted good. More than good. But the annoying man was right, the flavor held a little too much smoke.

It wasn't perfect. And that knowledge felt like a dagger stabbing at her chest.

That's why she was baking now. She'd tried sitting in front of her TV watching Netflix, but her mind kept wandering back to their meeting. Baking always made her feel more zen. The combination of measuring the right quantities, along with mixing everything together, helped her to zone out.

"What's up?" Van asked, her voice low. "You look sad."

"I had a meeting with my new boss today. He hates the new blend."

Van's eyes widened. "Nathan's brother? Mia told me about him."

It wasn't unusual for everybody in the family to talk about everybody else. Becca guessed that's why Van and Tanner had sworn her to secrecy about their pregnancy.

"He doesn't like me. Said I had a sweet tooth."

Van looked like she was biting down a grin. "Of course he likes you. *Everybody* likes you."

"Who doesn't like Becca?" Tanner asked, leaning over Van so his face was looming large on the screen.

"Nobody," Becca muttered. The last thing she needed was for her brothers to get wind of her meeting with Daniel. She wouldn't put it past them to go to the distillery heavy handed and strong arm him into apologizing. The thought of it was mortifying.

"This is girl talk," Van said, snatching her phone back from Tanner. "I thought you were watching football."

"End of the second quarter." Tanner smirked. "Come on, who've you upset, Bec? Want me to beat them up?"

"No, she doesn't," Van said, rolling her eyes at her husband. "And if she did, she'd ask Cam first. He's got way more muscles than you."

"Hey, I resent that." Tanner pouted.

"You're the brains of the family," Van murmured, inclining her head to kiss Tanner's lips. "That's why I love you." She looked back at Becca. "And you're the heart. Don't let this get you down. You'll have him eating out of your hands in no time, I promise."

"Who'll be eating out of her hands?" Tanner frowned. "I don't want any guy touching Becca's hands. Especially not with his mouth."

"One of the engineers at work asked me to make him a cake for his wife," Becca said quickly. "I forgot to confirm it with him. It's all good."

"Oh." Tanner looked bored. "Okay. I thought it might be juicier than that."

Becca shook her head. "Sorry to disappoint."

The timer pinged, telling her that the first batch of scones were ready. "I gotta go. My scones are ready."

"If there's any of those left tomorrow evening, I could probably stomach one," Van said, giving Becca a hopeful smile.

"I'll drop some around on my way home from work." Becca blew her a kiss. "I'll speak to you later. Take care of growing that baby."

"Love you." Van ended the call, and Becca slid her hands into her oven mitts, pulling the golden brown drop scones out of the oven. The smell of mature cheese and pastry filled her nostrils and made her stomach growl, reminding her she'd not eaten tonight.

Pulling off a chunk, she blew on it, before putting it in her mouth. It was fluffy on her tongue, but also deep and savory. It made her stomach growl with delight.

Sweet tongue? Ha! She'd show Daniel. Maybe she'd even leave one of these little babies on his desk. What guy didn't like being baked for?

Miserable ones, with faces like thunder, that's who. Ugh, she really wasn't looking forward to tomorrow.

CHAPTER FIVE

*S*he hadn't even gotten to work yet, but it was already turning out to be a *very* bad day. It started with sleeping through her alarm. She'd set it thirty minutes earlier than usual, determined that today would be the day when she actually did some YouTube yoga before work. She'd arrive all relaxed and limber and Daniel Carter's jibes would bounce off her like a tennis ball on a trampoline.

Great plan. Except her body decided that six-thirty was way too early to do anything but turn over and keep snoring, as she drooled onto her pillowcase. So when she finally opened her eyes, she had to make a breathless dash to the shower. Then, with one towel wrapped around her hair and the other around her body, she yanked open the closet door to discover she didn't have a clean polo shirt to wear.

Monday night was laundry night. Yet she'd spent yesterday evening covered in flour and fuming about Daniel's description of her sweet tongue.

Yanking clothes to the floor, she eventually found a clean white blouse. She had no white lingerie to go with it, but at the bottom of her drawer she found a black lace bra that would have to do. The blouse was thick enough for the undergarment not to show through too much.

The parking lot was half full when she'd arrived. She pulled into a space near the front entrance and rushed around to the trunk, sighing when she saw the scone box had turned over and slid to the back. It was her fault – she'd taken a couple of corners way too fast in her haste to get to work on time. Gritting her teeth, she rolled onto her tiptoes, her fingers outstretched to gain purchase on the box.

And then she heard a pop.

She froze in place and looked down at her blouse. The top button had flown off, landing on the black interior of her trunk. The fabric gaped open, revealing the scalloped lace edge of her bra as it barely covered the swell of her breasts.

Dammit!

Taking a deep breath in, she attempted to center herself. Okay, so she'd arrived at work with her half-dry hair flowing wildly around her shoulders and her blouse practically open to her breasts. But it was salvageable. Sandy would have a sewing kit. Like a Girl Scout, she was always prepared.

It'd take five minutes to sew the button back on in the bathroom and tame her hair into submission. Then she could start today all over again with the zen mindset her morning yoga was supposed to give her.

In the meantime, she'd use the box of scones to cover herself up. Sure, she had to squeeze her arms against her side and lift her hands to a stupid height, but it was better than flashing the entire workforce of GSC.

The double glass doors swished open and she stepped into reception, opening her mouth to ask Sandy for a needle and thread.

And then she shut it again, because Sandy wasn't alone.

Lounging on the reception desk, his dark tailored pant-clad legs stretched out to the floor, was Daniel Carter.

And he was laughing. *Actually laughing.* Not grimacing or glowering or shaking his head. Instead, there was a weird noise that sounded almost like a chuckle as his eyes sparkled and he said something to Sandy, who giggled back.

Becca hugged the box closer to her chest. She'd make a run for the bathroom and message Sandy from there. But as she moved her feet to the left to head for the still room door, two heads turned to look at her.

"Becca. What have you got there?" Sandy asked, a smile still lifting her painted lips. She turned to look at Daniel. "Did you know our Becca is an amazing baker? We call her the sugar queen."

Thanks, Sandy.

Daniel wasn't smiling any more. Instead, he was staring straight at her with those killer blue eyes. "I'd heard."

"Come over here and show us what you have," Sandy said. "I swear every time you bring food in I put on another pound. But it's worth it."

"That'll be the sugar," Daniel said. He looked Becca up and down and she tried not to react. "Okay, let's see what you've got."

"Actually, I need to go and do someth—"

Daniel reached for the cake box, his long fingers wrapping around the lid. Becca tightened her grasp and tried to take a step back, but his hold was surprisingly tight, stopping her movement.

Panicked, she tried to yank the box back again, but there was no give at all. Daniel's brows knitted, his grasp on the box loosening, right as her own fingers slipped on the plastic and the box tumbled to the floor.

"Oh my!" Sandy called out, standing up behind the desk.

Becca didn't need to look down to know another button had flown off her blouse. She could feel the rush of cool air against her skin. Her breath caught in her throat as she somehow brought her gaze to Daniel's.

And he was staring straight at her chest.

"Fu—" His eyes were dark. "Sorry." He blinked, thick lashes sweeping down. His cheeks were as pink as Becca's. But then his gaze locked on hers, holding it for a long, silent moment.

And she felt something weird. Her skin was all warm and tingly. Still, she couldn't look away. It felt like the world had narrowed to the size of a pin, containing only the two of them.

He ran the tip of his tongue along his bottom lip, and the movement made her heart clammer against her ribcage. Every nerve ending she had stirred and tingled, her body so aware of his.

His jaw was set, as though he was gritting his teeth, but their connection held strong. As though neither of them wanted to look away. Maybe they couldn't.

Why did he have to be so attractive? And so angry?

Slowly, he reached out, pulling the gaping edges of her blouse together, covering her exposed flesh, his fingers burning against her skin. Her flush deepened as she felt her nipples harden in reaction.

Daniel's eyes flashed with recognition. As if he knew the affect he was having on her.

With one hand still holding her blouse closed, he reached for her own, lifting it until her fingers could take his place. Then he stepped back, inhaling sharply before dipping down to pick up the box of scones, turning to put them on the counter as Sandy leaned down and searched through the desk drawers for her emergency kit.

What the hell just happened? Becca blinked, because she felt like she was floating. She had to look down to make sure her feet were still firmly touching the ground.

"I found it!" Sandy called out. Her expression held no clues as to whether she could sense the tension between Becca and Daniel. "Ooh, are they cheese scones?" She'd lifted the lid off the plastic box.

"Yeah. No sugar." She raised a brow at Daniel.

Was that a smirk on his lips? It was hard to tell. It could have been a new version of his scowl. He was so aggravating. How could he be so calm when she felt like she'd just been hit by a truck?

"Can I take another one for break time?" Sandy asked.

"Sure." Becca nodded tightly. The tension was slowly draining out of her. "Take one home for Marty, too, if you'd like."

"He'd love that. He's always asking me what you've been baking. That man has a hollow leg." Sandy smiled over at Daniel. "You should try one. They smell amazing."

"I'm watching what I eat." His voice was low.

Against her will, Becca's gaze moved to him again. He was all lean lines and thick muscles. Not an ounce of fat to be seen.

"Don't be silly." Sandy laughed. "Here, take one."

Daniel glanced at Sandy affectionately, taking a napkin-wrapped scone from her hand. Becca's brows pinched together. He was affectionate now? Did he even know that emotion?

Then he turned on his heel and walked toward the still room, his gait easy and smooth, unlike Becca's heart rate.

"There you go," Sandy said, walking around the reception desk to hand Becca the sewing kit. "Why don't you go tidy yourself up and I'll take the scones to the kitchen for you? We don't want to give anybody else an eyeful." Her eyes crinkled. "Though it's a very pretty eyeful. That bra is to die for."

"Thanks." Becca managed a grimace as Sandy handed her the kit. With a sigh, she hurried to the bathroom.

She'd already managed to flash her boss and she hadn't even started her work day. One thing was for sure – it was going to be a long day.

———

THERE WAS something wrong with him. A bug or a virus he'd picked up on the flight back from the UK. It was the only explanation for the way he'd behaved in reception.

Daniel leaned on his desk, staring at the cheese scone like it was the holy grail. He'd set it there ten minutes earlier when he'd basically ran away from Becca Hartson like he was in the playground and thought she had cooties. Jesus Christ, he needed to pull himself together.

It would help if every time he blinked he didn't see the soft curve of her breast beneath the lacy fabric of her bra. Or think of how warm and inviting her skin looked.

Damn. He needed to stop this. She was his employee.

He was a damn hypocrite, lusting after a woman who was too young and too wrong and who clearly thought he was an asshole. He dropped his head into his hands and breathed out heavily. Coming back here was a bad idea. He'd known it even when he'd agreed with his mom that Nathan deserved an adventure, and that he'd cover for Nathan the same way his brother had covered for him.

He should have stayed in Scotland. Life was easy there. Predictable. And he didn't go around getting hard-ons at the sight of the female body.

His stomach turned at the memory. He hated himself right now. Had she noticed the effect she had on him? For a moment, she'd stared right back at him, her eyes wide, her lips slightly parted, her chest heaving in a way he was trying really hard not to think about. And he'd wondered if she could feel the spark he'd been feeling.

No she couldn't because there was no damn spark. It was just jet lag. That was all. Next time he'd be on his guard. Walk away without even looking.

Next time? Dream on, man.

Grunting with irritation at his own damn thoughts, he pulled the cheese scone toward him, lifting it and inspecting the pastry as though it was something precious. It was lighter than he'd expected. When he tore a piece of the golden crust between his fingers he could see how fluffy it was inside.

Fluffy and fragrant. The aroma of cheese wafted over him, making his stomach gurgle in a reminder that he hadn't eaten breakfast this morning, having chosen to take a run instead.

Parting his lips, he pressed the morsel onto his tongue and had to stop himself from moaning. Soft and savory, it filled his senses, and before he even realized he'd finished half the scone.

Opening his eyes, he pushed the rest of the pastry away, disgusted with himself. He'd eaten it like he'd stared at her. With a hunger that couldn't be sated.

Shaking his head, he picked up the remaining portion of the scone and threw it in the trashcan. He wasn't going to eat the rest no matter how good it tasted. And he wasn't going to stare at Becca Hartson and wonder what her warm skin would feel like against his fingertips.

He was better than this. He'd be aloof and calm. He knew how to separate work and pleasure.

Standing, he caught a reflection of himself in the glass of his drinks cabinet. His hair was messed up, thanks to the raking of his fingers. He smoothed it back and straightened his collar, pushing his shoulders back.

She was a distraction, that was all. Like an annoying fly he could easily bat away. He had a business to run. To save, even. And it was going to take all his concentration to do it.

CHAPTER SIX

"This is going to involve a lot of investment," his mom said, reading the figures Daniel had printed off for her.

"I know. But we can't afford not to. Either we move forward or we die. You know that. The International Blend was always going to be a Band-Aid. A short-term fix. We need to plan a new product, and start working on it now. Using only the very best ingredients." Daniel had spent all week planning this out. Investigating the options, stalking the competition, all the while knowing that cashflow was tight thanks to the overspend on marketing. He loved his brother, but damn the man wasn't great at figures.

People, yeah. Numbers, no way.

Eliana nodded, her delicate fingers holding the printed paper. "You're right. I'd hoped the blend would be enough but..." She sighed heavily. "Is a single malt really the way to go? The investment will be huge. Sourcing barley, building a maltings, and then there's the springwater. It'll be hugely expensive to tank in."

"It's the best. There's no point in doing this unless I can

source the best water. We both know it's the surefire way to making a great whiskey." He'd learned that in Scotland, where they'd used the ice cold water from the mountains, filtered through volcanic rock and rich in minerals. It had been on their doorstep there, where the distillery was nestled into the side of the foothills, and the water flowed directly into their huge wells.

Here it would take either pumping the water from a source or having it brought in tankers. A third option – to build a distillery next to the water source, but that was too costly.

The idea of trying to reproduce a Scotch single malt here in GSC had come to him yesterday. Creating a true artisan blend that was brewed using the traditional Scotch methods, rather than the American way. There were only a few distilleries in the US doing it, and GSC had the edge of his experience.

He could make this work, if he had the investment.

Releasing the paper, his mom pushed it back toward him. "You know what you need to do."

"Persuade Lawrence and Nina." Nathan would agree, he knew that well enough. His brother was always on his side.

His mom gave him a soft smile. "Use your charm. I know it's in there somewhere."

"Charm might work on Nina."

"But not Lawrence." She sighed. "Can't the two of you bury the hatchet once and for all."

"I'm not the one who did the dirty on his half-brother," Nathan reminded her. "That's all on Lawrence."

"It was so long ago." She reached out to squeeze his hand. "When was the last time you two spoke?"

"Before I left for Scotland." It wasn't so much speaking as shouting at each other. Daniel blinked the memory away.

Eliana nodded, running her finger along her bottom lip.

"Maybe you should go to Charleston. Take Nina and Lawrence through the plans face to face. In person is always better than video. Maybe it'll give you the chance to build some bridges, too."

"What happened to me never talking to him again? I thought you disliked Lawrence as much as I do."

A ghost of a smile passed her lips. "I disliked what he did to you, but I still love your brother. I also know how much you love this business. If it takes charming Lawrence to get what you need, then that's what you should do. I'm all for being pragmatic." She squeezed his fingers again. "And maybe I'm sentimental, too. He's still your brother, even after everything that's happened."

Daniel sighed and slid the paper back into the file folder. "Okay, I'll go to Charleston and take them through it." The thought of heading to the state capital made him want to punch something.

Eliana beamed. "Good. It's the first step to making it work. Have I told you how pleased I am to have you home? Even if the other half of my heart is in Tokyo right now?"

"I don't think you have, no." He shook his head, unable to hide the smile on his lips.

"Okay then." She stood. "I'm so happy you're here. I've missed you. And now I'm going to head home. Would you like to join me for dinner again?"

"Not tonight. I have other plans." They involved a punching bag and his fists, as well as not thinking about Becca Hartson's open blouse.

"Another time then." She kissed his cheek and left the room in a waft of Youth Dew, lifting her hand to wave goodbye.

"Yeah, another time." He glanced at the trash can. The half-eaten scone was still laying at the top. He grabbed a piece of paper and covered it up, not really knowing why.

Maybe he didn't want to deal with Becca again. Or explain why he'd thrown her scone away.

Yeah, that was it. He'd do anything for a quiet life.

———

"So GIVE me all the details about this new project," Naomi said, lifting her cup to her lips. "I've been working on the numbers all week and I'm dying to know when it's going to start."

Becca tipped her head to the side. "What project?"

"The new Scotch single malt. If I have to calculate any more construction costs and commodity prices I think I'm going to pull my hair out. I know you guys go crazy about crops and the quality of the ingredients, but do you know how much it's going to cost to grow and malt ourselves? Surely you could just buy some on the market." Naomi shook her head, her pink lips curling into a smile.

Like Becca, Naomi had joined GSC straight from college. As a business major, she'd been a natural choice to become a junior accountant when a position opened in the finance department. Along with Mia, she was also one of Becca's closest friends at work. They'd been the inaugural founders of the coffee club, having bonded over their mutual disgust of the powdered swill that GSC brought in.

"I haven't heard about a project." Becca kept her voice light, but her chest felt tight. If there were plans, she *should* have heard of them. When Nathan was running operations, she would probably have been the first to hear. He liked to use her as a sounding board – that's how the International Blend came to life.

She wasn't expecting Daniel or Eliana to give her any special treatment. But she was one of GSC's best distillers, and it hurt to be cut out.

"Oh." Naomi's face fell. "I thought you would have. I figured you'd be involved in the planning. Especially after you did so well with the International Blend."

Talk of the International Blend still stung after her meeting with Daniel. "Maybe they want to keep their cards close to their chests. I'm sure I'll hear soon." She drained her cup and put it in the sink. "I should get back. I have a billion things to check before I clock out for the night."

It was already past six in the evening. Usually, she liked to leave early on Friday nights. It was the one night a week that all of Hartson's Creek got together at the water's edge to spend time together and drink sweet lemonade. Known locally as Chairs, because of the fact they all took their own chairs to place on the grassy lawns, it was a local institution. The women talked out their problems, the children played, and the men either threw themselves into it or grumbled about being dragged along.

Or, if they were her brothers, they headed to the Moonlight Bar instead.

"Oh, hey, I was going to ask you for a favor," Naomi said before Becca walked out of the kitchen.

"Sure?" Becca smiled at her. "What can I do?"

"Remember how Alex used to be in the Army?" Alex was Naomi's husband. The two of them lived in a pretty cottage on the edge of town.

"Yeah, I remember."

"One of his old buddies is flying in for a visit next week. We were wondering if you'd like to join the three of us for dinner?"

"As in a double date?"

"As in I thought we could have some fun. Shawn's a good guy, and he's only in town for a few days. If it's the three of us then the guys are going to end up talking to each other and I'll have to smile and nod in the right places. If you come we can dance and ignore them." Naomi looked at her imploringly. "Come, please?"

"Don't you have any other single schmucks for friends?"

Naomi grinned. "None as easy to persuade as you."

Becca laughed. "So you're saying you're only asking me because I'm a pushover?"

"I'm asking because I want to spend some time with you. It'll be fun." She grabbed Becca's hand and squeezed. "Say yes. Otherwise I'll pull all of my beautiful hair out."

Becca rolled her eyes at Naomi's dramatics, though a smile pulled at her lips. "Okay."

Naomi squealed and Becca shook her head. "I'm only doing this because I love you. And because you're going to keep me updated with what's going on with this new project."

"I'm not above a little corporate espionage to get what I want."

Yeah, and nor was Becca by the looks of it. She was still irritated by the fact she didn't have an inkling about this project.

"I'll see you later. Have a good weekend." Becca lifted her hand.

"Friday night. I promise it'll be fun. Shawn's off to the Middle East after his leave, so there's no commitments. We can wear pretty dresses and dance our asses off." Naomi lifted her brows. "That'll give him something to remember when he's in Afghanistan."

Becca shook her head and sighed. She'd wear the kind of things she always wore. Jeans and a cute top would work perfectly. "I don't need to show him my legs to give him something to remember." She blew Naomi a kiss and walked out of the kitchen, right into Eliana Scott-Carter.

The single malt – and her lack of involvement in it – was still playing on her mind. Her brows pinched together.

"Everything okay?"

Becca nodded, letting the frown wash off her face. None of this was Eliana's fault, she'd always been a big supporter of Becca's. "Everything is fine. I'm just trying to get things finished before the weekend." She waited for Eliana to give her customary nod and walk away, but instead her elegant uber-boss stayed exactly where she was.

"I imagine you have a busy weekend planned. With all your lovely brothers."

Eliana had met the Hartson brothers when they'd recorded an advertisement for the International Blend. It had featured Becca's four brothers sitting in Gray's backyard while they laughed and shot the breeze. Nathan had laughed that his mom had a thing for Gray, but she hadn't shown it. Just watched quietly, in her usual way, her blue eyes noticing everything.

Her eyes were the same color as Daniel's, Becca realized.

"I'll probably see them. But not until after I sleep-in tomorrow. It's been a long week."

"It's nice that your family is so close." Eliana showed no signs of returning to her office. This was probably the longest she'd ever spoken to Becca. "The way families should be."

Maybe Eliana was missing Nathan. Becca nodded, giving her a sympathetic smile. "I guess. Though we fought like cats and dogs when we were younger. And they still drive me crazy on occasion."

"Are they a little over protective?"

"That's an understatement."

"Give them time. They'll come around."

Becca bit her lip. While Eliana was in a good mood, maybe she should take the opportunity to find out some information. "Um, can I ask you a question. If you have time, that is?"

"Of course. Shoot. Or fire." Eliana frowned. "Whichever people are using these days."

"I heard about the new single malt." She wasn't going to tell her Naomi was the leak. "And I was wondering why I hadn't been involved as one of the distillers."

"You heard about that? I suppose things are never secret around here for long." Eliana patted her arm. "And the answer is because we haven't really done anything about it yet. It's an idea Daniel has, but it's in its infancy. You'll all be involved when it gets going, I'm sure."

"Oh." Becca breathed out a sigh of relief. "I was wondering if you were unhappy with my work."

"Of course not." Eliana shook her head. "Where did you get that idea from? Nathan always sung your praises very highly. And I'm sure Daniel will too when he gets to know you."

The mention of Daniel's name made Becca tense. "He doesn't seem very happy with the International Blend."

"Did he tell you that?"

Becca pulled her lip between her teeth, torn between telling the truth and covering up for Daniel. "Pretty much." Okay, so maybe it wasn't much of a choice.

"The International Blend is wonderful. It's received great write ups in the trade press and the marketing campaign has really done the trick. Daniel's a perfectionist. He always wants to make things better." She gave a tinkling laugh. "When he was a child it drove me mad. He'd rebuild a LEGO project about a hundred times, throwing away parts that wouldn't work exactly how he wanted. Do you know how painful it is to step on Legos in bare feet?"

Becca smiled. "I can imagine."

"Please don't worry about this. You're a valued member of the senior team." Eliana patted Becca's upper arm again, as though she had no idea what else to do. "Now it's late, and we should both be finishing up. I'm all for girl power, but we don't need to be the last people left in the building."

"Thank you." Becca nodded. "Have a good weekend."

"You, too, dear."

———

"No." Daniel shook his head, his jaw tightening.

"Why not?" His mother steepled her fingers together, leaning across the dining room table to look at him.

"I'm going to recruit for the lead distiller to work directly under me. Miss Hartson can stay working on the International Blend."

"I thought you didn't like her work on the blend." Eliana's lips twitched. "Or at least, that's the impression you gave her."

Daniel sighed. Why the hell were they talking about Becca Hartson on a Saturday night? Didn't she haunt him enough during the week, now he had to think of her over the weekend, too?

"I told her she had a lot to learn. Which she does. And that there are aspects of the blend that could be improved. Which there are." He ran his finger around the rim of his wine glass. "She's too green. Too eager to please. I need somebody who won't stop until they make the best glass of whiskey they've ever tasted."

"You're describing yourself, darling. And there's only one of you in this world."

Daniel arched an eyebrow. "Is that relief I hear?"

His mother laughed. "She's a good distiller. I don't understand why you've taken a dislike to her. Nathan was always singing her praises."

"I bet he was."

The smile slipped from her lips. "What's that supposed to

mean? Is there something going on between Nathan and Becca?"

"No." He wasn't going to tell his mom that Becca Hartson seemed overfriendly with the staff. Or that he'd caught her in Nathan's arms the night he arrived back. The memory tasted like bottom shelf liquor on his tongue.

"It wouldn't matter if there was, would it?" Eliana continued. "We don't have anything in our contracts that says staff can't have relationships. It'd be rather hypocritical, since your father and I met at the distillery."

"You *owned* the distillery. Or half of it. There's a difference."

"I owned nothing at the time. My father was still alive and your father's partner. I worked for him and Larry." Eliana smiled at Daniel over the rim of her glass. "So technically, Nathan and Becca would be no different than your parents."

"There's nothing going on between Nathan and Becca. Nathan assured me of that. They're just friends."

"So why have you taken a dislike to her?" Eliana put her glass down.

"I haven't. I just don't want her working on this project." It'd be almost impossible to avoid her. For the past few days he'd had good success at not being wherever Becca Hartson was. He'd even managed a few hours without thinking about her.

"Well, she deserves a chance at least. Along with anybody else who applies for the job."

"You want me to interview her for the role?"

"Maybe."

"But I know what she can do."

"Do you?" Eliana lifted an eyebrow. "Or have you made assumptions? The fact is, Miss Hartson is more than qualified for the job. We've trained her for this. If you don't interview her, you stand a good chance of being accused of bias."

"I'm not biased," he protested. "I just want the single malt to be a success."

"Then don't wreck it before it starts with any lawsuits or discrimination. Give her a fair crack of the whip, that's all I ask. If she loses the job fair and square, then I'll be happy."

Daniel looked at her carefully. "Why are you so keen on Becca Hartson all of a sudden?"

"I'm not keen on her. I just know a good worker when I see one. And the fact she's a woman makes me interested in her success."

"There are plenty of women working at G. Scott Carter."

"In the still room?"

Daniel frowned. "Well... no. But we have plenty in top jobs in the rest of the company. We're an equal opportunity employer."

"Then let's give her an equal opportunity."

He leaned back in his chair. He knew when he was defeated. Mostly because his mother was right. Becca did deserve a chance to show what she could do. And if she was anybody else, he'd be pushing for them to get the opportunity. But Becca Hartson... she made him second guess himself. She was attractive and aggravating and so damn eager to please everybody.

Except him. She never seemed that eager to please *him*. Maybe that's what was so annoying. He wasn't sure. All he knew was working with her would be dangerous.

"Okay." He said it with a sigh.

Eliana lifted a brow. "Okay?" she asked.

"If she applies for the job, I'll give her the chance to prove herself. But she might not want to. It'll involve working closely with me." He gave the smallest of laughs. "And I'm pretty sure she dislikes me."

Or maybe he hoped she did. Because that would be safer.

For him *and* for her.

CHAPTER SEVEN

The paper was folded neatly in two, the line so crisp she could probably have cut her fingers on it. Becca pulled it out of her locker in the still room and unfolded it, her brows knitting as she read the top line.

Job Description. Lead Distiller. Project A

THERE WAS no note to say who it was from, or an explanation for why it had found its way to her locker. Just a printed piece of paper with a list of required duties, knowledge, skills, and desirable qualifications written on it. Becca folded it back up carefully and slid it into her pocket.

"So you got it?"

Becca looked up at Garrett Rhys. He'd been a lead distiller at GSC for longer than she'd been alive. He worked on the GSC legacy lines, and was three years away from retirement.

"Did you put it in there?"

"Not me. Mr. Carter. He offered me a copy, too. I said thanks, but no thanks." Garrett flashed her a smile. "I like working on the current lines. By the time any new whiskey matures, I'll be long retired."

He wandered over to the mash tun, and Becca opened the description again. Why had Daniel not given it to her himself? Or emailed it to her – they so rarely printed things out nowadays.

It was like being back at school and having a boy pass her a note. Except she wasn't sure if this was a good or a bad thing.

There was only one way to find out. She flashed Garrett a smile and headed out of the still rooms, the warm malty air replaced by the airconditioned crispness of the office corridors. With the job description rolled up in one hand, she used the other to rap on Daniel's office door.

"Come in."

She pushed it open, arranging a neutral smile on her face. "Hi," she said before she'd stepped inside. "I was just wondering why you'd put this in my locker?" Then she realized Eliana was in his office, sitting in the leather chair opposite his, her ankles elegantly crossed.

"That's my cue to leave." Eliana's eyes were soft as she looked at her son. Then she smiled at Becca. "Let you two talk alone."

Daniel nodded, but his eyes were on Becca. They weren't the empty ones she'd seen before, but they weren't full of heat either. Just purely professional, cool and collected.

The way she wanted it.

Eliana patted Becca on the shoulder as she passed her. "Good luck," she whispered.

"Sit down," Daniel said, nodding at the chair his mother had vacated. Today he was wearing a dark blue shirt, open at the neck as always. It brought out the blue in his eyes, making them look more vivid than ever. His thick, dark hair was raked back off his face, and there was a hint of a shadow on his jaw.

Becca unrolled the job description. The neat line from where he'd folded it was still there. "Garrett said you left this for me."

"I did."

"There's no note attached," she told him. "Nothing to tell me why you left it."

The corner of his lip twitched. He was so damn distracting. She'd never met somebody who aggravated her so much. Or made her heart skip a beat every time their eyes clashed.

It was unnerving.

"Why do you think I left it?" There was a hint of amusement in his voice. As though he was playing a game she didn't know the rules to.

But she'd been brought up to play games. She knew them intimately. "Either you want to taunt me about a job that won't be mine, or you want me to apply for the job."

Their gazes connected and there it was again. The fizz of electricity that made her body react in ways she didn't want it to.

She kept her face impassive, not moving an inch. She wasn't going to be the one to look away first.

He didn't seem to be in a hurry to look away either. The corner of his lip was still lifted, his head tilted to one side. He had such delicious lips when they weren't twisted into a scowl. They held a hint of cruelty to them, but a fullness, too. And for a moment she wondered what they'd feel like on hers.

Focus, Becca.

Her eyes were feeling dry. Itchy. She had to clench her teeth in an effort not to be the first to blink. Her heart was racing, her legs squeezed together in an effort to ignore the warmth pooling deep inside her.

Why was she so attracted to this man? If he'd stood and pulled her over the desk right now she wouldn't have protested. Just the thought of it made her breath catch.

Her eyes were as arid as the desert. It hurt not to blink. And damn Daniel Carter was still half-smirking at her with no effort at all. He was going to win.

She didn't like that feeling at all.

"I want you to apply for the job."

The words didn't register at first. She was too busy blinking to take them in. But then her breath slowed and the rush of blood through her ears calmed down, enough for her to realize that he'd spoken.

And what he'd said.

"Are you okay?" The half-smile turned into a full smile as the other side of his mouth lifted. He was actually smiling at her. For the first time in two weeks. Becca gave a mental fist bump because it felt like she'd just won a gold medal.

"I'm fine." Apart from the blood heating up her cheeks and the pulse between her thighs, that was. "I was just wondering why you want me to apply when your opinion of me is so low."

The corner of his eyes crinkled. "Who says my opinion of you is low?"

"You said, and I quote, *'my best isn't good enough'.*"

"Maybe I don't think you've given us your best yet. And I only said you should apply for the job. Not that it's yours."

He was so damn irritating. Becca inhaled sharply and looked at him. This time she blinked slowly, letting him know she wasn't starting another staring battle. She needed all her energy for talking. "So let me get this straight. You don't think my best is good enough. You think I'm too young to be a lead distiller. And I'm too friendly with the staff and have a sweet tooth." Irritation washed over her.

He lifted an eyebrow. "On the plus side you have a very good memory."

"Thanks. I think. So why do you want me to apply for the job?"

"Because my mother asked me to give you a chance."

"Do you always do everything your mother tells you to do?"

He laughed. "Are you asking if I'm a momma's boy?"

She shrugged, even though she'd never met somebody less like a momma's boy in her life. "I was just wondering." She kept her voice nonchalant, even though it was taking a concerted effort not to show her surprise at his amusement. It was a game she was playing to win. "Because I'm not sure I want to work for a guy who takes all his direction from his mom."

He was smiling now. As though he was enjoying the back and forth as much as she was. Becca knew it was dangerous. He was the boss, he owned the business, if she pissed him off she could lose her job.

But he didn't look pissed off. He looked entertained.

In a weird and totally messed up way, she was, too.

"How about we agree that I want you to apply. Does that work for you?"

"What if I don't want to?" She arched an eyebrow.

For the first time he looked disconcerted. It was subtle, of course. A blink. A shift of his hands. The wavering of his smile. "Don't you want to?"

Of course she did. Even if it meant working closely with Mr. Hyde, because she still wasn't sure there wasn't a sweet Dr. Jekyll lurking beneath his pretty face. She loved her work. And she had a lot of ambition, even if people thought she was just a friendly, easy-going kind of woman.

The thought of being involved in this project made her

skin tingle. Almost as much as the thought of working closely with Daniel Carter did.

"I'll think about it." She lifted her chin, her gaze steady.

He looked like he was biting down a grin. His eyes boldly held hers, as though he was ready to battle with her all over again.

"Do you want to know why I had concerns about you applying?"

Sure. Hit her with it. As if he hadn't put her down enough already. "You look like you want to tell me."

"You're too willing to please. And that's lethal in a distiller."

Becca stared back at him, unflinching. "Do I seem willing to please you?"

A ghost of a smile passed his lips. "No. You don't. Why is that, do you think?"

It was like an elite game of tennis. He served, she volleyed. He hit back hard and she had to leap to keep up. She felt exhilarated.

"Maybe I think you're impossible to please." She arched an eyebrow.

He ran a finger along his jaw, his stare speculative. "You could be right. But I think it's more than that. I think you don't *want* to please me."

There was something in the way he said it that made her blood heat up. His voice was slow. Measured. And too damn sexy.

"Why would I want to please you?"

"You shouldn't. You should only want to please yourself. That's what I'm looking for in a distiller. Somebody who knows what they're tasting. Who understands what they like, and not because somebody told them to like it, but because every sense they possess delights at the flavor. Because they understand the pleasure that taste can give and can't live without the way their body feels when they experience it."

Her skin felt like it was on fire. "I understand pleasure."

"Do you?"

Their gazes locked. "Yes."

"Okay. We'll do a taste test as part of your application. Meet me in the barrel room on Friday evening."

Becca blinked. She was set to go out with Naomi, Alex, and his Army friend on Friday. She'd opened her mouth to tell Daniel she couldn't make that night, but she'd quickly closed it again. Because it would only confirm his prejudices against her.

"I'm free between six and eight p.m. After that I'll have to leave. I have a prior engagement." There was no way she was telling him about a date.

"Six it is then." He nodded. "Thank you for your time."

She knew when she was being dismissed. Becca nodded and stood, walking toward the door. "Thank you for yours."

As she walked out, she could have swore she heard him murmur, "It was a pleasure," but it might have been the blood still rushing through her ears. As she passed by Eliana's office – the door unusually open – the elegant lady beckoned her in.

"How did it go?" she asked.

"I have to do a taste test."

Eliana's lips curled. "You'll be fine. You're an excellent distiller. And don't mind Daniel, he can be an ass sometimes."

Becca bit down a laugh, because Eliana's thoughts echoed her own. "Thank you."

CHAPTER EIGHT

*B*ecca checked her make up in the bathroom mirror, touching her fingertip to her bottom lip to smooth away a lipstick smudge. She'd had to get ready for her night out while at work, as she'd have no time between her taste test and meeting Naomi and her husband at the bar. Glancing down at her tight jeans, off-white silky shell, and black wool jacket, she wondered if Daniel would think that she'd made an effort for him.

And then she decided she didn't care. He could think whatever he wanted. She'd do this stupid taste test then call a cab to take her to town, while messaging Naomi a drink order so she could down it as soon as she'd walked inside Moonlight Bar, because she was certain that Daniel Carter would have driven her crazy by then.

The thought of two hours alone with him in the barrel room – actually a separate building to the rest of the distillery – was enough to drive her to drink.

When she walked back out of the bathroom, Naomi was waiting for her. She let out a low whistle as she looked Becca up and down. "You look hot. Shawn won't know what hit him."

She'd forgotten about Shawn. Which was weird because all this effort was for him, right? "By the time I get there I'll probably look a mess. I'm not sure I'll even have any hair left."

Naomi grinned. "Daniel's not so bad. And at least you get to look at that face while he's putting you through the labors of Hercules. He asked me a question in our team meeting yesterday and it took me a whole minute to realize he was talking to me. Have you seen those eyelashes?"

"Shame the inside isn't so pretty." Becca shrugged.

"He seems okay. He asked Ryan about his father – even I didn't know he was in the hospital. And then he asked me about Alex and how he's handling life out of the Army."

Becca's mind wandered back to the day she lost her shirt button, when he was sitting on Sandy's reception desk and the two of them were laughing.

So it really was only Becca he hated. No, maybe hate was too strong a word. They clashed. Like a personality mismatch or something. Except for when she sparred with him.

Then he seemed to like it.

"You okay?" Naomi asked.

Becca gave her a genuine smile. If Daniel wanted to rile her up, she'd give it right back to him. "I'm real good. I'll see you some time after eight."

"Don't be late. Three's a crowd."

———

THE GSC BARREL ROOM – also known as the rickhouse – was more of a warehouse than a room. The four story wooden building loomed large at the rear of the estate. It was a traditional whiskey rickhouse – the barrels stored on their sides in racks, allowing air to flow around them as the whiskey inside matured. There was no climate control inside. The natural highs and lows of the West Virginian climate were used to drive the whiskey into the wood, creating an aged, oak flavor.

The rickhouse was labor intensive, thanks to the way the barrels were stored. It took two men to take a barrel from the racks and roll it to the floor. In the past they'd experimented with different storage – having the barrels upright on pallets that could be moved by forklift trucks – but in the end the flavor suffered.

The staff in the rickhouse were gone by the time Becca arrived. The door was unlocked, and she pushed it open, her heels clacking against the concrete floor as she walked inside.

The air surrounding her was temperate. In a few months it would be almost unbearably hot, especially in the upper levels. In winter, the temperatures plummeted, requiring the staff to wear thick goose down coats and hats to keep themselves warm.

But it was all worth it for the end result.

She called out, unnerved by the silence surrounding her. "Hello?" From the corner of her eye she saw some movement, and turned her head to see him standing there.

Dark tailored pants. A crisp white shirt unbuttoned at the neck. His sleeves were rolled up to right beneath his elbows, exposing strong forearms, warm skin peppered with hair, and a watch that looked like it cost her annual wage.

He was in the shadows so it was impossible to see his eyes. For a moment she felt exposed in her tight jeans and shell top. As though he was staring at her delicate throat and dark hair flowing over her shoulders in a cascade of waves.

She heard him inhale sharply.

"Did you dress up for me?" His tone sounded almost bored.

Becca bit down a smile. So they were playing again. "Nope. I have a hot date after this. You just get to enjoy me first."

She felt different wearing these clothes. Confident. As though she could rule the world.

He stepped out of the shadows. His thick hair was messy, as though he'd been raking it with his fingers. A single lock fell over his brow, and damn if the dishevelment didn't make him even more attractive. "I'll try not to delay you for too long."

Oh please delay me. She was really careful not to say it out loud.

Cool and calm. That's what she needed to be.

He took two glasses from the tasting table, passing one to her. "If you're going out later, we should get on with this. Pick a barrel that will impress me."

"I don't imagine anything will impress you."

A hint of a smile tugged at his lips. "Try me."

She looked at him for a minute, her eyes assessing. His dark hair gleamed beneath the low lighting of the rickhouse. The curve of his jaw twitched as though he was pressing his teeth together.

Equals. They were equals. "Okay follow me." She turned on her heel, heading toward the stairs.

Neither of them said a word as they walked, the only sound was the clack of her heels on the wooden floor. Daniel kept his eyes ahead, not looking at her, though she saw a flicker of surprise in his eye when she didn't turn left toward the vintage barrels that had been there since his father's time. Instead, she headed up the stairs to the second level, never once looking behind her to check if he was following.

There was something different about him. He was being less abrasive. She tried not to let it unnerve her.

When she turned left down an aisle, she saw him biting down a smile as if he knew where she was going.

The 2012 Small Batch Select. Her very favorite GSC whiskey. She reached out to touch the barrel, aware of his eyes scrutinizing her. Weird how much she liked that.

Holding the stem between her delicate fingers, she lifted the glasses to the barrel tap, filling them with the scantest of amber fluid before turning it off.

Her neck was straight, her jaw set, as she handed him a glass. Their fingertips barely touched but it was enough for her to feel it.

The pulse of electricity rushing through her body.

She looked up to see if he'd felt it, too, but his expression was unreadable.

He took a deep breath in, lifting the glass to his nose. "Tell me about your choice."

She ran the tip of her tongue across her bottom lip, her gaze catching his. "We had a lot of storms in 2012. I remember it well. I was seventeen at the time and every outdoor event at school was called off." Her eyelashes flickered. "How old were you then?"

"Twenty-four."

"Were you working here in 2012?"

He glanced down at her lips, as though they held all the answers. "Yeah."

"Then you should remember how humid and steamy that summer was. When you stepped outside it was like walking into a hot shower. The creek was so clear and pure. I guess all the water around here was like that." His eyes were still on her lips. Unmoving.

"I guess it was." His voice was low. Thick.

"And the crops grew like crazy. I know a lot of people

were worried they might rot it got so wet. But when it wasn't raining the sun was blasting down. And they kept on growing."

"What was your favorite subject at school?"

She blinked at his abrupt change in topic. "I liked practical things. Chemistry. Cooking. I even took Shop. I don't like sitting around that much. How about you?"

A wry smile pulled at his mouth. "I didn't like school very much. I spent most of my time working out how to get out of there."

"Did you go to a rich boy's school?"

"How did you guess?"

She lifted an eyebrow but didn't reply. She was supposed to be impressing him. Proving that she was the right choice for the job. "The rain is what made the 2012 batch so special." Her voice was low. He had to lean closer to hear her. "Along with the attention the distillers gave the small batch when it was created. Maturing it on the second level means it's had some temperature extremes, but not the intense heat and cold you get on the higher floors."

"Which means?" He tipped his head to the side.

Her lip quirked. "Which means it smells and tastes fucking fantastic."

Daniel blinked as though her words shocked him. And then he laughed. Not just a chuckle, but a full blown, head back laugh that completely changed his demeanor. The corner of his eyes crinkled, and his lips were turned up.

She wondered what kind of kisser he'd be. Soft and gentle or hard and demanding? Maybe both, enough to keep her on her toes.

What the hell was going on? Why was she thinking about him kissing her?

Becca took a deep breath, pulling her gaze from his lips. This was stupid. It was the atmosphere in here that was making her feel weird. The lights were low, the air was gentle and silent. It felt like they were the only two people in the world.

"Taste it," he murmured. This was a bad idea. She knew it as soon as his gaze caught hers. She slowly lifted the glass to her lips. He held his breath as she tipped it back, her mouth parting to allow the whiskey to flow over her tongue. She closed her eyes, her jaw moving as she savored, her cheeks pulling in as she swallowed. When she opened them, he was still staring at her.

His gaze dipped to her throat, watching it undulate.

"Tell me what it tastes like."

"It's soft. Not too delicate but not too overpowering. There's hints of vanilla. Not too sweet, just enough to make it feel like the whiskey's dancing on my tongue."

"Can you taste the almonds?"

"At the very end. It has a long finish. There are almonds and salt there. They're sticking to my tongue. It's delicious."

"Yeah. It is."

Every time their eyes clashed it felt like her skin was on fire. This weird, sensual connection between them was so much stronger than before. It felt like it had been distilled until it was almost overpowering.

Her breath caught in her throat, making her chest lift up with the need for air. Daniel's piercing blue eyes flashed like there was a fire igniting behind them. Neither of them said a word – she wasn't sure she could speak even if she wanted to.

There are moments when your body knows things that your mind isn't ready to consider. When every cell in your muscles ache to do the one thing your rational thoughts are screaming against. Becca's free arm slowly lifted up, reaching for him, her fingers desperate to feel the roughness of his jaw.

In an instant, his own hand shot up, fingers curling hard around her wrist, making her stop an inch short of his face. His grasp burned her, so tight it felt like a vice.

"Don't." It was somewhere between an order and a plea.

What the hell had she been thinking? She tried to pull away, but his fingers were unyielding. His jaw was hard and set, his eyes darker than she'd ever seen them.

When she tugged again, he released her, stepping back as though to put distance between them. Becca desperately tried to find the words to explain why she'd tried to touch him. But they weren't there. All she could see was a fog of panic. Because she'd ruined any chance of getting the job.

So much for cool, calm, and collected. She'd just acted like a damn school girl.

Daniel looked away, his profile illuminated by the soft lights above them. "This is my favorite whiskey, too."

"I…"

"Why don't you take me to the next cask? I want to taste the one you think is most overrated. The one everybody gushes about but you think tastes ordinary."

Becca inhaled a deep breath. His voice was completely unaffected. As though the last two minutes never happened. Okay then, two could play at that game.

"It's the GSC Vintage Gold," she said, keeping her voice even. "On the bottom floor."

He still wasn't looking at her. Almost certainly because he thought she was a complete idiot. "Okay. Let's go try it."

She swallowed hard, straightening her shoulders and walking back toward the stairs, not bothering to see if he followed.

The quicker she did this, the faster she could get out of here and pretend nothing happened.

And on the positive side? At least she wasn't going to get this job.

CHAPTER NINE

*D*aniel grabbed his keys and switched the lights off, leaning his head against the warehouse wall and taking a deep breath.

What a mess that was. He'd been inches from pulling her toward him and kissing the hell out of her. It had taken every ounce of willpower he had to release her arm and turn away.

So much for professionalism. At least it was the weekend. He'd have two days without having to see her. Two days of running, of beating the hell out of his punching bag, of doing whatever it took to wipe the image of her out of his mind.

But right now all he could see was the hurt expression in her eyes when he stopped her from touching him.

What had she been thinking? Had she even intended to touch him? He'd never know because his hand had shot up by instinct, in a desperate move to protect himself.

Because if she'd touched him, he would have been a goner.

After that, he'd cut the tasting short. Originally he'd been planning to make her taste at least six barrels, but three was more than sufficient to show him what he'd known all along, somewhere deep inside.

Becca Hartson was good. She didn't have a sweet tooth or an unmatured palate. She knew what she liked and why she liked it. And it pissed him off.

He'd wanted her to be bad. Wanted to make his decision easy, because he didn't want to work with her. Not when every time he saw her, he felt like he was out of control.

Shaking his head at himself, he exited the barrel room, setting the alarm and fastening the locks behind him. One of the guards would be around later to make sure everything was secure.

He stopped short when he saw Becca standing outside the warehouse, a soft breeze catching her long hair.

"I thought you'd be long gone," he said, taking care to keep distance between them. "Don't you have a hot date?"

"I'm waiting for a cab. There are only two in Hartson's Creek and they're in demand on Friday nights."

"You're not driving?" He frowned.

She shook her head. "I don't drink and drive."

"And exactly how much are you planning on drinking?" He felt more pissed off than ever. Didn't she know what guys were like?

Her eyes caught his. "A lot. It's been a rough week."

Yeah, and he hadn't made it any easier. "You should be careful."

"It's okay. Naomi will be there. And my date is a friend of her husband's, so…"

Daniel felt slightly better. "Is it a first date?" He was asking too many questions. But he was her boss – wasn't it appropriate that he cared about her welfare?

"First and last. He's heading to the Middle East next week. I guess I'm going to show him a little appreciation for all he does."

The tightness in his gut returned. "Appreciation?"

Becca smirked. "For his service."

Irritation rushed through him again. The thought of Becca showing appreciation to anybody made him want to grind his teeth.

Damn, it made him want to hit something. Or someone.

"I can give you a ride to wherever you're going," he found himself saying. "Save you from waiting." *Great idea. Be in another enclosed space with her. Let's see how well that goes.*

"It's okay, it should only be ten minutes at the most. You don't have to wait with me. I'll be fine."

"I'm not leaving you on your own, Becca." He liked the way her name felt on his lips.

"Stay here then." She shrugged. "It doesn't matter to me." She bit on her bottom lip, like she was trying not to smile. It was a little easier to ignore the atmosphere between them out here. Though the sky was darkening, the air was getting cooler. Like a cold shower for his soul.

When the cab arrived five minutes later, he wasn't sure if he was relieved or annoyed. They'd stood in virtual silence, both of them staring at the gate to the distillery estate like they could make a vehicle appear in front of them by sheer force of will. And he was so damn aware of her, even though they were four feet apart.

And so damn aware that she was about to go on a date with somebody else.

"Goodnight then," she said, looking over her shoulder at him as she opened the cab door.

"Goodnight." He wasn't smiling. He wasn't sure he could remember how. "And be safe."

Her lips curved into a smile. "I will. I promise."

He nodded, and turned away as she closed the door and the driver put his foot on the gas. Grabbing his keys from his pocket, he walked across the road toward the parking lot, pressing the fob to unlock his car.

He'd head straight to the gym and whack the hell out of a punching bag. Right now, nothing else would make him feel better.

———

IT WAS TURNING into the weirdest night ever and her date hadn't even started yet. Becca pushed open the door to Moonlight Bar and forced a smile onto her lips. The clang of rock music hit her ears, mixed with the rumble of conversation spiked with the occasional shout. It was packed, even for a Friday night. As the door swung closed behind her, she spotted Naomi and her husband, Alex, along with a sandy-haired guy who looked around thirty.

Naomi was the first to see her, standing up and waving wildly. Alex and his friend stood, too, making Becca feel self conscious as she weaved her way through the throng of people to their booth.

"You got out of there alive!" Naomi grinned. "How did it go?"

"It was fine." She had no idea how to explain what had happened between her and Daniel. That's if anything had actually happened. If you took it down to the basics, she'd tried to touch him and he'd stopped her.

The rest – the aching gaze, the intense electricity that seemed to heat the air between them, the way he held onto her like he didn't want to let go – was almost certainly a figment of her imagination.

Yet she couldn't stop thinking about it.

"Hey, Becca." Alex kissed her cheek. "It's good to see you again. This is my friend, Shawn Smith."

"It's great to meet you." She held her hand out to him at

the exact moment Shawn leaned in to kiss her cheek, and her knuckles punched his hard abdomen.

Her eyes widened. "Oh my god, I'm sorry."

Shawn chuckled. "It's okay." He stepped back, rubbing his stomach with his palm. "You have a strong right hook."

Becca was mortified. Had she really hit him the moment after they were introduced? Her cheeks felt like they were on fire.

"I was just going to shake your hand," she said faintly. "I really didn't mean to hurt you."

"It's the first date I've ever been on that started with physical violence."

"I guess the only way is up." Naomi shot Becca an amused look.

"Would you like to sit down?" Shawn asked her, pointing at the bench seat. "We ordered you a white wine. Was that alright?"

Becca exhaled softly. "Thank you. I just need to head to the ladies' room first. Freshen up a bit."

"Try not to hit anybody else on the way there," Alex said, giving her a friendly nudge with his shoulder. "Those fists should come with a warning sign."

"Shut up." Naomi rolled her eyes at him. "Can't you see she's embarrassed?"

"*Are* you embarrassed?" Shawn asked her, tipping his head to the side. "Because you shouldn't be. I've been hit much harder. I just wasn't expecting it, that's all."

"A little." But that wasn't the overriding emotion rushing through her right now. Compared to the mess her brain had become thanks to her tasting with Daniel Carter, punching a blind date she wasn't going to see again barely registered.

And let's face it, if her mind wasn't still completely preoccupied with her very good looking, very disinterested boss, she'd probably have noticed Shawn leaning in to kiss her, and held her hand back. But she'd been running on automatic, the same way she had been since she'd left the barrel room. Her body doing what it needed to do while her mind still thought about *him*.

"Are you okay?" Naomi murmured. Becca blinked. How long had she been standing there? She couldn't keep acting like this. Shawn must think she was crazy.

"Just trying to wind down from a heavy day." She made herself smile. "A splash of cold water on my face and a mouthful of wine should do it."

"I'll come with you to the bathroom," Naomi said, sliding her hand into Becca's. "I need to freshen up myself."

"Have you ever wondered what girls do in the bathroom together?" Alex asked Shawn as Becca and Naomi headed to the back of the bar. "Why can't they just do what we do? They'd be in and out in five seconds."

"I haven't wondered, no." Shawn sounded amused. "Because that kind of thing gets you in trouble."

"I've been in trouble since I've met Naomi."

Naomi turned around and blew him a kiss. "Yes you have, baby. Just remember that."

Despite the crowd in the bar, the ladies' bathroom was almost empty. One stall was taken, the other three empty. There was a girl putting lipstick on at the sink, smacking her lips together and blowing kisses at her reflection. Becca vaguely recognized her from high school.

After they'd both done what they needed to do, and were standing at the sinks, Naomi shot Becca a speculative look. "So, what happened in the barrel room?"

Becca frowned at her reflection. "What do you mean? I did the tasting, Daniel asked some questions, and then I headed straight here."

Naomi shook her head. "No, something happened. You were normal when I saw you a few hours ago. Now you're all breathy and shaky and hitting guys in the stomach. And I know it's not the whiskey that did it. You do tastings all the time. So what gives?"

Becca turned to look at Naomi, a long sigh escaping her lips. "I made an idiot of myself there, too." And if she thought about it, the same right hand was to blame. Would it hurt a lot if she chopped her arm off? "I went to touch his face and he caught my arm, then held it for too long."

Naomi's brows pinched together. "He held you? How?"

He curled his fingers around my wrist and made me wonder what it would be like to be naked in bed with him. "Like this," Becca said, curling her fingers around Naomi's wrist. "Except up in the air, so my elbow was bent and my hand was inches away from his jaw."

"I don't get it." Naomi shook her glossy dark hair. "Why did you want to touch him?"

"Because I'm an idiot."

Naomi laughed. "No you're not. Come on, why did you want to touch him? Was he annoying you? Did you want to slap him?" She tipped her head to the side. "Oh my god, do you have a thing for him?"

Swallowing hard, Becca slowly nodded. *A thing* didn't even cover it. She wasn't sure when it had happened. When the dislike had fizzed into something stronger. More spectacular. But the fact was, she had a huge, unmissable yearning for Daniel Carter.

"But you hate him. And he's been an asshole to you. Remember what he said about the blend?"

"I remember." Becca's voice was low. Rough. "And it doesn't matter anyway, because I'm being stupid. He's my boss, which is bad enough. But you're right, he's an asshole, too." Except he hadn't been an asshole to her tonight. He'd been different. He'd listened to her. *Intensely.* Yeah, that word summed Daniel up perfectly. He was intense in everything he did.

Would he be intense between the sheets, too?

"Becca? You zoned out again."

She really needed to stop doing that. "Sorry. I was thinking."

"About him?"

"About tonight. I'm sorry, I'm here talking to you about Daniel when I'm supposed to be on a double date with you and Alex."

Naomi waved her hand. "Ah, Shawn's a good guy, but he's leaving next week. Daniel, on the other hand, is staying right here. How are you going to deal with seeing him on Monday?"

Becca bit into the fleshy skin of her bottom lip. "I don't know. I might not even have a job when I go in on Monday. I touched him first. Or at least, I went to touch him first. If he complains about me, I'll be gone."

"He won't complain about you."

"What makes you think that?" Becca curled her fingers around the edge of the sink.

"Because he's not that kind of guy. If he had a problem with you, he'll say it to your face. Hell, he already has." Naomi grinned.

"True." Becca shook her head. "You know what? I want to forget about Daniel Carter for a while. And GSC. Let's go talk to the guys and have some fun."

"You know I'm always up for fun." Naomi shook her hair out, flipping it behind her back before turning toward the door. "But if you ever need to talk, I'll be there."

"**W**hat are you doing in Charleston?" Eliana's smooth voice echoed through the phone speaker as Daniel talked to her on Sunday. "Are you coming into work tomorrow?"

"You wanted me to meet with Lawrence and Nina, so I thought I'd strike while the iron's hot." Daniel leaned back on the soft cream leather sofa and looked out of the plate glass window of his hotel suite to the city below. He'd driven up this morning. Charleston was a two hour drive from Hartson's Creek, and he'd played loud rock music for every mile of it, determined to chase the thought of Becca Hartson out of his mind.

He'd spend a few days in his family's home city, get his half-siblings to agree to the new whiskey line he wanted to introduce, then go back to the distillery and forget anything ever happened between him and Becca.

The truth was, nothing really had happened. But it could have. There was a moment when all he could think about was kissing her. But then she'd reached out to touch him, and he'd stopped her by reflex.

He knew that if she touched him, he'd be a goner. He wouldn't have wanted it to stop at a touch; he wanted more.

And that thought made him grit his teeth with anger. Because he shouldn't want it. Not from her.

He was stronger than that.

"I wasn't expecting you to drive to Charleston so soon. You should have told me, I'd have come with."

Which was exactly why he hadn't told her. He needed to be alone right now. Needed the distance between him and Hartson's Creek to wash the memory of Friday night away.

"I have it handled. I'm meeting Lawrence and Nina for dinner tomorrow. We'll discuss the proposed plans and then I'll come home. I'm pretty sure you can handle the distillery without me for one day."

"Of course we can, darling. But I worry. You'll be outnumbered at dinner. Will Charles be there? And Melissa of course."

"They will." Charles was Nina's husband. Part of the Charleston aristocracy. Nina had married well. And Melissa was Lawrence's wife. And the less he thought about them the better.

"Are you sure you're ready to do this?"

"Yes, I'm sure. It's not a big deal. One meal and then I'll be home. So stop worrying."

"Do you have everything you need?" Eliana asked, sounding anxious. "Did you remember your—"

"Mom, stop. It's all good. I'm here, I'm ready, and now I'm going to hang up and head out for a run. You didn't worry when I was in Scotland, and you don't need to worry now."

"Scotland was out of sight, out of mind. It was easy not to worry about you when you were there."

"Why not worry about Nathan, instead. Have you heard from him?"

"He called this morning. His night time. He's settling in nicely."

"That's good." Daniel was happy for his brother. Sure, he wished Nathan was here with him to even out the numbers between their father's first family and his second. But if anybody deserved to experience new things, it was Nathan. He'd held the fort for too long.

"So I'll see you Tuesday?" Eliana asked.

"You will. I'll drive down in the morning, and should get to work by lunchtime. But if there are any problems, let me know and I'll leave early."

"There won't be any problems. Not here, at least." She sighed. "Please don't let Lawrence get to you this time."

"I won't." If anything it would be the other way around. He always knew what buttons to push with his brother.

Except for that one time that was better left forgotten.

He ended the call and walked over to the window, looking out at the city below. Night was falling, the sun dipping behind the Allegheny Mountains, their peaks silhouetted against the darkening sky. Like the rest of West Virginia, Charleston wasn't big. With a population of just over forty-five thousand, it would probably be called a town anywhere else. But it housed the State Capitol, and was the center of political life.

It was also where his father had grown up. And his father before him. Their ancestral home was on the outskirts of town, occupied by Lawrence and his wife. Even with its modern buildings and political life, Charleston was a slower way of life. Bloodlines were important, manners were everything. And backstabbing was practically an artform.

Maybe that's why he hated coming here. He always had. Even as a boy, he'd counted down the days to his summer vacations with a heavy heart, knowing that the family would decamp to the Jackson-Carter House, named after his great-

great-great grandparents, or something like that. It was an old fashioned home built twenty years before the Civil War, where Lawrence and Nina would join Daniel and his family for two months of family summers, tension, and acrimony sizzling beneath their perfectly polite smiles.

He hadn't been unhappy that Lawrence had inherited the home from their father. It wasn't somewhere Daniel ever wanted to spend time, anyway. That slow, humid, stiff-upper lip lifestyle that his half-brother and sister led held no interest for him at all.

But at least while he was here, he wouldn't be constantly thinking about Becca Hartson, and the way she'd stared at him as he held her wrist.

Or the deep, throbbing need he was starting to feel for her.

Shaking his head at himself, he tore his gaze away from the city scape and headed for the bedroom, changing into his workout gear and grabbing his ear pods. He couldn't box today, not with the way his hands ached from two nights of pummeling his punchbag. Running would have to do.

Right now, physical exercise was the only thing that was stopping him from going mad.

———

"BECCA, YOU HAVE A PHONE CALL." Sandy was huffing, as though she'd run from the reception into the still room. "You can take it in the office," she said, pointing to the small cupboard-like room that was supposed to be the still room office, but was barely used. "I've transferred it there."

"Do you know who it is?" Becca frowned. She wasn't expecting a call. If it was her family, they'd use her cell.

"Mr. Carter." Sandy smiled. "Daniel."

Oh. Becca felt her breath catch in her throat. It had been strange coming into work and Daniel not being here. She'd heard somebody say he was out on business, and she tried to feel happy about that, because it meant she wouldn't have to see him.

But instead she'd felt a little empty.

Becca winked. "You know, next time you could use the PA."

Sandy wrinkled her nose. "I hate it. If I wanted to hear my voice echoing out of the speakers, I'd have become a rockstar like your brother."

She bit down a smile at the image of Sandy rocking it until she dropped on a stage. "I'll go answer it now."

Sandy rushed back to reception. She hated leaving it unmanned. Not quite as much as she hated the PA system – hence the fifty yard dash.

Becca walked across to the office, her brain working overtime as she tried to discern why Daniel was calling. Closing the door softly, she walked the two steps it took to reach the desk and picked up the phone, pressing the button that was flashing. "Becca Hartson speaking."

Lifting a sheaf of paper out of the way, she sat on the corner of the desk. A cloud of dust lifted into the air.

"Becca, it's Daniel. I need a favor from you."

Well that was unexpected. "What can I do?"

"Are you in the middle of anything you can't leave right now?" He sounded strange. Almost urgent.

"Um, nothing I can't ask Garrett to manage. Why?" She noticed an old calendar hanging on the wall from 2016. This room really needed to be cleaned.

"Listen carefully. I need you to go to my office and open my refrigerator. You'll find a black insulated box in there. Then I want you to get in your car and bring it to me. I'm in Charleston, at the Ambassador Hotel. When you get here, leave the car with the valet and take the elevator to the penthouse. I'll meet you there."

Becca blinked, wondering if she'd heard him right. "You want me to drive to Charleston?"

"The one in West Virginia, yes."

"I wasn't thinking you were in South Carolina. It's going to take me a couple of hours to get there."

"It's okay. I can wait." His voice was low. Thick.

"What's in the black box?"

"Nothing you need to know about. Please don't open it. I need it to stay sealed." He cleared his throat. "And don't let my mother know you're coming. She'll worry."

Becca ran the tip of her finger along her lip. "So let me get this straight, you want me to sneak into your office without your mom seeing, take a box out of your refrigerator that I'm not allowed to open or see the contents of, then bring it to Charleston where I'll take it to the penthouse." She shook her head. "Either this is some kind of prank or I'm in the middle of a heist movie."

"It's not a joke. It's important. I need that box as soon as possible." His voice softened, became edged with honey. "I'd be really grateful if you can do this. I wouldn't ask if I didn't need it."

Becca exhaled heavily. It was going to take two hours to get to Charleston, then at least another two or three to get home in rush hour traffic. Okay, so she had nothing planned this evening apart from tackling a Mexican Chocolate Fudge Pie she'd found a recipe for. But still.

"You'll owe me."

"I'm perfectly aware of that."

She smiled at the tartness of his response. "All right then. I'll see you in a couple of hours."

———

EVERYTHING about the Ambassador Hotel screamed luxury. From the gleaming marble tiled floor and dark oak walls of the reception, to the sleek metallic lines of the elevator, with gold leaf patterns on the doors that slid silently to welcome her inside. The concierge had intercepted her as soon as she walked through the hotel doors, and upon ascertaining her name, escorted her to the private penthouse elevator at the back of the expansive, triple story reception. He slid his card slickly through the reader then let her step inside.

"Mr. Carter will be waiting for you," he told her. "So you won't need a code to unarm the alarm."

Becca nodded, clutching the black insulated box in her fingers. She was used to wealth. Her brothers made enough money, after all. Gray with his music career, Cam with his football, and both Tanner and Logan were successful businessmen. But she hadn't personally experienced luxury like this. She stood in the center of the elevator car as it rose seamlessly through the building, watching as her reflection stared back at her.

She'd made more of an effort than usual this morning, tying her hair back into a low bun, and wearing a black tailored shirt rather than her usual GSC polo top. It was cinched into a pair of tailored khaki pants, and belted at her slim waist. Of course, she still didn't look like she belonged in a hotel like this, but at least people wouldn't mistake her for maintenance.

The elevator came to a stop, the doors sliding effortlessly open. And on the other side, in the center of a lobby that was bigger than her kitchen at home, was Daniel Carter.

He didn't smile when he saw her. His jaw was tight and his eyes were dark, the way they always seemed to be when he stared at her. A stupid pulse of electricity shot through her veins.

When she stepped out of the elevator onto the tiled floor,

she noticed the dark circles beneath his eyes. Had he been as sleepless as she had been since Friday? His hair was messier than usual, as though he'd ran his thick fingers through it too many times. And his face – though still devastatingly attractive – looked pale.

"Are you okay?" she asked, expecting a smart reply.

"I will be." His attempt at a smile fell short. Maybe he really was sick. "Can I take this?" He reached out for the box. She slid it into his hands.

"I haven't looked inside." Though the temptation had almost killed her. But she'd made a promise and she always kept them.

"Thank you." Still no smart reply. Yep, there was definitely something wrong. "Take a seat," he said, pointing at a cream leather sofa in the center of an oversized living area. The wall in front of it was made of glass, looking out over the leafy city of Charleston. In the distance she could see the golden gleam of the Capitol dome. "There's water in the refrigerator if you're thirsty. I'll be back in a minute." He didn't wait for her to sit, just strode across the room with the box in his hand, heading for a door on the far side. His bedroom? Becca shrugged and walked over to the window to appreciate the view.

She was a little thirsty now that she thought about it. Turning on her heel, she walked to the kitchen area. Sure enough, the refrigerator was lined with bottled water. She grabbed one for herself, then took out a second in case.

"Would you like some water?" she called out. There was no response. Stupid oversized penthouse. If he was in a normal hotel room, he'd have no problem hearing her. She walked over to his bedroom door and knocked gently. Still no reply. Sighing, she pulled at the handle, opening her mouth to repeat her question.

Then closed it swiftly.

Daniel was standing in the middle of an opulent bedroom, his shirt open and his dark gray tailored pants unfastened at the fly, revealing a smooth, taut stomach and lean hips, with dips and muscles in all the right places.

Her breath caught in her throat as she saw him pinching his skin with one hand, the other holding a needle. At that moment, the point of the needle had made an imprint in his smooth skin. His body was as beautiful as his face. Sculpted and muscled. It made her heart speed, but for all the wrong reasons.

Pulling her gaze from his bare stomach, she took in his pinched brows and intense expression, his lips slightly parted as though he was concentrating.

And then he realized she was there and everything went to hell.

His eyes lifted, looking fiery as they met hers. Becca stepped back, her cheeks heating up as she realized she'd stepped into a scene she'd never expected to be part of.

"Get out!" Daniel snapped at her. "Now."

But she couldn't get her feet to move. It was like somebody had glued the soles to the carpet. Her heart was pummelling against her ribcage, blood rushing through her ears.

"Are you taking drugs?" she asked, her voice thin. Her hands started to shake. "Is *that* what I brought here? You made me traffic drugs!"

Daniel pulled the needle from his flesh, setting it in a tray on the dresser beside him. When he looked back at her, his eyes were as dark as ink. She could feel the disdain radiating from him.

"No, Becca, it's not drugs. I'm a fucking diabetic."

———

Daniel regretted his words as soon as they left his mouth. Not just because of the expression on her face – though that was pretty bad. But because she'd done something nice for him. Taken hours out of her day to bring his damn insulin and he'd thrown it back in her face.

"I'm sorry." His voice was soft. "I'm jittery. I haven't been able to eat until I could inject myself."

"That's insulin?" she asked, glancing at the syringe.

"Yeah. I thought I'd brought enough with me, but I ran out this morning. I'm an idiot." He blew out a mouthful of air. "Could you please give me a minute to tidy myself up?"

Her eyes were as wide as a doe's. "I should go anyway. It's a long trip back home."

His chest tightened. "Please stay. Let me explain."

"There's nothing to explain." She shook her head. "It's fine, honestly." She looked like she wanted to bolt.

"Then stay and let me thank you. But with my clothes on." He glanced down at his open shirt and pants. "If that's okay?"

She finally nodded, and relief rushed through him. As she left his bedroom, he walked over to the floor length mirror, taking himself in. He was a damn mess. Not just his clothes, or his ruffled hair, but his face, too. Pale from hunger because he hadn't dared to eat carbohydrates without having his insulin to control the sugar rush, and the slices of cheese he'd swallowed down just didn't cut it. Deftly fastening his buttons, he tucked his shirt back into his waistband and checked his appearance again. Better. Doing his best to rearrange his hair with his fingers, he walked over to the door, breathing a sigh of relief when he saw her sitting on the leather sofa.

So she hadn't run. Brave girl.

"I poured you a glass of water," she said, looking over at him. "It's on the counter."

"Thank you." He offered her a smile and grabbed the

glass, taking a healthy drink, then grabbed a banana from the fruit bowl, attacking it like he was starving to death. "Are you hungry?" he asked, when he'd swallowed it down.

"A little." She'd missed lunch to drive up here.

"I'll have some sandwiches sent up." He lifted the phone to reception and gave his order. "Would you like tea or coffee?" he asked, covering the mouthpiece with his hand.

"Coffee would be great."

"Two coffees as well, please. Can you make sure it's here in ten minutes?" he asked the woman on the other line. The banana should tide him over, but he needed to eat quickly after injecting. And anyway, he was hungry.

"Of course, Mr. Carter."

He hung up, carrying another banana over to where Becca was sitting on the sofa, her body leaning forward, her hands clasped tightly on top of her thighs. She was staring out of the wall of glass. When he walked in front of her, she blinked, as though surprised to see him there.

"I expect you have questions." He broke off a piece of the fruit and pushed it between his lips. His stomach gurgled as it welcomed the food.

"A few." There was no trace of a smile on her face. Not anger, either. Just a bewilderment that he too was feeling.

Damn, she was pretty. No, nix that. Beautiful. He wanted to trace the straight line of her nose with his fingertip, then press it against her swollen lips.

"Where should we start?" he asked, her ignoring the drumming need for her.

"What type of diabetic are you?"

Well that was an easy start. "Type one."

She nodded. "Why did you run out of insulin?"

He gave a rueful smile. "I thought I'd brought enough with me, but I was an idiot and ran out of my fast acting insulin. I should have packed more carefully. I usually do, but I was distracted as I left town."

"Fast acting insulin?" she echoed. "What's that?"

"I take two types, long acting insulin that keeps my levels regular during the day, and the fast acting insulin which I inject before mealtimes."

She ran the tip of her tongue along her lip. "But couldn't you have gone to a pharmacy here rather than call me?"

"I don't have a prescription in the States yet. I'm using up my Scottish insulin. Which was one of the reasons I didn't want you to tell my mother. Going to a doctor when I got back was the first thing I should have done."

Becca tipped her head to the side. "One of the reasons? What are the others."

"She worries about me and I don't want to cause her any more anxiety." He'd done enough of that over the years. "I figure what she doesn't know won't hurt her."

"Why did you call me? Surely you could've gotten anybody to bring it up." She was tracing a pattern on her thigh. It was distracting.

A half-smile pulled at Daniel's face. "I couldn't think of anybody else. I don't have a lot of friends." And maybe he'd wanted to see her. Even though she'd been the reason he'd left in the first place.

Her lips twitched. "Maybe you should be nicer to people."

He bit down a smile. She knew how to push all his buttons. "Maybe."

"What would you have done if I refused to bring it to you?" She tipped her head to the side, her eyes hooded.

"I would have called my mother's doctor and begged him to send through a script, and probably asked the kitchen to make me a protein based meal." He wrinkled his nose. "I guess at the worst I would have called my mom directly and opened myself up for a barrage of recriminations." He smiled again. "But luckily I didn't have to."

His legs were beginning to ache, but he didn't want to sit down. The distance between where she was sitting and he was standing was necessary right now.

"Do you always inject in your hip?" Her gaze dropped to his abdomen. He bit down a smile at the way her cheeks flushed at the memory.

"No. I inject in a lot of places. My outer arms, my thighs, either side of my abdomen. The trick is to not inject in the same place too many times, otherwise it causes problems. A build up of fat will stop the body from absorbing the insulin."

"Why do you keep your diabetes a secret?" She lifted her chin, looking at him carefully. There was something in her gaze that made him want to breathe her in. To touch her, to kiss her.

Damn it, he needed to get under control.

"I wasn't expecting this many questions." It was a joke, but it fell short. She lifted an eyebrow, giving him a pointed stare.

"I just drove two hours to give you life saving drugs. I figure I'm owed an explanation."

He exhaled softly, still drinking her in. "You are. And it's not a secret, I just don't want everybody knowing my business."

"Why not? It's an illness not a weakness."

Daniel gave a short laugh. "You obviously didn't grow up with my father."

Becca blinked, opening her mouth, then closing it again. For a moment there was silence between them. It screamed louder than their voices.

"How old were you when you found out you were diabetic?" Her voice was like a gentle caress.

"Seven."

"That's young." Her eyes were soft, too. "It must have been hard."

Yeah, it was. But he didn't want to talk about that. It was water under the bridge.

"I've learned to live with it. I have to take care when I'm sick, and if I get an injury it can be a pain. But it's part of me now."

She was looking at him carefully. Like she had a question she didn't want to ask. Daniel felt himself smiling again. She was so damn mercurial. One minute shouting at him, the next minute pulling back.

It was enticing. And exciting. Who didn't love the chase?

"What is it?" he asked her, eyeing her carefully.

"It doesn't matter."

"I said I'd answer your questions. So hit me with them." He ran a finger along his jaw, the roughness reminding him he hadn't shaved this morning.

"The diabetes. Is that why you're so…" She drew in a deep breath, as though to arm herself. "So cranky sometimes."

Daniel burst out laughing. "No, Becca," he said, shaking his head. "The asshole is one hundred percent me. Nothing to do with diabetes."

"Sometimes when you look at me, your eyes are so dark I think you're going to murder me."

They were? "If I murdered you, I wouldn't be able to ask you for help when I forget my insulin," he said lightly. A ping from the elevator made him exhale with relief. Saved by the food. "That's our sandwiches. Are we finished, or do you have anything else to ask?" He looked at her over his shoulder as he walked to the lobby.

"I'm finished, for now. But I may have more questions later."

He bit down a smile, relieved she couldn't see her face. "Something to look forward to," he murmured.

"**Y**ou eat like a maniac," Daniel said, as Becca swallowed the last bite of her sandwich.

"So would you if you grew up with four brothers. Either I ate fast or I starved when they stole all the food off my plate. I chose survival."

He smiled, and damn if it didn't make her whole body ache. It was like the tiniest chink in his armor had opened up, giving her a glance beyond the hard shell he projected. If she'd felt attracted to him before she'd arrived in Charleston, right now she was fighting it on two fronts.

Daniel being angry was exciting enough. Daniel being nice?

He was dynamite.

"Growing up with two brothers was enough." He shot her an interested look. "Your family seems close."

Becca smiled, relaxing now that she was on more comfortable ground. "It's huge and noisy and we have a lot of fun. They drive me crazy, of course, but since they've all moved back to Hartson's Creek and met their significant others they're a little more mellow. Plus I get the added bonus of having lots of nephews."

He blinked as though he didn't quite get the concept.

"How about your family?" she asked. "Are you close?"

Another laugh. She was getting used to the sound of them coming from his lips. "Not really. I'm close to Nathan, of course. But Nina and Lawrence... well we only saw them during the summer and holidays. They're older and Lawrence resented my mother, which led to him disliking Nathan and me, too."

"Why did he resent your mother?" Becca tipped her head to the side, licking the crumbs from her fingertips. Daniel's gaze dipped down and narrowed.

"You must have heard the stories. I thought they were rife at GSC?"

Becca shook her head. "Nope. And I'm not big into gossip, so even if I heard them, I wouldn't pay much attention."

He looked surprised at that. He was such a closed book. It was as though he hated anybody taking a peek he wasn't willing to show them.

And yet right now it felt as though he was opening. Just a tiny bit. Enough for her to see a pinprick of light on the inside.

"My father was married to Lawrence and Nina's mother when he fell in love with mine. It was a mess. Not just at home, but at the distillery, too. My mom's dad, my grandfather, was his business partner. He died within a year, and a lot of people say it was because of the stress my mom and dad's relationship caused." Daniel looked at her with those clear blue eyes. "The distillery nearly went under, and my dad's divorce with his first wife was apparently nasty. I don't know all of the details because I wasn't born yet, but I know that Lawrence and Nina suffered a lot."

"They can't blame you for that. You didn't even exist."

Becca sipped at her coffee, glad for the caffeine injection. It was going to be a long drive home tonight.

"You're assuming that people think rationally. They don't."

"That's very true."

Their gazes connected again. It was getting stupid how often it was happening. "I guess that's why you freaked when you saw me and Nathan hugging."

"I didn't freak. I was just surprised. Especially when I found out you were an employee."

"You're messing with the staff now? What kind of idiot are you?" Her impression of Daniel was woeful. But it made him smile.

"Is that what I said?"

She nodded. "Pretty much word for word."

"Well, he turned out not to be an idiot at all. Which is good." He looked down at his hands, the smile still playing on his lips. He was looking better now that he'd had something to eat. Less pale and sallow. His eyes were brighter, his jaw less tight. She glanced across at the windows to the skyline of the city.

"I should be going," she said, sighing softly. She really didn't want to leave. Not now that they were finally talking. "It's getting late and I don't want to be half asleep as I drive home."

He looked up, his eyes assessing. "You could stay."

Becca blinked with surprise.

"I mean, you can stay in the guest room." He pointed at the door opposite his own. "I'm having dinner with Lawrence and Nina tonight. Since you're so good with families, you could join me."

She was in shock at his offer, even if it was completely innocent. "I haven't got anything to wear." The words escaped her lips before she could think them through.

"That's easily remedied. If that's your only objection." He took their plates and put them back on the room service tray. "But don't feel like you have to stay if you don't want to."

Oh she wanted to. In a stupidly bad way. "I'd need a toothbrush," she said faintly. "And pajamas, too."

"Is that a strange way of saying yes?" He looked amused.

Becca took a deep breath in. "Yes." It felt more significant than it should. It was only dinner and staying in a bedroom that would otherwise be empty, nothing more. And yet there was a pulse in her throat that told her it wasn't just that.

It was the possibility of something. She just didn't know what.

"I'll leave first thing, so I can get to work on time." Her voice was soft.

"That would be sensible." He nodded. "Us arriving at the same time would cause unnecessary gossip. Something I think we'd both be keen to avoid."

She looked him straight in the eye. "We would."

He stood and wiped his hands on a cloth napkin. "I'll ask the concierge to bring you some things. What size are you?"

"Four." She felt amused that he was going to arrange clothes for her. Like she was in a regency romance and the duke was buying the beautiful-yet-destitute heroine a ball gown. "Eight in shoes."

He picked up the phone, pressing the zero. "We have a while before we need to leave. Why don't you go take a shower, relax a little? There's a robe in the guest bathroom, and toiletries, too."

Becca nodded. Right now a shower would be good. Maybe even a cold one. Because she needed something to shock her out of this mood. This weird, dreamy yearning she felt toward the man who she'd first thought was an asshole.

But now he was getting under her skin.

Yeah, a cold shower and a long hard look at herself. That should do it.

————

TWISTING the corkscrew into the bottle of Sauvignon he'd ordered, Daniel pulled it out and poured two small glasses. They probably both needed the liquid courage before heading out for dinner. Daniel because he was going to see family he hadn't set eyes on in years, and Becca because she didn't know what she was getting herself into.

He blamed himself for that. And yet the thought of having her beside him at the restaurant table calmed him.

Replacing the bottle in the refrigerator, he wondered what the hell he'd been thinking when he'd asked her to stay. Sure, he was worried about her driving home in the dark, especially when she'd spent almost three hours driving here without a break. But there had been other options.

He could have offered to pay for a separate room. Maybe even arrange a driver for her.

Or treated her like any other employee and not worried about how she was going to get home.

That way he wouldn't be staring at the guest bedroom door, knowing she was behind it and wondering how he was going to deal with that fact when they got back from the restaurant this evening.

As though she could feel the heat of his gaze through the hard wood door, Becca opened it, standing in the doorway, her green eyes wide as she looked at him.

The dress the concierge had ordered fit perfectly. The black silk bodice moulded to her every curve, the skirt flaring out at the waist until it stopped at her enticing thighs. Her hair was twisted into an intricate bun at the nape of her neck, exposing the smooth skin of her throat.

"Do I look okay?"

He looked down, surprised to see his fingers gripping the kitchen counter like he was about to fall back, his knuckles bleached white.

"You look beautiful." His voice was thick as he returned his gaze to hers. "We have five minutes until the car picks us up. Would you like a glass of wine?"

A smile pulled at her lips. "That would be lovely, thank you." When she walked over, he got a better view of her shoes. Black straps criss-crossed her tan skin, tying in a bow at the ankle. As she got closer, he realized she smelled as good as she looked. He'd have to ask the concierge the name of the perfume he'd brought up.

"I had to put my hair up," she told him as he handed her a glass. "I didn't have any way to curl it and I hate it when it's too straight."

He glanced at her neck again. "It looks perfect like that."

Sipping at her wine, she gave him an assessing look. "You're full of compliments tonight."

"I was brought up well."

"Is that what they teach you at prep school?" she asked. "No wonder the world is full of rich charmers."

The corner of his mouth lifted. "And what did they teach you at school?"

"How to avoid rich charmers."

He bit down a smile and clinked his glass against hers. "To rich charmers and fending them off."

She smiled. "To spotting bullshit from a fifty mile radius."

"You're going to be spotting a lot of bullshit tonight," he told her, putting his glass on the counter. "The place will be reeking of it."

"Why are you going out to dinner with your family if you don't like them?" she asked him. "Isn't life too short?"

"I need their support to move forward on the single malt. They own part of the business."

"And you and Nathan own the rest?"

"And my mother. She owns the majority share."

Becca frowned. "So why do you need their agreement? Can't you out vote them? I can't see your mom going against you."

"She always abstains. She has this thing about family being more important than anything." He shrugged. "Maybe it's the guilt that she broke their family up, I don't know. But unless I persuade Lawrence and Nina to agree, then the project is over."

Becca bit down a smile. "Your mom is a hardass."

"I know." He raised an eyebrow. "And it's damn annoying."

She put her empty glass in the wet bar sink, and turned. "Now I know where you get it from. Take me out to dinner and let me meet your family. I have a feeling they'll make mine look like the Brady Bunch."

CHAPTER TWELVE

Daniel climbed out of the back seat, extending his hand to Becca. She grasped it, trying to exit the car as elegantly as possible, considering she was wearing a short dress and sexy high heels. It felt natural to keep their hands clasped together as they walked up the steps to Jessie's Restaurant, an old colonial-style townhouse in the center of town.

Catching a glimpse of their reflections in the glass of the door, Becca swallowed hard. She looked like a different person in these clothes. More sophisticated and assured. In a weird way, she felt it, too.

Daniel was wearing a navy suit with slim pants that were expertly tailored to his body. With his pale blue shirt and burgundy tie he looked heartstoppingly handsome.

"You sure you want to do this?" he murmured as he pushed at the door. There was a quizzical expression on his face.

"Of course." She smiled at him, not willing to show any weakness. "I'm hungry."

The corners of his eyes crinkled. "Don't tell me that I didn't warn you."

There was this strange intimacy between them. Becca found herself liking it a little too much. Maybe it was the fact she'd driven over two hours to help him, or his confession about his illness that made her heart ache for his childhood self.

Or the fact that right now it seemed like them against the world. Whatever it was, he didn't seem in any hurry to release her hand as they walked inside and he spoke quietly to the maître d'. She wasn't exactly desperate to release his, either. She liked the warmth of his palm, the feeling of his fingers curled around hers. He had a firm grasp that made her feel secure.

"Ah, Mr. Carter." The maître d' gave Daniel a warm smile. "The rest of your party is already here. Let me show you to your table."

He walked them toward a large circular table at the center of the restaurant. Daniel's hold on her hand tightened a little as four people stood up. The man on the left was tall and slim – thin, even – his hair sandy and thick, and his long face tapered to a point at his chin. Next to him was a slim brunette, her dark hair was a cloud of waves to her shoulders. She was looking at Daniel with soft eyes, her lips slightly parted.

"Daniel." The tall man nodded, then slid his gaze to Becca, his eyebrow lifting. "We were wondering who the sixth seat was for."

"Lawrence." Daniel kept his voice even. "This is Becca Hartson. Becca, this is my brother, Lawrence." He gestured at the sandy haired man. Lawrence gave her a nod. "And next to him is Melissa." He paused for the slightest of seconds. "His wife."

Melissa's pink lips curled up as she looked at Becca. "Hello."

"And this is my sister, Nina and her husband, Charles." Daniel gestured to an older couple, the woman with a short sandy bob that held a natural wave. The man with her had a shiny dome of a head, with closely cropped hair along the sides.

"Becca?" Nina said. "Short for Rebecca?" She offered her hand to Becca, who shook it.

"Yes, but nobody calls me that. Unless I'm being yelled at." She smiled.

None of them smiled back at her. Okay, so humor wasn't going to cut it. Daniel slid his hand from hers and pulled out a chair, pressing his palm against the small of her back as she sat down. The others followed suit, as the waiter took her and Daniel's drink orders.

"Just a glass of wine for me, please."

"Of course, Madam. Would you like to look at the wine list?"

She shook her head. "House white will be fine."

"They do an amazing Californian Pinot here," Melissa said. She had a low husky voice. The kind that could lull you into a warm happy sleep. "You should try it."

"She can have the house white if she wants it," Daniel said, not looking at his brother's wife. "Choose whatever you like." He gave Becca a tight smile.

She could feel the stress wafting off him. The relaxed, smiling Daniel of only a few minutes ago had disappeared. So this was what his family did to him.

"What are *you* drinking?" she asked him.

"Something red," he told her. "And alcoholic." The last bit was said so low that only she could hear.

She gave him a smile. "Why don't you order for me, too?"

Daniel took the wine list from the waiter, shooting her a warm look. He quickly ordered and handed the list back.

"So, Becca, what do you do?" Nina asked, smiling tightly over at her.

"I'm a distiller at GSC."

Lawrence lifted a brow. "A workplace affair, Daniel?" From the corner of her eye she could see Daniel's jaw twitch.

"It's not an affair," Daniel pointed out. "Neither of us are married."

He hadn't denied a relationship between them, even though it would have been the truth. Becca tried to ignore the thrill shooting through her veins.

"Still, we all know that work and pleasure don't mix. Or they shouldn't." Lawrence lifted a cocktail to his lips, his knuckles white as he held the glass. "Isn't that right?"

Becca shifted in her seat. There was an undercurrent between them that she couldn't quite work out. It felt like more than bad blood over their parents' relationships.

"I didn't realize you were still interested in my love life." Daniel took his wine glass from the waiter, lifting it straight to his lips. When he'd taken a sip, he placed it on the table.

"I'm just making conversation." Lawrence shrugged. He looked at Becca. "Would you like me to change the subject?"

Becca lifted her chin and met his gaze. "Only if you want to. You're not making me uncomfortable."

"See?" Lawrence said to Daniel. "Becca's fine with the questions."

"Then ask her." Daniel's voice was low.

Melissa's arm moved beneath the tablecloth, as though she was squeezing her husband's leg. "What does your family do?" she asked, smiling at Becca.

Daniel gave a short laugh. "Why do you assume her family does one thing? Not everybody lives off their ancestral wealth. Some people make their own way in the world."

Damn he was stressed. Becca wondered what he'd do if she squeezed his thigh like Melissa was squeezing Lawrence's.

Have a fit, probably.

She smiled at Melissa instead. "I have four brothers. The eldest is a musician, my middle brother is a retired football player, and the other two are entrepreneurs."

"A musician?" Nina said, smiling. "How lovely." She exuded a motherly warmth.

"Where are you from?" Lawrence asked.

"She's one of the Hartson's Creek Hartsons," Daniel said. She couldn't tell if he was being sarcastic or not.

"Oh god, that's such a quaint little town," Melissa said. "Do you remember when I had to drive around for two hours trying to find a chai latte?"

Daniel nodded. "I remember."

Lawrence called the waiter over to take their orders. Melissa's hands were both on her menu now.

"What's it like working for Daniel?" Charles asked. It was the first time he'd spoke.

"Hell, probably," Lawrence muttered.

"Actually, it's been wonderful." Becca shot Daniel a smile. He was still stiff, as though somebody had shot a rod through his back. "He challenges me. I like that."

"But do you challenge *him*?" Charles asked.

"All the damn time." Daniel turned to Becca with a wry smile. She grinned back at him. Did he know how devastating his smiles were? Maybe that's why he didn't use them very much. The whole world would probably stop turning if he was always smiling.

"Actually," Daniel said, once he'd given his order. "One of the reasons I'm here is to talk to you about the new product we're working on. I need board approval for some changes."

"Do we have to talk about business now?" Melissa asked. "You've only just got here."

"Daniel doesn't know how to talk about anything else," Lawrence said smoothly.

Becca felt her own spine stiffen. God, they were horrendous. "Really?" She turned to look at Lawrence and his wife. "I find that Daniel talks about a lot of things." Reaching up, she cupped Daniel's cheek. This time he didn't stop her. If anything, he leaned into her palm.

His gaze met hers. She could see herself reflected in the darks of his eyes. "He's one of the most interesting men I've ever met," she murmured, staring straight at him. A ghost of a smile passed over his lips. She leaned forward, pressing her mouth to the corner of them.

"What are you doing?" Daniel murmured into her ear.

She turned her head so they couldn't see her. "Just go with it. Your family are assholes."

She felt his chest move with a chuckle. But he didn't pull away. Instead, he moved his hand to the back of her neck, his fingers stroking her skin. An electric shiver shot through her.

"I'm only interesting because you like me," Daniel said, his voice louder now.

"Is that right?" She smiled up at him. God, she wanted to feel his lips on hers again. Properly this time. How had she ever thought he was an asshole? Compared to his family, he was sweetness and light.

He dropped his brow until it was touching hers. She could feel the warmth of his breath against her skin. Then he tipped his head until his lips brushed against hers and she was on fire.

Okay, not literally. But damn, her whole body felt like it had been turned up twenty degrees.

Somebody cleared their throat. Daniel winked at her,

then released his hold on her neck, slowly pulling back, as though the world hadn't just tilted on its axis.

It took her a few seconds to remember how to send a message from her brain to her muscles. As she turned away from Daniel, she realized that all four of them were staring at them.

Charles was grinning. Nina looked surprised. Lawrence was shaking his head, and Melissa was glaring with narrowed eyes.

Becca felt Daniel relax beside her. "Sorry," he drawled. "I can't help it. She's beautiful."

They'd finished dessert before business was brought up again. In another time, the gentlemen would probably have left to go to another room for brandy and cigars while the women gossiped about them. Thank god it wasn't another time, because for some reason Melissa didn't like Becca. She could tell by the weird side glances she kept getting.

Maybe she was used to being Queen Bee around here.

"We still need to talk business at some point," Daniel said as he sipped his coffee. "When would be a good time?"

Lawrence smiled, though it didn't reach his eyes. "We're pretty tied up with the Charity Ball at the moment. It's this weekend." He blinked, as though an idea just hit him. "Why don't you join us there?" He glanced at Becca. "Both of you. Then we can take some time on Sunday to talk about the business."

Daniel swallowed. "I'm not sure. We'll have to check our schedules."

Becca leaned against him, kissing his cheek. "Don't be silly, darling. We'd love to, wouldn't we? I bet you look amazing in a tux." She bit down a smile. "And even better out of it."

Daniel coughed out a laugh. "Now do you see why I like her?"

"She's refreshing," Nina said, her voice warm.

"I like her, too," Charles said, nodding.

Neither Lawrence or Melissa said anything. They were too busy staring at each other, having an unspoken conversation.

Five minutes later, Daniel had paid for the bill, sliding a card into the leather folder so stealthily Becca hadn't realized it was there until the waiter brought over the slip for Daniel to sign. "We should get back to the hotel," Daniel said, standing. He held a hand out for Becca. "It's been a long day, especially for you."

She smiled up at him. "I still have some energy left."

Charles sniggered.

Daniel lifted a brow. "I know something that can help with that." He leaned forward, brushing his lips against her cheek. "The hotel has a good gym," he murmured. It was Becca's turn to bite down a grin. Touché.

Sliding his hand casually around her waist, Daniel nodded at his family. "Thank you for a pleasant evening."

They stood to say their goodbyes, Lawrence and Charles shaking hands, Nina hugging them both. Melissa gave air kisses.

"We'll see you at the ball," Lawrence said, giving Becca a nod.

"I'll try to remember my glass slippers."

Daniel grinned again, and pressed his palm into her back. "Come on, let's get you back to the hotel."

CHAPTER THIRTEEN

The car pulled away from the restaurant, driving through the empty roads toward Daniel's hotel. There was a half smile on his face as he leaned back against the seat, his long legs stretched out in front of him. He turned to Becca, looking casually amused.

"*I'll try to remember my glass slippers?*" he quoted. His thigh was pressed against hers, the warmth of him burning through his dress pants. She tipped her head and lifted a brow.

"It was funny," she told him. "Or at least you thought it was."

His smile widened. "I thought it was hilarious. It went over Lawrence's head though."

"Well, right now I'm wishing I had a crowd of willing mice to make me a dress. What do people wear to balls anyway?"

"I'll tell Lawrence you couldn't make it. You don't have to endure a second evening with my family. I'm pretty sure once was more than enough."

Becca looked at him carefully. "Are you afraid I'll embarrass you?"

His smile dissolved. "No." He shook his head quickly. "That's not what I'm thinking at all. I'll go to the ball for an hour, show my face, then meet Lawrence and Nina on Sunday. You shouldn't have to endure it for my sake."

"What if I want to go?" she asked him.

Daniel tipped his head, eyeing her carefully. "*Do* you?"

"Yes."

He turned to look out of the window. He could see the lights of the hotel in the distance. "You'll wear a gown to the ball. I'll pay for it."

"I can buy my own clothes."

"I know. But I'm already in your debt. I don't want to be any deeper."

The driver climbed out to open the door. Daniel took Becca's hand and led her from the car, sliding a tip into the driver's palm as he shook it.

"You hold my hand a lot," Becca said as he nodded at the concierge.

"Do you want me to stop?" He flexed his fingers. Her skin was soft and warm. It made him wonder what the rest of her felt like.

"No. I like it."

Pleasure pulsed through him.

He wasn't sure what he was doing here. Or what Becca was doing, for that matter. Since she'd started touching and kissing him in the restaurant, his mind was firmly in one place. It was taking a force of will not to pull her against him, so he could feel the softness of her curves against his firm chest.

"Can I ask you something?" Becca said, as he pressed the button for the penthouse elevator.

"If I said no, would it stop you?"

She laughed. "Probably not. Why didn't you just tell your family to go to hell? You don't usually have a problem speaking your mind."

His eyes caught hers. "Because I want something from them. And that desire outweighs the need to tell them they're assholes."

"Are you always so singular when you want something?"

The elevator pinged as the gold patterned doors opened. He gestured for Becca to walk inside first. He joined her and the doors slid closed, the car gently beginning its ascent.

"Nearly always," he said, in answer to her question. She was leaning against the side of the car, her arms behind her, fingers wrapped around the rail. In the warm light of the elevator, her skin looked almost luminescent.

"What's the exception?" Her gaze held his.

"When I want something I can't have." His voice was low. Thick.

Her lips parted as she exhaled softly. "Can't have? Or shouldn't want?" Her eyes reflected the overhead light. The tension between them grew and twisted. He could feel it deep inside him, churning. Damn, he wanted her. Needed to feel the softness of her skin. Hear her ragged gasp as he kissed her until she couldn't remember her name.

"Both." He hit the stop button, halting the elevator. He wasn't ready to end this conversation. She looked at him with hooded eyes, her skin blushing and pink and so damn touchable. "I have a question for you."

"You do?" She moistened her lips with the tip of her tongue. He could feel a muscle ticking at the edge of his jaw.

"What do *you* want?" he asked.

"*Now?*"

"Right now." His eyes bore into hers. He wanted her to say it. To tell him. To give him the green light his body was aching for. Her consent was the key, and he needed her to turn it over willingly.

Otherwise he'd walk away. Even if it killed him.

"I want you to kiss me."

He was mere millimeters from her before the last word had escaped her lips. Sliding his hand behind her neck to angle her face to his, he pressed his body to hers with sweet relief.

Her eyes closed as he traced his finger down her back, following the dip of her spine and the gentle curve of her ass. He brushed his lips against her neck, her jaw, drawing a line of fire to the tender skin beneath her ear. Her breath escaped in a rush as she curved into him.

"Do you know how much you rile me up?" he asked her, dragging her earlobe between his teeth.

Her lips curved at that. Her eyes were still shut, her skin flushed. He pressed his fingers into the softness of her flesh and lowered his mouth to hers, feeling the rush of air against his skin as he closed the minute distance between them.

Her lips were soft and sweet. They parted on a sigh and he slid his tongue against her, inside her. Blood rushed to his groin as she licked him back. Cupping her jaw with his strong palm, he kissed her confidently, his mouth curling against hers as she moaned softly and wrapped her arms around him.

His heart raged against his ribcage, hot blood pumping through him as she arched her body against his. He was achingly hard, the throb between his thighs matching the pulse in his neck. Becca's hands slid inside his jacket, her fingers tugging at his shirt until she touched his skin. She rolled her hips and the pressure sent him crazy, kissing her harder until he couldn't remember where she ended and he began. It was a dance as old as time. Choreographed by their intense need for each other. There was only one ending, and he knew he would make it good for her.

"Mr. Carter, is there a problem?" The voice echoed through the speaker. He looked up and saw a camera, his eyes blinking in surprise.

"Damn." He pulled away from her, tugging her dress down from where it had ridden up against him. Becca's eyelids opened. She looked dazed.

"No problem," he said, pressing the speaker, followed by the penthouse button. His voice was thick with need. "Goodnight."

"Goodnight, sir." The speaker clicked off and a moment later the doors to the penthouse lobby opened. Daniel stalked out, his jaw tight, his body still reacting to Becca's closeness.

He heard her exit behind him, her heels clicking against the tiled floor. For a moment he kept his back to her, willing his body to calm.

When he turned around to look at her, there were two red circles on her cheeks, and her hair was falling out of her curled bun. She was staring up at him, as though she was waiting for an explanation.

One he had no idea how to give.

"I'm sorry." He shook his head. "I overstepped." He pressed the code to the door, standing aside to let her in. "You should go to bed."

Becca stopped walking. He hated the hurt expression in her eyes. She'd done nothing but help him today. From the moment he'd called her at the distillery, all through the interminable dinner with his family. And even then, in the elevator, she'd been the bravest person he knew.

He's asked her what she wanted and she'd told him. He'd given it to her. And now he was going crazy. Torn between wanting to taste her all over again and doing the right thing and heading to bed.

Not to sleep, because god knew he wouldn't be able to. But to put distance between them. And two thin walls. The only defenses he had left.

"I need to check my insulin levels and take a shower," he said, as much to himself as her. "Do you have everything you need?"

She nodded silently.

"If you don't, please call reception and have it billed to the room." He was aware of how clipped his words were. Like he was talking to an employee.

Which was exactly what he was doing, dammit.

Becca swallowed and nodded again.

"Good night." He felt like an asshole. Maybe because he was exactly that. His eyes softened as he looked at her, taking in her wide eyes, swollen lips, and messed up hair. "And thank you," he told her. "For everything. You were wonderful tonight."

He turned and opened his bedroom door before she could say anything, gently pulling it closed behind him.

———

THE BED WAS TOO BIG. And too hard. She felt more like Goldilocks than Cinderella as she twisted and turned, the sheets tangled between her legs as she tried in vain to find a comfortable position.

She'd been trying to sleep for two hours now. The alarm clock told her it was one in the morning. In a few hours she'd need to get up and drive straight to work. Unless she got some sleep now, she was going to be a wreck.

Sighing, she dropped her head back on the pillow, gazing up at the ceiling. The kiss in the elevator was playing over in her mind. The way he'd tipped her head with his demanding fingers, as though her lips were made only for him. The way he'd pressed his body against hers so she was left in no doubt exactly how turned on he was.

He'd kissed her softly at first, then harder until every line between them blurred. As she'd stroked her fingers over his warm, muscled stomach, it had seemed inevitable that they'd end up in bed together.

Yet now she was here alone.

She glanced at the clock, disappointed that only one minute had passed since her last time check. She gave a grunt of annoyance and sat up. This was stupid. When she was little and she couldn't sleep, Aunt Gina always told her she needed to break the pattern.

"Come downstairs and have a cup of hot chocolate, then try again. I bet it works the second time around."

And it always did. Becca doubted there was any hot chocolate in the elegant suite kitchen, but she knew for sure there was ice water. That would have to do.

The living area was dark when she walked out of her bedroom. Only the light from the city outside helped her find her way past the sofa to the kitchen area, her feet padding softly against the cool tiles. She'd reached out for the light switch, sliding her hand up and down the wall until she finally found it.

And then she'd jumped like hell, because Daniel was sitting on one of the leather stools, leaning on the breakfast bar and staring out of the windows.

"You nearly gave me a heart attack." She pressed her hand against her chest, feeling her heart hammer against it. Daniel's gaze followed her movement.

"Sorry." His smile was almost boyish. "I kept the light off because I didn't want to disturb you." He looked a little gaunt beneath the harsh strip light. His hair was mussed, and he was wearing a black t-shirt and grey sweatpants. It was the most casual she'd ever seen him.

"Are you feeling okay?" she asked. "Have you checked your blood sugar?"

He lifted a brow. "You sound like my mother."

"I'm just worried, that's all." She opened the refrigerator and grabbed a bottle of water.

"My levels are fine. I checked when I came in here." A smile played at his lips as he looked at her. "Thanks to you."

Silence fell between them. A trail of condensation ran down her hand from where she was holding the bottle. "I guess I should go back to bed," she said, twisting the bottle in the air as though it explained everything. "Good night."

She turned to go and he called out to her. "Becca?"

"Yeah?" She looked over her shoulder.

He lifted his head, his eyes catching hers. They looked bluer, less dark than earlier. "What's keeping you awake?"

She turned around, her fingers still curled around the bottle. "Knowing I have to get up early tomorrow."

"You don't have to get up early. You can sleep in."

She shook her head. "I need to leave first thing. I have a hundred things to catch up with at work."

"Because I dragged you away at lunchtime yesterday."

She smiled. "Something like that."

"At least stay for breakfast. I'll order in. If you're desperate to leave you can go after that."

She nodded. "Sounds good."

She took half a step back, but didn't turn away from him. There was something softer between them now. Not the heat of earlier. But more of a gentle cotton sheet that caressed and soothed her.

He exhaled heavily. She could see a cord of muscles in his neck. "We should probably talk about what happened earlier."

Becca's chest tightened. "Should we?"

He gave a little laugh. "Maybe something to talk about when it isn't the middle of the night."

Her muscles relaxed at the reprieve. She really didn't want to hear him telling her what a mistake it was. It had been written on his face as he ran away from her earlier. "My job's okay though, right?"

He blinked, absorbing her words. "Of course your job's okay. What do you take me for?"

"I don't know." She tightened her grip on the bottle. "It's just that I love working at GSC. It's important to me."

His gaze locked on hers. "Your job's not in danger. Not only because you could sue me if it was."

"Oh." She pulled her lip between her teeth. "I see."

He raked his fingers through his dark hair. "That didn't come out as I'd intended. I just wanted you to know you're protected. You don't need to worry about your job."

"It's fine." It really wasn't. She took another step back. "I'm going to try to get some sleep."

"Good night." He turned away from her, frowning at the breakfast bar.

"Sleep tight," she whispered, though she was pretty sure he hadn't heard her.

CHAPTER FOURTEEN

"What do you want?"

Becca blinked her eyes open at the sudden sound. She looked around, trying to center herself. It took a moment to remember she was in the guest room of Daniel's hotel suite.

"Is that any way to greet me? You were eager enough to open the door." A woman's voice. Vaguely familiar. Becca sat up and twisted until her feet hit the floor.

"I thought it was room service. I'm hungry." Daniel sounded almost bored. "Is this a social visit? Because I'd have put a tie on if I'd known you were coming."

Becca padded across the bedroom, putting her ear against the door. Why didn't they put peepholes on interior doors? It would make eavesdropping so much easier.

"I was on my way to the gym, thought I'd drop in and say hello. Where's your friend? Did she go home?"

"Her name's Becca. As you well know."

"It's a cute name. She's a cute girl."

"Is that why you're here? To tell me you like her? Because

you didn't show it last night. And since when do you go to the gym, especially at seven a.m.?"

"Since Lawrence decided to renovate the west wing. My yoga studio is out of bounds. So I have to go to the club instead."

Becca's eyes widened in recognition. Melissa, Lawrence's wife.

"Don't let me stop you." There was a click, as though Daniel had opened the door to the lobby.

"Oh stop being such a grump. I only stopped by to see how you are. You were in a terrible mood last night. No wonder Becca didn't stay."

"I'm fine."

There was a shuffle of feet, then silence for a moment. One of them cleared their throat.

"I miss you," Melissa said, so softly that Becca had to push her ear against the wood until it hurt.

"Don't." It was the same tone he'd used on Becca the time she'd tried to touch him in the rickhouse. It made her grit her teeth together.

"I miss you smiling at me the way you used to," Melissa said, her tone full of sugar. "Why didn't you smile at me last night?"

Becca's heart was hammering against her ribcage.

"You should go to yoga." There was that bored tone again. Becca almost smiled at the sound of it.

"We should dance at the ball. To show everybody there's no hard feelings. I'll save one for you."

"But there *are* hard feelings, Melissa. For both of us I imagine."

"Are you ever going to forgive me?"

"There's nothing to forgive. It's history."

Her voice dropped so low that Becca couldn't hear what she was saying. She heard Daniel say something in response, but she couldn't make that out either. Frowning, she slumped down on the edge of the bed, trying not to imagine his sister-in-law touching his chest with her elegant hand. Or Daniel gazing down at her the way he'd looked at Becca last night.

What an idiot she was. No wonder there was bad blood between Daniel and his half-siblings. He'd lied to her, told her it was all about his mother. He'd let her touch him and kiss him and pretend to be his girlfriend, all while he was sitting opposite Melissa.

They must have all been laughing at her behind those excruciatingly polite stares. He should have told her. Warned her. Was that why he played along? To hide his feelings for his brother's wife?

Not wanting to hear anymore, she rushed through her morning routine, showering and brushing her teeth at light speed. Putting on the same clothes she drove up in yesterday – nobody except Mia and Naomi would even notice at the distillery – she looped her hair into a bun and slid the dress Daniel had bought her onto a hanger, leaving it in the closet.

When she walked out of the bedroom, Melissa was gone and the breakfast had arrived. There was way too much for just the two of them. The pastry platter could have filled every stomach in the still room at GCS. It didn't stop her stomach from rumbling to look at it.

Daniel turned around, his brows knitting as he saw her slide her purse up her shoulder. "Breakfast is ready. You can sit down."

She gave him a smile. "I think I'm going to head back to the distillery now."

"Aren't you hungry?"

Another twist of her stomach told her she was. "I'll take something to go." She grabbed a danish from the pastry tray, wrapping it up in a napkin. "Thank you for dinner. And for a bed for the night."

His jaw twitched. "Is there something wrong?"

Becca shook her head. "No. I just need to get to work, that's all."

He poured a glass of juice, tipping his head to the side. "You heard Melissa." It was a statement, not a question.

Becca put her hands up, giving him a shrug. "What you do with your brother's wife is your business."

"I'm not doing *anything* with my brother's wife." His eyes looked dark.

"That's not what it sounded like to me."

His eyes narrowed. His stare was uncomfortably piercing. "You think I'm sleeping with Melissa?"

The harshness of his words were like a bucket of ice water. "I don't know..." she stuttered. She just wanted to go home.

"Jesus, is that what you think of me? That I'm having an affair with my brother's wife?" He stood up, his face flaming as he pressed his hand down on the breakfast bar.

Becca took a step back. He was too big, too angry, too menacing. "I..." She glanced at the door, trying to work out how quickly she could get to it.

"Get out."

Her heart started hammering against her ribcage. He was angry. Maybe she was, too. "I was just about to."

"Good." He turned away from her. She could see the tenseness of his shoulders. She'd almost made it to the door when he spoke again. "And for the record, I'm not sleeping with Melissa. I *slept with her. Past tense.* When we were in a relationship years ago. Before she decided my brother was a better bet."

Her hand froze on the handle as his words seeped in. Her stomach churned as she realized he wasn't the one doing the cheating. She'd made assumptions. The wrong ones.

Becca looked over her shoulder. Daniel had walked over

to the huge window, and was staring out at it, his hands jammed into his pockets, his shirt taut across his back. The sun was shining brightly, casting a halo around his rigid body

"I'm sorry. I shouldn't have assumed." Her chest felt achy. Tense.

"Just go."

But she couldn't. She felt so damn bad. "Daniel, I…"

"Go!" His voice was harsh. Loud. It sent a shiver of fear down her spine. With a shaking hand she managed to open the door to the lobby, hearing it swing softly closed as she jabbed her finger on the elevator button.

CHAPTER FIFTEEN

He drove like a maniac back to Hartson's Creek, testing out his new Corvette Stingray to the limit. Not that it made him feel any better. The combination of last night's tense family dinner followed by the goddamn aggravating events of this morning were still rushing around his mind as he parked at the distillery just before lunchtime.

Not to mention the memory of that elevator kiss.

And that was all before Becca realized how messed up his family was.

Her car was parked in its usual spot, to the left of the main door. He'd gotten used to checking if it was there every morning. The sun was reflecting off the red hood, making him squint.

Sandy smiled at him as he walked through the sliding glass doors. "How was Charleston?"

He inhaled deeply. "Charleston was… interesting."

"Well it's good to have you back."

"Is my mother in today?"

Sandy nodded. "Her driver dropped her off this morning."

"And is there anything else I need to know?" *Like whether Becca Hartson is feeling as fucking confused as I am right now?*

"One of the stills stopped working, but Joe got it up and running half an hour ago. I heard Becca say we'd be running it until late tonight."

The sound of her name danced through his ears. He curled his fingers, giving no other visible sign that it affected him. "What time did Miss Hartson get in this morning?"

"Just after ten. She said she'd been running errands for you."

"Yes, that's correct." He nodded. "I'll be in my office if you need me."

"Sure thing."

There was no sign of Becca in the still room as he walked through. He'd stopped to talk to Garrett Rhys about the broken still, and authorized the overtime it would take to meet today's production numbers. Then he walked into the administration wing, glancing at the kitchen to see it empty, and pushed through the door to the executive corridor, stopping to look through his mother's door.

"You're back. How did it go?" Eliana stood and walked over to him, turning her head so he could kiss her cheek.

"As expected."

"How were Lawrence and Nina?" She walked back to her black leather chair, taking a seat, and gesturing to him to sit on the chair opposite.

"Again, as expected."

She looked at him carefully. "And Melissa?"

"Was there." His voice was short.

A smile played at her lips. "I can always rely on you to regale me with a story." She lifted an eyebrow to let him know she was joking.

Daniel ran his finger along his jaw. It was freshly smooth

from his morning shave. "Nothing was decided. I have to go back for the weekend. I agreed to go to Lawrence's ball."

"I know. His assistant called me this morning and asked if I'd mind you sitting at my table."

"*You're* going?" Daniel asked, surprised.

"I always do. You haven't been here to notice. And don't look so shocked, it's for charity. I can sit there and deal with Lawrence's glares for a couple of hours. And he likes my donations too much to turn me away."

"I'll never get why you put yourself through all this family bullshit." He only had last night and that was already enough.

"The same reason you do. Pride." She glanced at the paper in front of her, then back up at him. "You're bringing a plus one, they said?" Her voice was even, but he could tell from the spark in her eyes that she was desperate to know more.

"I was thinking about it. But I'll probably go alone."

"Becca Hartson?" She wasn't letting it go. Daniel sighed heavily.

"It's a long story. And as I said, it's likely I'll go solo."

"You should bring her. Becca's a lot of fun. It'd make a dull night a little lighter." There was a hint of hope in her voice. The sort that needed to be quashed immediately or it would grow like crazy and ruin his life forever.

He shook his head. He'd learned by experience that it was better not to run headlong down his mother's rabbit holes.

"Maybe I'll ask her as *my* guest," Eliana said, looking carefully at him to gauge his reaction.

"Don't." His voice was firm.

"But, darling," she protested. "I want her to be there."

He shook his head. "It's complicated, and I don't need you making it worse. So no, don't ask her."

His mother sighed. "I wish you'd let me in a little more. It's like talking to a brick wall. Or your father."

Daniel's nostrils flared. "Thanks for that comparison."

"Your father had many good qualities. And so do you. But communication isn't one of them."

Daniel stood and tapped her desk with his fingers. "In that case, I guess I should get back to work. I've got a lot to catch up on."

"I'll keep the seat free. In case you change your mind."

"I won't." He headed to the door, shaking his head. His mother was obstinate. When she got something in her mind it was almost impossible to get her to let go.

"Oh, and you can stay at my place in Charleston this weekend," his mother called out, "I'll have Rona make up the guest rooms."

"Room. Singular." He turned to raise an eyebrow at her. He knew exactly what she was doing, and he wasn't having it. "For one person only."

"That's what I meant, darling. Have a good afternoon. Dinner tonight?" She gave him an innocent smile.

"Not tonight, I have things to do." Like pull his eyelashes out one by one. Or stare moodily at the wall and determine why the heck he couldn't stop thinking about a certain distiller.

"Okay then." She smiled, as though she'd won a game he hadn't even known they were playing. "Maybe tomorrow."

———

THE FLOWERS ARRIVED right before five that evening. Sandy called her to the reception desk, beaming madly as Becca took in the elegant white arrangement sitting on the center of the desk.

"These are for you," Sandy pushed the arrangement toward her. "Aren't they beautiful?"

Becca gaped at them. She hadn't expected an apology from Daniel. Not this fast, anyway. And maybe she didn't even deserve one. She wasn't sure who owed who what. This morning's argument felt hazy, and she couldn't quite figure out who was in the wrong. She'd made assumptions, but then he'd yelled at her to leave.

Maybe neither of them owed each other anything. Wouldn't that be nice and easy?

"I didn't know you have an admirer," Sandy said. She was wearing her jacket as though she was about to leave, but she didn't seem in a hurry.

"Me either." Becca lifted the envelope from where it was nestled amid the blooms. Loosening the flap, she pulled the card halfway out, being careful not to let Sandy read over her shoulder.

THANK YOU FOR AN AMAZING EVENING. *I was smiling all weekend.*

Shawn

IGNORING the weird pang of disappointment tugging at her gut, Becca slid the card back into the arrangement. The weekend felt like forever ago. She'd danced with Shawn but nothing more had happened. She could barely remember what he looked like with her thoughts full of twisted lips and dark eyes. "Can I leave them behind your desk and pick them up on my way out?"

"Are you working late tonight?"

"No, Garrett's covering the late run. I just need to finish a few things up."

Sandy curled her hands around the vase. "You should really put these in fresh water. But I guess they'll be fine for an hour. Make sure you cut half an inch off the stems when you get home. They'll last longer that way."

"Sure. Have a good evening." She gave Sandy a wave and headed back to the still room, checking in with Garrett and the two operators who'd finish the run that evening. There were a few more tasks she needed to do before she could leave – making sure they had enough ground corn to start the next run in the morning, and a quick chat with Mia, her almost-sister-in-law, about some marketing they were doing for the International Blend.

"I hear you're making some tweaks to the blend," Mia said when Becca caught up to her twenty minutes later. She was pulling her jacket on, ready to leave.

"Just a few. Daniel suggested them." Even saying his name made her chest ache a little. It was all too awkward to think about. This was why people said not to mix business with pleasure. They had a point.

"Are you two talking to each other now? I thought you hated him."

"It was him hating me. And we're working together, so we have to talk." Or were they? Maybe he wouldn't want her on the project now that she'd pissed him off all over again.

"Well, it sounds good. I like the idea of putting less of the scotch in to make it really stand out. I can go with that." Mia grabbed her briefcase. "Are you heading out now? We can walk together."

Becca nodded. "Sure. I need to pick up my jacket on the way."

They made it through the still room and into reception before Becca remembered the flowers she'd left there. She glanced at Mia. "You go on ahead, I have to pick something up from behind the desk."

"Okay. Have a good evening." Mia gave her a hug. "Do you have much planned?" she asked, releasing her.

"I'll probably do some baking. Or maybe go for a walk. It's a nice evening." Anything to not think about last night. Or this morning.

"You're always welcome at ours. Cam and Michael are at some football thing, so it's just me and Josh. We'll probably watch something on Netflix. Come over if you're bored."

Becca flashed her a grateful smile. "I might do that."

Mia walked out of the main door as Becca made her way to the back of the desk, where Sandy had set the bouquet. She hunkered down to pick the vase up, right as Daniel walked through from the still room.

It was the first time they'd laid eyes on each other since their argument in the penthouse. She felt her fingers tremble as they held the flower box.

He stilled, his eyes raking her face, then dipping to the flowers.

"Yours?" he asked, unsmiling.

"Yes." She gave him a sickly sweet smile of her own to make up for it. "They arrived today. Complete surprise. Aren't they beautiful?" If this was a game, she'd just served an ace. For a moment she felt invincible.

But his face was devoid of emotion. Why was it that her heart always jumped like a kid on a trampoline whenever he was around? She wanted to dislike him. It was so much easier when she did. Because this weird, frantic need was impossible to ignore.

"I'm going home." She had no idea why she said it. Maybe to break the silence that was killing her.

"Have a good evening." He still wasn't smiling. *Bastard.*

"You too."

He nodded and turned to walk back the way he came, whatever he'd come to do in the reception forgotten. Sighing, Becca hitched the flowers in her arm and walked around the desk and out of the door, exhaling heavily when she reached her car from holding her breath for too long.

He made her feel things she didn't want to feel, and it was annoying as heck. Not because the attraction to him wasn't delicious, because it was. It made her feel more alive than she'd felt in years.

And she knew she couldn't have him.

ONE JAB TO THE BAG. Then another. Enough to make it swing back from his punch. Follow it up with a dodge and an attack so damn hard that it made his muscles ache and his forehead break out in a sweat.

Sparring with the punching bag wasn't cutting it. Just like the run he'd gone on as soon as he'd gotten home hadn't cut it earlier. He hit the bag again, hoping that this one would push her out of his mind, but instead she loomed larger.

Damn it. He needed to stop thinking about her.

He'd started training with a punching bag when he first moved to Scotland. It had been a way to stop being so wound up about the life he'd left behind. The only way he could control the anger that threatened to consume him.

Escaping to the gym had allowed him to regain control of his life. To be only mildly pissed off instead of constantly irate. But now it felt like he'd regressed, and nothing was helping him calm down. All he could think about were those damn flowers Becca had received.

Who were they from?

He should have been the one to buy her flowers. He owed her an apology, after all. But instead he'd stared at them and walked away, afraid that if he opened his mouth he'd piss her off even more.

Pulling his gloves off, he threw them on the floor and

stalked over to the bathroom he'd installed in his home gym. Stripping off his workout clothes, he threw them into the hamper before walking into the double length shower. He turned the water to cold, to try to shock himself out of his fury, but it did nothing. Just made him shiver.

Once dressed, he ran his hands through his damp hair to try to get it under control, as he walked into the living room and switched on the TV. Almost immediately he turned it off again, and strode to the kitchen, yanking open the refrigerator and staring into the abyss. He didn't even focus on the food. He was too busy thinking about all the breakfast food he'd left for housekeeping to clean up at the hotel this morning.

Because *she* didn't stay.

Because *he'd* upset her.

Letting the door swing shut, he stomped to the hallway and grabbed his keys, desperate to get out of this house. It felt too big and too small all at the same time. Fresh air would work.

Or a drive in his car, foot down as he cruised up the highway.

Maybe then he could start to think properly.

CHAPTER SIXTEEN

Pulling a tray of fragrant cranberry and white chocolate muffins from the oven, Becca slid off her oven mitts, transferring the muffins to a cooling rack. She'd come straight home and pulled the ingredients out, determined to do something other than think about today.

And last night.

Not that it was working. Every five minutes or so he'd flash into her mind, that blank expression on his face when he'd seen her flowers in reception. She'd hoped for anything other than blankness. She would've been happier if he'd shown her his usual pissed-off frown. Because at least then he'd be feeling something.

And she *wanted* him to feel something when she was around. The same way she did whenever his name was mentioned.

Shaking her head at herself, she decided to take Mia up on her offer. A movie with her and Josh was preferable to sulking in her apartment all evening.

Sliding her feet into her sneakers, she grabbed a light jacket from the hook beside the front door and jammed her arms into it. Then she ran back to the kitchen and grabbed a container, putting four of the still-hot muffins inside. If she took them out when she got to Mia's they should still be yummy.

With the tub in one hand, she opened the front door with the other, and nearly dropped the damn muffins when she saw Daniel standing only inches away from her.

With an expression that looked like it could kill anybody within a hundred yards.

"Oh."

Daniel's lips twisted into a frown. "Becca." There was a masculine deepness to his voice that made her pulse race. "Are you going somewhere?"

She looked down at the muffin tin. "To see a friend."

"Can I talk to you for a moment before you leave?"

"Um, I guess." She didn't move, though her pulse was nearing critical levels. "How do you know where I live?"

He lifted an eyebrow.

"My personnel file?" Had he looked inside it? Weird how warm that made her feel.

"Actually, I got it from your aunt. I called the number listed in your file and she said you'd moved out a few months ago. You should probably update your details."

"Is that why you're here? Because I didn't put in a change of address form with HR? Are you going to discipline me for it?" Her voice was more tart than she'd intended. But damn, would it kill him to give her a smile?

"I bought you these," he said, picking up an arrangement of white lilies. They were pretty and huge and she had to remember how to breathe. "As an apology for this morning." He ran the tip of his tongue along his bottom lip. "And because nobody buys you flowers but me."

"Oh." She had no idea what to say.

"I also want to talk to you."

"Now you want to talk." She shifted her feet. "You didn't seem very talkative earlier when you threw me out of your hotel room." The memory of it stung her.

He lifted his hand to his temple and took in a deep breath. "Why is it that every time you open your mouth you drive me crazy?" he murmured, then frowned at his own words. "Jesus, I'm supposed to be apologizing, not making it worse."

"Maybe I just naturally annoy you." She shrugged. "It's my superpower. I just never needed it until now."

"You do annoy me." His voice was low. "So damn much you wouldn't believe it."

She stared back at him, her chin lifted, her eyes narrowed. "The feeling's mutual."

"Do you know how hard it was to keep away from you last night?" he carried on as though he hadn't heard her. "Knowing you were so close yet so far."

"Why didn't you come get me?" There was so much tension in the air it was getting hard to breathe. And a little madness in his eyes. The same madness she felt rushing through her body whenever he was near.

He hated her. He liked her. Neither of them mattered right now. Because whatever this thing between them was, it was making the air around them fizz and crackle.

He's bad news.

Yeah, but bad news had never looked so delicious.

"I didn't come to your room because I would have been lost."

It was strange, with *been* in the sentence. She'd understand it if he'd said he would have lost. But *would have been lost?* What did that mean? Because it felt like a game they were both about to lose.

The door from the unit across the hall opened. Just the tiniest gap, but enough to let her know that prying ears were trying to listen. She reached forward and yanked him inside, and slammed the door behind him.

Daniel looked down at her hand, still circling his wrist. "Problems?"

"My neighbor works at my brother's farm." When he still looked confused, she added, "Well, his and his wife's."

"And you don't want them to know I'm here." He looked over her shoulder, taking in the apartment. Her living space was all one room, small enough to fit inside the suite he'd stayed in last night, and still have room left over.

"Your hair is wet," she murmured, more to break the silence than anything else.

"I was working out. Took a shower." A ghost of a smile crossed his lips. "I thought it would help relieve the stress."

"Then you decided to come around here and let your tension hit the roof all over again."

He moved the arm she was holding and put the flowers on the side table. Then he took the tin of muffins from her hands and put them down, sliding his fingers through hers. "I came here because you're like a damn magnet I can't avoid. No matter how hard I fight, I keep ending up right in front of you."

"Why are you fighting?" she asked, confused. "Why do you keep pulling away?"

"Because I'm no good for you."

Becca lifted a brow. "You don't strike me as someone who cares how good he is for people."

"Okay then, you're no good for me."

"Ouch."

He closed his eyes, inhaling sharply. "That didn't come out right. You're a good person, Becca. Too good. Like some kind of flame that lights up every dark corner you find. But some darkness can't be lit. And I'm so damn afraid I'll end up breaking you."

"I'm not that breakable." Her voice was low. Soft. "And what right do you have to decide whether or not I want to be broken?"

He lifted their joined hands together, pressing the back of her palm against his cheek. He breathed in, then exhaled slowly, not releasing his hold.

"I don't want to be like my family, messing lives up. I promised myself I wouldn't. I'm not a nice person. I'm definitely not the kind of guy you should be looking for. I'm the one in the shadows who should give you the creeps."

She slid her fingers from his, turning her hand so her palm was cupping his jaw. He squeezed his eyes shut, as though it hurt. But he didn't push her away.

"You don't give me the creeps."

He leaned his face against her hand. "I should frighten you." His voice was raw. "You should run away. I'm not the guy next door. I don't believe in relationships. I don't believe in happily ever afters. I've seen what they do to people. And I don't want to hurt you, I really don't."

"You're hurting me by pulling away."

"Becca..." it was a breath. A plea, maybe. She felt his words curl around her, heat her skin and make her own breath catch. Bold, she took a step closer, until she was inches away from him. He was looking at her, eyes dark, imploring.

As though she had the strength to walk away.

She didn't. Not now.

Without batting a lash, he slid his arm around her waist, pressing his strong palm to the small of her back. But he didn't close the gap between them. And she really wanted him to.

"Kiss me," she whispered.

He grimaced. "I can't."

"Why not?" She tipped her head up. His gaze was fixed on her mouth.

"Because if I kiss you, I'm going to carry you to your bedroom and strip your clothing off and neither of us will survive it."

"So that's it. We go to work and pretend this never happened? Just smile politely at each other across the still room?"

There was a rumble in his chest. As though he was trying to laugh but couldn't. "I don't know. I guess…"

"Maybe if we kissed again it wouldn't be so good. We could get each other out of our systems." It was a lie. She knew it and he did, too. She was bargaining, trying to find a way to feel his mouth move against hers again. Anything to quench the constant, pulsing need rushing through her body.

She was an addict desperate for a fix.

He pressed his hand against her back, pulling her closer, until her soft body was against his. She could feel the ridged plane of his abdomen, the thickness of his chest muscles, and the hard, aching need, that he was feeling for her.

"You want to know what I did when I got back to the office today?" he asked, his voice thick.

She blinked at the abrupt change in conversation. "What?"

"I spoke to my lawyer. Talked about ways to pay you off and get you to leave the company. How to avoid getting sued for being an absolute asshole."

"I'd never sue you."

"You should."

She shook her head. "And I wouldn't leave either. I love my job."

"I know." He sounded lost. "And that's why I told him it was impossible. You love your job, I own the company. We're at an impasse."

She could smell the scent of his soap. Clean and woody. It filled her senses, the same way he did. "The ball's going to be interesting," she murmured.

"You're not going."

"Yes, I am. My invitation arrived by courier today."

The corner of his lip twitched. "Lawrence always did like to make sure he got what he wanted."

"I don't care what Lawrence wants." She felt emboldened by his touch. By her need. "I care what *you* want."

"I don't want you to go."

"Why not?"

He dropped his brow to hers, closing his eyes as he breathed her in. "Because I won't be able to stop from touching you."

"You're touching me now."

"I'm leaving in a moment. I can do that much at least."

"We'll be in public at the ball. It won't matter if you touch me. If you kiss me, even. You won't be able to throw me over your shoulder like a caveman." Although now she had that image in her head, and she couldn't get it out.

"True." He ran his fingertip along her jaw, looking at her through his thick lashes.

"Take me to the ball," she urged. "After that, I promise I won't push you anymore. I'll avoid you if I need to. If that's what you want."

His fingertip stopped at the corner of her mouth. His brows were dipped, as though he was concentrating. Taking in every one of her features.

"Okay. You win." He pressed his lips to the tip of her nose. Then to her eyelids, his kisses so soft they sent shivers down her spine. "I'll take you to the ball."

CHAPTER SEVENTEEN

*H*ad he really agreed to take her to the ball at his brother's house and be seen together in public? Daniel sat back in his office, raking his fingers through his hair, still trying to work out what had happened last night.

He'd sat outside her building for half an hour before he'd given up fighting himself and walked to her condo, letting the dark side of him win through as he knocked at the door.

It wasn't a lie when he told her she was a magnet. His thoughts always ended with her. She was an attraction he couldn't shake.

And maybe he didn't want to.

So now he was taking her to Lawrence's charity ball because being in public with her was the only way he trusted himself to behave.

Sure. Because you're always an angel in public.

Why did the voice in his head sound *exactly* like Nathan?

Not that it mattered. After Saturday, he was pretty sure Becca would be avoiding him for the rest of her time on Earth. Seeing his messed-up family in all its glory should do the trick. He wouldn't have to do a thing to deter her, the Carters would do it all for him.

Which was a good thing. His family messed people up. You only had to look at his parents' rocky relationship to know that. Not to mention the messed up relationship between him, Lawrence, and Melissa.

He'd take Becca to the ball, give her the night of her life, then it would be over. He'd go back to his miserable life and live alone, the way he should.

And maybe then he wouldn't be sitting in his office at seven in the morning thinking about the way her dark hair shone beneath the lights in the still room.

His phone beeped, and he picked it up. His mother's name appeared on the screen. Saved by the bell. At least if he was talking to her he wouldn't be thinking about Becca.

"Hi, Mom."

"Darling, sorry to call so early. I just want to let you know I won't be in work today."

"Are you okay?" Daniel frowned.

"I'm fine, not sick. I just have a lot to do. I'm heading up to the city to help Rona get things ready."

"You're going to Charleston? But the ball isn't until the weekend."

Eliana laughed gently. "I know, but I want to make sure the guest rooms are aired out and made up. And it'll give me the chance to catch up with some friends, too. I assume you and Becca will want separate rooms? I could put you in adjoining ones, just in case."

"Becca will be staying at a hotel, as will I," Daniel said dryly. "And I won't even ask how you know she's coming now."

"For the record, I wasn't certain she was coming. But you've confirmed it," she said archly. "And Becca can't stay in a hotel. And nor can you. You have to stay with me, I insist.

You'll be in the guest wing, so if you need privacy you'll have it.

He rolled his eyes at her insinuation. "I don't need privacy. I just assume Becca will want some space. She'll be better off at a hotel. Our family is a lot to take."

"I know, darling. But we also welcome our guests with open arms, and I can't have Becca staying at some anonymous hotel. So I'll be asking her to stay with me. You're welcome to stay if you want to."

"I'll stay." He sighed. Maybe it was better this way. If they weren't at a hotel, he wouldn't be staring at her door wondering whether she was asleep. What she wore to bed. Whether he was a goddamned moron for thinking about knocking on the door just to confirm if she was as beautiful as he remembered.

"Perfect. And you can use the dining room for your meeting with Nina and Lawrence on Sunday. I'll arrange for brunch to be served."

"You have it all figured out." He swallowed down his amusement. Eliana Scott-Carter never did anything halfway.

"Oh, I wish that were true. I can't figure you out at all, I never have."

"It hasn't stopped you from trying."

"Becca's a lovely girl," she said wistfully.

"Mom." His voice was a warning.

"I just wish…" She sighed. "You'd be a little more open. Lighter. I only want to see you happy."

"I'll be happy when Lawrence and Nina have agreed to the single malt." But that wasn't what was nagging at his mind right now. It was Becca, wearing a ball gown, walking into his family home on his arm. The thought made him squeeze his eyes shut.

It was a sham. A charade he'd put on to get what he wanted from Lawrence. That was all, nothing more.

And if he and Becca kissed in public and neither of them felt anything? It was game over. His life could continue as normal and he could stop feeling so damn messed up.

It was win-win. Bring it on. After this weekend, everything would be going his way.

———

GRAY: **Becca, are you free to babysit the twins on Saturday? I want to take Maddie out for our anniversary.**

LOGAN: **Dammit, I was about to ask if she was free. Didn't Becca babysit for you guys last month? We need to start a rota or something.**

TANNER: **Guys, relax. Becca's going to be too busy making cakes for me because I'm her favorite brother. Right, B? xxxxxxxxxxxxxxx**

CAM: **What kind of anniversary are you celebrating, Gray? You two aren't married yet.**

LOGAN: **The kind that involve two people, one bed, and a lot of smiles after, I imagine. If anything's worth celebrating it's that, right?**

GRAY: **Actually, it's the first day we met. That's what we're celebrating, numbnuts.**

· · ·

TANNER: You met her when she was like twelve or something. You still celebrate that?

GRAY: Okay, the second time. Or whatever. Can you guys stop now? Just because I got in with my babysitting request first doesn't mean you all need to get pissy. Next time I'll message Becca directly.

TANNER: Nope. No fair. No off-group chat talks. How else am I going to know what's going on in Hartson's Creek?

LOGAN: I have an off-group chat with Becca.

CAM: Me too.

GRAY: Yep. That's where we all share our deepest darkest secrets about you, Tanner.

LOGAN: Like the time Cam jumped out at Tanner wearing a Santa beard on Christmas morning and he peed his new pjs?

TANNER: Okay, first of all, I didn't pee my pjs. I spilled milk down myself. And second of all, do you guys really have off-group chats with Becca? I feel wounded. Or cheated on. Or something. WE NEED TO TALK!

. . .

BECCA SIGHED as she read the messages. No wonder her phone had been beeping non stop while she worked in the still room that morning. It had been like carrying a little tweety bird in her pocket. Putting her finger to the screen, she scrolled down, shaking her head as the banter continued.

LOGAN: **Hey, is Becca all right? She hasn't replied.**

TANNER: **Becca?**

CAM: **Becca? You okay?**

GRAY: **Should I call her? Make sure she's not ill?**

CAM: **Hold on. I'll message Mia, she can check on her.**

TANNER: **Well? It's been five minutes, is she okay?**

CAM: **According to Mia, she's working in the still room. She has a break at one, and she'll probably get back to us then. So could you all calm yourselves down and stop panicking?**

BECCA CHECKED HER WATCH. Cam's last message had been sent twenty minutes ago. If she didn't reply soon, they'd probably send a SWAT team to the distillery.

· · ·

BECCA: **Guys, some of us have to work for a living. Can you stop with the protective big brother panic now? And I can't babysit for any of you on Saturday, I'm busy.**

TANNER: **What are you doing on Saturday? Can you still make me a cake on Sunday?**

SHE SHOOK HER HEAD. **Nope. I'm busy then, too.**

SHE CONVENIENTLY IGNORED his other question. She wasn't ready for them to know anything about Daniel Carter. The thought sent shivers down her spine, and not in a good way.

GRAY: **Well, I know you're not going out with the girls, because I asked Maddie.**

TANNER: **Wait. Are you going on a date? Is it that guy from the other week?**

CAM: **He flew to Afghanistan, numbnuts.**

TANNER: **So who's she going on a date with?**

ROLLING HER EYES, Becca tapped out a reply.

.   .   .

Becca: It's not a date. It's a work thing, idiots.

She was already regretting joining this stupid group chat. It had been Gray's idea to add her to the brothers' group. She had a feeling he was worried about her being lonely when she moved out.

Right now, the chance to feel lonely would be a wonderful thing. It was almost impossible to do anything without them knowing. To the rest of the world they were chilled, handsome guys who were laid back to the point of falling asleep. But to Becca they were like annoying flies she couldn't quite bat away.

Cam: Mia didn't say anything about working on Saturday.

Oh shit. There went *that* plan. She had a feeling that as soon as Mia got home, Cam would be asking about whether the distillery was running that weekend. Maybe sooner – she wouldn't put it past him to call her now and check. Becca locked her phone and slid it back into her pocket, then grabbed the soup she'd just warmed up and carried it to Mia's office.

"Do you have five minutes?" she asked, when Mia looked up from her laptop.

Mia smiled. "Sure. Sit down. What's up? Oh, did Cam get ahold of you? He called me earlier. It was weird, because he sounded all panicky and wanted me to check on you."

"Yeah, I replied to their group chat." Becca rolled her eyes.

"I know he's your fiancé, but he's such an ass sometimes. They all are."

"Hey, you have my sympathies. I can imagine how annoying they can be. I'm just glad I'm an only kid." Mia folded her laptop closed. "So, what's up?"

"I need you to lie to them for me."

Mia started to laugh. "You're not serious."

"I am. If Cam asks you whether I'm working this weekend, please tell him yes." Becca offered her a pleading smile.

"But you're not working." Mia frowned. "Unless there's a backlog I don't know about. We caught up on the schedule, didn't we?" As the marketing manager for GSC, Mia wasn't involved in the production, but the distillery was small enough that everybody knew what was happening and when.

"There's no backlog. And I'm not working." Becca traced the line of her phone in her pocket, then looked up with a sigh.

"So what are you doing?" Mia leaned forward, her eyes wide. "It's something you don't want your brothers to know about, so it has to be good. Come on, tell me, I'm all ears."

Becca took a deep breath. "I'm going to Charleston to a charity ball."

"Oh wow!" Mia grinned. "What kind of charity?"

Becca blinked. "I've no idea." She needed to find out. No doubt there would be a silent auction and other fundraising – she'd need to donate something.

"I didn't really care about the charity," Mia admitted, threading her fingers together, her gaze fixed avidly on Becca. "What I'm more interested in is why you don't want your brothers to find out."

Because they'll tear Daniel apart with their bare hands. No, that wasn't right. Her brothers may have been like overprotective bears, but she couldn't picture them hurting Daniel.

He was a stalking lion. He'd dance around them then bite until they bled.

She shivered. "I'm going with Daniel." Sometimes honesty was the best policy. Except where her brothers were concerned.

"What?"

"You want me to repeat it?" Becca clenched her teeth.

"*Daniel.* As in Daniel Carter?" Mia blinked. "Our boss, Daniel Carter?"

"That's the guy. Tall, dark, and always grimacing." Becca bit down a smile at that description. Add devastatingly handsome and it would be him to a 'T'.

"Okay, we need to back up. I'm completely confused. You hate Daniel. Or at least I thought you did. And you told me the feeling was mutual."

"It is." Becca nodded, her expression serious.

A slow smile broke out on Mia's lips. "Oh my god, you like each other."

Becca's chest tightened. "I'm not sure *like* is the right word," she said, not ready to admit that. "There's just this thing. I don't know." She shook her head. "It's like wanting something and not wanting it." She was still waiting for the not wanting part. Maybe it would come after the weekend.

One night together. Would it be enough?

Mia's mouth dropped open. "Oh shit. You hate-like him." She shook her head.

"Is that bad?"

"It's the worst. You need to tell me everything now. How did he end up asking you to the ball?"

Mia listened as Becca described her trip to Charleston to deliver Daniel's medication. Their strange and loaded evening out with his family. And that elevator kiss.

"Whoa, they make you Hartsons sound like the Waltons,"

Mia said after Becca told her about Melissa and her early morning hotel room visit.

Becca's brows knit together. "That's kind of what I said."

Mia chuckled. "So this weekend is all you're going to have? You go to the ball with him, he gets the go ahead for the new single malt from his family, then you come back here like nothing ever happened. No dating, no relationship, just boss and employee?"

"That's pretty much it." When Mia said it out loud it sounded stupid. Even if there was no other choice. "He's made it clear he's not interested in a relationship."

"How about you?" Mia asked softly, tipping her head to the side.

Becca shrugged. "It is what it is. I get to play Cinderella for the night, and mingle with the rich and benevolent of Charleston. Then I leave and come home. Nothing changes." She shrugged. "I couldn't cope with his mood swings anyway." Lies, all lies.

Mia eyed her carefully. "I'm worried you're going to get hurt. And then Cam finds out and I'm going to get hurt for not telling him about all this."

Reaching out across the table, Becca squeezed her friend's hand. "Nobody's going to get hurt."

Mia squeezed her hand back. "If you're sure…"

"I am."

"Then I'll evade Cam's question. I can't lie to him, I'd hate that. But this really *is* kind of a work thing, isn't it? You're going to Charleston to help Daniel win his family over. If that isn't work, I don't know what is."

"Of course it's work." Becca nodded, trying to reassure her.

"So, what are you wearing to the ball?"

"I don't know. Daniel offered to get me a dress, but that's weird. I was going to call Laura this afternoon and see if she had anything suitable." Laura's Dress Shop was the favorite haunt of the ladies in Hartson's Creek. Though most of her clothing was casual, she had some formal wear in the back.

"You don't need to do that. I have a dress from that charity evening I went to with Cam a few months ago. It'll fit you. I even have matching shoes. I'll sneak them out to my car while he's not looking."

"Are you sure?"

"Yep." Mia nodded with a smile. "Daniel Carter won't know what's hit him."

It was weird, but Becca liked the sound of that.

CHAPTER EIGHTEEN

"I'll pick you up at ten tomorrow morning," Daniel murmured. Becca froze where she was bending over to check the still, her heart rattling against her chest at the sound of his voice. She exhaled softly and turned to look at him.

He was wearing a pale blue shirt, unbuttoned at the neck as always, tucked into navy pants that skimmed his slim hips and hugged his thighs. His arm muscles looked bigger than she remembered, or maybe his shirt sleeves were tighter. He also smelled like heaven in human form. She swallowed hard, pulling her gaze away.

"I'll drive myself," she told him. It was almost six. They were probably the only two people left in the distillery right now. "What time do you want me there?"

Daniel frowned. "Why would you drive yourself? I'm going the same way."

"Because by the time we get to Charleston, one of us is likely to end up dead." She kept her voice light, but she meant it. The atmosphere between them was getting thicker every day. It felt as though it had a life of its own. It buzzed and hissed and made her body ache for things she shouldn't want.

He'd been walking through the still room a lot these past few days. It was amazing how long they could stare at each other silently before he turned to do whatever he came in for.

His eyes crinkled with amusement. "Will we be dead from murder, or from something else?"

"Either. Both. I just don't think we should risk it. What time should I get there?"

He didn't look pleased. But she needed the drive to center herself. It was one night, and it was all pretend. She needed to get used to that.

"Can you arrive by three? I'll send you the address."

"It's okay, your mother already sent it to me."

Daniel gave her a sidelong glance. "You've spoken with my mother?"

Becca managed not to smile. "Extensively. I can't believe you let her show your naked baby photos to strangers. Especially when you were such an ugly kid."

His lips twitched. "I was a beautiful baby. Everybody says so."

A lick of flame rushed through her blood. "It's weird how looks change as we get older. Some people grow into their beauty and some…" She gave a dramatic sigh, and patted his rock hard bicep. "At least you have your memories."

His muscle flexed beneath her palm. It made her feel sweaty. An image of him flashed through her mind, naked above her, his arms on either side, his biceps tense and sinewy as he slowly moved inside her…

"Becca?"

She blinked back to reality. "Sorry, I missed that."

He gave her a cocky smile, as though he knew exactly where her thoughts had been. "I asked you about your dress. You haven't sent me the receipt for it."

"I didn't buy one. I figure a skirt and blouse will be okay, right?"

His eyes dipped down, scanning her body. "I'm sure you'll look beautiful in anything."

Gah, he wasn't easy to bait.

And she was sure he was going to be devastating in a dinner suit and crisp white shirt. "Thank you. And for the record, I'm borrowing a dress from Mia."

"She knows you're coming to the ball?" He didn't seem annoyed, just surprised.

"I had to tell her. But she won't tell anybody else. She's discreet."

"What's there to be discreet about?" he asked, his voice low. "We're just going to an evening at my brother's. It's not like I'm taking you to a sex den and tying you to the wall."

Her body pulsed. Damn, what was wrong with her? "I'd rather my brothers didn't find out."

"Why?" He seemed genuinely interested. As though he couldn't figure her out.

"Because if they find out, they're going to grill me. And it's not worth it, because after Saturday you're just my boss, right?"

"Right." His voice was low. Gritted. His dark eyes swept her face.

"That's the deal, isn't it?" she asked softly. "We go to the ball, we dance together, then it's done. Over. You get the refinancing, I get to lead the project."

His mouth tightened. "Is that what you want?"

"To dance with you?" She shrugged. "I can endure it. For my job."

"But you might not survive it," he murmured. "That's what I'm worried about. You'll probably die and I'll end up one distiller short."

Becca grinned. She liked dark and dangerous Daniel. But she loved it even more when he teased her. "I'll pull you down with me. We can die together. It'll be a scandal Charleston whispers about for years. The infamous night when two people were slayed by a dance."

"I can live with that." He lifted a brow. "They talk about me anyway. At least this will liven up their boring lives."

"What do they say?"

"About me?" A flash of something she couldn't quite understand crossed his features. "If I told you, you wouldn't come."

"And you want me to come?" She tilted her head. "Interesting."

"I'm planning on using you as a human shield, to stop all the matriarchs from throwing their eligible daughters at me." He lifted his arms up, his hands curled as though he was holding an imaginary Becca in front of him. He moved them from side to side as though he was protecting himself from flying potential dates. "Bam, bam, take that you Mariannes and Elizabeths. You're no match for Becca Hartson."

She shook her head. "You're weird."

"I know." His glance was almost fond. "I'll see you tomorrow, Becca." Then he was gone, and she was thankful that the still room was empty, because there was no hiding her blush.

———

THE LAST TIME she drove to Charleston, she hadn't really taken in the timeless splendour of the town. She'd been too busy eyeing her GPS and feeling jittery about the box Daniel had asked her to bring, to notice the pretty, leafy city in her full glory. Built in the late seventeen hundreds where the Elk and Kanawha Rivers joined, the city had begun as so many back then as a fort, occupied by Colonel Savannah Clendenin and his company of Virginia Rangers.

The city's buildings were a strange mixture of old and new, sleek towerblocks dwarfing quaint nineteenth century churches, with the golden dome of the Capitol glinting in the afternoon sun. Becca followed the directions to Eliana Scott-Carter's tall redbrick manor, parking her car in the driveway alongside Daniel's sleek Corvette and an elegant black town car. She switched off the engine and looked up at the sweeping white stone steps that led to a stucco porch. If the door opened and a nineteenth century belle ran out, holding her crinoline skirt to stop herself from tripping, she wouldn't look out of place.

Climbing out of the car, Becca patted her hair, making sure it was still as shiny and wavy as when she'd left the salon. She'd given her stylist Lainey – who happened to be best friends with Courtney, Logan's wife – a tall story about a trip to Charleston where she was to attend a company dinner. She'd even lied to her Aunt Gina, the woman who'd brought her up since she was a toddler. She wouldn't be surprised if lightning struck her down.

The front door opened, and Daniel walked out. The waning sun caught his dark hair, bouncing off it, casting a shadow on his face as he stalked toward the car. Her heart skipped again. She was getting used to it now. Maybe she'd always feel like this, even when she was seventy and retired and occasionally saw him at the grocery store.

"How was your trip?" he asked, leaning into her trunk as she popped it open. He carefully pulled out the dress bag, looping the hanger over his finger, then took her overnight suitcase in his other hand.

"Slower than yours, obviously. But that wouldn't be difficult."

He smiled. "You have a terrible opinion of my driving. I kept to the speed limit all the way."

"I imagine that's not easy." She glanced at his car. It looked as dark and foreboding as he did.

"Come inside," he said smoothly, inclining his head at the house. "I'll have Rona take your dress to your room. Do you need it steamed?"

"Rona?" Becca walked up the steps.

"The housekeeper." As if by magic, she appeared. A fifty-something lady, by the look of her. She gave Becca a warm smile and took the dress from Daniel.

"There's sweet tea and cookies in the day room," she told them. "Would you like me to make some sandwiches?"

"Not for me, thank you. But the cookies sound delicious." Becca returned her smile.

"We're fine. Thank you, Rona." Daniel gave her a nod.

"Well, let me know if you change your minds. I'll be in the kitchen if you need me." She gave Becca another smile – and maybe a little scrutiny, too – then turned to carry the dress away.

"Is your mom here?" Becca asked him.

"She's at the salon in town. Said to give you her apologies, but she'll be back by five." Daniel put her case down. "Would you like a tour of the place while we wait?"

"I'd like that very much."

He was casual today. In a grey t-shirt and washed out jeans, his hair its usual messy glory as he raked his hand through it. "Well, you've seen the hall," he said, leading her down the wide corridor. Her shoes clacked against the marble tiles. "At the very end is the kitchen and scullery. That's where you'll find Rona if you need her. She's always happy to cook, so if you're hungry, go see her."

"I will."

"Through here is the drawing room." He opened a heavy oak door, taking her into an oversized living space, filled with what looked like antique chairs and tables, with heavy silken drapes framing the Georgian windows. "And through that door," he walked over, pushing it open. "Is the dining room."

"The scene of tomorrow's duel at dawn."

His lips twitched. "We'll be using our wits instead of pistols, but yeah, that's where I'm meeting Nina and Lawrence."

Becca followed him around the rest of the house, taking in the beautiful artwork, the polished antique furniture, and the maze of rooms that led from one to another. "How long has your mother had this place?" she asked him, as they emerged back into the hallway. "Didn't she live with your father in the Jackson-Carter house when he was alive?"

"You remember. Very good. And yes, we lived there when we visited Charleston. But this house is from my mother's side of the family. She inherited it when her own mother died. She made this her Charleston residence when Lawrence took over the family estate."

"That must have been hard for her to leave." Even though this place was huge.

"I imagine so." Daniel's voice was dry. "But she didn't get a choice." He inclined his head at the stairs, pressing his hand against Becca's back as they walked up the wide staircase. "My mother's suite of rooms is in there," he said, as they passed a closed door. "Including her office." They turned a corner, past more doors. "These are bedrooms. Family ones, originally. Now they mostly house old furniture and art."

He pushed his hand against another door, stepping through. "And this is the guest wing. Where we'll be sleeping."

It smelled fresh, as though it had just been cleaned. But there was an emptiness in the area that wasn't present in the other parts of the house. As though it was barely lived in.

He opened the first door. "My room," he murmured. She looked over his shoulder. Inside was an oversize bed and modern furniture.

He continued down the corridor, past two more doors. "And yours," he said, when they reached the final one. He pushed the handle down and walked inside. Sunlight streamed through the tall windows, bleaching the cream carpet to a paler white.

"It's a long way from your room. Is she worried I might steal your virtue?" Becca teased.

Daniel grinned. She'd forgotten how heartbreaking his smile was. When he was in Scotland, he probably left broken hearts scattered all over the highlands. "Maybe she's worried I might try to steal yours."

"Will you?" She looked at him, a smile playing at her lips. He swallowed hard, his throat undulating.

"It's tempting."

Her heart did a little leap. She could feel the electricity flowing between them, making her skin heat up. He said nothing, his dark eyes wary as he scanned her face.

"Are you afraid of me?" she whispered, trying to work out his emotions.

He shook his head. "I'm afraid of *me*," he said gruffly, then took a step back. "You have your own bathroom," he continued, as though their flirtation hadn't happened. "Fresh towels are in the closet, and there are toiletries in there if you want them. We'll have a light meal at five and leave at seven."

"Won't we be eating at the ball?" Becca asked.

Daniel snorted. "There'll be food there, if that's what you're asking. But nobody really eats it. They're too busy gossiping and networking to spear a chicken tender with their fork. Plus, the drink my brother serves is potent. So we eat before we go."

"And too busy dancing," Becca prompted.

His chin lifted as he looked at her. "Possibly."

"And kissing." She was playing with him now. Like a cat and a bird.

"Kissing?" His brow arched. "Will there be kissing?"

"I know you'll be thinking about it all night." She leaned back against the wall, flattening her hands against the painted plaster.

"Is that right?" He seemed amused. "Because I notice that you're the one who brought it up. Not that I blame you after the last kiss. I saw how it affected you."

"It affected you, too."

He swallowed. "It did. But tonight we'll be in public. So unless you plan on tearing my clothes off in the middle of the ballroom, I imagine it won't be quite so… potent."

Becca shrugged. "If you say so. I'm not the one who refused to kiss again because, and I quote, *If we kiss I'll carry you to your bedroom and strip your clothing off and neither of us will survive it.*" She smiled smugly. Game, set, and match.

He stared at her for a moment, his lips soft, his eyes narrowed. He was so damn masculine she could feel his potency pulse in the air between them. "Freshen up," he said, "And then come down. I'll ask Rona to make us some coffee."

"What are we going to do, then?" she asked. "It's a couple of hours before I need to get ready."

"You could make use of the library. Or we could play a game." He shrugged.

"What kind of game?"

He chuckled. "The board type of game, very boring, I know. We have everything here. Chess, Scrabble, Monopoly, there's even an old Ludo set somewhere."

She smiled, because he had no idea how much she loved

board games. She'd spent most of her childhood running around after one brother or another begging them to sit at the table and play. She was a scion at Monopoly, a ninja at Scrabble. She could even muster a passable Queen's Gambit if she concentrated properly. But there was one thing she loved more than anything else.

"Do you have a pack of cards?" she asked, trying to keep the excitement out of her voice.

"About a dozen of them."

"Okay then, I'll be down in ten minutes."

———

BECCA HARTSON never ceased to surprise him. Daniel bit down a smile as she laid out her hand, squealing with excitement when her straight flush beat his three of a kind.

"Dammit, I should have made a higher bet," she said, pulling the pile of matchsticks toward her. "I always under-call the worth of my hand."

"I didn't expect you to be so competitive." He pulled the cards toward him, shuffling them easily.

"You forget I grew up with four brothers. I spent hours teaching myself poker just so they'd let me join in on their card nights." She played with a matchstick, twirling it between her fingers. "Anyway, you're as bad as me. I saw you fist pump when you beat my three aces earlier."

"You noticed that? I'll have to be more discreet next time." She looked so happy, gazing down at her matchsticks as though they were worth something more than kudos. It made him feel warm inside. What would it be like to make her smile like that every day? "And for the record, I'm worse than you. I was competitive from the moment I was born. Before, probably."

She blinked. "How so?"

It was so easy to talk to her. He had to be on his guard to not let too much slip. "Let's just say I had a role to play from day one. To vindicate and validate my parents' relationship. To be the best son in the family." And it almost ripped him to shreds.

She leaned her jaw on her hand, propping her elbow on the card table. Her dark hair flowed in waves past her shoulders. "And Nathan? Did he have the same role?"

"You're still interested in my brother?" It was a tease, but also a little stab in his chest.

"Not in that way, no." She smiled. "And you know it. Nathan and I have only ever been friends."

He tipped his head to the side, noticing a pulse dancing on her throat. "How about us?" he asked. "Are *we* friends?"

She tapped her fingertips against her cheek. "That's an interesting question."

"Is that a no?" There was a tightness in his chest that he wasn't expecting.

"Do you want me to be your friend?"

"I don't know." He smiled gently. "Maybe. I guess I don't have that many around here. Hence why I asked you to bring my insulin up last week."

She pulled her lip between her teeth, gazing at him intently. He could feel the pull between them again. He was getting used to it now. Had stopped fighting it. It was a battle he was never destined to win.

"Daniel? Becca?" His mother's voice echoed from the hallway. "Where are you?"

He pulled his eyes from Becca's. "In the library. We're playing cards."

Eliana pushed the door open, smiling when she saw them sitting at the old baize-topped card table. "How lovely," she said. "Nobody's used that table for years. Remember when you and Nathan used to play Snap on there?" She moved her attention to Becca. "I'm so glad you're here. Do you have everything you need?" She took a breath. "Please tell me Daniel has at least showed you to your room."

Becca's eyes flickered, meeting his. "He's been the consummate host."

A smile ghosted his lips. "You've been an easy guest. Even if you do insist on trouncing me at poker."

"Is that what you're playing?" Eliana asked, walking into the library, looking elegantly put together.

"Your hair looks beautiful," Becca said. "Have you had it colored?"

"Just a little tint." Eliana touched the back of her head, her gorgeous white bob looking sleek beneath the library lights. "I was worried it would be too much."

"Not at all. It's perfect. And I love your dress. You always have the best style."

"You should bring Becca home more often," his mother said to Daniel. "She's wonderful for my ego."

"I don't think I can afford the matchsticks," Daniel said dryly.

"Well, I need to go get ready. I'm going to the Richardson's for cocktails." Eliana shot them a smile. "I'm so glad you're both here. I'll see you at the Jackson-Carter house at seven."

"You're not coming in the car with us?" Daniel asked.

"No, darling. I'll send the driver back once I'm at the Richardson's, they have a space for me in their car. You two will make a better entrance without me there."

Becca looked from Eliana to Daniel, her expression neutral. He wondered how she felt about making an impression.

"It was funny, because I saw Janet Sutherland at the salon.

She asked me about your new girlfriend." Eliana's brows knitted together. "I fudged an answer, but I'm not sure she bought it."

Becca kicked him softly under the table with her bare foot. A teasing smile played around her lips.

"We're friends," she told Eliana. Another shot of warmth rushed through him.

"Okay. I guess that works." She patted her hair again, walking over to kiss Daniel on the cheek. "Don't forget to shave, darling."

"Thanks, Mom. I don't know how I'd adult without you." His voice was deadpan.

Eliana rolled her eyes, looking over at Becca. "I hope he's nicer to you than he is to his mother."

Becca kicked him again. But he was ready for her this time. He caught her by the ankle, circling her soft skin with his fingers. Her eyes flashed as she tried to tug her leg back, to no avail.

Eliana raised an eyebrow but said nothing.

"No, I'm pretty sure he's horrible to everybody," Becca said with a grin.

"Be nice," Eliana said, patting Daniel's face again. She looked so happy to have him home. "Or Becca won't come again."

"Maybe that's what he's aiming for," Becca said. She'd given up struggling, letting him take the weight of her leg in his palm. He rubbed the pad of his thumb on the sole of her foot. Her lips parted at the touch, and he remembered how they tasted.

"Not at all," he said softly.

Eliana gave him a sideways glance, then smiled at Becca. "I'll see you both later."

"Yes, you will." Daniel watched as she gracefully walked to

the door, giving them both a warm smile before she left the room.

"One more hand?" he asked Becca, releasing her foot.

"Go for it. It's your funeral."

Yes it was. But what a good way to go.

CHAPTER NINETEEN

Becca took a deep breath and stared at her reflection. She looked like a fairytale version of herself. Her hair fell in perfect waves past her shoulders, the tips barely touching the decolletage of the gown Mia had loaned her.

It was beautiful. The bodice was made of mesh, the transparent fabric covered with thousands of tiny pearls that caught the light as she moved around the room. It was tight on the chest, giving her the kind of cleavage she'd always dreamed of, then nipped in at the waist. The skirt was draped with layered champagne tulle, flowing to the ground in a cascade of fabric. And around her neck were her mother's pearls. She touched them carefully, hoping they gave her strength.

A gentle knock at the door alerted her to Daniel's presence. She walked across the carpeted floor in her bare feet – the shoes Mia had given her were perilously high. She'd only put them on when she had to.

Her heart did a flip as soon as she opened the door. She'd always found tuxedos a little comical before. Grown men wearing little bow ties that made them look like the mouse from *Tom and Jerry*, tied up and presented like a Christmas gift. But now she understood the hype. Because Daniel Carter was as far from a cartoon as it was possible to be.

He was breathtaking.

Becca reached out and touched his sleeve. The fabric was thickly expensive. "Tailor made?" she asked.

It took her a moment to realize he was silent. She looked up to see him staring at her, his neck undulating as he swallowed hard.

"You're beautiful."

Becca blinked, hoping her cheeks weren't too red. "Thank you. I just need to put those on," she said, pointing at the shoes. "Then I'll be beautiful and dangerous, because I'll probably be falling all over the place."

"I'll catch you."

"Why are you being so sweet?" A little thrill rushed through her at his words.

"Because my mother brought me up to treat my dates well." He bent down and picked up her shoes. "Not glass," he murmured, before standing. "Did you want to bring a spare set? In case these ones really do kill you?" The ankle straps dangled from his fingers.

"It's fine, I'll get used to them. Plus, I have you as a human walking stick." She looked at him through her mascaraed lashes. "I'll have to ask your mother why she didn't teach you to be sweet at work, too."

"That's all my father's doing," he said lightly. "The car's waiting outside if you're ready."

"I'll just grab my purse." She picked up the matching champagne clutch, sliding her phone and a lipstick inside. Daniel held his arm out, and she curled her hand around his bicep, enjoying the steel-hard feel of him against her palm.

The Jackson-Carter house was on the outskirts of

Charleston, the white stuccoed building towering high against the backdrop of the Allegheny Mountains, its expanse framed by verdant sycamore maples.

At the front was a huge portico, held up proudly by tall Grecian columns. They joined the row of cars lined along the drive, waiting for each to pull up to the sweeping stairs where their passengers would alight. Becca shifted in her seat and glanced at Daniel.

"Are you okay?" he asked. He was sitting completely upright.

She smiled softly at him. "I'm fine."

When they reached the front of what felt like the world's longest kiss-and-ride line, Daniel opened the door and climbed out, turning to offer Becca his hand. Behind him, she could see elegant couples lingering on the steps as they waited to walk inside. The sound of a band playing echoed in the air.

As they walked up the steps, Daniel slid his hand around her, pulling her close so she could feel the warmth of him through his tuxedo. The evening air was cool, making her shiver, so he pulled her even closer. She breathed in, inhaling the deep musk of his cologne.

"Daniel." Lawrence held his hand out to his brother as they reached the door. "I wasn't sure you'd come."

Daniel's fingers twitched on her back. "I wouldn't miss it for the world."

Becca bit down a smile at the dryness of his voice.

"And Becca. We're delighted to have you here." Melissa smiled, though it didn't reach her eyes. "Has Daniel told you the history of this house?"

"No he hasn't." Becca's smile was perfectly polite. "We were a little... busy this afternoon."

Daniel chuckled at her insinuation. Even if it was a complete lie.

Melissa's poise slipped. Only for a moment. "Maybe you can come see us another time and I'll arrange for a tour." Her eyes flickered to Daniel's. "We'd love to host the two of you."

"That's a very kind offer. Thank you." Becca had no plans of coming back. She was already feeling like she had insects crawling on her skin.

"We'll see you later," Daniel murmured, steering her away from his brother.

"Make sure you save me a dance," Melissa called after him. Lawrence murmured something to her, and she whispered furiously back at him.

"I guess all is not well in the Jackson-Carter house," Daniel said, picking up a glass of champagne from a tray and handing it to Becca. His other arm was still wrapped around her. She liked it. Maybe too much.

As they made their way to the ballroom, people greeted Daniel like he was their long lost friend, asking about Scotland, about Nathan, and the distillery. "So much for having no friends," Becca said pointedly, as they approached his mother's table.

"They're acquaintances at best," Daniel told her. "The problem with Charleston is that everybody has a great memory. Some of them stretch back about three hundred years."

Eliana rose to greet them, hugging first Becca, then Daniel. Then she introduced them to the other guests at the table. Of course they all knew Daniel, and Becca marveled again at how pleased they seemed to see him.

So he really was just an angry man at work, then. Interesting.

"Oh good, you're sitting next to me," a smiling woman said as Becca took her seat. "I'm Julia. Usually, I get the old leeches who pat my thigh about a hundred times before I threaten to kick them in the nuts."

Becca grinned. "Well you do have nice thighs."

Julia filled both of their wine glasses up. "So I see you're with Daniel. Have you two been dating for long."

Becca looked at Daniel. He just shrugged. *Thanks for your help.* "We work together," Becca said, turning back to Julia. Maybe if she answered every awkward question with a change of subject she'd survive the night. It felt better than lying, anyway.

"It's nice to see him with somebody so smiley for a change." Julia said. "Which brings me to my next question. Have you met Melissa yet?"

"Yes she has," Daniel said, rolling his eyes at Becca. "And it's always a delight to sit with you, Julia." He lifted a brow. "Becca, this is Julia Raymond. Charleston's finest gossip queen. And my mother's best friend, which is something I've never been able to work out."

Julia laughed. "Oh, I've missed you."

"Be careful what you say to her. She has a mind like an Excel spreadsheet. She knows the names of who's slept with who in Charleston for the last four centuries." He lifted his glass to his lips, his warm eyes belying his fondness for her.

"People just seem to confide in me." Julia shrugged. "I can't help it if I have one of those faces."

As Daniel had promised, the guests barely touched the food, though the wine flowed like water, bottles constantly being replaced by the wait staff. By the time coffee was served, the buzz in the room had reached a crescendo, edged with the tinkling of laughter and the occasional shout.

"And now it's time for the whole of Charleston society to get their dicks out and wave them around." Daniel leaned over to whisper in her ear.

"The auction?"

"Yes. By tomorrow morning half these people will be fighting headaches and trying to get through to their bank manager to ask for a loan to cover the jet ski or the Bahamas vacation they bid on. It'll probably take them an hour to remember it's a Sunday."

"Will you be getting your dick out?" She tilted her head, amused.

"Are we talking literally or metaphorically?"

She shrugged. "Whatever floats your boat."

Daniel's eyes caught hers. For a moment it was only the two of them. Everything else faded away. "I'll bid on something appropriately expensive and completely useless," he murmured, his gaze unwavering. "And probably never actually use whatever it is."

"How boring."

"It really is. Shall we go home and play more poker instead?"

Becca grinned. "I think you'll save money by staying."

His eyes crinkled. He leaned to brush his lips against her shoulder, sending a shiver down her spine. "Touché."

———

As soon as the auction was over, Becca excused herself to go to the bathroom. Daniel watched as she walked across the ballroom, admiring the proud way she held her shoulders, her dark hair tumbling around her creamy skin. Her dress looked almost luminescent – the bodice would be scandalous if it wasn't for the hundreds of pearls stitched in patterns across the mesh, but every now and then the pattern allowed for a bare patch that revealed her body beneath.

She was beautiful. He ran his finger around the rim of his glass, exhaling slowly through his nose. He'd had to curl his hands into fists on the drive over to stop himself from touching her. In a few minutes they'd be dancing, and he'd have no choice.

He feared for both of their sanities.

"She's delicious," Julia said, leaning in with a smile. "I love her."

"I thought you might." He bit down a smile.

"Did you see the way people looked at her as she walked past. The whole room is buzzing. They want to know who this woman is that captured the ice king's heart."

"No they don't," he said softly. "They all know I don't have a heart."

Julia sighed. "They might think that, but I know better. I once saw you hold a bird with a broken wing for hours, tears in your eyes."

"I was seven years old. I was probably crying because I wanted to play on my Gameboy."

She tipped her head to the side, giving him a speculative look. "You don't like being vulnerable, do you?"

He turned to give her his full attention. Julia had been a part of his life since he was a baby, thanks to her friendship with his mother. And like Eliana, she was predisposed to think the best of him.

"I find that people like to project their feelings onto me. You want me to be kind, so I'm kind. You want me to love animals, so you remember that bird I nursed, rather than the fact I just ate a chicken breast, which also comes from a bird."

"To be fair, you didn't eat it." Julia smiled. "None of us did."

"A good point. But it doesn't mean it isn't true."

"Maybe I just want you to be happy. The way your mother does." Julia shot a look at Eliana, who was talking with the Richardsons.

"And you think I can only be happy if I throw myself at Becca's feet?"

Julia poured herself a glass of wine, lifting it to her lips. "I think she's the first woman I've ever seen who gives you as good as she gets."

"So I can only be happy if I date somebody who's as much of an asshole as me?"

Julia laughed. "Maybe."

Daniel leaned toward her. "Well unfortunately, Becca's not an asshole. She's a good person. Wants to make everybody happy, even when it's to her own detriment. So your hypothesis fails."

"Maybe she makes you happy by challenging you."

Daniel blinked. For a moment he couldn't think of anything to say. Could Julia be right?

"You look horrified," Julia pointed out. "Is it so bad if she wants to make you happy? Isn't that what happens in relationships. You make each other happy, become a team. You against the world."

"You've been watching too many Hallmark Movies," Daniel said playfully.

"And you're still a cynic."

"Can you blame me?"

Julia sighed, putting her glass on the table. "No, but maybe this time it will be different."

"As I said, Hallmark." He smirked.

The band started up again, drowning out her response. Chairs scraped against the floor as guests stood and made their way to the dance floor, more than one of them stumbling on their heels thanks to the copious amounts of wine they'd consumed.

Daniel stood, unable to sit and wait for Becca any longer. "Excuse me," he murmured, leaning down to give Julia a kiss on her cheek. "I'm going to find my date.

"Make sure you save me a dance," Julia said. "If you can spare one."

"For you, anything."

CHAPTER TWENTY

"Becca." The soft voice came from the hallway as she walked out of the bathroom. Becca looked over to see Melissa, her dark hair pulled back from her delicate face and wound into a plaited bun, a polite smile painted on her lips. She was wearing a navy dress that suited her peach complexion. Right now, she was glowing.

"Hello." Becca forced a smile onto her lips. "Is everything okay?"

"Everything is fine." Melissa slid her arm through Becca's. "I just wanted to thank you for coming tonight. I know it must be hard trying to fit in, and Daniel isn't exactly the most helpful guy I've ever met. If you're feeling lonely or ignored, come find me. I know a lot of interesting people." She took a step forward, leading Becca through a door. The room behind it was cool, the walls lined with old paintings and antique mirrors, the floor filled with furniture that looked like it could have been purchased hundreds of years ago.

"I'm not bored." Becca's cheeks were starting to ache from holding the smile. "How could I be?"

Melissa's eyes crinkled. "The offer stands. I don't know if Daniel's told you, but we used to be a couple. I know what he's like. He promises to be somewhere and never turns up. He takes you out for a date and spends all evening on his phone trying to sort out a production problem. And then there's his moods. The black ones. They can last for days." Melissa squeezed Becca's arms. "We girls have to stick together. So if you need to talk, let me know."

"Thank you," Becca murmured. She had no intention of ever confiding in Melissa. It would be like a fly confiding to a spider that it needed a rest. "But Daniel isn't like that with me. He's kind and funny and has a lot of time. Sometimes I have to remind him he still has a job."

The smile on Melissa's face wavered for a moment, before she remembered to tense her cheek muscles. "I guess these are still the early days. How long have you two been seeing each other?"

Becca couldn't remember what they'd said at the restaurant. Had they even said anything at all about that? "A while."

"Well it can't be too long, since he's only been back home for a few weeks. Seriously, call me in a few months. Unlike him, I always pick up my phone."

The door opened, light spilling in from the hallway. Daniel stepped inside, his eyes darker than dark. "Am I interrupting something?"

Becca let out a lungful of air. Just being close to him made her body tense. It was strange how contradictory her reactions to him were. A little bolt of fear rushed through her, because he held an air of menace, and then warmth because somehow his mere presence made her feel safe.

It was like a python winding itself around her neck and making her happy because it was warming her up. Before it squeezed.

"I was just telling Becca how pleased I am that you both came," Melissa said smoothly. "I wasn't sure you would."

Daniel was still staring at Becca. She stared back, her skin tingling.

"Great. Now that's done, I'm stealing Becca. I want to dance."

He held out a hand, and Becca stepped toward him, slipping her own against his palm. He folded his hands around hers and gave a little tug, enough for her to step forward again. "Goodbye, Melissa," he said, his voice firm.

He was silent as they walked back to the ballroom. She could feel the tension in his body wafting through the air. "Was she unkind to you?" he murmured, as the sound of the band heightened.

"No. She was worried you'd ignore me."

He lifted an eyebrow. "How could I do that?"

As soon as they made it onto the dance floor, he swept her into his arms, his fingers folding over hers as he slid his right hand down her spine. Becca leaned her cheek against his lapel, feeling the smoothness of the fabric against her skin. The sound of violins filled her ears as he stepped back, twirling her across the floor, moving easily, as though she was as light as a feather.

"You can dance." She inclined her head to look up at him.

"Yes, Ma'am. Miss Mary's School of Ballroom. Class of ninety-nine."

"I must thank your mother. *Again.*"

He twirled her once more. Even though the dance floor was full, people parted as they danced, whispering softly to each other as they glided past. She felt like she was in a fairytale, the beauty dancing with the beast. Except this beast was already transformed.

When she looked at him again, his eyes were soft. Light.

Her lips parted, her chest felt full. No, he definitely wasn't the beast.

"Everybody's looking at us," Daniel said, though he didn't seem to mind at all. "Wondering what a beautiful woman like you is doing with an asshole like me."

"I guess they don't know that assholes are my kryptonite." She moved her hand from his shoulder, pressing her palm against his neck. Her fingers brushed his hairline, making him swallow hard.

"I have no idea what you're doing to me." He danced so easily. Like it was his second language.

"The same thing you're doing to me."

"Is that right?"

"I think so." Her voice was soft.

He closed his eyes for a second. "You make me lose control."

She pressed her cheek against his chest again, breathing in his warm masculinity. "And that's a problem?" she asked.

"It is where you're concerned. Maybe you're my kryptonite, too."

"Then stop fighting it." She closed her eyes, letting him lead her. She was like putty in his hands.

"I have. I'm giving in."

"To me?" Her lips curled against his chest.

"No, to *me*. I'm not fighting anymore. I've forgotten why I was fighting to begin with." His hand pressed tighter against her back. She could feel the hard planes of him against her. And a thick ridge that made her breath catch in her throat. He made her feel like a woman, in a way she never had before. Like a delicate glass he could easily crush. Yet he didn't. Instead he guarded her, protected her, made sure nothing hurt her.

She tipped her head up again. "Kiss me." Her voice was

thick with desire. She'd thought about this moment all week. Fantasized about his mouth and what it could do.

A half smile pulled at his lips. His eyes were heavy lidded, his long eyelashes obscuring her view of them. She could feel a pulse in her neck, dancing to the rhythm of the music. She was full of him. Every sense reacted to his nearness. The sound of his breath, the feel of his strong hold, the manly aroma of him. It all made her want him more.

He paused. It wasn't a hesitation, she could read that much in his dark eyes. It was more of a savoring. Tasting the moment, the possibilities, the need that rushed through both of their bodies. He was a man who knew how to give pleasure, and knew that so much of that was in the anticipation.

Her skin felt like it was boiling beneath his scrutiny.

"So beautiful," he murmured, pressing his brow to hers. "The way you look at me, with those wide eyes, makes me want to carry you out of this room and lay you on the nearest bed."

The thought was like a stab of desire to her belly. "The gossips would have a field day."

"I don't give a damn. Do you?" He stopped dancing, pulling her against him.

No, she didn't. There was only one person she cared about in here, and right now she was in his arms. She could feel his warm breath against her lips, the thrum of blood through her veins reaching a crescendo.

Their first kiss was in an elevator. Enclosed. Full of hot desire. But now they were in a wide open room, surrounded by people. And all she could see was him.

When his lips brushed against hers it made her toes curl. He let out a groan, then brushed them again, the soft, almost-there, pressure maddeningly light. She tightened her fingers on his neck, rolling onto her toes to get closer. He released her hand, sliding his palms down her side, holding her hips to steady her.

As they stood in the middle of the floor, couples danced around them, the world carrying on even though her own had stopped. She arched her body against his, a soft sigh escaping her lips as he kissed her again. Firmer this time, the slide of his tongue against her mouth, both a request and a demand. She opened her own, welcoming him in, feeling the sensual throb of her body as he claimed her mouth, ruining her for anybody else.

Time stood still as they kissed and kissed, her world shrinking to the sensation of his mouth against hers. Heat sparked, excitement pulsed, making her nipples hard and her thighs ache. As though he could feel her need, he pressed his muscled thigh against her.

And it helped. A little.

When he pulled back, she blinked, slowly coming back to reality. The music had changed beat. People were dancing faster. Daniel's eyes were hazy, as thunderstruck as hers. He looked at her questioningly, as though he was trying to work out what just happened.

You just rocked my world, buddy. The same way I rocked yours.

"You can dance, you can kiss." Her voice was thick. Ragged. "Is there anything you can't do?"

A ghost of a smile passed his lips. "Maybe I'll show you later."

———

"MAY I HAVE THIS DANCE?"

Becca was still in Daniel's arms, her lips swollen and parted from the way he'd kissed her. Thoroughly and without mercy. She turned, still dazed, to see Lawrence standing next to them, an amused smile curling his lips.

"We were just going to get some air." Daniel held her tightly.

"Oh come on, just one dance. To show there's no hard feelings." Lawrence's smile didn't waver.

Daniel looked down at her, a question in his eyes. She shrugged. "It's okay by me." She needed the space to think about what just happened. Because that wasn't a random kiss.

It was life changing.

"Just one," Daniel said. "Then I want her back."

"Of course." Lawrence chuckled. "I wasn't planning on keeping this one."

Ugh, he was odious. But at least he was a good dancer, too, though not as effortless as Daniel. His long legs were stiffer, less at ease. "Are you having a good time?" he asked, as though he hadn't insinuated he could keep her if he wanted moments earlier.

"Any time I'm with Daniel is a good time." It wasn't a lie to rile him, though she did relish the short-lived surprise in Lawrence's eyes. The fact was, she craved his brother. One taste, and she'd become addicted.

"Your home is beautiful," Becca said, in an attempt to soothe the wound. "It must take a lot of work to maintain."

"It does. You don't own a house like this, you're a guardian of it. Keeping it up and going for the next generation. We do tours in the summer if you'd like to see the rest of it."

From the corner of her eye she could see Melissa talking to Daniel. He nodded unsmilingly, then took her in his arms.

A shot of jealousy racked through her. Melissa danced as well as Daniel. With her dark hair and pale skin she looked like a Hollywood princess in his arms. "I suppose you know that Melissa and Daniel were a thing once," Lawrence said, following Becca's gaze.

Daniel looked at her over Melissa's shoulder. His eyes were dark again. Narrowed. Did he feel as jealous as she felt right now?

She hoped so.

"I know." She nodded. "A long time ago."

"She broke his heart," Lawrence said, his voice full of an emotion she couldn't quite place. Was it relish? "Made him run away to Scotland. I guess it took this long for it to finally mend."

"I didn't know that's why he went to Scotland." Becca blinked. Lawrence's hand was sweaty as it held hers.

"He was always a sore loser. It's the first time he couldn't even bear to be in the same country as me, though."

Melissa laughed at something Daniel had said, her head tipping back, revealing her slender neck. Daniel's face was impassive.

"He learned a lot about Scotch Whisky while he was there," Becca said, ignoring the tightness in her chest. "So I guess it was good that he went."

"Maybe."

Daniel was looking at her again. She stared back, her eyes full of emotion. She didn't want to be here anymore. Didn't want to be in his brother's arms, or watching as he danced with Melissa.

She wanted it to be the two of them in their own little world again.

As though he could sense her stare, Lawrence spun Becca around. But her gaze automatically reconnected with Daniel's. He looked as pained as her. It was a small consolation.

When the dance came to an end, Becca politely pulled herself from Lawrence's hold.

"Thank you." His smile was smug.

She nodded, then searched for Daniel. He was on the side

of the dance floor, talking to Melissa. Becca tried to ignore the pain stabbing at her chest as Melissa rolled onto her toes and pressed her lips against Daniel's cheek.

"Well, it looks like we're all friends again," Lawrence murmured, flattening his palm high on Becca's back so he was touching bare skin. Trying not to tense, she stepped forward, away from him. He smiled, as though he was enjoying her discomfort, leaning down to whisper in her ear. "You and Daniel should come over some time. I'd like to get to know you better."

Even though he was too far away to hear his brother's words, Daniel's gaze lifted, the smile slipping away from his lips when he saw Lawrence so close to Becca. Without saying goodbye to Melissa, he stalked across the dance floor toward them, Becca's heart slamming against her ribcage in rhythm with his steps.

"Excuse me," he murmured, barely giving Lawrence a glance. "I'd like her back."

"Of course." Lawrence sounded smug. "She's a beautiful woman, who wouldn't want her?"

Daniel took Becca's hand, his fingers tense as they threaded through hers. "Would you like some air?" he asked, not waiting for her answer. Instead, he pulled her through the ballroom to the open glass doors at the far side, walking out onto the paved patio area, the music fading away behind them.

The cool air was a shock against her skin, but the jealousy still burned inside her. Daniel guided her along a path, toward an old summerhouse. Once they were at the door to the small building, he wrenched the door open and they stepped inside. "Did he upset you?" he asked, his face twisted with anger.

She shook her head. "No. He tried to get a rise from me but I batted it away."

"What did he say?" There was a twitch in Daniel's cheek. He looked like he wanted to hit something. She knew how he felt.

"Something about you being a sore loser. That you were so upset to lose Melissa that you ran away to Scotland."

Daniel snorted. "Anything else?"

"Um…" She wracked her brain. "He talked about the house. Said we should come over for dinner some time."

"Fat chance." Daniel shook his head. "I didn't like seeing you in his arms."

"It didn't mean anything." Her voice was soft. "I didn't like seeing you dance with Melissa either."

He inhaled deeply, shaking his head. "She means nothing."

"You were in love with her once."

"I don't know what love is. I'm not sure it even exists, but if it does, I never felt it for her."

Becca's head felt dizzy. "Did you go to Scotland because you were heartbroken?"

"No. I ran away because Lawrence won and I lost. It could have been a game of cards or a woman, it didn't matter. It pissed me off. I told you I'm competitive." He raked a hand through his hair. "And I'm aware of how fucking nuts that sounds. But you had to grow up here to know what it was like." He pressed his lips together, as though in pain. "Seeing you in his arms, it made me angry."

"I'm not his." It was a whisper.

"No. You're mine." His voice was low and harsh. "That's all I could think about when you were in his arms. That he was finding out how soft your skin is. How good you smell. That he got to look into your eyes instead of it being me."

"I was looking at you." A hot pulse danced in her neck.

She could feel the tension radiating from him. It matched her own. Ever since they kissed, it was as though the world had tipped sideways. Like one of those rides that whipped you around and round until you were barely clinging on.

Daniel stepped toward her, a lion stalking his pray. His hand cupped her jaw, his fingers hot and needy against her skin. He tipped her head, staring down at her with flinty eyes. "I could get so damn lost in you," he whispered.

"You could be found, too."

"You're the sweetest thing." He brushed his finger over her lips. It was enough to make her heart leap in her chest.

When Daniel kissed her this time, it felt like coming home. He tasted of wine; his lips demanding and hot as he took everything she wanted to give him. He slipped his arms around her waist, pulling her closer, taking more. Her hands tangled in the hair at the base of his skull, tugging him closer, needing more. So much more.

With one hand on her head, he slid the other up her side, his thumb gently brushing the swell of her breast. The touch made her gasp against his lips. He brushed again, closer to her nipple, and she let out a needy cry, desperate for his touch.

When it came, his caress sent a shot of pleasure through her body, making her toes curl as he tugged at her, rolling her between his thumb and finger. She arched against him, her lips moving against his, begging for mercy, for release, for something to sate this desperate need.

When he pulled back, she could see the fire in his eyes. Could see the evidence of his excitement in the thick line of his pants. He shucked his jacket off, throwing it on one of the old wicker chairs, loosening his tie before he kissed her again.

His lips slid from her mouth to her jaw, kissing and nipping his way down her neck to the dip at the base of her throat. Her chest rose and fell as she gasped for air, her heart beating so fast that one thump ran into the next.

Then he was kissing the top of her breasts, her impressive, forced cleavage, his hand scooping inside the mesh of her bodice until his fingers found what they were looking for. Without the fabric barrier between them, her response was fast. Heightened. She cried out again, arching against him as he freed her breast from its fabric prison, dipping his head to capture her nipple between his lips.

And she was gone. Not sure if she was in heaven or hell, her body began to throb, the need rushing between her legs. It was an itch she could never sate, no matter how much she pushed against him. She needed him above her, inside her, everywhere he could be.

"Daniel." She gasped as he flicked against her with his tongue. Her hands threaded into his hair, holding him to her chest.

"Hush, I've got you," he whispered against her skin, circling her waist with his hands.

"I need…" Another gasp. "Daniel, I need you."

His gaze flickered to hers. She could see herself reflected in the ink of his eyes. "I'm not going to take you here."

Her mouth dropped open. She needed him. Didn't he know? If he kept going like this she would explode.

"But…" She sighed as he freed her other breast, cupping it with his warm palm. Sucking her hard, until her head tipped back with pleasure.

"Sit down." He nodded at the wicker bench behind her. She was too wound up to do anything but obey. To her surprise, Daniel dropped to his knees in front of her, sliding his hands up her calves, thumbs brushing the sensitive underside of her knees before he reached her thighs.

His fingers dug into her flesh as he parted her legs, swallowing hard as he exposed her white lace lingerie. "Beautiful." His voice was raw. "So damn beautiful." He pushed her thighs apart further, leaning in to press his nose against her, inhaling sharply as he pressed his lips against her laced panties.

It was mortifyingly sexy, watching him breathe her in like air. Seeing his eyes darken even further as he leaned back to hook his fingers around her panties, sliding them easily down her legs. She lifted her feet as he pulled the lace scrap over her shoes, leaving her bare and exposed.

He touched her first with an outstretched finger, like he was writing in the sand. "You're wet."

"For you," she breathed.

"Yes." He dipped his finger deeper, then pulled it back to her sensitive nub. An electric pulse shot down to her toes, making her gasp again. Then he put his finger into his mouth and licked it, making her blush.

She reached for him, her hand curling around his wrist. "I want to touch you."

He shook his head, understanding exactly what she meant. "Not here." His voice was rough. "I wouldn't be able to control myself."

Pressing a kiss against her knee, he brushed his lips upward, until he reached the apex of her thighs, breathing her in all over again. She was squirming on the bench, her body a bundle of desperate need, and when he finally pressed his lips to her it felt like a blessed relief.

But only for a moment. Because then he started to tease her with his tongue, swirling it between her folds, his face pressed against her like she was his favorite meal. His hands slid beneath her, angling her body to suit his needs, his tongue and lips taking everything he wanted, giving her intense pleasure in return. Her head tipped back against the wooden wall of the summer house, her awareness of her surroundings disappearing as Daniel's tongue lashed against the pinpoint of nerves between her legs.

Heat coiled inside her, spitting and sparking as he took

her to the edge. She rolled her hips against him, earning her a murmur of approval. "Daniel…"

"Hush, I'm here. Not stopping." He slid two fingers inside of her, the rhythm of his tongue never wavering. His finger tips curled, intensifying the sensations, sending her over the edge. Then she was flying and falling at the same time, fireworks exploding behind her closed eyes, her breath stuttering as pleasure crashed over her again and again.

He didn't stop. Not even when she tried to sit up. "More." He slid his tongue against her sensitive skin, eking out the pleasure, growling against her with his own.

"I can't… it's too much."

"Trust me, you can."

Every part of her was pulsing with pleasure. Her body felt so sensitive that she was moments from screaming out. He curled his fingers again, twisting them in a maddeningly delicious knot that made her blood feel like it was on fire. And then she was coming again, hard and fast, her body boneless as he pulled his fingers from her, spasms wracking through her body until she slowly came down.

"You're addictive. You're not kryptonite, you're crack." His lips were glistening with her. "I don't know how I'm ever going to get over you."

CHAPTER TWENTY-ONE

They'd almost made it back to the ballroom when Becca stopped. Daniel turned to look at her. She was glorious. She'd done her best to smooth her hair down and fix her lipstick, but anybody who noticed her flushed skin would wonder exactly what she'd been doing.

Not that he cared. Let them gossip. He was too busy trying to figure out how quickly they could leave. He didn't want to make chitchat or smile politely at another old friend of his late father.

He wanted to be with her. Alone.

"We have to go back to the summer house," Becca said, her eyes wide.

A slow smile curled his lips. "You want more?"

"No!" Her lips almost trembled. "I think you've wore me out. I can barely walk right now. We need to go back because I left my panties there."

"No you didn't." He patted his pocket. "I have them."

A mixture of relief and shock washed over her features. "Give them to me."

"You want me to give your panties to you here?" He

inclined his head at the open glass doors in front of them. "In front of everybody."

"Oh god, no. Not here." She looked around. "When we're inside. Slip them to me and I'll put them on in the bathroom."

"We could do that if you like." His voice was mild, but his body felt more alive than it had in years.

"What's the alternative? Leave?"

He shook his head. "I keep your panties and know that you're walking around without them." He slid his hand in his pocket, feeling the lace against his fingertips. "You'll know, too."

Her chest hitched. "I'll be bare beneath my dress." She'd already shown him she was braless, thanks to the cut of her ball gown.

"Yeah." His voice was rough. "I know."

She stared at him, her eyes still glazed from their activities. "Would you like that?" she asked, her voice a whisper.

His eyes flashed. "I would. But only if you would, too."

She shifted her legs, as though she had an itch she couldn't scratch. He could see the flush of desire wash over her again. How had he stopped himself from touching her before? It was hard to remember. Because now that he knew how she tasted, he wanted so much more.

Everything.

"Let's go dance while you think about it," Daniel suggested, leading her to the center of the ballroom. He had to do something to take his mind off the desperate urge to kiss her, to taste her, to feel himself get lost in her. Just like before, she fit him like a glove, her sweet body pressing against his as he led her around the room.

Every time his thigh touched hers, she gave a little shudder. As though the sensation was too much for her. She was unsteady on her feet. He liked to think he'd made her that way.

"Can I ask you something?" she asked, as they spun away from the band.

"Of course."

"Why did you do that in the summer house?" Her eyes didn't quite meet his. "You made me feel good and you ended up frustrated."

"Because it's polite to put ladies first."

Becca smiled. "I'm pretty sure that's not something you were taught by your mom."

Daniel grimaced. "Definitely not. And now I'm wondering what kind of guys you've been dating where you're surprised that I enjoyed tasting you."

Her flush deepened. "I don't date that much."

"But you're not a virgin."

Becca shook her head. "I had a boyfriend at college for a while. He lasted for about eight months before he met my brothers and got spooked."

"Doesn't sound like much of a guy."

She sighed. "I guess he wasn't. I've had a few other boyfriends and some dates. Mostly assholes who got annoyed that I didn't put out on the first date. Nobody special."

"I don't understand how you got to your mid-twenties without anybody special." His brows knitted together. "You're like a ripe fruit."

"Waiting to be plucked."

He grinned. "Your words, not mine."

"Maybe I'm discerning." She pressed her cheek against his shoulder. He could smell the scent of her shampoo. Damn, she was intoxicating.

A rush of anger went through him at the men who hadn't treated her the way she deserved. "Don't ever let a guy take without giving." His voice was hard. "You deserve more."

Her gaze lifted to his. "Is that why you did it? Because I deserve more than a quick romp?"

"Maybe I did it because you deserve to be pleased, rather than pleasing everybody else."

"I'd like to please you." Her voice was low. It went right to his core. He could feel himself harden against her.

"Becca…"

"I'd like to taste you, the way you tasted me. To wrap my lips around you, and slide my tongue up and down."

He inhaled sharply. Didn't she realize what she did to him? He was throbbing. "I'm half a minute away from taking you back to that summer house."

"Not the summer house." She pressed a kiss to his jaw. "I want to see you above me, all angry and concentrated. I want to watch your face as you c—"

He released his hold on her back, spinning her around and leading her off the dance floor. The song hadn't even ended. A smile pulled at her lips as he held tightly to her hand, walking over to their table to bid farewell.

"So early?" Eliana said, looking at them with a confused smile.

"Becca's hungry." He shot her a look, and Becca squeezed his hand. "I need to get her something to eat."

"Well that's understandable." Julia lifted her glass to them. "The food here is terrible. And it's no place for young lovers. Off you two go. Have a good time."

Eliana pressed her lips against Daniel's cheek, then hugged Becca. She whispered something in Becca's ear that Daniel couldn't hear.

And then they were heading to the car, waiting for them at the base of the steps thanks to Daniel's quick text. He opened the door and helped Becca in, then walked around to the driver to speak quietly to him.

When he climbed into the backseat, Becca slid her hand

back into his, resting her cheek on his shoulder. A strange emotion rushed through him. Was it contentment?

"What did my mother say to you?" he asked her.

Becca bit down a smile. "Nothing important."

He blinked at her refusal to tell. The driver pulled away, down the graveled driveway and out of the huge cast iron gates. Becca curled against him, and he wrapped his arm around her, marveling again at how perfectly she fit against him. Her skin was warm, her hair soft against his cheek, her hand softly resting on his thigh as the driver made it to the outskirts of Charleston.

Five minutes later they came to a stop. Becca looked out of the window and back to Daniel with confusion.

"The Ambassador Hotel?"

"I figure it's better not to make you scream in my mother's house."

"Do they even have a room?"

He nodded. "I texted them while we were driving. The penthouse is ours."

A slow smile pulled at her lips. "Like a do-over of last week. But with less angst and more pleasure."

"I certainly hope so." His voice was smooth. Sexy.

He helped her out of the car and led her into the hotel, where the concierge nodded at them both, slipping a card into Daniel's hand. "The code is your usual."

"Thank you."

It was only a short wait for the penthouse elevator, but every second felt tangible, like it stretched for minutes. Becca was still holding his hand, standing close to him. He usually hated being too close to his dates. But with her it was different.

Then the gold leaf doors opened and they stepped inside.

———

BECCA WALKED to the back of the elevator and turned until her back was pressed against the rail, her hands reaching behind her to curl around it. Daniel stepped inside, his jaw sharp and tight, his eyes dark and delicious as he scanned her face.

"When you look at me like that it makes me want to take you against the damn mirror," he growled.

"Like what?"

"All doe eyed and innocent. Like you're half afraid of and half desperate for me."

"That's exactly how I feel," she told him. "Like you're a predator and I have no idea what you have planned."

"I have a lot of plans." He glanced at his watch. "For the next few hours."

Her breath caught in her throat. The memories of his face between her thighs, his lips and tongue taking and giving until her body was drowning with pleasure flashed through her.

"What are you thinking?" he asked.

"That I might not get out of here alive."

His face relaxed into a smile. "I fear for my own life more than yours."

She loved the way he was looking at her. He was so intense, so dark. Yet there was a softness there, you just had to find it. He gave her pleasure first, because he wanted to.

And now she wanted to see his pleasure written all over his face.

"They'll find our bodies in a few days still sweaty and flushed."

"Our faces still full of pleasure."

He took a step forward, reaching out to cup her cheek. "Where did you come from?"

"I've been here all along. It's you who came back."

He inhaled sharply. "I don't know what's going to happen

between us after tonight." His eyes gazed at her, as though he was trying to tell her more.

"I don't want anything from you after tonight. You're more trouble than you're worth."

He chuckled. "Touché."

"And while we're talking about trouble, do you have any insulin?"

His eyes softened at her question. "I checked my levels earlier. I'm good."

"Okay then."

He stepped even closer. Enough for her to lift her head to look at those dark eyes. He was overwhelming. Not just in height, but in everything. Definitely trouble with a capital 'T'.

The doors pinged as they opened behind him. He leaned forward and her breath caught. Was he going to kiss her again? Instead, he slid his hands beneath her, lifting her up and carrying her out of the elevator, his sudden movements shocking the air from her lungs.

"Five five seven eight," he said, dropping her enough so she could punch the number into the keypad. The lock clicked, and Becca pushed down the handle, Daniel kicking the door open with his foot.

He carried her inside, stalking across the living room of the suite toward the door of his bedroom, dipping her again so she could press down on the handle.

"You could put me down," she murmured against his cheek. "It would probably be easier."

"If I put you down, I don't trust myself not to take you. And I want to see you on my bed."

Sure enough, he headed straight for the king in the center of the room, carefully laying her on the smooth bedsheets, stepping back to look at her like she was an installation at an art gallery.

He stalked around the bed, his gaze still on her, as though he wanted to see her from every angle.

"Still a predator, circling your prey."

"Just trying to work out the best way to die."

She lifted herself up on her elbows. The fluffy tulle of her skirt was wrapped around her thighs. Her breasts were fighting to escape the bodice. "This must be how it feels to lose your virginity on prom night," she said, as he pulled at his bow tie and unfastened his top button.

His eyes crinkled. "Who took you to prom?"

"You don't want to know." There was no way she was going to admit it was Tanner.

"You're keeping all the secrets tonight."

"Maybe I want to be more like you. Strong and silent."

He shook his head slowly. "You really don't." He shucked his jacket off, then toed off his shoes. If he'd looked glorious in his full tux, now he looked dangerously sensual. White shirt, loose tie, and pants that hugged his hips as though they never wanted to let go.

"Who did *you* take to prom?"

"I didn't go. I was going through a rebellious phase."

Becca grinned. "I'm not sure you grew out of it."

He reached the base of the mattress, his eyes scanning her. She knew how she looked. Louche, needy, dirty. Her legs splayed, her dress half off her body, her hair a mess of waves as it tumbled over her shoulders.

He dropped to his knees, leaning forward and circling his hands around her thighs, pulling her toward him, his thumbs digging into her skin. She tried to slide her shoes off her feet and he stopped her.

"These stay on."

Damn, even the way he talked sent shivers down her spine. "What if I want you to keep your shoes on, too?" She raised an eyebrow

He laughed. "Not the same." Running his fingers along her inner thighs, he leaned forward to press a chaste kiss against her.

"Not again. Please. I'm ready for you."

"Maybe I'm not ready. Maybe I want to taste you again."

She sat up, hooking her legs around his waist, pulling him forward until their faces were almost touching. "Kiss me."

Something flashed behind his eyes. "You're giving the orders now?"

She ran the tip of her nose against his. "I'm asking nicely."

His mouth curled, as he slid his hand into her hair. He tipped her face back and kissed her throat, his lips demanding and hot.

Becca's nipples tightened, rubbing deliciously against her dress. "I should take this off," she said. "The dry cleaning bill is going to be astronomic."

"I'll buy you a new dress." He continued kissing her neck, reaching behind her to unzip the mesh fabric, pushing the straps down her shoulders. The rush of cool air made her nipples tighten more.

"Then I'll buy you a new tux. This needs to come off," she muttered, tugging at his open tie and flinging it on the floor. Then she tried to unfasten his buttons, but he wouldn't let her lift her head to see what she was doing, too busy kissing her jaw, her cheek, the corner of her lips.

There was a movement as he took over, shrugging his shirt off. This time she made sure she looked, and she was so glad she did.

Thick, muscled shoulders. Warm skin stretched over rippled pectorals, with dark nipples that made her mouth water.

She could never get bored of touching a man like him. Her breath caught as she reached out, tracing her finger over him, loving the feel of his skin.

His erection jutted proudly against his pants. She touched that, too, and he let out a strangled moan.

"I want this," she said, tracing the line of it again. "Now."

"So demanding," he murmured, unfastening his fly.

"I just want to see if you taste as bitter as your personality."

He laughed, the deep chuckle filling the room. His fly was open, revealing black shorts that did nothing to hide the size of him. He leaned over, stroking her face softly before pressing his lips against hers.

"What are you doing here with me?" he asked, kissing her again. She curled her arms around him, her thigh pressing against his groin, and he let out another groan, circling his hips as though he had no choice.

"It's a fight to the death," she whispered.

He kissed her again. "La petite mort."

"Are you trying to seduce me with your language skills? Because if you haven't noticed, I'm already seduced."

He pushed her bodice down, jaw tightening as he took in her breasts. "It's the French word for orgasm. If you translate it literally, it means little death." He dipped his head, sucking at her nipple, growling approvingly as she arched herself against him.

"I'd like to die a little tonight with you."

"Or a lot." He sucked at her other nipple. How did they end up like this? She was supposed to be tasting him. Teasing him. Seeing how dark she could make his eyes. Instead, she was at his mercy, subdued by his teasing lips.

He peppered kisses across her chest and she reached down between them, sliding her hand beneath the waistband of his shorts. He was thicker than she realized. His hot skin was tight as her fingers circled him. Slowly, she ran her palm down him, loving the way his kisses stilled against her.

"Stop." His voice was urgent. He pressed his hand against

hers. "Damn, I should have knocked one out at the summer house."

She laughed with delight, loving that he was on the edge of control. That she could do that to him. "Come between my lips." She sat up, wriggling the dress off her waist, putting it gently down on the floor because it wasn't hers.

"No. Inside you." His voice was ragged. "Just give me a minute."

He breathed in and out, as if centering himself. Then he turned his attention to her again. Circling his hand around her wrists, he pushed her back on the mattress, her hair spreading out beneath her as he scanned her from face to feet. She stared back at him, loving the way he stared at her. Loving how he held himself above her, back in control once more. Daniel the predator, sizing up his prey.

"This will help," he muttered, pulling a foil package from his wallet. "A little." He slid it on, encasing his magnificent erection, doing nothing to diminish its beauty to her. Then he was back over her, still holding her wrists with one hand, the other sliding down between her legs, his eyes closing as he felt how wet she was.

How ready she was for him.

He slowly circled his thumb against her, making her thighs tense with desire. His touch was soft, too soft for her to get the satisfaction she needed. She rolled her hips in an attempt to get friction.

Despite the cool air surrounding them, she could feel herself begin to sweat. He slid two fingers inside of her and it made her cry out.

"Please…"

"Please what?" He crossed his fingers, the knotty pressure of his knuckles sending sparks of electricity down her thighs.

"I need you inside me, please," she gasped. How could he

bring her to the edge with only a few touches? How many little deaths was she going to have tonight?

"I need you ready."

"I've been ready since the first time you scowled at me." Her words were breathless. He was still teasing her, coaxing pleasure.

"I was scowling because I wanted you."

"I wanted you, too." It was more than want. It was need. She needed him inside her like she needed air. A smile flitted over his lips. He curled his fingers, finding the spot inside her that nobody had discovered before, and she convulsed beneath him, pleasure washing over her as he kissed her breasts, her throat, as his hand slid beneath her thigh to gently part her legs.

She could feel the weight of him against her, even though he was bracing himself with his elbow. The warmth of him, too. His hard body pressed against her, his thickness slowly spreading her apart as he gently eased himself inside, his face contracting with pleasure as his hips grazed hers.

She felt so full, the sensation of him causing her muscles to ripple around him. He pulled back and pushed forward again, his fingers digging into her behind, his lips capturing hers as he muttered soft oaths against her mouth.

When their eyes met, she felt something inside of her twist. Her chest felt tight, as though she was falling. He pulled her hips higher, until he was rolling his body against her in a maddeningly delicious rhythm, making every muscle inside of her tighten.

"Daniel," she breathed.

"I've got you." He dropped his brow against hers, his breath stilted, his body covered with a sheen of sweat. She held onto his shoulders as though she was clinging to life, the roll of her hips urging him deeper, harder, and her stilted words begging him not to stop.

Oh god, oh god, it was happening again. This mort wasn't petite. It was big and rolling and it was going to kill them both. Her cries were loud, her grip on him hard. He cupped her jaw, slipping his thumb between her lips, groaning as she sucked him. Then he reached down, touching her as they moved together, his thumb circling and caressing until she could only babble incoherently.

She was flying. She was falling. She was everywhere and nowhere. He tensed against her, an animalistic grunt escaping his mouth, his arms circling her waist and pulling her against him as he spilled inside her. Her perspiration mixed with his, their bodies slipping and sliding as his face contorted with pleasure. Slowly he released her, until her back fell against the mattress.

"Dear Lord," she whispered. "You killed me four times tonight."

"Give me five minutes and I'll work on a fifth." He rolled onto his back, pulling her against him. She waited for him to laugh, but he didn't. Was he serious? Didn't he know she might *really* die this time?

He brushed the hair away that was sticking to her cheek, dipping his head to press his lips against her. "You're beautiful," he whispered. His eyes fluttered closed, his breath evening out as he regained composure.

"Your mom told me I'm the only person who's ever made you smile this much," Becca whispered, not sure if he even heard her. Maybe it didn't matter. The words warmed her anyway.

CHAPTER TWENTY-TWO

Daniel walked into his mother's dining room, nodding at Lawrence and Nina who were already sitting at the table, sipping at their coffees. He poured himself a cup from the pot on the counter, not bothering to add any cream as he took a seat opposite them. Nina gave him a smile. Of the four siblings, she was always the one to try to smooth things over. She and Nathan had gotten all of their respective mothers' peacemaker skills, and Daniel and Lawrence got their father's drive and harshness.

"You look tired," Lawrence said, his eyes scanning Daniel's face. "I guess that's what happens when you spend the night wrapped around a younger girlfriend."

"Lawrence." Nina wrinkled her nose. "Don't be disgusting." She turned to look at Daniel. "He's right, though. There are shadows beneath your eyes. Have you tested your blood?"

"It's fine." He brushed her enquiry away with a soft smile. "My levels are right where they should be. You don't need to worry."

"I do worry." She sighed. "I was the only one who took it

seriously when you were younger. Apart from your mom, but when she wasn't around it fell to me."

"Remember when Dad took your insulin away and said your body would adapt if you stopped injecting?" Lawrence exhaled through his nose. "Man, you got sick that time."

There was a relish to his voice that Daniel ignored. He glanced at his watch, it was almost eleven. He wanted to be on the road by lunchtime. Becca had already left, and he wanted to see her again. Just to check that she got home safely. And then he'd beat the shit out of his punching bag.

Something had to happen with all this excess energy he had.

He took a sip of coffee and opened the file he'd brought in, passing a sheaf of paper to his siblings. "Hopefully you've had a chance to study the figures. Initial costs, projected revenue, suggested sources of investments."

Lawrence didn't glance down at the paper. "I've read it. But what I don't understand is why you want to make a single malt Scotch over here. The company has barely broken even on the International Blend, and now you want to spend more money?"

"The International Blend will be in profit by next quarter. And since there are no more development costs associated with it, the profit should continue. But it won't grow the business the way I want to. The International Blend appeals to the occasional whiskey drinker. It has a cachet to it, thanks to the marketing campaign. It's the kind of drink people order in bars to make themselves look good."

Nina smiled wryly. "Charles ordered a bottle when we were at Annabel's Club last week."

"There you go." Daniel nodded. "But we need something to appeal to the dedicated whiskey drinker. The ones who buy a thirty year old bottle because they can tell the difference between that and one made last year. Scotch is for connoisseurs. Those who can tell a peated from a non peated, or a burgundy cask from a reused rye one."

"But we won't see any profit for seven years," Lawrence pointed out. "That's how long you have to let it sit in the barrel if you want it to be a single malt." He frowned. "And even then, it wouldn't be classified as a single malt under strict Scottish rules. So you can't even market it like that."

"I've been speaking to some other producers. They've been campaigning for a single malt classification here in the US. If that comes to pass, we'd get our own space on the shelves in liquor stores. People would actively search our bottles out."

"It sounds like a gamble," Nina said. She always was the most cautious of them. Maybe it came from seeing her world tip upside down as a child.

"I guess it is. But all leaps forward are gambles, aren't they?" He tipped his head to the side, scrutinizing them.

"And the investment money? You have it secured?"

Daniel nodded. "Yes. Along with the loans, we'll be pre-selling some casks. With a name like ours, speculators will see them as assets. With interest rates low, commodities like ours are in demand. If things go the way I project, the profit we make will be enough to fund GSC for the foreseeable future."

Nina took a bite of pastry. "And Becca will be the lead distiller?"

Daniel nodded, his face impassive. "If she accepts the role."

"Well I guess I'm okay with it." Nina shrugged. "Daddy always loved that distillery. If you say it'll work, then I believe you."

Lawrence looked carefully at Daniel. "Go for it," he said with a nod.

Daniel tried not to smile. "That's a yes?"

"If it brings in more money, who am I to refuse?" Lawrence stood and dusted crumbs from his shirt. "Now, I need to get home. I have a ball to clear up from."

"No you don't. You always make Melissa do the work." Nina laughed. "It's more like you have a ball to recover from. I saw how much champagne you drank."

"I need to get home myself." Daniel nodded. "I have a lot of work to do."

"Don't work too hard," Nina chided as she stood and folded her napkin. "You need some rest."

Daniel walked around the table to see them out, kissing Nina on the cheek and holding his hand out to Lawrence. His brother hesitated for a moment, then took it, giving him a limp wristed shake.

Not that Daniel cared. The shake could be as weak as he wanted, the deal was still his. Even if it didn't quite feel like a victory.

―――――

"You must be delighted." Eliana's eyes crinkled as she lifted her tea cup to her lips. The sun was shining through the tall windows of the library, creating a long shaft of light on the polished wooden floor.

From the corner of his eye, he could see the card table he'd sat at with Becca yesterday. The thought of her made his blood heat up. He could still taste her on his lips, still hear her soft sighs in his ear.

Still see the way she smiled at him when he'd kissed her brow after they'd taken each other over the edge.

"It's a good deal for everybody," Daniel said, trying to push Becca out of his thoughts. "They'll make money without having to lift a finger." The truth was, Lawrence's acceptance of the plan felt anticlimactic. Daniel had thought he'd have to fight for it.

But his brother just acceded.

"But it's nice to have their blessing. It's good to see you all getting closer."

Daniel stood, unable to sit still any longer, striding over to the shelves lined with books and photographs. There was one of him and Nathan in their school uniforms, their hair neatly brushed back and polite smiles on their faces.

Next to it was one of Daniel as a baby, cradled in his Eliana's arms. She was looking down at him, her eyes full of love.

Then there was one of Lawrence and Nina, his sister awkwardly holding a toddler Daniel as Lawrence pulled his brows together, no smile lifting his lips.

It was impossible to remember a time when things between him and his half-siblings were civil. The circumstances of his birth had seen to that, as well as the rivalry his father had encouraged between him and Lawrence.

Two firstborns fighting it out for their patriarch's attention. In the end, they were both losers.

Yet yesterday hadn't been half as bad as he'd been imagining. And that was thanks to Becca. Her smile, her laugh, her warm palm clasped in his. She made everything feel lighter. Softer.

Better.

"Did you have a nice evening?" his mom asked, looking at him over the rim of her teacup.

"It was tolerable." He gave her half a smile.

"You looked like you were enjoying yourself. And Becca was delightful."

He swallowed. "Yeah, she was."

"I like her a lot."

His lips twitched. "I get that impression."

"How about you?" Eliana tipped her head to the side, scrutinizing him. "Do you like her?"

He looked at another photograph. This one was posed. His father and the four siblings, sitting around him like planets orbiting the sun. The older Larry Carter looking so damn smug as Lawrence and Daniel stood on either side of him, Nina and Nathan on chairs in front.

Once upon a time, even looking at that photograph would make him want to smash the glass. It was all a lie. The perfect family on the outside, a torn up mess on the inside.

But it didn't matter, did it? His father was gone. The game was over. Neither he nor Lawrence had won.

The door opened and Rona walked in, carrying something in her hands. "I found this in the guest bedroom," she said, carrying it over to where Daniel was standing. As he realized what it was, a huge smile pulled at his lips.

A shoe. Or a glass slipper. Damn, it was Cinderella playing out in real life. If Cinderella was a gorgeous brunette distiller who knew exactly how to make his body surge with pleasure.

But it was more than a shoe. It was an excuse to talk to her. And he wanted it, badly. Because Becca Hartson made everything better.

What happened to no promises after last night? He shook his head at his inner voice. Last night changed everything.

She lit up his dark world.

"I guess she forgot to pack it," he murmured, taking the shoe from Rona. "I'll take it back to Hartson's Creek. Make sure she gets it."

And while he was there, he'd find a way to persuade her to see him again. Because she was still a strong-as-heck magnet. And he wasn't ready to give her up.

———

BECCA TURNED her car onto Gray's driveway, waiting for the gates to open before she pressed her foot on the pedal and drove inside. All of her family was here, from the number of cars parked outside Gray's sprawling ranch house. She could see Tanner's car next to Logan and Cam's, along with her aunt's brand new Ford that Gray had insisted on buying her. He'd tried to buy Becca a car, too, but she'd turned him down. The same way she'd turned down all their offers of help when she bought her condo.

She loved them, even though they were too much sometimes. And right now her family was exactly what she needed to take her mind off last night and this morning.

And Daniel Carter.

She hadn't stopped thinking about him for the entire drive home. A hot, steamy shower did nothing to help, other than to remind her of how slippery their bodies were as they came together for the third time last night.

Her lips twitched as she remembered them sneaking back to his mother's house like teenagers, her giggles muffled by his lips as he kissed her all the way up the stairs.

She'd been surprised when he'd followed her into her bedroom, taking his clothes off – again – and climbing into her bed, wrapping his arms around her as she nestled against his warm chest.

When she'd woken this morning he was gone. Eliana had gracefully offered her breakfast in the kitchen, and then she'd gone to pack. They'd agreed it was for the best if she left before he did, but it still made her chest ache to go.

She walked around the side of Gray's house, hearing the sound of talking and laughter drift through the air from his yard at the back. Mia was the first to see her. She was sitting with Maddie and Van, and shot up as soon as Becca walked around the corner, hurrying to catch her before she could join them all.

"Oh god," she whispered, holding Becca's hands and backing her up. "They've been incessant. Constantly asking why you had to work and where you were working at and whether they should contact your boss and tell him to stop riding you so hard."

Becca had to smash her lips together to stop herself from laughing. "Riding me hard?" she finally said, swallowing down a laugh.

Mia looked at her carefully. "No," she whispered. "You didn't."

"I totally did." Just saying it made it feel more real.

"Of course you did. You're glowing like the sun. I need all the details."

"*Now?*"

Mia shook her head. "Definitely not now. Look at your brothers, they're all staring at us."

Sure enough, as Becca looked over her shoulder she could see them watching her. She rolled her eyes at Tanner, who rolled his eyes back.

"How was work?" he called out.

"Fine."

"Where was it you were working again?" Cam asked. He folded his arms in front of him, his muscles popping.

"In Charleston."

"Right." Logan nodded. "And where did you sleep last night?"

Becca sighed. Maybe this hadn't been such a good idea after all. She was a bad liar when it came to them. "At my boss' house. Eliana. You remember her, right?" She looked at Gray. He'd met Eliana a few times after he became the face for the new International Blend.

"Yeah, I know her." Gray ran his finger along his jaw. "I'll have to give her a call. Thank her for taking care of you."

"He won't. I'll speak to Maddie. She'll stop him," Mia

whispered in Becca's ear. "But if you don't stop looking so guilty, they'll guess anyway."

Her Aunt Gina was sitting next to her father. Becca kissed their cheeks, and Gina squeezed her arm. "You look so beautiful," her aunt said. "Radiant, even. What's happened to make your eyes sparkle like that?"

"Nothing." Becca shifted her feet. How do you stop your eyes from sparkling? She needed to work that out, stat. Aunt Gina knew her too well. She needed to get away without her guessing Becca's secret.

As if she could sense Becca's thoughts, Maddie stood, hitching one of the twins onto her hips. "You must be hungry after all that driving. Come inside and I'll plate you up some food."

Becca's other two sisters-in-law, Van and Courtney, stood too, muttering something about dessert. They followed Maddie, Becca, and Mia inside to the kitchen.

"What's going on?" Maddie asked as soon as the door was closed. "You two look so guilty."

Mia glanced at Becca. "Nothing." She shifted her gaze away so none of them could catch her eye.

"Were you really working last night?" Van asked, leaning on the counter.

They were all staring at her expectantly. This was probably the most fun they'd had all day.

"Sort of," Becca admitted, rolling her bottom lip between her teeth.

"What does that mean?"

"It means, I went to a charity ball with Daniel Carter." She'd lasted two minutes. She'd make a terrible spy.

"Daniel Carter?" Van frowned. "As in your boss?

"The asshole?" Maddie added. "Didn't he make you cry the other week?"

Mia coughed away a laugh.

Becca looked down at her hands. "And I slept with him." She needed her sisters-in-law on her side. If it meant telling them the truth, so be it.

A collective gasp filled the room. Maddie was the first to recover. "Oh my god!" she whispered. "You did?"

Courtney squealed loudly. "You slept with your boss?" She clapped her hands together with glee.

"You've got to tell us all about it," Van said, grabbing Becca's hands. "Does that mean he's not an asshole any more?"

"He's definitely still an asshole," Becca told her. One she liked very much.

"You had hate sex!" Maddie laughed. "That's the best kind of sex. So dirty and animalistic. Whenever Gray and I argue we always end up in bed…"

"Ugh, please." Becca put her hands over her ears. "You guys need to stop talking about your love lives with my brothers."

And it wasn't hate sex, anyway. It was so different from that. Intense, deep, his eyes staring into hers. There was a connection there that she could still feel pulling at her chest.

"What are you guys squealing about?" Tanner asked, pushing open the glass door. "We can hear you out there."

"Nothing," Becca said quickly, aware she looked as guilty as hell.

"Oh come on. I haven't heard so much squealing since Logan and Courtney bred their prize boar."

Van patted Becca on the shoulder, sending her a message with her eyes that Becca couldn't quite understand.

"It's okay," she said. "I'll tell him. He'll be fine."

"No!" Becca shook her head. "Please."

"I told them about the baby," Van told Tanner, ignoring Becca's desperate tug on her hand.

"You're pregnant?" Maddie's mouth fell open, then realizing what she said, she quickly added, "I mean, you're pregnant. Congratulations, Tanner. We're all so excited for you." Her face was so red she looked like she was going to burst.

"I can't believe it," Mia said, hugging Van tightly. "Congratulations! Again." Her lips twisted at their subterfuge. "And congratulations to you, daddy," she told Tanner, who was frowning.

"I thought we were going to announce it together, babe," he said. "Once we reached the second trimester."

"*We*?" Maddie said, trying to hide a smile. "Why is it *we're pregnant* until the vomiting starts and the nightly trips to the bathroom happens and your pelvic floor gets ruined?"

"Your pelvic floor gets ruined?" Tanner blinked. "What does that mean?"

"I got one word for you," Mia said. "Kegels. Look them up. And bribe her to do them if you have to."

Tanner pulled his phone out and swiped his finger across the screen, frantically pressing against the keyboard. Realization slowly washed over his face, much to everybody's amusement.

"Thank you," Becca mouthed at Van.

"You owe me one," Van mouthed back.

"Everybody okay in here?" Gray asked, walking inside. "You guys sound like you're going crazy."

Behind him, Logan and Cam were peering in. "Tanner, why do you look like you've just seen a naked photo of Aunt Gina?"

"Did you know pregnancy can ruin a woman's pelvic floor?" Tanner asked. "Why didn't you guys warn me?" He glanced at Van. "Sweetheart, we need to go home. You have exercise to do."

Van smiled. "How do you know I haven't been doing them?"

Tanner blinked again.

"What's Van been doing?" Gray asked, looking from Tanner to Van.

"You should tell him," Van prompted.

"Oh shit. Yeah." Tanner nodded quickly. "So we have an announcement."

"Van's pregnant," Cam said.

"Yeah, totally pregnant," Logan agreed. "You can see it in her eyes."

"She's blooming." Gray winked at her.

"You guys knew?" Tanner looked at his brothers, hurt in his eyes.

"We kind of guessed. You keep asking us questions about when our kids were born," Logan told him. "And last week you asked how long we waited until we announced."

"You are such a terrible secret keeper," Van said, hugging Tanner. Her eyes were bright with amusement.

"We both are, babe." Tanner kissed her softly.

"So, are we gonna drink to the new Hartson or what?" Gray asked, pulling a bottle of champagne out of the refrigerator. "Who's going to go out and tell Aunt Gina and Dad? I don't want to give them a heart attack before I give them the champagne."

"We'll go," Van said, grabbing Tanner's hand. "At least we get to announce it properly to them."

"Yeah." Tanner nodded. "Let's do it."

Becca's phone rang as her brother and Van walked outside. She pulled it from her purse and checked the caller.

Daniel Carter.

A little shiver of anticipation washed through her.

"Is it him?" Mia asked quietly.

Becca nodded.

"Go take it. Pretend you need to use the bathroom or something."

Thank goodness for her sisters-in-law. They almost made up for her over protective brothers.

"Just a minute. It's work," Becca called out, walking into Gray's elegant hallway. She accepted the call and lifted the phone to her ear, letting out a breathy *hello*.

"Did you make it back okay?" Daniel asked her. His voice sounded warm. Soft.

"I got home about an hour ago. The traffic was light. How about you? Was your breakfast meeting all right?"

"It was fine. Lawrence and Nina agreed to go ahead with the investment."

"That's amazing." Becca grinned. "You must be happy."

"I'll be happy when I see you again. Are you at home?"

A thousand fireworks exploded in her chest. He wanted to see her again? She'd take it, even if it was an abrupt change from what he said yesterday. "I'm at my brother's house. Tanner's just announced his wife's pregnancy. There's a lot of celebrating going on."

"How long will you be there?"

"I don't know. Are you bored already?" she teased.

"Rona found one of your shoes beneath the bed. I thought you'd want it back."

Becca blinked. It must have been thrown under there when they got home last night. "How very Prince Charming of you."

Daniel laughed, deep and low. It sent a shiver up her spine. "I'd better get it back to you before you turn into a pumpkin."

"I can tell you don't have nephews and nieces. Cinderella didn't turn into a pumpkin, her carriage did."

"What did Cinderella turn into?" He sounded amused.

"Nothing. She's still Cinderella. Just a little more casually dressed."

"That sounds like a terrible story." He cleared his throat.

"Did you know in the original one, her sisters chopped their toes off to fit in the shoe? That's how desperate they were for Prince Charming. I can only assume he had a big…" She let out a low laugh.

"Well, I won't make you chop your toes off. But I would like to entertain you with my big…"

"Stop it!" She laughed again. "But I do need that shoe back. It belongs to Mia."

"I can drop it off tonight. Maybe bring something for us to eat. I miss you."

Those three words made her chest feel tight. "I miss you, too," she said softly. "But I was planning on making it an early night. This guy I met kept me awake until the early hours of the morning. If I don't get some sleep, my boss is going to kill me at work tomorrow."

"He sounds like a bastard."

"He is. Demanding, overbearing, and so good in bed I won't be able to walk for a week."

"That should make for an interesting few days at the distillery. Maybe you should put in a complaint."

"I have no complaints," Becca said. "That's the problem."

"Let me come over tonight. I promise not to be demanding. I'll bring your shoe, you can make me a cup of coffee, then I'll leave like a good boy."

"You're nothing like a good boy."

He chuckled. "Then I'll leave like a bad boy."

"Okay. I'll be home around seven."

"I'll be there at five past."

Becca grinned, because he wanted her as much as she wanted him. Last night hadn't been a one off, no matter how much they'd tried to resist the lure of each other. Some things were just too intense to contain.

"You're very eager."

"For you, yes."

A thrill shot through her. "I'll see you later."

"You will." It felt like more than a promise. Her heart thrilled at his words. She was still smiling as she ended the call and put her phone back into her purse, turning around to walk back to the kitchen.

And that's when she saw Gray, standing a few feet away from her in the hallway, his eyes narrowed as he glared at her, frowning.

Oh shit. She had some explaining to do.

CHAPTER TWENTY-THREE

hen Becca opened the door, her face was covered with a fine dusting of flour, a black apron tied around her waist with the slogan *'no bitchin' in my kitchen'* written in white lettering across the front.

"Nice apron," Daniel said, as she stepped aside to let him in.

"Thanks." She glanced over at the kitchen. "I'm just making some cupcakes."

"I thought you weren't getting home until seven?" He glanced at his watch. It was five past, as he'd promised. If he'd known she was getting home earlier, he would have come to see her. He'd been practically twiddling his thumbs at home.

"I did. I came straight to the kitchen." Her voice sounded a little off. Sure enough, her shoes and jacket were abandoned next to her sofa, her purse laying haphazardly on the floor next to them. "I'm stress baking."

"What's that?" His brows knitted as he followed her to the kitchen. She pointed at a stool in front of the breakfast bar.

"Sit."

His lips twitched, but he did as directed, putting the shoe

he'd brought with him on the stool beside him. "Are you okay?"

"No, I'm not." She lifted the bowl and a balloon whisk. "But if you don't want me to take it out on you, just let me whip this batter for a while."

He watched as she attacked the contents of the bowl with the metal whip, her teeth gritted as the batter came together in a pale yellow mass. A small piece landed on the tip of her nose, but Daniel decided that right now wasn't the time to tell her. She looked like a woman on the edge.

By the time she started scooping the batter into the cake cases, her shoulders had relaxed a little. She opened the oven, sliding the tray inside, then turned to look at him.

"You have a…" He gestured at her nose.

She reached up and wiped it with her finger, scowling as some batter came away on her tip. "Why didn't you tell me?"

"I just did." He gave her a half smile. "And anyway, you looked cute."

"Well, I won't be looking cute for long." She turned the timer on the oven, then sighed visibly.

"What have I done to annoy you this time?" She'd seemed so happy to hear from him earlier.

"It's not your fault." She took her apron off and hung it on a hook. "Well not entirely." She bit her lip and finally brought her gaze to his. "*They know.*"

Bemusement washed over him. "Who knows? And what do they know? This is like a mystery game."

"Gray heard me talking to you on the phone. He knows I was with you last night. And so do the rest of my brothers."

"Okay." He still couldn't figure out why she was so jittery. "Is that a problem?"

"Of course it is." She grimaced. "I couldn't tell them it was just a one night thing. They would've been around your place with blazing torches. I made something up about it, but of course they want to know *everything* about you."

"You made something up?" He tipped his head to the side, scrutinizing her. Though her shoulders were more relaxed than they had been, he could tell she was still tense as hell. He wondered how much baking it would take for her to smile again.

She swallowed hard. "I told them it was just a first date. That I wasn't sure if there'd be a second."

He ran a finger over his bottom lip. "Why would you say that?"

"Because…" she hesitated, shaking her head. "Calling it a hook up is a surefire way to get your ass beaten by my brothers."

He lifted a brow. "I'm not afraid of your brothers. I'm more concerned that you think it was *just* a hook up."

"Wasn't it? You said you couldn't make any promises last night."

His eyelashes swept down. "Yeah, well I probably said a lot of shit last night. But I want to see you again." His gaze flickered up to hers. Her lips were open, her brows dipped. "How do you feel about it?"

Her hands trembled as she looked down at them. He immediately missed her gaze. "Becca, look at me."

Swallowing hard, she looked up again.

"Taking you to the ball last night was the most fun I've had in a long time," he said softly. "Having you on my arm made it all feel okay. And then later?" He shook his head, remembering the feel of her body against his. "It was the best night I've had for as long as I can remember. And I don't want it to stop. I don't want to go back to just being your boss, or your pet asshole, or whatever I was. I want to see you. To spend time with you. To be inside you again. So no, you're not *just* a hook up. You're more."

Her eyes looked glassy. "I am?"

"Yeah."

She exhaled raggedly, the smallest of smiles pulling at her lips. "Oh!"

"And you? How do you feel?" He needed to hear.

"I feel... exhausted. Wrung out and emotional. My thigh muscles ache like I ran a marathon last night. And it was the best night I think I've ever had, because you were there, and I was so scared you wouldn't want to see me again."

He shook his head. "You're crazy, you know that? Why wouldn't I want to see you?"

"I don't know." She shrugged. "Because you got what you wanted?"

"You think all I wanted was sex?" He frowned. "Is that what you think of me?"

"No." She leaned forward on the counter, the breakfast bar separating them. "But the last time you were here you told me you were bad for me. That we shouldn't be together. So I'm wondering if last night was enough for you."

"I *am* bad for you," he told her, his gaze not wavering from hers. "But I'm also selfish enough to want to see you again. So I guess it's up to you. Do you want me, too?"

"Of course I do."

He exhaled with relief. Not that he'd planned to give up even if she'd said no. He would've wooed her. Sent her flowers. Waited for whatever it took. Last night changed everything.

Now she was his.

"I want you, too." His voice was low. Thick.

"How much?"

"Come around here and I'll show you."

Her smile was genuine. And wide. "Enough to come meet my family next Saturday?"

"What?" His own smile froze.

"My brother Logan has invited us all to his farmhouse restaurant. They want to meet you."

"Okay." He nodded.

Her eyes softened. "That doesn't scare you?"

"Should it?"

"Most guys hate meeting my family."

"How many guys have met them?" he asked, reaching out to trace his finger over the back of her palm. Just the feel of her skin relaxed him.

"Only one. And he got scared off."

"Well, if my family didn't scare you off, I don't expect yours will scare me." He'd do whatever it took to be with her. How strange was that? "Now, are you coming around here, or do I have to come over there and get you?"

An eager expression washed over her. "Is it wrong that I like the chase?" she said, not moving.

He stood, walking around the breakfast bar, his finger trailing across the surface of the counter. His face was unsmiling as he walked toward her. "Not wrong at all," he said softly. "I like it, too."

She was still as he traced the line of her cheekbone, her nose, her jaw, then her lips, leaning in as he cupped the back of her head. "I like the capture even better," he murmured, brushing his lips against hers.

Becca melted against him, her mouth parting with a sigh as he deepened the kiss, her arms looping around his neck to pull him closer.

"I thought you wanted an early night," he murmured.

"I do." Her lips curled against his. Then she pulled back to look at the oven. "We have thirty minutes before the cupcakes are due to come out."

"Thirty minutes?" It was nowhere near enough time. But then he wanted *all* her time.

"Yep."

He lifted her into his arms, making her giggle. "Okay, I can do something with that."

———

"Tell me about your family," Daniel said, as Becca nestled against his chest. It was Thursday night and they were in his queen size bed, his cool white bedsheets wrapped around their legs.

All week it had been the same. They'd try to ignore each other at work, then go home only to find the other there waiting for them. Except for tonight when they'd both managed to go to their own homes for an hour before Daniel caved and called her, inviting her over.

He was an addiction she wasn't ready to kick.

"Why?" She smiled curiously.

"Because if I'm meeting them on Saturday I need to know a little bit about them." His voice was warm. Maybe with a hint of fondness. She snuggled closer.

"Okay, but this could take a while. I've told you about my mom dying when I was a kid. So I was brought up by my dad and my Aunt Gina, my mom's sister. She took care of us all and still lives with my dad, though there's nothing going on between them."

Daniel shrugged. "Your family is already more normal than mine."

"Then there's my brothers. I guess I'll start with Gray. You know him from the marketing campaign, of course. And you may have heard his music."

"Of course I've heard his music."

"I wasn't sure if he'd reached Scotland," Becca said.

"It's not Mars. We have radios and streaming. The Scots are huge music lovers. Some of the best bands come from there. Anyway, he was big before I even left the states."

"Was it as beautiful as it looks over there?" She drew a circle with her finger on his chest. He'd injected himself earlier, before they ate dinner. It had been strange watching him pierce this hard, taut skin.

"Yeah. I'll take you there sometime."

She smiled at his talk of the future. "I'd like that a lot."

"But now you need to tell me about your brothers if I'm going to survive the weekend."

She laughed. "Well, Gray's now married to Maddie, and they live in a beautiful ranch house with a music studio on the edge of town. They have two little boys – twins – Presley and Marley. They're completely crazy but adorable."

"How old are they?"

She looked up, amused. "You're really taking this thing seriously."

"I just want to know which brother is hitting me," he joked.

Her eyes crinkled. "That'll probably be Cam. Or Logan. Gray is calmer than they are. He only gets riled up when you really piss him off. Like when he caught me on the phone with you in his hallway."

"He's protective. That's natural. I was the same with Nathan growing up."

"You're still protective of him. Remember how you reacted when you thought we were a couple?"

He brushed his lips over her brow. "I'm very glad you weren't."

"Me, too." She sighed softly. "Next are Cam and Logan. The twins."

"More twins?"

She shrugged. "They run in the family. What can I say? So, Logan runs the farm and restaurant we're going to visit this weekend. It was originally his wife's first husband's farm, but he bought it out."

"His wife's first husband?" Daniel's brow lifted. "Maybe your family is as complicated as mine."

She pressed a kiss against his chest. "Nothing is as complicated as your family. So, Courtney is Logan's wife. Her first husband died. She was still living on the farm when she and Logan met. He used to run restaurants in Boston, but now he lives here with her and their son."

"What's their son's name?"

"George."

"Okay. So there's Gray with Maddie, Presley and Marley. Logan with Courtney and George. Who else?"

She lifted her head from her comfortable spot on his chest, gazing up at him. "You have a very good memory."

"I do when it comes to you." He trailed his finger down her arm, sending shivers through her.

"Cam used to play safety for the Boston Bobcats before he retired. Now he's engaged to Mia, who you know from work. They met when her kids threw a ball against his new car. He was so pissed."

Daniel chuckled. "I would have been, too. So they're his stepkids?"

"Yeah, Michael and Josh. Really lovely boys. They both love football, which makes Cam very happy. And I think they'll have more kids soon."

"Damn, I don't want to lose Mia. She's a good Marketing Director."

"Cam insists he's going to be a stay at home dad. So you won't lose her." Becca shrugged.

"Interesting."

"And then there's Tanner. My nemesis."

She felt Daniel's chest rumble beneath her. "Nemesis?" he repeated. "How?"

"We're the two youngest. We used to fight like cats and dogs when we were kids. He was bigger so he'd usually win.

But now I have him exactly where I want him because his wife is pregnant and the only thing she can keep down is my carrot cake. Which means he has to suck up majorly to me." There was more than a hint of pleasure in her voice.

"And his wife? What's her name?"

"Van. Short for Savannah. She was a tomboy growing up, so we all called her Van."

"You knew her when you were younger?"

Becca nodded. "She was Tanner's best friend. Then the two of them didn't talk for a few years before they made up and got together."

"So you have…" His brows pulled together as he thought things through. "Five nephews and one on the way."

"We don't know if Tanner's having a girl or a boy. It's too early to know. But I'm hoping it's a girl because I sure could use some female support."

Daniel tucked a lock of hair behind her ear, his finger lingering there. "How about you? Do you want children?"

Becca shifted against him. Her stomach tightened at his question. It felt like a trap. Say too much and he'd think she was trying to pin him down, too little and she wouldn't be honest.

She chose honesty.

"Yes, I do. I love my nephews. They bring so much happiness to everybody, but especially to their parents. When I see the love my brothers have for their kids, it makes my heart stop." She looked up. His expression was unreadable. "How about you? Do you want children?"

"I've never really thought about it." He combed his fingers through her hair, massaging her scalp, his expression unreadable. "I haven't had a lot to do with children. I don't have nieces and nephews."

"Do you think Lawrence and Melissa might have some?"

"I have no idea." His jaw tightened, a tic dancing in and

out. "You'd have to ask them that." His tone was flat. As though he didn't want to continue this conversation.

Becca swallowed. Did he still have feelings for Melissa? The thought made her chest feel tight.

She ignored the warning, swallowing it down. "Well, the good news is that I'm not planning on having kids for a long time. I have a distillery to keep running. The boss there has all these crazy ideas about brewing single malts and using barley, which, by the way, you should talk to Logan and Courtney about. They know a lot about grains."

"That's a good idea." His voice warmed at her abrupt change of subject. "It's always nice to have an icebreaker when meeting the guys who want to cut off your balls."

She exhaled. Crisis averted. Daniel slid his hand down her back, cupping her behind to pull her naked body over his. She could feel the hardness and warmth of him against her, sending shots of pleasure to each of her nerve endings, making her want him all over again.

He tipped her head up and brushed his lips against hers. He still wanted her. And she wanted him, too. Sliding her knees beneath her, until she was straddling him, she could feel his desire surge, hard against her softness, hot and demanding as they kissed, all wet lips and tongues.

"Again?" she murmured breathlessly when she pulled away to catch some air.

"Again." His voice was deep and rough, his fingers digging into her as she slid herself against him, lining her body up against his in a way that would bring them both pleasure.

The weekend didn't matter. Nor did the future. Because what they had now was everything. It was time to stop worrying and start living.

And as he slid inside her, making her full and breathless and flushed with pleasure, she'd never felt more alive.

———

"So, Mom called," Nathan said, his voice echoing through the phone line. It was eight in the morning in Hartson's Creek, and Daniel had just arrived at the office when his phone started ringing. Becca would arrive twenty minutes later in an attempt to hide the fact they were sleeping together every night.

"Good for you," Daniel said. It was strange how he couldn't get the smile off his face nowadays. Strange and *good*.

"And she told me you took Becca Hartson to the gala." Nathan's voice rose up at the end. He sounded disbelieving.

Daniel shook his head. "So *that's* why you're calling me at nine o'clock at night your time? I thought it might be something important."

Nathan laughed. "It *is* important. I'm starting to wonder if I'm living in a parallel universe where you've turned into somebody else. What was it you said to me when you thought I was sleeping with Becca? Something about me being a complete idiot."

"You're an idiot without sleeping with anybody," Daniel pointed out. His chest felt tight at the memory of Becca in Nathan's arms, and how he'd come to the wrong conclusion. He didn't want her to be in anybody's arms but his. "And are you really calling just to ask me about Becca?"

"Pretty much." Nathan sounded like he was grinning. "Mom said she's never seen you as happy as you were at the gala. So, you and Becca are a thing now?"

Daniel blinked. "Yeah. We are." It felt weird to admit it out loud.

"Wow."

"And what's that supposed to mean?" Daniel frowned.

"I never thought I'd see the day where you fell for an employee, that's all. Or for anybody, come to think of it."

"Who said I've fallen for her?" Daniel sat on his desk, shaking his head.

"You did. You said you were a thing. And I know you wouldn't be a thing without falling for her. You'd be fighting it all the way. I'm guessing you probably hate yourself for being so human right now." Nathan laughed again. "I knew it would happen eventually."

"Well, I'm glad to have proven you right."

Nathan's voice softened. "I'm really happy for you, bro. Becca's an amazing woman, and you're a good guy. Just make sure you treat her right."

"She already has four brothers, I'm not sure she needs another," Daniel said lightly.

"Yeah, but I know you. And your past dating history."

Daniel inhaled sharply. "That has nothing to do with anything."

"Does she know about Melissa?"

"Yeah." Daniel raked his hands through his hair.

"You told her everything?"

"There's not much to know. And that's old history. Melissa and Lawrence have been married for years."

Nathan sighed. "I know. I bet they were shocked to see you at their gala with somebody."

Daniel's mind flickered to his dance with Melissa. "I guess they were. But their opinion doesn't matter to me." It hadn't for a long time. It was his own opinion that had stung. But now he felt optimistic. Happy. Like the future was something to welcome instead of avoid.

"So when's the wedding?" Nathan asked.

"Get out of here."

"Hey, I'm just making sure you don't do anything rash

without telling me. It's a thirteen hour flight. I need enough notice to get back to be your best man."

"I promise if I ever get married, you'll be the third to know."

"Good." Nathan sounded mollified. "Now, I gotta go. There's this great karaoke bar down the road. Be good, okay?"

"Always am." Daniel rolled his eyes.

"Oh! One more thing, have you met Becca's brothers?" Nathan asked.

"I'm meeting them this weekend."

Nathan started to laugh.

"What?" Daniel sighed. His brother was beginning to piss him off.

Nathan coughed loudly. "Well, good luck with that."

CHAPTER TWENTY-FOUR

"Have you checked your glucose levels?" Becca asked, as she climbed into Daniel's car.

"Yes, I have." He smirked. "And you sound like my mother."

Becca winced. "Sorry. It's just that Logan's food is irresistible. And full of sugar. I don't want you to become comatose."

"I have it under control." He kissed her cheek then closed the passenger door behind her, jogging around to climb into the driver's seat. "But I like that you worry about me. So thank you."

He'd showed his diabetes kit to her earlier in the week. Demonstrated how he washed his hands, not only to clean them, but to warm them, too. "It helps the blood flow," he explained, as he put a lance into the lancing device. "I try to always prick the side of my finger, there are less nerve endings there."

She'd watched as he wiped away the first drop of blood, pressing the second against the strip he'd loaded into the blood sugar monitor, then threw away the tissue and sharp needle into the special bin he kept in his bathroom. When the reading came up, he showed her. "I put this number into the app on my phone. Then I'm done."

"What if the number is bad?"

"It needs to be between seventy to one-thirty if I haven't eaten. Up to one-eighty if I have. If it's too low, that's hypoglycemia. I can eat or drink something sugary to raise it up. Like juice or a snack bar. I also carry an emergency kit just in case."

"And if it's too high?"

"Then I take some insulin and recheck in thirty minutes."

She'd pulled her lip between her teeth. "What happens if you don't?"

"When my glucose levels are too high that's called hyperglycemia. I've been hospitalized with that a few times with DKA. It can come on with things like stress, or when I'm sick with a cold."

"DKA?" she'd asked.

He'd smiled gently. "Sorry, I keep forgetting you don't know the jargon. That's diabetic ketoacidosis. It can happen with high glucose levels."

"So it's worse if your glucose is too high than too low?"

"No, they're both bad. With hypoglycemia – low glucose levels – I can black out. It happened a few times when I was younger. And at college when I didn't always manage my levels properly. But now I can look at a plate and my glucose levels and work out exactly how much rapid insulin I need to take before I eat."

"Except for when you forget your meds," she murmured.

"Thank god you came to the rescue." He'd kissed her, then they'd ended up in the shower, water pouring down their naked bodies as he showed her exactly how grateful he was.

And now he was coming to meet her family, and she was jittery. From the corner of her eye, she looked at

Daniel as he drove them away from her condo and into the main part of Hartson's Creek. Flowers were blooming in the town square, people sitting on benches and sipping coffee as they enjoyed the spring air. Somebody was coming out of the *I Can Make You Beautiful* salon, patting her hair and beaming widely. On the other side of the square, an old man was brushing the steps of the First Street Baptist Church with a huge broom, dust clouding the air as he worked.

"Have you always lived here?" Daniel asked, noticing she was smiling as she looked out of the window.

"Apart from college, yes. I love it. So many memories." She grinned, pointing at Murphy's Diner. "That's where Gray and Maddie fell for each other. She was a waitress and he was trying to hide from his fans." Then she pointed at a poster, advertising the spring season at the Chaplin Drive-In Theater. "Tanner and Van run the drive-in, but they also used to work at it as kids."

"And Logan and Cam? Did they meet their partners here, too?"

"Yep. Logan and Courtney met on the road to their farm when a hen ran in front of his car. And you know that Cam met Mia when her kids threw a football at his car."

"You're a country girl at heart."

She laughed. "Does that scare you?"

He shook his head. "Not at all." He ran a finger down her thigh. "It must be nice, feeling like you belong somewhere."

There was a wistful tone to his voice. She wanted to ask him about his family, his life, but whenever she'd tried, there was a block there. He'd either change the subject or kiss her.

They were on the road toward Creek Edge Farm. Becca pointed out the drive-in theater as they passed, then directed him left, down a dust track that led to the Creek Edge Restaurant. The fields were bursting with green crops.

Beyond them, he could see a beautiful farmhouse looming in the distance.

"You can park here," she said, pointing at an empty space in the makeshift parking lot. "Logan keeps talking about getting this repaved, but then he gets distracted by other things."

"There's a lot to be distracted by," Daniel said, looking around the wide expanse of fields. "How many acres are here?"

"I've no idea. I forgot to bring my measuring tape."

"Smartass."

"And you love it."

He kissed her temple, his breath warm against her. "I do. Now let's go in and meet your family."

She gave him a side glance as he climbed out of the car. "You're very eager."

He opened her door. "The sooner we get this done, the sooner I can take you home. I have plans for later."

Becca climbed out, smiling. "What kind of plans?"

"The kind I'm not stupid enough to say out loud within distance of your brothers." He slid his arm around her waist. "Let's do this."

"Are you afraid?" she asked.

He shook his head. "No."

"But you made those jokes about them cutting your balls off. And asked me all those questions about them."

"I'm interested in them, because I'm interested in *you*," he said, as though it was obvious. "And it's hard to be scared when I don't actually care what they think of me. Except if it influences how you feel about me."

Becca flushed, hoping he thought it was the warm spring breeze rather than his words that were affecting her this way. He looked amazing today, wearing a pair of jeans and a pale grey sweater that was tight enough to show the lines of his muscles through the knit fabric. His dark hair was tamed, though some locks were lifting in the air as the wind blew in from the fields. But it was the smile on his face that made him look so damn delectable. She was getting used to it now.

Nobody else has ever made him smile this much. His mother's words echoed in her head. She loved that she was the one who made him happy. The one who took down his defences until he was almost exposed.

Almost. If only he'd let those last shields dissolve.

As he opened the door to the restaurant, the loud echo of voices and laughter spilled out, along with the delicious aroma of food. The restaurant was built on the site of an old cottage where Logan's wife, Courtney, once lived. It was a low, cosy building, keeping with its heritage. No fuss, no glamor, just good company and great food.

"From the earth to the plate," Daniel murmured, reading the information on the wall. The menu was designed around the crops and livestock grown on the farm, changing seasonally to provide nothing but the most delicious meals.

"Logan doesn't like to do things halfway." Becca smiled. "Remind you of anybody?"

"No." He cocked an eyebrow. "Nobody at all."

"You made it," Courtney said, walking over to them with George in her arms. He immediately reached for Becca, babbling something that sounded like her name. Becca lifted him from Courtney, and kissed him on the cheek, laughing as he pulled at her hair.

"Courtney, this is Daniel Carter," she said. Daniel reached forward to shake Courtney's hand. "And this is George." She turned to him and he swallowed hard, as though surprised at the sight of her with a baby in her arms.

The moment passed as the rest of her family joined them, and she introduced Daniel to Aunt Gina and her dad, and then her brothers and their partners in turn. Mia's sons,

Michael and Josh, were at the table, leaning over Michael's phone, as they watched something on the screen. Presley and Marley were fighting over a toy one of them had stolen from Maddie's bag of entertainment, neither of them willing to give in. She could tell from Daniel's shifting eyes that he couldn't keep up with them all.

She hadn't noticed how loud and overwhelming her family was, until she tried to see it from somebody else's point of view. She tried not to compare it to the elegant ball Daniel's brother had thrown. There were no screaming babies, no sister-in-laws squeezing Daniel into a bear hug, and no brothers giving him the third degree in Charleston.

Just a brother he couldn't stand and an ex that made her jealous. Becca couldn't help but think she'd gotten off lightly compared to him.

"We should sit down," Gray said, after they had all shaken Daniel's hand. Logan had closed the restaurant for the evening – wisely deciding not to antagonize any of his customers by having them spend time in the midst of a Hartson family get together.

Becca slid her hand into Daniel's and squeezed it. He squeezed back, and she felt it again. The connection, the need. "You can sit with me," she told him.

"Oh no, we've got the guys at one end, the girls at the other." Gray gave Daniel a smile. "That's not a problem, is it?'

Daniel seemed unperturbed. "Not at all."

Becca gave her eldest brother the stink-eye. "Be nice," she warned him.

"I always am." With a lopsided grin, he walked over to where Cam and Logan had taken a seat, Presley and Marley on their laps, still fighting.

Daniel kissed Becca on the cheek, and George grabbed his nose. "Stop worrying," he said softly, tickling George under the chin. "I promise not to die from Hartson overload."

"If they get to be too much, send me a signal."

"What kind of signal?" He grinned.

"Send me a text. Or scream. Whatever."

He laughed. "Go sit with your family and have fun. I won't need to text. How bad can it get?"

"Bad. Very bad. I'm going to owe you big time." Becca grimaced.

"Then I look forward to claiming my favors." He kissed her again, and walked to the table, looking as casual as could be.

A complete contrast to her body full of nerves.

"Let me take this guy," Courtney said, lifting George from Becca's arms and sliding him into a highchair, grunting as she tried to fasten the straps around his wiggling body. "At least dinner will be fast. Logan told the chefs he wants it to be done in an hour, otherwise the kids will start to go stir crazy. And by the way, your boyfriend is gorgeous."

"I'm not sure that he's my boyfriend," Becca murmured, a frown pulling at her lips.

"Of course he is," Maddie said, sitting on Becca's other side. "Do you see the way he keeps looking at you? Oh, I remember the days when it's impossible to keep your hands off each other."

"To be fair, you and Gray still can't keep your hands off each other," Becca teased. "Remember the last time I babysat? I found you guys half naked in your car, your ass pressed against the horn."

Courtney spluttered out her water. "Man, I would have paid money to see that."

Van laughed, too, though she was looking a little green. Becca hoped the second trimester treated her better than the first.

"Tanner can keep his hands off me for the rest of our

lives," Van said, as though she could read Becca's mind. "I can't go through another pregnancy like this one."

"I'll make you another carrot cake tonight," Becca told her.

"And this is why I love you."

Logan had wisely decided on a family-style menu, putting various dishes on the table for them all to help themselves, rather than wait for everybody to make up their minds and order. Beautiful buttermilk chicken nestled against creamy mashed potatoes, along with steak fillets and fries so crisp you could hear them crackle as you pushed your fork into them, and so many veggies it looked like a harvest table.

The family dug in, laughing and joking as they ate, the men drinking beer and sodas as the women – minus Van – sipped wine. Every now and then, Becca would look over at Daniel to check that they hadn't killed him.

So far, so good. She liked him alive, with his balls intact, thank you very much.

And then dinner ended, and Gray stood, a mischievous look in his eye.

———

THE MEAL HAD PASSED without any big surprises – and more importantly, without any punches and with his balls still intact. Daniel looked across the table to Becca, who was laughing with her aunt and one of her sisters-in-law, baby George once again nestled against Becca's chest.

A weird shiver snaked down his spine at the sight.

"Okay," Gray said, standing with a grin. "It's football time."

Daniel looked around for a television.

"Now?" Maddie said, looking up from where she was trying to entertain her twin sons. "But we're eating."

"We've finished. A little sport will help the digestion, right?" Gray looked at Cam, who nodded, a smile playing at his lips.

"Sounds good." Cam grinned, looking at his twin.

"I'm up for it," Logan said, stretching his arms. "All these months of throwing hay have to have been good for my fitness. How about you, Tanner?"

"Sure." Tanner stood, rolling his shoulders. "Who doesn't like football?"

Then they all turned to look at Daniel, who was watching them with a bemused smile. Everybody stopped talking, their eyes on him.

"No." Becca was the first to speak. "No way."

"What?" Gray said, his voice light. "Daniel, you know how to play football, right?"

"I played a little at school." This was a set-up, plain and simple. A way for Becca's brothers to get him alone. He had two choices, say no and look like an idiot or say yes and look like… an idiot.

But at least he'd be an idiot who didn't back down.

"Great. Hey, Michael," Cam said, looking at his step-son. Becca had told Daniel that Michael was only fifteen, but he already looked like a man. "You playing? That way we can go three against three."

"Sure." Michael nodded. "If you guys can keep up with me, let's do it."

"Can I play?" his little brother Josh, asked. "Please?"

Gray exchanged a look with Logan. "Maybe later. We don't want you to get hurt."

What kind of game were they planning? Maybe it wasn't a game, but more of a test.

To see what kind of man he was. Whether he was worthy of their sister. Part of him was pleased that they took her happiness so seriously. The other part? The part that hadn't picked up a football in about ten years? It was slightly more concerned.

"You don't have to do this," Becca said. "We've had a nice meal. We can all go home and relax."

"It's fine," he reassured her, trying not to smile at her obvious distress. "I'm happy to play."

Logan walked into the kitchen and came out carrying a ball and a duffle bag, as though it was normal to keep sports equipment in his restaurant. Daniel followed the five of them out of the door, noticing they were all wearing athletic shoes.

A spontaneous game of football? Sure. Tell that to the judge.

Logan led them to an empty field about a four minutes walk away, with a makeshift goal at either end. "We need to pick teams."

"I'll take Daniel and Cam," Gray said. "You can have Michael and Tanner." He looked at Daniel. "No tackling, no kicking. We throw and we score touchdowns. That's it."

"Sounds good to me." Especially the no kicking part.

They started off with a warm up, Logan throwing the ball to Michael, who threw a hard lob at Tanner. The youngest brother dodged to the left, avoiding the catch, and they all laughed loudly.

"Hey, take it easy. I'm not the guy messing around with Becca," he complained.

Gray shot his brother a dark look. "Just catch the damn ball, Tanner," he muttered, picking it up and throwing it to Cam. The ex-professional football player caught it easily, then turned to Daniel with a speculative glance.

"How hard should I throw it at you?" he asked Daniel.

"As hard as you want." He wasn't backing down. And he wasn't going to dodge it. They wanted to test him? Fine. He'd take a beating if he needed to.

Cam's throw was fast and pointed. The ball careened

toward Daniel, who shot his hands up, wincing as the heavy leather slapped against his skin. A smile tugged at his lips as he caught it, and Cam gave him an unsmiling nod.

One brother down, three to go.

"Okay, we'll start," Gray said, handing them each a handkerchief. "Your flags. Put them down the back of your pants."

"We're playing flag football?" Daniel did as he was told, placing the fabric square into the gap between his waistband and back.

"Cam played professionally. Logan nearly did. If they tackle you, you'll feel it. Instead, we take the flag and that means you're down."

"Or I take the flag," Daniel pointed out, "and they're down."

"Touché." Gray nodded. "Now let's play."

Ten minutes later, Gray's side was winning by six points. Michael and Cam were pretty much leading each team. Logan was doing his best – though you could tell by the way he ran that he had a bad knee. Tanner wasn't really bothering, having too much fun making his brothers shout at him. Gray was good – but no match for Cam and Michael.

As for Daniel, he was just glad for all the boxing and running he did. He wasn't the most skilled footballer, but he could keep up.

He was throwing the ball to Cam when he saw movement from the corner of his eye. At first he thought it was a flock of birds, swooping down to eat seeds from the earth. But then the flash got closer, the pink color becoming clearer, and he frowned, calling out to Logan who looked to see what was up.

"Oh shit. The pigs." Logan's eyes widened. "How the hell did they escape their pen?"

Cam hadn't noticed, as he was too busy making a run for the goal, Michael fast on his heels. But Tanner had. He'd stopped running, and was staring at the oncoming stampede with his mouth open.

Daniel had always thought pigs were slow, lazy animals. But the twenty or so beasts running toward them looked fast, their trotters kicking up dust as they ran past the goal and a surprised looking Cam, heading right toward where Logan, Daniel, and Tanner were standing.

"Hot damn." Tanner turned on his heel and started to run, squealing louder than a pig ever could.

Logan swallowed hard. "We gotta turn them back," he muttered. "Before they reach the road."

"How do we do that?" Daniel asked.

"We run *at* them." Logan spoke through gritted teeth.

Daniel lifted his gaze to the pigs. Their bodies undulated as they ran, their curled tails bobbing. They were closer now, their mud-covered bodies looking menacing as they continued their onslaught across the grass.

"You ready?" Logan asked.

Not at all. But he wasn't backing down either. "Sure." His heart started to hammer against his chest. The closest he'd ever come to a pig was on his breakfast plate.

"Okay, let's run," Logan shouted, and Daniel took off, running straight toward the oncoming pigs, his lungs protesting at the sudden burst of energy. As he got closer, he could see their beady eyes and their twitching snouts. A few of them stopped running and looked up at him expectantly.

But there were more behind them, their pink bodies still hurtling across the field. One of them was heading straight for him, and Daniel had to dodge to the left, his shoes sliding against the muddy field, making him slip and fall to the ground in a puddle of mud.

That's when he heard the laughter. Five deep chuckles coming from a few yards behind him. Groaning, Daniel rolled to his knees, wincing as he looked down at his mud-coated jeans. When he lifted his head, he saw Becca's brothers and Michael standing in a group, as Logan gently turned the pigs around and directed them back to the end of the field.

Gray wiped his eyes and walked over to Daniel, offering his hand to pull him up. "You really ran at them, man. I'm impressed."

Daniel stood, dusting himself off, though it was a futile gesture. He was caked with mud. "Thanks. Just trying to help."

Cam walked over, and shook his hand. "You're okay," he mumbled. "I like you."

Tanner was still laughing loudly. "Jesus, Becca's going to kill us all."

In the distance, Daniel could see one of the farm hands ushering the pink horde through a gate. So it *was* a set up.

"No hard feelings?" Logan asked, slapping Daniel on the shoulder. "We just wanted to see what you were made of."

"I'd say he's made of steel, with a little kick ass thrown in," Michael said, grinning. "I like him."

"I like him, too." Tanner nodded. Then they were all slapping Daniel on the back, and he felt like he'd completed some Labor of Hercules. Proved himself worthy for the princess, gotten the respect of his fellow warriors, and ended up caked in mud and pigshit.

Great.

"Uh oh." Gray looked over Daniel's shoulder. "Busted."

Daniel turned to see Becca storming up the field, followed by her sisters-in-law, carrying their children. Aunt Gina and Becca's father must still be in the restaurant.

"This time, I really recommend running," Logan murmured. "When Becca's pissed, it's a scary sight."

CHAPTER TWENTY-FIVE

"My brothers are assholes. All of them. I'm so sorry." Becca winced at the memory of Daniel running at the pigs while the four of them watched, laughing their ugly heads off. "I can't believe they planned that all out. I'm going to kill them all very slowly. And record it with my camera so I can relive the excitement over and again."

Daniel rubbed his damp hair with a towel. "It's fine. It was kind of funny if you think about it. And I suffered worse at prep school. Not to mention college."

"Yeah, but you were a kid then. They're all grown men now. Or they were. I don't know what they'll be once I chop their balls off."

"You're kind of hot when you're angry, you know that?" He brushed his lips against hers. "Now relax. I'm clean, I'm fine, it's all good, apart from a bruised ego. And that'll heal fast."

"Maybe I could massage it better." She gave him a tentative smile. They'd driven straight to his place from the farm, as he needed fresh clothes and a shower. She'd fumed all the way, imagining painful ways to exact her revenge on all four of them. She'd let Michael off this time – she knew Cam had led his step-son astray.

"I'm all for some therapeutic relief." Daniel winked.

She exhaled softly. "I think you deserve it after what I put you through." She wasn't sure she'd actually get over it. "It's mortifying."

"Come here," Daniel said softly, tipping her chin until her gaze met his. She tried to look away, but he leaned forward, until all she could see was him. The warm smell of soap and shampoo wafted from him, his t-shirt and sweatpants soft as his body touched hers. "I'm not angry. I'm not fed up. You're worth a hundred stampedes from the pigs. If I had to do it again to be with you, I would."

The intensity of his stare made her chest ache. He was overwhelming. Not just in how he looked or smelled or felt, but because of who he was. She'd won him over, somehow or other.

And now he was trying to win her back.

"Your family or mine?" she murmured. "Which one is worse?"

"There's no contest." His lip curled. "Definitely mine."

"Yours didn't make me play football then arrange for an animal stampede."

"But don't you see?" His eyes softened. "They did that because they care. In their own, weird way, they wanted to test me. To make sure I'm good enough for you. My family doesn't give a shit about me. Not like that."

"Your mom does."

He nodded. "Yeah, she does. And Nathan, too, but you've already met them. I'm talking extended family. My brother and sister."

And Melissa. She didn't vocalize it though.

"Nobody has ever fought for me the way your brothers

fight for you. I'm glad you have them. You deserve to be loved and protected. Even from a guy like me."

"I don't need protecting from you," she whispered, her breath quickening as he softly stroked her hair.

"Don't you?"

"No." She shook her head resolutely. "I'm not afraid of you."

"Maybe you should be. *I'm* afraid of me. Of hurting you so much you won't ever look at me like this again."

"Then don't. Don't hurt me. Be my protector, too."

Something flashed behind his eyes. He cupped his hands over her jaw, dropping his brow to touch hers. "I want to," he whispered, his breath caressing her skin. "I want to be the man who deserves you."

"You are." Her throat felt tight. "You don't need to prove yourself to me, you're the only one I want."

His lips were soft and gentle against hers. She could feel the hard ridge of him digging against her stomach. His fingers tangled into her hair, his lips sliding across her jaw and down her neck, making her gasp as he dragged his teeth against her. "What are you doing to me?" he murmured. "I don't know who I am anymore."

She gasped as his fingers grazed her hips, pulling her even closer. His lips were worshipping her throat, sending shivers down her spine. The need for him curled and pulsed inside her, making her thigh muscles tense and her nipples harden.

He unbuttoned her jeans, sliding his hand inside, sighing softly as his fingers grazed her. "I can never get enough of you."

She closed her eyes at the pleasure his fingers were already dragging from her. "You don't have to."

Her words disappeared because he knew exactly how to make her feel good. Her knight in tarnished armor. Her once-enemy and now-protector. He made her world shrink until all she could see was him.

And it was the most beautiful sight she'd ever laid eyes on.

———

"BECCA?" a voice called out as she walked down the corridor from the kitchen. It was Monday afternoon and the coffee just wasn't cutting it. She blamed Daniel for keeping her awake for most of the night on Saturday, his demands so sweetly dirty it made her breath catch in her throat at the memory.

"Hi." Becca arranged a smile on her face as her eyes met Eliana's. "How are you?" *Please don't ask me about Daniel. I can't lie to save my life*

"I'm as good as it gets on a Monday." Eliana laughed. "They're not my favorite day of the week." She took Becca's hand. "Could we have a quick chat in my office? There's something I want to ask you."

Becca's stomach tightened. She wasn't sure what Eliana knew. She hadn't seen her since the weekend before last. "Of course." She followed Eliana down the corridor and through the door to the executive offices. Daniel's door was shut, and Becca wondered if he was behind there, or somewhere in the distillery. They'd agreed to keep it professional at work, but it didn't stop him from messaging her.

In fact, her phone had been lighting up constantly. If it wasn't Daniel asking her if she wanted to go out for dinner and to spend the evening at his, it was one of her brothers begging for her forgiveness. She still wasn't talking to them, but she knew she would eventually.

Just as soon as she could think of them without wanting to hit them.

"Take a seat," Eliana said, gesturing at the leather guest chair at her desk. "Can I get you anything to drink?"

"Thanks, but I just had a coffee." Becca shot her a smile.

"Ah, the famous coffee club. Is it still no guys allowed?" Eliana lifted a brow, walking around to her seat. Everything in here was elegantly neat. The large windows at the back of her room overlooked green fields, the barrel room just visible on the far left.

"We were debating letting them in, but then they launched a full scale assault on the donuts." Becca laughed. "So now they're excluded again."

"They should start their own club."

"That's what I told them." Becca shrugged. "But they refuse to put in any work. They want the women to organize it."

"That sounds familiar." Eliana gave a wry smile. "Which is kind of why I wanted to talk to you."

Becca braced herself for Eliana's questions, ready to bat them off with a few nonchalant words.

"It's my birthday on Saturday and I'm hosting a dinner at my house in Charleston, and I'd love for you to join us."

Becca blinked. She wasn't expecting that at all. Shifting in her chair, she tried to think of an appropriate response.

"Don't look so worried. I spoke to Daniel earlier and asked him to invite you, but I know what he's like. It would be so lovely to have you there. My friend, Julia asked if you were coming – she enjoyed sitting next to you at the ball. I know it's a drive, but I'll have a room made up for you. Or for you and Daniel." Her voice lowered. "Whichever you prefer."

"I should… talk to Daniel." Becca shifted awkwardly.

Eliana nodded, a smile pulling at her lips. "Of course." She lifted her elegant chin, looking Becca in the eye. "I meant what I said to you before. You're good for him. He's so much more relaxed than I've seen him in years. And he might not say it out loud, but he cares for you. A mother can tell these things."

Becca's chest tightened. She so wanted Eliana's words to be true. "He's a good man."

Eliana pressed her lips together, her eyes shining. "I can't tell you how long I've wanted to see him happy. Thank you for making him smile again."

It was strange how awkward this conversation was, yet it warmed her, too. When she was in Daniel's arms, everything felt right. But when they weren't together, she found herself wondering if she was exaggerating the pull between them, or the softness in his eyes when he gazed at her. Last night he'd cooked for her, and she sat in his gleaming kitchen, smiling at how at ease he seemed with a griddle pan and a steak. Yes, he could be difficult, and he clammed up when she asked questions he didn't want to answer, but he was also soft and loving, and always put her comfort first.

And he'd sacrificed himself for her family's approval. Let himself be covered in mud to gain her brothers' respect. He wouldn't have done that if he didn't feel something for her, would he?"

"Can I let you know tomorrow about your birthday?" Becca asked.

"Of course. But if anybody can persuade him, you can." Eliana leaned on the table, the sun behind her catching her white hair. "It would mean a lot to have you both there. And maybe one day Nathan will be there, too. I feel like I'm finally getting my family back, and a lot of that is thanks to you."

"Family is important." Becca didn't know what else to say.

"Yes, it is." Eliana nodded. "I didn't know how important until mine started to crumble. So thank you. For bringing him back to me."

"He came back of his own accord."

Eliana laughed. "I don't mean bringing him back from Scotland. I mean bringing back the man who knows how to smile."

Becca shifted again, looking down at her hands. "I should probably get back to the stills. We're on a run."

"Of course." Eliana stood, and Becca followed suit. "I'll hopefully see you on Saturday."

"Okay, then." Becca lifted her hand in goodbye, hoping she didn't look as uncomfortable as she felt. Maybe this was why they said not to have relationships at work. Because when your big boss was your boyfriend's mother, it made everything feel awkward as heck.

———

"No."

He didn't even look up from his laptop as he said it. Becca shifted on the sofa to look at him, folding her legs beneath her.

"Why not?"

Daniel sighed, pressing the laptop screen down, the back light diminishing to a single line before fading away. "Because we're even. You did my family, I did yours. I'd rather spend this weekend the two of us, preferably naked and sweaty between the sheets."

Her lips twitched. She secretly liked it when he was grumpy. It reminded her of those days when he couldn't look at her without a scowl. "It's your mother's birthday," she reminded him. "You can't miss that. Especially with Nathan in Japan. You're the only one of her sons who can celebrate with her."

Daniel sighed, running his fingers through his hair. Today they hadn't even bothered to pretend to go to their own homes. Daniel had messaged her this morning asking her to stay at his, suggesting she bring a few things to leave at his place, but she'd countered that it would be easier for him to bring a few things to *hers*.

It was simple, guys needed less things than girls did. And she liked seeing him wince every time he tried to get comfy in her small double bed.

"Why is it that you're happy to please everybody else in the world but me?" His eyes were dark.

She tipped her head to the side, grinning. "Because it's so much more fun riling you up. And you should be pleased I don't try to always give in to your requests. I keep you on your toes." She leaned forward and kissed him lightly on the cheek. "Don't tell me you hate the challenge."

He shook his head, his eyes soft. "I love the challenge," he murmured. "Except for when it comes to my family. I don't want to go, and I'm almost certain you don't want to go either. So why put ourselves through it?"

Becca sat back on her heels, studying him carefully. "I'm going whether you are or not."

He pinched the bridge of his nose between his finger and his thumb, grimacing as if he was in pain. "Becca…"

"What?"

"Why can't we just stay here?"

"You know why. Because it's your mom's birthday and she'll be hurt if we don't go. This is what families do, Daniel. They celebrate together. They have fun. I'm happy to go see your mom, I like her."

He stared back at her, his brows knitting together. "Okay." He exhaled heavily. "The truth is, I don't want to go because Lawrence and Melissa will be there." His voice was low. "My mother has this stupid idea that we're becoming closer as a family. She thinks that since we were civil at the ball and they agreed to the single malt that we can play happy family. And I don't want to."

His words felt like a punch to her gut. "Why?" she asked, ignoring the tremors in her voice. "Why would you avoid them?"

"Because they're old history. And I'm not interested in getting closer to Lawrence. We share blood, but nothing else."

That wasn't quite true. They also had Melissa in common. The thought made her throat feel tight.

"Are you still in love with Melissa?" she asked, wincing as his expression darkened.

"What kind of question is that?" he snapped. "Of course I'm not."

His answer didn't feel like the salve she'd hoped it would be. Her body still felt on edge. Like she was on a boat constantly tilting to the side. "Then why avoid them? If they mean nothing to you."

"Because Lawrence enjoys making people feel bad. I saw the way you looked when you were dancing with him. You didn't enjoy it and neither did I. He's been like this as long as I can remember. He's competitive and nasty, the way our father made him. And I don't want you being exposed to him more than you have to."

"I'm a big girl," she reminded him, her voice soft. "I can deal with your brother. It's *you* I find hard to understand. I just wish you'd talk to me, open up. Tell me what it is that makes you so uncomfortable around them."

He slid the laptop onto the table beside the sofa, taking her hand and pulling her on top of him, until her knees were straddling his thighs. She could feel the hard muscles of him against her soft behind, as he brushed the hair from her face.

"It's old history," he told her, leaning forward to kiss her, his lips warm and demanding. "They're the past. We're the future. I don't want to talk about them. I'm more interested in us."

She knew he was avoiding her question, but his lips and hands were so damn teasing. He knew exactly where to kiss her so she'd forget every thought in her head. Exactly where to touch her until her body began to sing.

Her head fell back as he kissed his way down her throat, his hand pushing up her blouse so he could trace the circle of her breasts. He hardened against her, the thick ridge of him digging into her exactly where she needed him. Her body began to move against him, making him groan.

Somehow, she managed to form a coherent thought. Cupping his rough jaw with her hand, she lifted his face to kiss him again, breathing in his masculine scent.

"Just say yes," she whispered, undulating against him again.

"To what?" His voice was thick. He grabbed her hips with his hands, fingers digging into her soft flesh as he pulled her closer against him.

"Take me to your mom's birthday." She gasped as he slid his hand inside her bra.

"You're a jezebel, using your body against me," he muttered, sliding his thumb across her nipple. The sensation made her body jerk against him, making him harder.

"Yeah." Her words were as thin as gossamer. "But isn't it worth it?"

He captured her lips with his mouth, sliding his tongue against hers, kissing her until she was breathless.

"I'll take you to the dinner," he said, when their lips parted. "But you'll owe me. Big time."

She smiled, pressing her chest to his, hearing him groan as she slid against him. "Of course," she whispered, kissing his jaw with soft, feathery caresses. "And I look forward to repaying."

CHAPTER TWENTY-SIX

Her Bluetooth connected and her phone rang out over the stereo speakers, Daniel's name flashing across the display screen on the front of her car. Becca accepted the call, smiling as Daniel's voice echoed through the speakers.

"Where are you?" he asked.

"About thirty minutes out. How about you?"

"I just arrived." He sounded tetchy. "And I still can't figure out why you wouldn't let me drive you."

"Because you should spend some time alone with your mom tomorrow. It will make her happy. And since you'll be doing such a nice thing, that will make me happy, too."

"What makes you think I want to make you happy?"

She smiled at his grumpiness, feeling the heat of the spring sun radiating through the window, landing on the side of her face. It was a beautiful Saturday morning. The forest lining the sides of the road were full of verdant trees, their leaves dancing in the breeze as she whipped past them. "You wanted to make me happy last night," she reminded him.

"I wanted to make you come."

"And that made me happy. See how easy it is to be nice?" She loved teasing him. Finding the little chinks in his grumpy exterior and pushing her way in. "Now go in and see your mom and I'll be there in half an hour."

"Did you deliberately leave late so I'd have to do this without you?"

She laughed. "No. I'm not manipulative, I'm just a slower driver than you. Now I'm going to hang up so I can concentrate, so goodbye."

"Becca?"

"Yeah?"

"Press that pedal a little harder. It's completely legal to drive faster than forty miles per hour."

Her chest rumbled. "Stop it. And *go inside!*"

"Shit. My mom's walking down the steps. I should go."

"Yes, you should."

"I'll see you in thirty."

She managed not to laugh this time. "Yes you will."

"And I haven't forgotten that you owe me. I'm still planning on collecting. Very soon."

He ended the call before she could respond. And maybe that was for the best, because his low-level threat sent a thrill through her, making her cheeks flush.

If Grumpy Daniel was fun, Passionate Daniel was everything. She liked them both. But the one she loved most of all was Happy Daniel.

She hoped to see a lot more of him.

———

DANIEL TURNED to see Becca walk out of the little dressing room connected to her bedroom. She was radiant. Wearing a white cocktail dress that molded perfectly against her breasts and slim torso, then flared out to her knees, with embroidered flowers lining the hem. Her slender legs were exposed and tanned, and her feet were encased in pale pink shoes he wanted to see wrapped around his hips later.

He was wearing a suit. Dark blue, with a crisp white shirt. Becca had insisted on knotting his grey tie for him, her fingers sliding against his neck as she twisted the fabric under and over. He'd inhaled deeply, loving the soft floral notes of her perfume, and the way she stared up at him with those big eyes.

He could never get enough of her. She was the only one who could make him do things he didn't want to do. He blinked at the thought of it. She was the sunshine to his darkness, the smile to his frown.

She warmed him in a way nobody ever had before.

"Come here," he said softly, holding his hand out to her. She took it, and he pulled her toward him, circling his arms around her waist. "I've decided on what you owe me."

A smile curled at her lips. "You have?"

"You tied to my bed for all of next Saturday, so I can do what I please with you."

"That sounds very boring." Her flashing eyes told him she was lying. "How about I tie *you* to the bed and make you watch all seven seasons of the *Gilmore Girls* with me?"

"That sounds like torture. What I have planned is all about pleasure," he murmured, kissing her softly.

She arched against him, kissing him back, then drew away when the sound of the doorbell echoed through his mother's house. "Saved by the bell," she whispered, smiling.

"Not saved. Just postponed." He took her hand. "Come on, let's get this over with. And by the way, my mother may have made up two rooms for us, but you're sleeping with me tonight."

"All right, but no funny business, not with your mom here."

"You owe me funny business," he whispered in her ear, pushing the door to his bedroom open so they could walk down the hallway toward the stairs. "You owe it to me big time."

The guests were milling about in his mother's drawing room, a low hum of conversation echoing through the doors as they made their way inside. The room was beautiful, facing west, so the setting sun cast a warm glow through the glass doors that led to the gardens.

Daniel poured a glass of water for himself and a gin and tonic for Becca. She smiled with appreciation as he passed the glass to him.

"Darlings, I was about to come searching for you." His mother walked toward them, a big smile on her face. "Though I would have knocked first, of course."

Daniel rolled his eyes. "Happy birthday. Again." He kissed her cheek, and she patted his. "Can I do anything?"

"Just be here. That makes me happy enough. Dinner will be ready in twenty minutes," she told him. She knew he'd need to inject his fast acting insulin before they ate. He glanced at his watch, noting the time.

She turned to hug Becca. "I'm so glad you're here. Thank you for coming."

Becca shot him a smug glance. "I wouldn't have missed it for the world."

"And thank you for your gift. The flowers were beautiful and that vase is perfect."

"You're so welcome. The painted ceramic reminded me of the beautiful plates you have on the walls. I thought it would fit in nicely."

"It really does. And as for you," Eliana turned to Daniel. "You spoiled me. A week in Tokyo?"

"It was from Nathan and me." Daniel shrugged, avoiding Becca's knowing smile. Okay, so it had been her idea. But he'd organized and paid for it. "He can't wait for you to visit."

"I'm so excited. I just wish you two could come, too." She pouted a little.

"Who would run the distillery?" Daniel asked, his voice light. "And anyway, it's your gift, not mine."

The doorbell rang again, and Eliana nodded at one of the staff, who walked into the hallway to answer. A moment later he walked back in, followed by Nina and Charles, along with Lawrence and Melissa, the four of them standing together in silence as they looked around the room.

Daniel exhaled slowly, keeping his expression impassive. Becca hooked her finger through his, and it made him relax.

"I'm so pleased you could make it," his mom said warmly, as she walked over to greet his siblings. "Nina, you look beautiful. Where did you get that dress?"

"I see the McHaggersons have made it," a throaty voice whispered in Daniel's ear. He turned to see Julia grinning at him and Becca. "I told your mom to give up on the happy family harmony, but she still keeps trying."

"She's very trying." Daniel lifted a brow.

"Becca, how are you, darling?" Julia asked, leaning forward to kiss her cheek. "I'm so glad you came. I have a feeling you're the reason this grump is here, so thank you. Eliana's been so excited that you're both here to celebrate with her."

"I'm glad to be here." Becca smiled. "I love your hair. Is that purple?"

"Pink and purple streaks." Julia patted her head. "I figure I may as well grow old disgracefully."

Daniel could see his family moving toward them from the corner of his eye. A better man would have walked over and welcomed them effusively. But then he'd never pretended to be that.

"Daniel." Lawrence nodded at him. "Ah, and the beautiful Becca." He leaned in to kiss her cheek, and Becca held her breath until he'd moved away. For a moment there was small talk, as Nina and Charles hugged them both, and Becca spoke softly to Julia about something he couldn't quite hear.

Melissa was silent. She looked strange, her eyes red rimmed as though she'd been crying. Not her usual unflappable self, at all. Not that it was his problem, but it made him feel awkward.

"Can I get you a drink?" he asked.

She shook her head. "One of the waiters is bringing them over."

"Are you all right?" He frowned. To his left, Becca was still holding his finger. She squeezed it and he squeezed back.

"I have a headache." She glanced over at Becca who was deep in conversation with Julia, then touched her forehead, wincing. "I wasn't sure I should come."

"Are you upsetting my wife again?" Lawrence asked, sliding his arm around Melissa's waist. A grimace flickered over her features, as though she hated him touching her. "Darling," Lawrence said, kissing her cheek. "Are you feeling any better?"

"I'm just feeling a little weak," she said, exhaling softly. "Maybe Daniel could take me to the library, and ask one of the staff to make me a cold compress. I'll rest for a little while." Her smile was tremulous. "Hopefully, I'll feel better by the time dinner is served."

She really did look faint. Her face was pale, her lips almost blue.

Daniel looked at Becca and pulled his finger from hers. "I'll only be a moment." His smile was tight.

Becca nodded, her brows pulled with concern. "Is everything okay?"

"It's fine. I'll be back. Don't move." He kissed her cheek and he felt her skin tighten beneath his lips. She was smiling. Good. He'd take Melissa to the library and then take his rapid insulin in the kitchen. Rona would be able to find a cool cloth for her, make her feel better.

"Okay." He nodded. "Let's go."

Melissa slid her arm through his.

———

"Interesting, aren't they? Your boyfriend and my wife." Lawrence's voice was low. Becca was still standing with him, along with Charles and Nina. Julia had gone to find Eliana to see if she needed help with anything.

"In what way?" Becca curled her hand around her glass. She hadn't drunk her gin and tonic at all. Daniel's water was on a table where he'd left it to escort Melissa to the library. Ten minutes ago. She could see Eliana looking at her watch, as though she was about to call everybody through for dinner.

"I guess there's still a pull between them," Lawrence said, his voice almost whimsical. "That happens when you're with somebody for years. Your lives become intertwined, your emotions, too. Suddenly you don't know where one ends and the other begins, even after years apart."

Becca tried to ignore the twisting jealousy in her gut. Lawrence was being Lawrence. It wasn't as though Daniel hadn't warned her. "You don't seem very sure of your wife's attachment to you," Becca murmured, looking around to find an escape from him.

"Oh, she loves me. The same way an abandoned puppy loves its rescuer. She's grateful to me. I've given her a beautiful home, a lifestyle she always wanted, and more importantly, I'm there for her. Daniel ignored her for years. And then of course, everything went wrong. She was heartbroken when she came to me. I took her in, made her feel better, made her want me." He shrugged. "Sometimes the good guys do win."

"Daniel's a good guy," she said softly.

"Are you sure about that?" Lawrence looked at her, his expression full of sympathy. "Do you know why she left him?"

Becca frowned. "For you."

"You see, that's *not* quite true. She left him and came to me, yes. But that wasn't the reason they imploded. I simply took care of her when she needed somebody. When he wasn't there."

Her throat felt tight. Like there wasn't enough space for oxygen to get through. "It doesn't matter. It's history."

"History's replaying itself in the library right now. If you're so sure of him, why don't you go see what they're doing?" He lifted a pale brow.

"Your wife is the one who's ill. Why aren't you checking on her?" She didn't like what he was insinuating. But she also didn't like the thought of Daniel and Melissa being alone either. Her hands felt shaky.

"That's a good point." A smile played on his thin lips. "We can go together. Give them a surprise." He held his arm out. "Shall we?"

She'd been played. Either she refused to go and all but admitted she didn't trust Daniel. Or she went along with Lawrence, no doubt making him happy because he'd gotten what he wanted. *Again.*

"All right." She ignored his proffered arm. "I'll see if he needs any help." She stalked across the drawing room, turning left at the hallway, her heart hammering against her chest as she heard Lawrence following close behind. The last time she'd been in the library was to play games with Daniel. Was that only two weeks ago? It felt like a lifetime. The day that intersected her life before him, and her life after. The pivot on which her world turned.

She stopped outside the door. Inside, Melissa was sobbing softly. For a moment she wondered if Daniel was in the kitchen, getting the cold compress she'd asked for. But then she heard his voice. Low but clear.

"Why her? I thought you were too busy for relationships. Too focused on work to think about anybody else. So why did you bring her here tonight?"

"That was a long time ago. I've changed. She's changed me."

"So why couldn't you change for me?" Melissa cried.

"I'm sorry. I'm so sorry." He sounded almost tender. It made her heart ache. "For everything."

Another sob from Melissa. "I just can't get over what happened. No matter how much I try. And I do try. I do. I was so happy then. Before we lost her."

"I should have been there for you and I wasn't. None of this was your fault." She could almost picture him, wringing his hands.

Lawrence shifted next to her, his beanpole body a few inches from hers. If he touched her, she thought she might scream.

"Do you think about her?" Melissa whispered.

Daniel cleared his throat. "Of course I do."

Becca could feel the heat of Lawrence's gaze on her face. She turned to look at him. There was a cruel smile pulling at his lips. "She lost a baby at twenty weeks," he told her. "And he wasn't there for Melissa. By the time he made it back and to the hospital, it was over."

"A baby?"

"*Their* baby. She was pregnant with their child. A time for celebration, you'd think? But not for Daniel. He was too busy trying to prove himself to take care of his girlfriend." He sounded almost pleased about that.

Becca's chest felt like it was going to explode. Daniel had lost a child and he hadn't told her? Her eyes stung with tears. She blinked them back, knowing Lawrence was enjoying this. Like a vampire, he fed off her.

"You didn't know, did you?"

Becca ignored him, trying to catch her breath.

"I wonder why he didn't tell you," Lawrence mused. "I guess there's only one way to find out." He leaned across Becca and she almost jumped out of his way, watching with horror as his long fingers curled around the door handle, the hinges creaking as he pushed it open for them both to look in.

Daniel was standing in the center of the room, next to the table where they'd played cards. Melissa's tear-ridden face rested on his chest, her body shaking as she cried. Her hands clutched at Daniel's shirt, bunching the cotton against her palms.

It took them a moment to realize they were being watched. But when they both looked up, Daniel's eyes darkened as he saw them standing in the doorway.

Becca had to curl her fingers around the doorjamb to stop herself from sinking to the floor. Her legs trembled beneath her, her breath caught in her throat. All she could think was that Daniel had lost a child and never told her.

She lifted her hand to her mouth in shock.

CHAPTER TWENTY-SEVEN

"Becca, wait!" Daniel called out, as she stepped backward, her fingers reluctantly releasing her hold on the doorjamb.

She shook her head, not because she was answering him, but because she couldn't think straight. Maybe movement would help, because right now everything felt blank. She didn't run. She walked. Down the hallway and to the stairs, her blood pounding in her ears as she took them one riser at a time in her pretty shoes. Only an hour ago she'd walked down them, feeling so damn happy in his arms.

And now all she wanted to do was curl up and cry.

"Wait." It was a command. She could hear his breath as he ran up the stairs to catch up with her. "That wasn't what you think."

"What do I think?" Her voice was stretched thin. Maybe he knew, because she sure as hell didn't.

"I'm not having an affair with Melissa. There's nothing going on."

"I know." She'd reached the top of the stairs. Daniel was a

step behind her, his breath caught, his face creased into a frown.

"Then why did you run?"

"Because..." She sighed heavily. She wasn't ready to put her feelings into words yet. They were too strong, too painful. "I just need to be alone."

"No." He shook his head almost frantically. "I need you to talk to me. What's going on?"

"You want *me* to talk?" Her voice rose up. She knew how hysterical she sounded. "I'm not the one with all the secrets here." She pushed open the door to the guest wing, letting it fall close behind her. Daniel must have caught it, because she could hear the slap of his dress shoes against the floor. "Please, let me be alone. Go down to dinner. You'll be missed."

"I'm not going down there without you."

She turned to look at him, and he winced at the tears falling down her cheeks. "I can't go back to the party. I'm not making a scene on your mother's birthday. Please, Daniel."

"I'll go if you tell me what's going on." He leaned around her, opening her door. She stepped inside and he followed, pulling the door shut behind him. He took her hand, pulling her toward him, but she resisted his tug.

She couldn't think when she was this close to him. His body called to her like a siren on a rock. She needed space. Needed to think.

"Becca?"

"Why didn't you tell me about your baby?" She wiped the tears from her cheeks with the back of her hand. A black smudge of mascara stained her skin.

Daniel grimaced. "You heard us?"

"A little. Lawrence filled in the blanks."

"Fucking Lawrence." Daniel shook his head. "I'm going to kill him."

"No." Her voice was firmer than she'd expected. "It isn't his fault. You're the one who should have told me. You had plenty of chances."

"When did you want me to say something?" His eyes were narrow. "When we were having sex at the hotel? When my head was buried between your thighs at my place? Maybe you wanted me to walk into the still room and make an announcement. Would that have been the best thing?"

She hated the way he was looking at her. His eyes were cold and dark. "You asked me about children. I told you I wanted some. Do you know how much guts that took? Everybody knows that you don't tell guys you want a family too soon. That you hold back, as to not scare them." She shook her head. "But I wanted to be honest with you. I thought the truth was important. So I told you and exposed my biggest damn fear. Maybe then you could have told me. Or last week when I asked you why you didn't want to come to this dinner party. You could have told me any time, but you didn't." She wiped her eyes again. "Do you know how much enjoyment Lawrence got from telling me?"

"I can imagine." There was a tic in his jaw.

"Why didn't you tell me?"

"Because..." He sighed and turned away, raking his fingers through his hair. "I was protecting—"

"No, don't you dare say you were protecting me." Her voice was hard. "Because that's a damn lie."

He spun to look at her. The darkness in his eyes felt like it was getting bigger. She almost didn't recognize him. "I was protecting myself." His voice was as harsh as his expression. "Does that satisfy you? I was protecting the one good thing that has happened to me in years. Because I knew as soon as I told you, you would have left."

"You don't know that at all." She shook her head.

He gestured at her. "You proved me right. You heard it and you ran."

"But not because you lost a baby. I'm not that cruel."

"So why are you shouting at me? Why are you looking at me like I'm a piece of shit?" His face was red. She noticed his fingers were trembling.

"Because you lied to me. By omission, at least. You hid something important from me, and let me find out in the worst of ways."

"Because I knew you'd leave."

"I wouldn't have."

"Yes, you would." He spat out the words. "You would have left, and you should have left, because you deserve so much more than me. So much more than the kind of guy who was too busy to be with his girlfriend when she lost their baby."

His words felt like a body blow. She tried to catch her breath, and failed. "She was alone," she said raggedly, remembering Lawrence's words.

"I was traveling. She kept calling and asking me to come back." He scrunched his face together. "I was too busy working to bother listening to what she had to say. She was having cramps, and I told her it was fine, probably growing pains. I'd take her to the doctor when I got home. That it would be nothing to worry about." He shook his head, lost in his memories. "I was so damn full of myself, I didn't think of her or our child. And that's why she left me. Because I'm a heartless asshole who puts himself above everybody else. Is that what you want to hear?"

Becca's heart was hurting. For him, for Melissa, for the baby that never got to live. "Daniel…" She reached for him, and he pulled away.

"Please don't touch me." He wouldn't look at her. She hated not being able to connect her gaze with his.

"I should have told you, I know that. But I also knew what

it would cost me. And I'm still enough of an asshole not to want to pay the price." His smile had no happiness in it. "And now here we are. You know who I am, and you should leave."

"No." She couldn't catch her breath. "We should talk." She reached for him again, and he winced.

"*Leave!*" he shouted, the sudden noise making her jump. "I can't stand you looking at me like that. I don't want your pity. I don't need it." His whole body was shaking, as though his anger was uncontrollable.

There was a tentative tap at the door. Daniel's head snapped around. Without saying a word to her, he stalked over and opened it.

"Julia."

"Eliana was wondering where you are. Dinner's about to be served." Julia glanced at him and then at Becca, her eyes widening when she saw the tears running down her face. "Is everything okay?"

"Everything's fine. Please tell my mother I'll be down in a moment. Becca isn't feeling very well."

Becca tried to smile through her tears. It was a big fail.

"Okay," Julia said, frowning. "I'll let her know."

As soon as she'd gone, Daniel closed the door softly. "I need to go downstairs."

"Yes. Please do."

"And you?"

"I should leave." She wanted to go home. To think. To be away from the intense emotions Daniel stirred up in her. She couldn't stay here, not now. She needed the comfort only her home could give.

I'm a heartless asshole who puts himself above everybody else. Is that what you want to hear?

She didn't believe it. But she also didn't know how to make this evening better. She'd go and give them both some space. Eliana deserved an evening with her son. It was her birthday, after all.

Daniel stared at her, unspeaking. He didn't beg her to stay. Or tell her he'd call her later, or say anything else that might have given her the tiniest seed of hope she so desperately wanted. Instead, he opened the bedroom door and turned to look at her, his face blank.

"Drive carefully."

———

HE LASTED fifteen minutes before something broke inside him, and the emotions made him start to shake. He was sitting next to his mother, an empty chair next to his own, as the waiter walked around with a pair of silver tongs, offering bread to each guest.

"I need to go," he said, looking at his mom. "I just made a huge fucking mistake."

"Daniel!"

"Sorry." He wasn't even aware that he'd sworn. "But I can't stay. I can't."

Eliana put her hand over his. "Is it Becca?"

He nodded.

"She isn't sick?"

"No. I asked her to leave. She's angry with me. She found out about the baby Melissa and I lost."

"You hadn't told her?"

He pressed his lips together. His hands really needed to stop shaking. "No. I'm an idiot."

"Yes, you are. You need to go see her. How long ago did she leave?"

"About ten minutes ago, I think." At least that's when he'd heard the front door open and close.

She squeezed his hand. "You have time to catch up with her if you leave now."

He stood right as the waiter reached him, shaking his head at the offer of a roll. "Are you sure you don't mind?"

She smiled softly. "I'd mind more if you stayed. Thank god you came to your senses. Now go and get her."

He kissed her cheek and grabbed his phone, ignoring the raised eyebrows of the other guests as he passed them, the handset pressed to his ear. His mother called out something, but he didn't hear her, as Becca's recorded voice filled his ears

"Hey, it's Becca, leave a message."

"It's me. If you get this, please call me back. I'll be in the car. I'm coming to find you. I'm so damn sorry. For everything. Please let me see you and explain, okay?"

"Are you leaving?" Nina asked, as he passed her, ending the call and sliding his phone into his pocket.

"Yeah."

"Lawrence and Melissa left, too. Your poor mom." She sighed in sympathy.

"I'll make it up to her."

Nina smiled. "I know you will. You always were a good kid."

He gave her an absentminded nod and headed to the hallway, not bothering to stop to get his travel bag. He'd worry about that later. Right now he needed to find his girl.

To somehow persuade her to listen to him. Give him a chance to finally talk.

The empty space next to his Corvette made his chest hurt. He pressed the button on his keyfob and climbed inside, his hands shaking so damn much it took him two attempts to close the door behind him. Damn, he was a mess. He needed to see her *now*. He couldn't function without her.

Pressing the ignition, he reversed out of his spot and sped

down the driveway, out of the gates and onto the street. It was killing him to keep to the speed limit. She couldn't be that far away. He was sweating. He reached up to wipe his brow with the back of his hand as the houses thinned out on either side of him, and he reached the city's edge, taking a right onto the road out of Charleston.

It was dark enough that he had to concentrate to read the license plates of each car in front of him. Dammit, where was she? He checked to make sure his Bluetooth was connected, then gritted his teeth because it was.

When he reached the highway, he pulled into the fast lane and put his foot down, his hands shaking as he held the steering wheel straight. A bead of sweat dropped into his eyes, and he had to blink to stop it from stinging.

Exhaling heavily, he glanced at the dashboard again. It was almost eight-thirty. His teeth started to chatter. Damn, he'd injected his fast acting insulin when he'd gone into the kitchen to get Melissa a cool compress. He should have eaten something before he left.

He glanced at the passenger seat, grimacing as he realized he'd left his emergency kit at the house. There was no food in here. Nothing to bring his sugar up. He needed to pull over and call somebody.

It took an act of will to keep his hands on the wheel as a wave of dizziness came over him. He lifted his gaze to the mirror, the reflection blurry, and signaled, moving his car to the right, while biting on his lip to keep himself conscious. With his foot on the brake, he slowed the car, his indicator still on as he began to pull over to the soft shoulder. Knowing he was still driving too fast, the treeline looming large as his car hit the grass.

Then everything went black.

"I'm sorry," Becca breathed into Mia's shoulder. "I didn't know who else to call."

"There's no need to be sorry," Mia's voice was soft. "I'm glad you called. Nobody should be this upset alone. And anyway, the guys were watching some shoot-em-up movie. It was a good excuse to get out of there." Becca had called Mia on her Bluetooth as she'd driven back from Charleston. She'd been waiting for Becca when she arrived back at her condo.

"Does Cam know it's me you're with?" Becca looked up, her eyes rimmed red.

"No. I told him it was a girl emergency, and that shut him up. You know your brothers and girl stuff."

Yeah, she did. And she was glad Cam had no idea, because she couldn't cope with her brothers right now. They'd get angry and she couldn't deal with it. She just wanted to cry.

"So Daniel left a message on your voicemail saying he was coming to see you?"

"He did." Becca checked her watch. That was hours ago. "He should be here soon, unless he's changed his mind. He was so angry with me, you should have seen him. And he was right to be. I should have been understanding, but instead I accused him of lying to me."

"He should have told you before. That was a horrible way to find out." Mia rubbed her back. "I can't believe he hid it from you."

"I think he was embarrassed."

"I guess so. Maybe you should try calling him. See if he's still planning on coming here."

"You're right." Becca sighed, and lifted her phone to her ear. It rang then went to voicemail. "Um, it's me. I made it home. Call me back when you get a chance." How lame was that? She sighed and hung up.

Somewhere between Charleston and Hartson's Creek, she'd realized how stupid their argument was. He'd asked her to leave, but she should have stayed. Talked it out with him. Instead, she'd gotten hysterical.

"Maybe I'm just really bad at relationships," Becca muttered, shaking her head as she sat down next to Mia.

"They take work. And getting to know each other. I don't know a single relationship that doesn't go through ups and downs. Look at me and Cam. We separated and he went back to Boston after Michael found out about us." Mia rubbed her arm gently. "And then there's Van and Tanner. Look how many years they were apart."

Becca squeezed her eyes shut. "I can't imagine how painful that was." The thought of not seeing Daniel for years made her chest ache.

"The first argument is always the toughest. It's when things get real. It's not that the fairytale is over, so long as you pause it occasionally to face your differences head on. Working through your differences together is what separates successful relationships from the ones that will never work."

"I didn't work through it. I walked out." Becca squeezed

her eyes shut, not wanting to remember their explosive argument.

"Sometimes you need a break from each other, too. Look how much good it's done you already. You've had a chance to think things through." Mia smiled gently. "Maybe you know yourself better than you realize. You said you couldn't think there, and that's why you came home. Maybe that was the best thing to do."

"How did you get so wise?"

Mia laughed. "I'm older than you. And I learned from all my mistakes. And for what it's worth, I really like Daniel. Any guy who's willing to go up against all four of your brothers at once is a keeper. He must really like you to do that."

Becca's heart clenched at the memory. "Or he has a death wish."

Mia stood, pulling Becca up with her. "How about I make us some tea and a sandwich or something? If you left before dinner, you must be starving. We'll put on a movie and wait for Daniel to call you back. Or show up. And then I'll melt away into the distance and leave you two alone.

"You're a good friend." Becca hugged her. "But I'll make the food. It's my condo, after all."

"Hey, I never turn down your cooking." Mia held her hands up, smiling.

Making a light supper for herself and Mia was the perfect way to keep busy. Becca sliced some of the sourdough bread she'd made, layering it with ham and lettuce, sprinkling some cheese on the top before grilling it. Pouring some glasses of sweet tea, she laid them out on a tray, while Mia scrolled through Netflix in search of the perfect easy watch.

"Do you want a movie or a series?" Mia called out.

"I'm fine with either." Becca laid the tray on the coffee table just as her phone started to ring. She almost ran for the phone, her brows knitting together when it wasn't Daniel's name on the screen.

It was Eliana's.

Mia leaned over to look. "Maybe his battery died or something."

Becca shrugged and accepted the call. "Eliana? Hi. I'm so sorry I didn't stay for dinner. I wasn't feeling well."

Mia wrinkled her nose at Becca's obvious discomfort. It was kind of true, but it still felt like a lie. And she didn't like telling untruths to her boss.

"It doesn't matter. None of it does," Eliana was almost breathless. "The police have just called. Daniel's been in an accident. They've taken him to Charleston Memorial Hospital."

———

Mia insisted on driving her to Charleston, batting off Becca's protests as she opened the car door. "We don't need two of you in the hospital. You haven't eaten either and you're in no state of mind to drive."

"But you should be with Cam and your boys."

"I'll call them and let them know what's going on. Now, are we going to Charleston or what?"

The roads were thankfully empty. In less than two hours they were back in the city, a sense of déjà vu wafting over Becca as Mia followed the directions on her GPS.

The Charleston Memorial Hospital was a sprawling modern sandstone building, with a glass frontage that sparkled as it reflected the night sky. Becca twisted her fingers, and swallowed hard. Somewhere in there was Daniel.

In what state, she had no idea.

"I'll drop you at the entrance then park," Mia said, as

Becca shifted in her seat again. "Go straight to him. I'll find you."

"You don't need to stay."

"I'm not leaving you alone." She pressed her lips together as she drove around the circle to the entrance. "Now go find him, okay?"

"Okay."

The Emergency Room was full of Saturday night casualties. Mostly alcohol related, from the sound of slurring words and wails. At the front desk, the receptionist directed Becca to a family waiting room on the far side. When Becca walked in, she saw Eliana sitting there, Nina holding her hand.

They both looked up as Becca approached, and Eliana patted the empty seat beside her.

"Is there any news?" Becca asked her.

"He'll be okay. They're treating him now." Eliana breathed out heavily.

Becca pulled her lip between her teeth. "Do they know what happened?"

"They found his car on the shoulder of Route Sixty. He'd crashed into a tree. When the EMTs got there he was unconscious, his head against the deflated airbag. They gave him a glucose injection and brought him straight in." She squeezed Becca's hand. "He was coming to see you. To apologize for the things he said."

Becca's eyes stung. "Do they know what caused the accident?"

"He was hypoglycemic. He must have injected himself but then forgotten. He ran out before dinner was served. He was so worried about you. So angry with himself. He could barely sit still he was so agitated."

"This is my fault," Becca whispered. If only she'd stayed.

"No, it isn't." Nina gave Becca a sympathetic smile.

"Daniel's a grown man. He knows how to manage his diabetes. And this isn't the first time we've been here for him, is it?"

Eliana sighed. "No, it isn't."

"And some of that's because Dad refused to see it as a disease." Nina's eyes met Eliana's, and some unspoken communication passed between them.

"He was wrong," Eliana said gruffly.

"Yeah, he was."

Finally, a weary doctor finally walked into the waiting room. "Mrs. Carter?"

Eliana looked up. "I'm Daniel Carter's mother."

The doctor walked over, her hair pulled into a tight black ponytail. "Is this your family?"

"Daniel's sister and his girlfriend. And her friend." Mia had come in shortly after Becca, and had been holding her hand in support ever since.

"I'm Doctor Nixon. I'm pleased to tell you that Daniel is stable. We've gotten his blood sugar levels under control and treated his wounds. His injuries are mostly superficial. I want to monitor his levels overnight and send him for a brain scan in the morning to make sure his hypoglycemia hasn't caused any damage. But there's nothing for you to worry about, all the signs are looking good."

"Can I see him?" Eliana asked, her breath catching.

Doctor Nixon looked at the four of them. "Yes, but only you. It's late and most of the patients will be asleep. I suggest you all go home and do the same. Then come see Daniel in the morning."

Eliana nodded. "You should go home," she said to Nina. "Thank you for staying to take care of me."

"Are you sure?"

"Yes, darling. I'm sure. I'll call you if there's any change."

Nina gave her a hug.

"You should go, too," Becca told Mia. "Cam will be worried."

"Come home with me," Mia urged. "I'll bring you back tomorrow."

Becca shook her head. "I'm staying." The thought of going home to her empty condo made her feel ill. She wanted to be where he was. Even if she couldn't see him, it gave her comfort to know they were beneath the same roof.

Half an hour later, Eliana came back, her eyes heavy and weary. "He's asleep," she told Becca, who was sitting alone. The waiting room had thinned out. "Why don't we go back to my house and get some sleep, too?"

Becca shook her head. "I'll stay." There was no way she was leaving. She wanted to be near him, however stupid that sounded.

"I'd stay, too, but my bones are too old for these plastic chairs." Eliana kissed her cheek. "Please call me if anything happens."

"I will."

"Thank you for being here. Daniel cares for you a lot."

"He does?" Becca's eyes watered.

"Yes. I wasn't lying when I told you he was agitated tonight. I don't know what happened between you, but I haven't seen him like that before. My cool, calm, and collected boy in a mess over a girl." Her lips curled. "And such a beautiful, lovely girl at that." She cupped Becca's cheeks with her palms. "Try to get some sleep. He'll need you tomorrow."

"I will." She'd already folded her jacket into a makeshift pillow. She'd curl up over a couple of chairs and wait.

CHAPTER TWENTY-NINE

"Should we wake her up?"

"I think we should. We don't want her McMuffin to get cold."

"I'll eat her McMuffin if she doesn't want it. I'm starving."

"Get your hands off Becca's breakfast. You've already eaten two of the damn things. You don't need a third."

"I'm having a baby. I'm eating for two."

"Van's the one eating for two, not you, numbnuts."

"Well she's not keeping anything down. So really I'm eating for three. Give me that damn McMuffin. The baby needs it."

It took two blinks for Becca's eyes to open. They were stuck together with what felt like glue. She ran her tongue along her dry lips and tried to sit up, her muscles aching from being curled against plastic for hours.

All four of her brothers were leaning over her. Gray was holding a McDonald's bag, and Logan had a tray of coffees in his hands. Tanner was leaning over his shoulder, staring at Becca with wide eyes.

And Cam was Cam. Silent and strong.

"What are you all doing here?" she asked, her voice raspy from sleep. She managed to sit up, her socked feet hitting the cold tiled floor.

"We heard you'd decided to hang out at the hospital. Thought we'd bring you some breakfast." Gray held the bag out to her.

"What time is it?"

"Seven."

"How did you guys get here so early?" The room was flooded with early morning light, forming a halo behind her brothers' heads. It made her want to smile, because those four definitely weren't angels.

"Gray drives like a maniac." Logan shrugged. "We stopped to get some breakfast though, because none of us can stand Tanner's bitching."

"Cam was hungry, too," Tanner protested.

"Yeah, but he was silently hungry. We like that in a brother." Logan jabbed Tanner with his elbow.

"You okay, kid?" Gray asked softly, ignoring their brothers' bitching as he sat down next to Becca.

"Yeah." But her stinging eyes said otherwise. So did her aching body, her tight chest, and the throbbing in her head.

"Come here." Gray pulled her into his arms, resting her face against his chest. He kissed her hair. "It's okay. Everything's going to be okay."

She could feel hands patting her back. Her brothers. They'd come all this way to be with her. That made the tears start to flow, because she'd been so damn alone for the past few hours.

"What happened?" Gray asked, stroking her hair. Becca gave them a brief rundown of the doctor's report from the previous night.

"And have they been in to update you since?"

She shook her head. "I went to the desk a couple of times

and they promised to send somebody to update me, but I guess they're too busy."

Gray's jaw tightened. "Cam, can you come sit here?" He stood and Cam took his place, folding Becca in his arms. Everybody knew that Cam gave the best hugs in the family. He didn't ask questions, didn't give advice, he just held you hard until you felt better.

"Where are you going?" Logan asked.

"To use a little of the Hartson charm on the medical staff. Becca needs an update."

Cam chuckled, and it made her body shake. "Try not to dazzle them too much. They have a job to do, remember?"

Of course he would. Gray dazzled everybody. He's been known to make grown women become mute. And right now she was so happy he was here. If anybody could charm some information out of them, it was him.

Five minutes later, he was walking back into the waiting room, closely followed by a different doctor who was staring up at him with wide eyes. "Miss Hartson?" she said breathlessly.

"Becca." She stood, Cam and Tanner flanking her.

"I've just come on shift, so I haven't had much time to see Mr. Carter yet, but everything I've seen is looking good. We'll be giving him some breakfast soon, then we'll take him for a scan. If all is clear, he'll be released to go home."

"Can Becca see him now?" Gray asked.

"Let me see what I can do. We don't usually allow visitors in before rounds."

Gray smiled, and the doctor's chest lifted. "I'd be so grateful if you could help my sister," he said, his voice low and graveled. "She's been here all night waiting to see him."

The poor woman put her hand on her chest. "Of course," she said breathlessly. "Give me five minutes."

Gray's expression was smug as the doctor hurried out of

the door. "And that, ladies and gentlemen, is how you get what you want."

"It's how *you* get it," Tanner said. "The rest of us have to wait our turn."

"*I* don't." Cam shrugged. "Gray's way has always worked for me."

"And for me." Logan grinned. "We learned it from the best."

Becca patted Tanner's arm. "Don't worry, it doesn't work for me either."

Tanner huffed. "Hey, are you going to eat or what? That McMuffin must be freezing by now."

"You have it." Becca passed him the bag. "Your need is greater than mine." She rolled onto her tiptoes and pressed a kiss against his cheek. "I'm so glad you're here." She looked around at them, circling her like they were her bodyguards. "I'm so glad you're *all* here," she told them. She hadn't known how much she needed her brothers until they turned up.

"Yeah, well we wouldn't let you do this alone. And we're worried about Daniel, too." Logan shrugged. "Who's gonna herd my pigs for me if he's not around?"

Cam sniggered, and Becca arched an eyebrow at him.

"Seriously. If he's the guy you want, that means he's one of us." Gray rubbed her shoulder. "And we'll be here for as long as you need us."

———

THE FIRST THING Daniel noticed was the piercing light. Quickly followed by the dryness in his mouth and the constant tugging on his arm. It took him a moment to realize he wasn't in his own bed, and that the person tugging was a nurse, taking blood from the catheter on his hand.

The nurse smiled as he tried to pull his arm away. "Mr.

Carter, you're awake. Let me go tell the doctor. Don't move, okay?"

"Wasn't planning on it." He reached his hand up to touch his face, wincing as pain shot through his cheekbone. He'd been driving, he could remember that much. Had he been in an accident? Was anybody hurt. He tried to sit up, but his head was too dizzy.

"Mr. Carter," a warm voice said. "I'm Doctor Reynolds. It's good to see you awake."

"How long have I been here?"

"You were brought in last night. Do you remember anything from then?"

He shook his head, and immediately regretted it.

"You were in an accident on the highway. From your glucose levels when you were brought in, we believe you were having a hypoglycemic episode which led to you losing consciousness. The good news is that you were already driving toward the shoulder, and that no other vehicle was involved." She gave him a tight smile. "The bad news is you drove into a tree at around twenty miles an hour. According to the police, your car didn't make it, but I'm glad to say that you did."

Was that her attempt at humor? Daniel wasn't sure if he was supposed to laugh.

"We just ran your blood, and your glucose levels are normal now. We'll be taking you down for a brain scan to make sure nothing was affected by the hypoglycemia and the crash. You're a little beaten up, and needed some stitches to your face, but all in all you had a lucky escape."

"I can go home?" Damn, he needed to leave now.

"If we're happy with the results of your scan, yes. But you'll need to take good care of the wounds and come back if there are any problems."

"Can I call somebody? My… friend was expecting me last

night. She's probably worried about me." Damn, he hoped she was.

"Is her last name Hartson?"

"Yes." He didn't try to nod, assuming it would hurt.

"She's here. Been here all night according to the nurses. Kept asking about you. Her brothers are here, too." The doctor blushed. "Would you like to see her?"

His throat tightened at her words. "I would. Please."

As he waited for Becca to come up, memories of last night flooded into his mind. Becca's discovery of his loss, her reaction to it. *His* reaction to her understandable shock. He'd been an asshole. So afraid that she'd find out who he really was. The man who couldn't even be there when his girlfriend was losing their child.

The self centered sonofabitch that pushed everybody away, because his father had taught him he'd never be good enough. He'd fulfilled that prophecy himself, thanks to his stupid decisions.

He should have told her about the baby. Not because he was ashamed, but because that loss was part of him, and he wanted her to know all of him.

Even if he'd lose her when she did.

"Here he is," he heard a voice echoing from the hallway outside his door. "He's awake but a little beaten up. There are bruises and cuts on his chest and face. They should heal quickly, but he'll need to rest today. We'll do a scan and release him as soon as we can."

"You think he could have brain damage?" Even though Becca's voice was asking that question, his body stilled at the sound of her. She was close. It was all he needed to know.

"All indications say no. But it's prudent to check."

"He has an emergency pack. There are glucose tablets and raisins in there. Wasn't it in the car?"

"Nothing was found on him apart from his wallet and

phone. There's an emergency card in there. That's how we contacted his mother. I'm glad he has a pack, though he needs to remember to take it with him."

"He will," Becca growled. He smiled at the vehemence of her words. Smiled even wider when she walked into his room, the light of the morning streaming in with her. Her hair was pulled into a messy bun, her face free of makeup. She looked about twenty standing there with her hands pressed to her hips, a mixture of relief and anger washing over her face.

"Hi."

She exhaled heavily. "Hi." Walking over to his bed, she grimaced at the sight of his face.

"Is it bad?" he asked.

"You've looked better. But to put it in perspective, you're still the most handsome man I've ever seen."

He tried to laugh but it hurt. She grimaced in sympathy.

"I'm sorry," he croaked, when she took his hand in hers. "So damn sorry."

"You should be. You know better than to go anywhere without your emergency pack. You could have been seriously hurt." Her eyes shone as she looked at him. "You were lucky."

He was just so glad he hadn't hurt anybody else. He was a goddamned idiot, he knew better than to mess with hypoglycemia. "I don't care about me. I'm sorry about last night. About not telling you the truth. About pushing you away when I should have pulled you closer." He squeezed his eyes shut. "I shouldn't have done that."

A nurse walked in and pulled a thermometer out. Becca swallowed, but the pain didn't leave her eyes. He hated that he'd put that there. "Maybe we should talk about this later?" she said, glancing warily at the nurse.

"There'll be a later?" Something like hope lit up inside of him, mixing with the exhaustion he felt.

Becca nodded slowly. "Yeah." She looked as tired as he was.

"I can't believe you were here all night."

"Just because we argued doesn't mean I don't care about you." Her eyes were soft. As though there was so much more she wanted to say.

He knew how that felt.

There was that hope again. Lighting a little fire in his chest. "I care, too," he said, his voice graveled. Becca ran her tongue across her lip, her eyes catching his.

Even without sleep and wearing rumpled clothes she looked beautiful. He couldn't believe he'd hurt her. Not only because he'd pushed away the one perfect thing in his life, but because she was such a good person. She didn't deserve to have red rimmed eyes or lips that trembled when she looked at him.

She deserved to always be happy. And he wanted to be the one to make her that way.

"I know you care." Her voice was soft. "But now you need to concentrate on getting better. You scared me last night. Scared all of us."

Daniel nodded. "I know."

"We'll be taking you for your scan in a moment, Mr. Carter," the nurse said. "And your mother called to say she'll be here in an hour. She's delighted to hear you're awake."

"Thank you." Daniel smiled at the nurse, and a blush stole up her cheeks. "I appreciate that."

"We'll be in to get you very soon." The nurse glanced at Becca with an embarrassed smile, then scurried out of the door.

"Still got it," Becca murmured.

Daniel shook his head at her. "Will you stay?" he asked. "Until I've had the scan."

"Of course."

He slid his fingers between hers. "Thank you," he said softly. "For being here. For caring."

She pressed her lips against his brow and he closed his eyes for a moment, savoring the feel of her mouth against him. He wanted more, but not yet. Only once he'd apologized properly. Told her everything she needed to know.

Maybe then she wouldn't want him. It was a risk, he knew that much. But one he had to take.

He'd fight until he had no fight left inside him. Do whatever it took to be worthy of this beautiful woman with the mossy green eyes.

Last night he'd pushed her away. Now he needed to figure out how to get her back again.

CHAPTER THIRTY

It was almost nine by the time her brothers left the hospital and headed back to Hartson's Creek. Becca had insisted they go spend time with their families. "I don't think I need your dimples and sexy smile any more, as useful as they were," she told Gray with a smile. "Go home and give those twins a huge kiss from me."

One by one, they'd hugged her and told her to call them as soon as she got home. She rolled her eyes at their protectiveness, even though it secretly made her feel warm inside.

When they'd finally walked out of the hospital, Becca returned to Daniel. His mom had arrived around when he was due back from his scan, and she'd insisted on Becca going to get some breakfast and a coffee while she took over.

"I think you've aged me ten years." Eliana's voice echoed out of Daniel's room as Becca approached it. She slowed her steps, they were obviously in mid-conversation. No need to interrupt them.

"You still look about forty. I saw the way that technician was looking at you," Daniel teased.

A Daniel that teased? That was new. Becca smiled at the development.

"Don't try to win me over with flattery. I'm your mother, I know how you work. You have to take better care of yourself, or god help me I'll start calling you every hour."

"Becca's already read me the riot act."

Eliana laughed. "Good for Becca. Somebody needs to take care of you." Her voice lowered, and Becca had to lean closer to the door to hear. Yes, eavesdropping was wrong, but they were talking about her now.

And she really wanted to hear what they had to say.

"Speaking of Becca, have you two made up?"

There was silence, save for Eliana's high breaths, and Daniel's lower ones. "We've agreed to talk. Later."

"Oh, darling. Does that mean there's hope for you two?"

"If I stop being an ass, then maybe." He cleared his throat. "I hope so, anyway."

Becca held her breath. She hoped so, too.

There was another silence, as though they were communicating silently. "What happened with you and Melissa, it was heartbreaking. But you two were never meant to be." Eliana's voice was soft.

"I know that. I think I knew it all along. It was easy to get swept up in everything, and then she got pregnant and there was no choice..." Daniel sighed.

"I can't lose you again, darling. Not the way we lost you when you left for Scotland."

"I didn't leave because of Melissa. I left because of me. I'd failed everybody. I could barely stand to look myself in the mirror, let alone have you look at me."

"You didn't fail me. You never have. I love you. And I know you and Melissa weren't supposed to be because you never looked at her the way I see you look at Becca."

"Is that right?"

"You think you're being so damn clever walking through the still room looking at her when you think everybody is busy. But these things don't escape me. I know you too well. You're in love with her."

Becca's eyes widened. She could feel her spine tingle.

"Yeah, I am."

Her breath caught in her throat. He loved her? It felt like the sun bursting through the clouds of her heart.

"You should tell her."

"I will. But not when I'm wearing a damn gown in a hospital bed."

Eliana laughed. "Okay, then. Do it your way. You always do."

Trying to rearrange her features, Becca made a show of stomping the last few feet to Daniel's room, smiling nonchalantly as she walked inside.

"You're back. How was the scan?" She kissed Eliana's cheek, and his mom hugged her back.

"So are you." He smiled and it made her heart skip. "And the scan was fine. The technician saw no problems, but the doctor will look at it before I'm discharged."

"That's good." She shot him another smile.

All she could really think about was that he loved her. And she loved him too, and she needed to tell him soon.

Some secrets weren't meant to be kept.

———

"I WISH he'd let me take him home," Eliana said to Becca as they waited outside for Daniel to dress. "He's so stubborn sometimes." She took one look at Becca's amused smile and added, "Actually, he's stubborn all the time. He hates being sick, he always has. He makes the worst kind of patient."

"I'll stay with him," Becca said. She'd already said she

would to Daniel. Neither her nor Eliana wanted him to be alone.

And it would give them time to talk. Time they both needed.

"Thank you." Eliana gave her a grateful smile. "My driver will take you both. I'm so glad he has you to take care of him. He's different when he's with you. I know he isn't always the easiest man in the world, but you're good for him."

Becca's chest tightened. "He's been good for me, too."

"I hope the two of you work things out." Eliana patted her arm. "I can't tell you how long I've waited to see him happy. If I had known you were the one to make him smile again, I would've sent you to Scotland years ago." She shook her head. "No, actually, it happened as it was meant to. The last person he ever listens to is his meddling mother."

"He loves you a lot. Talks about you all the time. I believe he has you to thank for his dance skills."

Eliana shook her head, amused. "He hated those dance lessons. It was a battle of wills every Saturday morning."

"And yet he learned how to dance anyway."

"His father told him Lawrence was a wonderful dancer. That's all it took for him to push himself hard." Eliana sighed. "My late husband encouraged their rivalry. Enjoyed it, even. I think he liked having two boys constantly vying for his attention. But it didn't do either of his sons any good." She smiled sadly. "That's why I keep encouraging them to build bridges now that their father has gone. Though I'm not sure if I only make things worse."

"Families are difficult," Becca sympathized. "So many dynamics going on under the surface."

"I knew you'd understand." Eliana nodded. "Though your family is lovely. That's all I really wanted. A husband who loved me and children who were happy. Including Lawrence and Nina."

"Maybe they *are* happy. Nathan's enjoying himself in Tokyo. Nina seems fairly content with life. And Daniel..." Becca smiled wryly. "Is Daniel. Lawrence has Melissa, that must make him happy."

"Lawrence and Melissa suit each other."

Becca lifted an eyebrow but said nothing. Her jealous feelings about Melissa still weren't resolved. She knew she needed to work on that.

"I don't mean they deserve each other in a bad way." Eliana shook her head. "They just like the same things. The old fashioned life. Keeping history alive in their home. Being part of the social scene in Charleston. Daniel hated all that. The only thing he loved was making whiskey. Until you."

Their eyes met, an understanding flowing between them. Eliana pressed her lips together, her eyes shining, full of words she didn't vocalize.

Please forgive him.

I'm going to try.

Don't hurt him.

I don't want to. I love him, too.

The door to Daniel's hospital room opened, and he walked out, wearing clothes Eliana had brought him. Dark jeans and a t-shirt, his hair brushed and raked back from his face, revealing the bruises and cuts caused by the airbag.

"Everything okay?" His gaze slid from Becca to Eliana and back again, eyes narrowed as though he knew they'd been talking about him.

"Yep." Becca smiled, her throat tight as she took him in. Even damaged, his face was beautiful. "Your mom says you're not to give me any problems while I'm playing nurse."

His lips twitched. "And I always do what my mom tells me."

"You should." Eliana kissed his cheek. "I know best, after all."

"Shall I take your bag?" Becca asked, reaching for the duffle. Daniel refused to pass it to her, hooking it over his shoulder and wincing.

"I'll take it," he muttered. "I'm not a patient anymore."

Eliana winked at Becca. "He's all yours." She hugged her tightly. "Call me when you get home. And if there are any problems." She lifted a brow at Daniel. "And you're not to come into work tomorrow."

"Of course I'm coming to work. I'm fine."

"Good luck," Eliana whispered.

"Thanks." Becca nodded. "I have a feeling I'm going to need it."

CHAPTER THIRTY-ONE

It was early afternoon by the time the driver pulled up outside Daniel's house, climbing out of the car to take Daniel's overnight bag out of the trunk. Becca was glad he'd opted to go to his home rather than hers. The thought of being so close to him in her apartment was too much. They both needed space – or as much of it as they could get while they were sitting together.

"Would you like a glass of tea? Or some water?" she asked him once they'd made it inside.

Daniel shook his head. "I'm going to take a shower and check my blood." He shifted his feet. "Are you sure you're okay with staying?"

Becca nodded her head. There was no way she was leaving now. Not after everything they'd both been through. Yes, it hurt to feel that she didn't know everything she needed to about him, but his health was more important than anything else. The memory of the phone call from Eliana last night was like a vice to her chest. "I already messaged Mia to have her to go to my place and pack a few things."

"You could have left me for five minutes," he said, his voice soft. "I wouldn't have gotten into any trouble."

Her lips twitched. "Experience tells me otherwise."

He let out an amused huff, his eyes catching hers. And she ached to throw herself into his arms. But he was still weak, and she still needed answers. Her heart was tender, she needed to protect it.

She walked into Daniel's beautiful kitchen, memories of their nights here surrounding her. Pulling a glass out of the cupboard, she filled it with sweet tea from the refrigerator, gulping it down as she leaned against the counter.

Overhead she could hear the faint rush of water as Daniel took his shower. She wondered how bruised his body was. Part of her wanted to go up to check. To climb into the shower with him and put her arms around his waist until she couldn't work out where her own body ended and his began.

A knock at the front door brought her out of her thoughts. Becca opened it to see both Mia and Aunt Gina standing there, Mia holding a bag, Aunt Gina holding a casserole dish with foil covering the top.

"Sweetheart." Aunt Gina gave her a soft smile, and Becca felt herself crumble. Aunt Gina cupped her cheek and clucked. "You look so tired. What's happened, baby girl?"

"Sorry," Mia mouthed. Then, louder, she said, "Gina was at ours when I got your message. She insisted on picking up a casserole from the freezer."

"If in doubt bring a casserole, am I right?" Gina smiled at her. "Now are you going to let us inside or what?"

"You're lucky I dissuaded your brothers," Mia whispered in her ear. "They were all up for another game of football in Daniel's back yard."

Becca squeezed her eyes shut. Her brothers were so predictable. "They must have only just gotten home."

"Yeah, but you're their baby sister." Mia smiled. "You bring out all their protective instincts."

Aunt Gina was already pouring herself and Mia a glass of tea. How did she even know where everything was? As a child, Becca had thought her aunt knew everything. Maybe she'd been right all along, she certainly could sniff sweet tea at thirty yards.

"Hi." Daniel walked into the kitchen, his brows pulled together when he saw Gina and Mia sitting at his breakfast bar. He was wearing a towel slung around his waist, another around his shoulder, his chest damp and pink from the shower.

There was a bruise running from his shoulder to his waist where the seatbelt must have pressured his skin, and the cuts on his face she'd already seen. But apart from that he looked unaffected.

And good. So good. She had to swallow and pull her gaze away.

"I… ah… came to get my kit," he said, looking down at the bag he'd thrown on the floor when they'd walked in.

"Be our guest." Aunt Gina lifted a brow, her eyes sweeping over his torso. "You should put some arnica cream on that. It'll help the bruising fade within a couple of days."

Daniel gave a half smile. "Thank you. I'll try that."

"Are you okay?" Mia asked. His eyes met hers and he gave her a slight nod.

"I'm fine, thanks to the EMTs and doctors." His eyes lifted. "And to Becca."

"I didn't do anything," she pointed out. She was still trying hard not to ogle his body. He was hurt, but damn, did he look good.

"You did." His voice was soft. "More than you know."

His eyes caught hers, and she felt breathless. The corner

of his mouth lifted, and she mirrored his action, blood rushing through her ears.

"We should go," Mia said, hastily standing up. "We have lots to do, remember?"

"We do?" Aunt Gina asked. "Like what?"

Mia rolled her eyes. "Like tidy your garden. And there's that jigsaw you were halfway through. And I need to go home and make sure Josh and Michael are doing their homework."

Aunt Gina huffed. "I haven't even finished my tea."

From the corner of her eye Beccca saw Mia shake her head. "I'll make you some, now lets go." She pulled at the sleeve of Aunt Gina's dress. Aunt Gina huffed again, slowly rising up.

"I don't know why everything has to be such a rush nowadays," she complained. "I just wanted to stay and admire the view."

Daniel's eyes caught Becca's once more, and she had to swallow down a laugh. Mia looked almost fraught as she hustled Gina over to the kitchen door. "No need to see us out," she shouted. "We'll just close the door behind us."

"Why are you shouting?" Aunt Gina asked her.

"Because I'm making a point. Come on, let's go. Those two need to be alone."

"Why?" Their voices were getting fainter, but their conversation was still audible. Becca was torn between laughter and embarrassment. Daniel was still looking at her, his eyes soft.

"Because they need to talk."

"They can talk with me here," Gina said. The sound of the front door opening came as a relief. Surely she couldn't make things any worse. "Anyway, I was enjoying looking at that young man. Did you see his chest? Reminded me of a young Burt Lancaster."

"You can stay over and ogle Cam's chest instead," Mia said, sounding as though her teeth were gritted.

"He's my nephew. That's disgusting." The door closed and their voices were gone.

Becca lifted her hand to her mouth, mortification winning out over amusement. "Oh my god," she whispered, her eyes wide.

"I love your family," Daniel told her. "And I love you."

Her mouth dropped open. All thoughts of Aunt Gina flew out of her mind. "You do?"

He nodded. "Yes, I do. And I'm so damn sorry about last night. I can't stand that I hurt you. You're the best thing that's ever happened to me, and I messed it up." He was standing ten feet away from her, but she could feel the warmth of his words curl around her. "Can we talk? I really want to explain."

"You need to check your glucose level." Her voice was faint. He was actually admitting that he loved her? Her chest felt so full it could burst.

"I know. And I should probably get dressed, too." He looked down at his bare, bruised chest. "Will you give me ten minutes?"

Becca nodded.

His lip curled. "Thank you. I'll be right back." He glanced over his shoulder as he carried his overnight bag out of the kitchen, his eyes catching hers once more.

"I'm one lucky sonofabitch that you'll even listen to me," he told her. "This time I'll try not to mess it up."

———

HE LOVED HER. She couldn't stop smiling as she waited for him, putting the casserole Aunt Gina had brought into the refrigerator and carrying her own bag to the bottom of the stairs. Daniel was walking down, wearing a pair of grey sweats and a dark blue t-shirt, rubbing his hands through his damp hair.

"Hey." He smiled at her, his eyes crinkling. "I didn't expect you to wait at the bottom of the stairs." He inclined his head toward the living room. "Shall we go sit down?"

She nodded. "Yeah, that'd be good."

Truth was she was exhausted. After her fractured sleep last night, and the sheer rush of emotions she'd been feeling since leaving Charleston yesterday evening, she felt like she could sleep for a hundred years.

She sat on his black leather sofa, and he dropped down next to her, taking her hand into his as though he couldn't bear to not be touching her. He circled her palm with the calloused pad of his thumb, sending shivers down her spine, as he opened his mouth to talk.

And then somebody knocked at the door.

"Oh my god," Becca said, shaking her head. "If that's another member of my family I'm going to kill them."

Daniel's lips twitched. "They just love you. And I can't blame them."

"I'll get rid of them and then we can start again." She stood and pointed at him. "Don't go anywhere."

He grinned. "I wouldn't dare."

She stomped over to the hallway, gritting her teeth as she yanked open the front door. To her surprise, it wasn't her brothers, but Nina standing on the doorstep.

All the fight sank out of Becca. "Hi." She smiled. "Is everything okay?"

Nina nodded. "I'm sorry for arriving unannounced. I just wanted to see if Daniel's okay. And if you are, too."

"Come in." At least Daniel was dressed this time. "Daniel's in the living room."

He looked up with surprise as his older sister walked in.

Her face crumpled when she saw him, and she rushed over to throw her arms around him, burying her face in his chest.

He winced, and Becca grimaced in sympathy. Those bruises looked painful. "Hey," he said, stroking Nina's hair. "What's all this?"

"I'm just so glad you're okay," Nina said, her voice muffled. "You had us all worried."

"I know." His voice was gritty. "I'm sorry."

"No, I'm sorry," Nina said softly. "What happened last night should never have happened. All of it. Lawrence and Melissa, you and Becca… I can't help but feel it's my fault."

Daniel frowned. "How did you figure that out?"

"Can I get you some sweet tea?" Becca asked her. It felt like a brother-sister moment. She should know, she'd had enough of them.

"Tea would be lovely." Nina gave her a half smile. "Thank you."

As she walked to the kitchen, Becca could hear the low hum of their conversation. The way Daniel spoke to his sister, the way he held her, made her chest contract. He could be the gentlest of men when he wanted to be.

Even if it scared him to be vulnerable.

She took her time in the kitchen, not wanting to disturb them. She emptied the glass Aunt Gina hadn't finished and slid it into the dishwasher, along with Mia's used glass. Then she washed the counters down, drying them until they sparkled. When she finally poured Nina's sweet tea, five minutes had passed.

Daniel and Nina were still talking quietly when she padded down the hallway.

"Lawrence knows how badly he behaved," Nina was saying. "I left him in no doubt that this is all his fault. I think I hit a nerve because he actually asked to come with me to see you."

"Why didn't he?"

"Because I told him to shut up and stay home. He's done enough damage." Nina sighed. "I blame myself. Even when you two were children you were at each other's throats. I was the eldest, I should have stepped in."

"You were a kid, too. We all were," Daniel told her. "It wasn't our faults. Not then."

"Yeah, well Lawrence is a grown up now. He should know better. I have no idea why he thinks everything's a competition. Dad isn't even with us any more."

"He's not the only one who behaved badly." Daniel breathed heavily. "I've not been an angel."

"Yeah, but you grew up a lot while you were away. It did you so much good. And then there's Becca." Her voice was warm. "She's so beautiful and good for you. I've never seen you happier than you were at the gala." Nina lowered her voice, saying something Becca couldn't hear.

"Thank you." Daniel's voice was choked. "That means a lot."

"There's one more thing. I'm calling my lawyer tomorrow to have my shares in the distillery transferred to you and Nathan equally. Lawrence has agreed to do the same. We discussed it this morning before I came here."

"Why?" Daniel sounded incredulous.

"Because I don't want it to be the thing that tears us apart. There's been too much of that. You and Nathan put in all the work, you deserve to have the shares. And it's not as though Lawrence or I need the money."

"I can pay you."

"No." Nina's voice was firm. "It's not about money, it's about family. That's what we are, even if it doesn't feel like it sometimes." She sighed softly. "And maybe you can come and see us sometimes just because you want to see your sister, not because you want the go ahead for something at the distillery."

"I could do that." Daniel's voice cracked.

"I know you and Lawrence will never see eye to eye. And you don't have to. But I love you both and want you to be happy. Maybe one day that happiness will include forgiving him for what he did."

"For Melissa?" Daniel asked. "I forgave him for that long ago."

"No, I mean for Becca. For trying to split you apart. That was so much worse, because she means something to you." Nina cleared her throat. "And now I need to go home. Let you recuperate."

"You can stay."

"No, darling. But don't be a stranger, okay?" The sound of footsteps echoed from the living room and the next moment the door opened. Becca stood there, holding the sweet tea Nina probably didn't want anymore.

Nina's lips twitched when Becca handed her the glass. She took a polite sip. "Thank you." Inclining her head to the door, she smiled at Becca. "Will you walk me out?"

"Of course."

They walked together to the door. Becca opened it and took the glass from Nina.

"Are you all right?" Nina asked her. "After last night?"

Becca gave her a half smile. "I will be."

"I'm so sorry you got caught up in all that sibling rivalry."

"I'm kind of used to it with four brothers," Becca said, shrugging.

Nina's eyes were warm. "He's a good man, you know? He's been hurt and he doesn't always know how to do the right thing, but he has the kindest heart when he lets it show."

"I know." Becca's throat felt tight.

"He and Melissa were never right. I could tell that from the start. She's so much happier with Lawrence. He gives her the life she always wanted, at the center of Charleston society." Nina exhaled softly. "What happened last night was just her getting caught up in the past. It hurts when a guy passes you over and chooses somebody else. Even when you're married." Nina smiled.

"I know." Becca nodded. It was true. She knew Melissa wasn't really a threat. She also knew she over reacted last night.

"I told Daniel something that I want to tell you, too." Nina was on the front step. A light breeze lifted her hair. "I've never seen him look at anybody the way he looks at you. He's so in love with you, Becca. If you can, please find a way back to him."

Becca's lip trembled. "I will," she whispered.

"Good." Nina smiled. "Now go back inside. I have a feeling you two have some talking to do."

CHAPTER THIRTY-TWO

He'd never get sick of seeing Becca Hartson walk into his living room, her dark hair flowing over her shoulders, a smile curling at her lips. Damn, she was beautiful, and he didn't deserve her.

But he wanted to be the kind of man who deserved to have this beautiful, sensitive, funny woman on his arm.

He'd spend the rest of his life proving it to her, if she'd let him.

He held his arms open, and she stepped into his embrace, her head soft against his chest. Lowering his head, he breathed her in, the ache in his ribcage lessening as he curled his arms around her.

"I'm so sorry," he whispered into her hair. "I'm sorry for hurting you. For driving when I shouldn't have and making you scared." She looked up at him, her eyes shining, and his stomach contracted because she was so beautiful. He cupped her face, lowering his lips to her brow, kissing her softly. "I'm sorry for not being honest."

"Can you tell me about the baby?" Becca asked him.

Every cell in his body was telling him not to. But he knew

they were wrong. If he wanted to deserve this woman, he had to show her who he was. He needed to be honest and vulnerable.

Even if it killed him.

"Let's sit down again." His lip quirked. "Hopefully nobody else will be knocking at the door."

"We'll ignore it." Becca's eyes narrowed. "People need to learn to call before they come over."

They sat down, and he pulled her close, unwilling to be apart from her again. He cleared his throat, sliding his fingers between hers. "Melissa and I were on the verge of splitting up when she discovered she was pregnant," he said, swallowing hard because this was so damn difficult to talk about. "It came as a shock to us both. But she thought it would bring us closer together, while in reality it tore us apart."

Becca leaned her head against his shoulder. "Do you think she planned it?"

"I don't know. She said she didn't. And in the end it doesn't matter, because it takes two to make a baby."

"Can you back track a little?" Becca asked. "Tell me how you met Melissa."

She wanted it all. And he'd give it to her, whatever it took. It was painful knowing that back then he wasn't the man he should have been. He fell short so many times. How could Becca love him if he couldn't love himself?

"Melissa was an old family friend. Our fathers knew each other for years. That's how Lawrence and I met her. We dated for two years. For most of that, I was working all the hours I could. I started off in the sales department. I traveled all over the country, sometimes all over the world, talking to clients, getting orders in. And it didn't leave much time for relationship. Melissa resented that, but I didn't change a thing." He blew out a mouthful of air. "We should have split up long before we did. But my father liked Melissa, and then there was Lawrence…" He sighed. "Even after Dad died, I didn't do the right thing until the truth was hitting me in the face. And when I tried to end our relationship, she told me she was pregnant. And I felt trapped."

Becca squeezed his hand. "But you were going to stay with her?"

"I thought it was the honorable thing to do. But I didn't stop traveling or working every hour I could." He shook his head. "I worked harder than ever. Because when I was working, I didn't have to think about what a mistake we were making. We were arguing a lot by that point. We couldn't even agree on where to live. She wanted to buy somewhere in Charleston, I wanted to be near the distillery. Then she gave me an ultimatum. Either I moved to a job in the distillery that didn't involve traveling, or she left me."

"And you refused?"

"I saw red. Told her not to pin me into a corner. We didn't talk for days, and then I left for a meeting in Toronto. That's when the phone calls started. She tried everything. Begging. Arguing. Pleading. And eventually she started telling me she was feeling ill. That I should come home in case something happened to the baby."

Becca's face fell. "Oh god…"

Daniel's breath felt ragged. "I told her she was imagining it. That she was fine. I'd take her to the doctor when I was back. I was still going to be there for the baby, even if the two of us didn't make it." He glanced up, his pained gaze catching Becca's. "Then, in the middle of the night I got the phone call from the hospital. She'd lost the baby." There was a softness to his voice that made her ache.

Becca blinked back tears. "I'm so sorry."

"It was my fault. I should have been there when she needed me."

"It wasn't your fault." Becca was vehement. "These things happen. They're nobody's fault."

"I still should have been there." Daniel curled his fingers around hers. If she pulled away now, he wasn't sure he could take it. "And I truly regret that I wasn't."

"What happened next?"

"Lawrence was there for her when I wasn't. Took care of her, showed her love. Within a month of her leaving me, they were engaged."

"Did she do it to hurt you?" Becca asked, frowning.

"I don't know. Maybe." Daniel shook his head. "It doesn't really matter. The truth is, they're more suited to each other. It never would have worked between us. But it still didn't stop me from feeling like a failure. And when I heard the distillery in Scotland was looking for a new director, I jumped at the chance to get away." He looked at her through his thick lashes. "And now you know what a mess I was. Still am."

"I know what a *human* you are," she said, her voice raspy. "I just wish you'd told me about it before Lawrence did."

"So do I. So much. But I was so afraid of losing you if you knew the real me. I wasn't prepared to take that chance."

"I *want* to know the real you." She shook her head. "I'm not afraid of your past, Daniel. I'm not going to run away because you've made mistakes and have been hurt."

"But you left last night."

"I wanted to leave because you lied to me. Or lied by omission, anyway. It messed up my mind. I couldn't think properly. I didn't leave because of the baby. I'm so damn sorry about the baby. I can't even imagine the pain that kind of loss causes." She brushed her lips against his. "I just wish you'd told me."

"I've spent my life trying to be perfect. It's hard to admit that I'm not."

"But nobody's perfect. We can't be. Why is that so hard for you to admit?"

He ran the tip of his tongue over his bottom lip. "I guess I always felt like that's the only way to be loved. My dad…" He shook his head, sighing. "It's always the damn parents, isn't it?"

She smiled softly. "So I hear. Your mom said something about your dad pitting you and Lawrence against each other."

Daniel nodded. "I can't remember a time when I wasn't compared to him. Wasn't told that I needed to be better, faster, stronger than him. To be fair, Lawrence probably had it worse. He was the oldest son, therefore he should have been all those things. Yet he was constantly compared to me, too."

"Your dad got off on your rivalry." Her voice was low.

"I guess he did. He enjoyed having us compete for his love. Encouraged it. Even after he died, Lawrence and I still hated each other. And then things started going wrong between Melissa and me, and I guess he saw his chance."

"I don't like Lawrence."

Daniel chuckled. "Good. And you don't have to. He's not a big part of my life."

"Nina wants him to be. So does your mom."

"My mom wants everybody to be happy. She adores you, by the way. Thinks you keep me on my toes."

"I like her, too."

"Does that mean there's a chance for us?" His chest felt like a vice was wrapped around it.

Becca nodded. "I think there is," she whispered. "If you promise to stop clamming up when I try to talk to you about something difficult. I can't take you telling me to leave again. And if I try not to overreact every time something goes wrong."

He winced at the memory of their argument. "I don't want you to leave. Ever. I've never wanted anything as much as I want you to stay with me. I love you."

Tears filled her eyes. "I love you, too."

He brushed the teardrops from her cheeks with the pad of his thumb, then softly kissed her, marveling at this beautiful woman loved him.

Warmth rushed through him as she pulled away from their kiss, smiling shyly up at him. He reached out to trace the line of her lips with his fingertip. "You don't know what that means to me. I don't know what I did to deserve you. I'm so afraid of messing this up."

"Maybe you could change your thinking," she told him, her lips moving against his finger. "Rather than being afraid of messing up, figure out how you'll make it better when you do. We're not perfect, we're going to make mistakes. I'm going to get angry with you sometimes. And you'll get furious with me, I've no doubt. But if we keep talking, if we're honest with each other, maybe we can really make this thing work."

"I want that more than anything," he admitted, his voice gruff.

Her heart gave a little leap. "So do I."

"How did you know that you'd fallen for me?" he asked her, his expression so open it made her heart hurt. Vulnerable Daniel might be her favorite.

"I'd been thinking about it for a while. But the moment I was certain of it was when I saw you covered in mud, your jeans stinking of pigs and farms. I never thought anybody would go up against my brothers for me. But you did, and I fell for you." She pulled her lip between her teeth. "And you? When did you know?"

He closed his eyes, a smile playing on his lips.

"When I saw how competitive you were at board games."

Her mouth dropped open. "*That's* what did it?"

Daniel shook his head. "It was the last piece of the puzzle. You amazed me. I knew before we even spoke that you were kind. It radiates out of you. And then I learned you were funny, enough to make me laugh just remembering the things you said to me." He pressed a kiss to the tip of her nose. "You're brave, too. You never back down from a confrontation with me, not just last night, but at work, too. The competitiveness was the cherry on top. It's what makes you so damn perfect."

"I'm not perfect."

"You're perfect for me. That's what I'm trying to say. And after that afternoon in the library I was done for. I stopped fighting my feelings."

"You make my heart soar," she told him softly. "Not just because you say the sweetest things, but because you're kind and funny and brave. You're willing to do things you're afraid of, to be honest and open and reveal your imperfections." She stroked his cheek tenderly. "I love you so much I could burst."

The warmth of her words were like a caress. He leaned toward her, his lips pressing against hers. He curled his hand around her sweet face, angling her so he could deepen the kiss, brushing his tongue against hers until they were both short of breath.

"I'm the luckiest man that ever breathed," he told her, kissing her again. "Thank you for giving me another chance."

———

BECCA TIPTOED UP THE STAIRS, wincing when one of the steps squeaked under her weight. She'd sent Daniel up to sleep hours earlier. He was exhausted after dinner – Aunt Gina's beef casserole, of course – and she knew he needed to rest.

He'd smiled when she told him she had some calls to make, anyway. He was getting used to how chatty her family was. So while he slept she phoned each of her brothers in turn to thank them for being there at the hospital and to give them an update on Daniel.

It touched her heart how they all sent their love to him. Sure, they could be asses sometimes, but she loved those boys.

Daniel's door opened, and he stepped outside, his hair a sleepy mess. "Are you going to bed?" he asked her.

"Yeah, I was just heading to the guest room. I didn't mean to disturb you." She wasn't sure why she was whispering. Maybe the sight of him bare chested in a pair of black pajama pants took her breath away.

"Sleep with me." His eyes were soft. "Please."

"You need to recover."

He reached for her hand, pulling her toward him. His torso was warm against her body. "I'll recover better if you're with me."

She smiled. "Okay. Give me ten minutes. I need to shower and brush my teeth."

"Take your time."

He was laying on the mattress when she walked back into his room, his beautiful, muscled body stretched out on top of the sheets. He rolled over and held out his hand, his eyes warm as he took in her silky nightgown.

"You look so damn gorgeous you drive me crazy," he told her, his voice rough. She climbed into bed beside him, and he pulled the covers over them, sliding his arm around her waist to pull her body to his. He let out a low growl as he slid his palm down her back, his movement aided by her silken nightgown.

He buried his face in her throat, his lips kissing her skin. "You smell amazing."

She felt a sharp jab of arousal between her thighs. "Daniel, we can't. You just got out of the hospital."

He laughed against her neck. "I'm feeling pretty damn good right now." He pressed a kiss to her ear. "Thank you for taking care of me."

"I was expecting more of a fight, to be honest." She smiled at him.

"Are you disappointed I didn't give you one?"

"I figure you didn't have the energy. And there'll be plenty more fights to be had." She slid her fingers into his silky hair, and he groaned as the tips massaged his skull.

"Keep doing that and I'll never fight you again." He could smell the sweet fragrance of her as she leaned over him. The neckline of her nightgown gaped, and he glanced down at the soft swell of her breasts. His eyes were heavy lidded as he brushed his hand down her side, his thumb feathering her nipple.

"Daniel…" A pulse throbbed at her core, matching the rhythm of his touch.

"It's okay." He captured her lips, sliding his hand down further, hitching her thigh over his hip. She could feel his excitement press against her, hard and thick. He kissed her again, swallowing her sigh as he slid his hand inside her nightgown and cupped her breast.

"Daniel," she was breathless. "You need to rest."

"Tell my body that."

She reached down to feather her fingers against his erection. "You're so hard."

"Don't you know how you affect me by now? It's like your body sings to mine."

"I guess it could be therapeutic," she murmured. "If you stay very still."

He blinked. "Therapeutic?"

"You've had a hard day." Her lips curled at his surprise. "You need some stress relief."

He took her face between his palms, looking into her pretty eyes. "Are we okay?" he asked her, an edge to his voice.

"We're more than okay."

"You don't hate me anymore?"

"Only a little bit."

He laughed, and it hurt his bruised ribs. "I'll take that."

"I love you, too."

Daniel inhaled sharply, his eyes so soft she could lose herself in them. "I love you more."

He pulled her on top of him, sliding his hands along her thighs. She straddled him, her hips circling.

"I thought you didn't believe in love." She rolled her hips again

"Did I say that?" He curled his hands around her waist. Steadying her. Taking control.

"You said you didn't know what love was, if it existed at all."

He tugged at her nightgown, pulling it over her head. His breath caught as his gaze slid over the curves of her breast, her tight stomach, the flare of her hips.

"I know what it is." His gaze was intense. "It's like being stabbed and kissed by the same person. It's being so happy you can't figure out how you ever didn't feel this way. It's seeing somebody smile and your heart stopping because you put that damn smile on their face. It's knowing you can't live without them, and being terrified you'll really fuck it up next time."

She brushed her lips against his, smiling. "There's going to be a next time?"

"I can almost guarantee it. The sun rises, the world turns, Daniel Carter fucks things up."

"I have something you can fuck up."

He laughed, looking surprised at her swearing. "You do?"

"Mmhmm. So why don't you stop all this emo stuff and take me already?"

He slipped his thumb into the waistband of his pants, wriggling it down his hips. Becca pushed herself above him, letting him kick them down past his feet. He looked up at her breasts, propping himself up on his elbows to capture a nipple between his lips. Her head fell back as she whispered his name, her hands grabbing at the sheets in an attempt to steady herself.

He slid his fingers between her legs, his lips curling softly as he felt how ready she was for him. Flicking her with his thumb, he kissed her hard, not caring about the cuts on his face, or her worried glances. He wanted to give her pleasure, to feel her submit to it. To feel her ripple around his fingers until she couldn't form a coherent sentence.

And once he'd done it, she leaned forward, her lips trembling as she kissed him softly. A moment later, he heard the rip of foil, and felt her hands sliding the condom over his hardness. Soon, her palms were replaced by the warm sheath of her over him, her tightness taking his breath away.

"Does it hurt?" she whispered, when he gasped.

"So good."

She laughed and rocked her hips, making him groan louder.

"Don't leave me again," he said, his palms cupping her hips, stilling her so he could take over the rhythm. His eyes closed tight at the pleasurable pressure they were creating.

"Never."

He thrust inside. "Not even when I'm an asshole?"

She gasped. "I like it when you're an asshole."

"I don't want to be an asshole," he murmured against her lips, kissing her again because he could never get enough of her. "I want to be good enough for you."

"You can be both." She was breathless, her cheeks flaming, her eyes shining.

She began to undulate around him as the pleasure built, her head tipping back as he held her up, giving her everything she needed. From the darkness in his eyes, he could feel it, too. This never ending desire, coiling in the pit of her stomach, in her breasts, all over her body.

"Daniel…" she was breathless.

"I've got you," he said, his voice gritty. He really did. And when she soared, her body tightening around him, he found himself following moments later, pleasure wiping out the pain they'd both been feeling since they'd been apart.

He had her now and forever.

He kissed her hot and fast. "Baby, I'm never going to let you go."

EPILOGUE

SIX MONTHS LATER...

"BE CAREFUL," Eliana warned as Becca walked up the executive corridor. "He's in a terrible mood."

Becca bit down a smile, because those five words sent a little thrill through her. Dark-Eyed Daniel was back, even if only for a few hours.

"Thank you." She lifted her brows at Eliana. "I'll try to get out of there unscathed."

She rapped her fingers lightly against the door, her smile deepening as she heard a growled, "Come in." Pushing down the handle, she walked inside his office, spotting Daniel standing in front of the window that overlooked the G. Scott Carter estate. He turned around, and sure enough his mouth was twisted into a scowl, his eyes dark as they roamed over her.

"What's got you all messed up?" she asked softly. "Everybody said you've been snapping at them."

"The first run was terrible."

She stepped forward, running her tongue along her dry lips. "Of course it was. First runs usually are. That's why we take our whiskey from the heart of the run. You know that."

"It was a damn stupid idea, putting so much money into the single malt."

"No it wasn't. We've made adjustments, run it again. You should come try it now."

"What kind of adjustments?" Daniel frowned.

"Nothing major. Just come see." She held out her hand. "Before you combust."

He walked over to her, his expression still tight. She put her hands on his chest, feeling his heartbeat through his white shirt. "You need to stop catastrophizing everything," she murmured, pressing her lips to his. "You nearly made Garrett cry when you snapped at him."

Daniel squeezed his eyes shut. "Sorry."

"Tell it to him, not me."

He dropped his brow to hers, staring at her through thick eyelashes. "I will. But I'm sorry if I upset you, too."

"Don't be. I like it when you're all dark and moody."

His lip quirked. "You do?"

"Yeah. It means we're in for a fun evening." She smiled. "I like the way you take all your frustrations out on me. Have you tested your glucose levels, by the way?"

"Half an hour ago. All good."

"Then let's go try some whiskey." She laced her fingers through his, and led him out of the office. Nobody gave their linked hand a second glance, they were used to their relationship by now. The gossip had disappeared about a week after they went public. It was amazing how boring a good relationship was to people.

"You calm me, you know?" His voice was gritty.

"Yeah, I know." And he calmed her, too. Held her when

she cried. Whispered soft words when she was afraid. Made her feel safe in a way she never had before.

When they walked into the still room, it was a hive of activity. With their hands still intertwined, Becca led him to the spirit still and poured out the clear liquid, which contained the distilled water, malted barley, and sugar, heated and condensed before being turned to liquid again. Holding up the glass, she gave it to Daniel, who lifted it to his nose and inhaled deeply.

"What do you think?"

"It's better." He nodded.

The whiskey was fiery and potent, not yet mellowed by years of resting in an oak barrel. They'd chosen three different barrels for the single malt to age in, a bourbon, a virgin oak, and a burgundy cask. Each would impart a different flavor, and once mature, they'd mix the single malt to the right taste.

"It's going to be a long wait," Becca murmured, as the still men worked hard, piping the whiskey to the casks, where they'd be taken to the barrel room to mature. "In seven years I'll be in my thirties." She lifted a brow at Daniel. "You'll be almost forty."

He shook his head, amused. "Thank you for the reminder."

"Ah, you'll age well. You know you will. A few sexy greys at your temple, and maybe some deeper lines." She grinned. "And you know what they say, you're only as young as the woman you live with."

"That's the only reason I'm keeping you around."

She arched a brow. "The only reason?"

"That and your baking." He'd stopped teasing her about having a sweet tooth and started asking when she was making her next batch of treats. She'd known she'd win him over to the dark side in the end.

Even after six months together, he could still make her weak in the knees with a single glance. And though he seemed mollified, she knew he was still a little pissed about the first run. Maybe tonight she'd rile him up a little more.

Let him take it out on the punching bag, then indulge her in her favorite kind of pastime. Turning Daniel Carter's dark eyes light.

They balanced each other. She was slowly learning that she didn't have to be a people pleaser, starting with him. And he was learning that she wouldn't run screaming if he showed his weaknesses. Instead, she'd give him advice that he'd listen to and absorb.

Seven years. That's how long they had to wait for the whiskey to mature. Maybe longer, if it hadn't aged to where they wanted it to be. It was all about patience, trusting the process, and not rushing things that didn't need to be rushed.

Having faith in something you couldn't see with your naked eye.

And she had faith in them. They'd gotten through the worst night of their lives together, and each day after that had been a step toward the happiest of futures. Of course, it wasn't perfect. Lawrence and Daniel still hated each other, but at the rare time they saw each other at Nina's house, they were scathingly polite.

It helped that Lawrence, along with Nina, had signed his shares to Daniel and Nathan and didn't have to pretend to show an interest in the distillery any more. And that Melissa had apologized quietly to Becca about her behavior. There'd been no repeat of it since.

Garrett Rhys walked into the still room, blanching when he saw Daniel standing there. He glanced at Becca, and she nodded in an attempt to tell him that Daniel was calmer now.

"Garrett?" Daniel said, putting the glass of distilled whiskey down.

"Yes, Sir?"

"I apologize for biting your head off earlier. It wasn't your fault. You're doing a good job."

Garrett blinked, as though shocked. He wasn't officially working on the new single malt, preferring to be the lead distiller for their traditional lines until retirement. But he'd stepped in to help Becca while she was in the office calling for more supplies, and had inadvertently taken the heat.

"That's okay." Garrett nodded. "Whiskey does that to all of us."

Daniel smiled. "I appreciate you helping out. How are those grandchildren of yours?"

Becca listened as Garrett described a birthday party he'd been to the previous weekend. Daniel looked at the photos on Garrett's phone, his expression interested. He was learning to be human. And it warmed her heart.

———

THE NEXT MORNING – Saturday – was sunny and bright. Becca grinned to herself as she stepped out of the shower and saw Daniel sleeping. He dreamed like he did everything else in life. With passion and energy. His legs were twisted in the sheets, his arms flung out on the mattress, his hair a mess that only a shower could cure.

She'd moved into his place a month ago. It had been a wrench to leave her condominium, though she'd leased it out rather than sold it. They'd talked about finding somewhere new together, but for now Daniel's house was the more sensible option. It had space and light, plus a gorgeous yard that they spent their evenings in, watching the leaves rustle and the sun dip below the mountain peaks.

And he had one killer of a kitchen. She was constantly filling it with new appliances, loving having all the space she needed for her latest experiments.

"Hey." His eyes blinked open, the corners crinkling as he saw her standing there in a towel. "Come back to bed."

"Nope. I don't have time. I promised Van I'd get to the restaurant early to help decorate."

Daniel sat up. "The baby shower. I forgot about that."

She smiled. "No such luck, pal. On the plus side, it's only a few hours and then we can come back here."

"That makes it sound slightly more appealing."

"I also made my brothers promise that there won't be any shenanigans. No football games, no pig stampedes. You'll leave as unblemished as you arrive."

He grinned. "I'm not afraid of your brothers."

No, he wasn't. They'd welcomed him into the family with open arms, treating him like one of them. One by one, they'd told her how much they liked him, and what a good guy he was.

It made her warm inside.

"Are you going to meet me there?" she asked, unravelling the towel, and ignoring the way his eyes darkened as he watched. She slid her underwear on, then pulled a dress over her head, searching in the dresser drawers for her hair dryer.

"Yeah, there are a couple of things I need to do first."

"At the distillery?" she asked, looking over her shoulder at him.

"Nope. In town."

"Don't tell me, you're going to the salon for a back, crack, and sac wax."

Daniel grinned. "I'm not a masochist. Gray wanted some help with something at the studio. Maybe he's taking some equipment to the restaurant, I don't know."

Becca shrugged. "Okay. I'll see you at the restaurant this afternoon."

Daniel climbed out of bed and kissed her cheek. She could feel the warmth of his skin against hers. "That you will. By the way, you look beautiful."

"My hair's wet and I haven't put on any make up."

"Exactly. *Beautiful.*" He winked and walked over to the bathroom, his swagger making her smile. Damn, he was gorgeous, even in his black jersey shorts, his hair all mussed. Her mouth felt dry as she watched the muscles in his back ripple as he pushed the door open.

"I know you're looking at me," he said, still staring ahead.

"I'm just wondering if I'll look that old when I get to your age," she teased.

He laughed. "I'm looking forward to finding out."

———

FIVE PAIRS of eyes stared back at him. Five mouths unspeaking. Daniel crossed his legs and bit down a smile. It was like being at an interview, but worse, because he knew he didn't deserve this job.

But he wanted it anyway.

"I'm not asking for your permission," he said, his voice deep. "I'm just showing you respect by informing you of my intentions. Any permission has to come from Becca."

Their father stood, and gave Daniel a nod. He'd quietly accepted Daniel into the family, saying hello whenever Daniel came to his house for dinner. Aunt Gina, on the other hand, always gushed over him. It made Becca laugh when she tried every way she could to see Daniel's chest again. "It's fine by me," Becca's father said. "Now I need to find my paper. I was halfway through my crossword."

He left the room, so there were only five of them left.

Daniel and Becca's four brothers. He looked at Gray. The eldest and the spokesman for them all.

"You'll treat her well?" Gray asked."

"As if my life depended on it."

Gray nodded.

"What about kids?" Tanner asked. "Are you planning on having any?"

"Can you shut up about kids?" Gray said, shaking his head. "First of all, that's their business. And second of all, you haven't got any yourself yet."

"I will in a few weeks." Tanner crossed his arms over his chest, a smug smile breaking out on his lips. "And I'm only asking because I know Becca wants a family."

"I intend on making Becca very happy. If she wants a family, I'm good with that."

An image of her pregnant with his child flashed in his mind. She looked all swollen and radiant. He would be more than good with that. He wanted a family with her.

Wanted to be the father he never had.

Logan shrugged. "Anybody who runs head on at a herd of stampeding pigs is good with me." He gave Daniel a crooked smile. "You have my blessing, for what it's worth."

"And mine." Cam nodded. "Especially if you're serving whiskey at the wedding."

"So easily bought." Tanner shook his head.

"Says the guy who begged Daniel to save him a barrel of the single malt."

Tanner shrugged. "It's an investment." He cleared his throat. "But yeah, you have my blessing, too."

Daniel looked at Gray, the final brother. "And you?"

"You love her," Gray said. It wasn't a question, but Daniel nodded anyway.

"More than anything. And I know how much you all love her. How protective you are of her. But the most amazing thing about Becca is that she doesn't need our protection. She's strong enough to protect herself."

"I can't believe she's old enough to be in a relationship," Gray muttered. "What happened to the little kid who hated me pulling her pigtails?"

Daniel smiled at Gray's wistful expression. "She grew up into a beautiful woman."

Gray's eyes met his. Their gazes held, an unspoken understanding forming between them. Gray had taken care of his siblings all his life, and now he was having to let go.

Having to trust Daniel to be the one to take care of Becca into the future.

Until death do they part.

A slow smile pulled at Gray's lips. He stood and held his hand out, and Daniel shook it firmly, a rush of warmth speeding through his veins.

"Welcome to the family," Gray said.

"She hasn't said yes yet," Tanner pointed out.

No, she hadn't. Maybe that's why he wasn't intimidated by her brothers, or their grilling of him when he'd told them he bought an engagement ring. As he'd said to her before, so many months ago, it was her opinion that counted.

In a few hours, he'd find out exactly what that was.

THE SUN WAS SETTING behind the mountains, casting a fiery glow on their peaks. Becca was standing outside Logan's restaurant, the baby shower over, her family whispering behind her as Daniel suddenly dipped to one knee.

Her first thought was that he had fainted. But then he was smiling up at her, his eyes crinkled and warm. No sign of darkness at all.

"Becca Hartson, will you do me the honor of becoming my wife?"

Her heart started to hammer against her ribcage. She felt like she was going through an out-of-body experience, watching the two of them in the cornfield, Daniel looking at her as though she was the most beautiful thing he'd seen.

She opened her mouth to answer, but no sound came out. Instead she nodded, and Daniel's smile widened into a grin. He rose to his feet and took her hand in his, sliding the ring onto her slender finger. She swallowed hard, looking down at the square cut diamond, then back at him.

"I…"

"She's speechless. Damn." Logan was laughing. She turned to look at her brothers. "You knew?"

"I asked for their blessing. And your dad's," Daniel told her.

"Not their permission?"

He shook his head. "Only you get to give me that."

"I do." She nodded, so full of love for him. "And I do."

Daniel laughed, pulling her into his arms. She exhaled heavily, loving the way he held her. The way he kissed her softly. She could never get enough of him.

And now she didn't have to. *Ever.*

"You really want this?" she asked him, her eyes shining.

"I do." His voice was solemn, but his grin was wide.

"You know if you marry me, you marry my family."

"I understand." He glanced at them all standing there watching. Gina was dabbing her eyes with a handkerchief.

He kissed the corner of Becca's lips. "As long as I don't have to consummate the marriage with them, I'm good with that."

She laughed. "I never thought I'd meet somebody who'd take all this on."

He stroked her cheek tenderly. "I never thought I'd meet

somebody who'd make me want to take this on. To be part of something bigger. But then I met you and everything changed. *I* changed. I want this, because I want you. And maybe one day we can make our own family, too."

Becca blinked, her eyes stinging. "I want that."

"So do I." His voice was thick. He kissed her again. "I live to make you happy. Who knew I was even capable of that?"

"I knew," she told him, a half smile on her face.

He nodded. "And that's why I love you. Because you make me want to be a better person. The kind of person who deserves you."

"And that's why I love you," she whispered, looping her arms around his neck and smiling up at him. She felt radiant. More alive than ever, thanks to him. "Because you *do* deserve me."

He brushed her cheek with his lips. "And will you feel that way forever? For the rest of our lives?" he murmured.

She lifted her hand from his neck, turning her fingers to admire the ring. It was beautiful, just like him.

Joy bubbled inside her, as she inclined her head, brushing her lips against his. "I will."

AUTHOR NOTE

Thank you for taking the time to read Becca and Daniel's story. In WHEN WE TOUCH, Type 1 Diabetes has played a huge part in Daniel's life. 1.25 million people in the USA currently suffer from this autoimmune condition, including more than 200,000 under 20 years old.

I'm very grateful to my friend, Jennifer Locklear, for her time in sharing her experiences with me as a mother of a young man who lives with Type 1 Diabetes. She gave me a huge insight into the challenges he faces, and how he manages these. Any mistakes I've made in the story are mine and mine alone.

If you wish to find out more about Type 1 Diabetes, here are some links:

The American Diabetes Association - https://www.diabetes.org

AUTHOR NOTE

Diabetes UK - https://www.diabetes.org.uk

World Health Organization - https://www.who.int/health-topics/diabetes#tab=tab_1

DEAR READER

Thank you **so much** for reading Daniel and Becca's story. If you enjoyed it and you get a chance, I'd be so grateful if you can leave a review.

When We Touch is the last book in the Heartbreak Brothers series, but if you'd like a sneak peek into the Hartson family's future, you can read a bonus epilogue featuring all the Heartbreak Brothers (and sister!) you can type the following link into your browser: https://dl.bookfunnel.com/a7lc36iqqh

I'm also delighted to announce that I have a BRAND NEW series called WINTERVILLE. It's set in a small wintry town, and features all the gorgeous things you expect from me, including big families, kick-ass heroines, and gorgeous heroes you'll fall in love with.

To keep up to date on this new series, and ALL my news, join me on my exclusive mailing list, where you'll be the first to hear about new releases, sales, and other book-related news.

To sign up you can key this into your web browser:
https://www.subscribepage.com/carrieelkshbb

I can't wait to share more stories with you.

Yours,

Carrie xx

ABOUT THE AUTHOR

Carrie Elks writes contemporary romance with a sizzling edge. Her first book, *Fix You*, has been translated into eight languages and made a surprise appearance on *Big Brother* in Brazil. Luckily for her, it wasn't voted out.

Carrie lives with her husband, two lovely children and a larger-than-life black pug called Plato. When she isn't writing or reading, she can be found baking, drinking an occasional (!) glass of wine, or chatting on social media.

You can find Carrie in all these places
www.carrieelks.com
carrie.elks@mail.com

A heartwarming small town beach series, full of best friends, hot guys and happily-ever-afters.

Let Me Burn

She's Like the Wind

Sweet Little Lies

Just A Kiss

Baby I'm Yours

Pieces Of Us

Chasing The Sun

Heart And Soul

Lost In Him

THE SHAKESPEARE SISTERS SERIES

An epic series about four strong yet vulnerable sisters, and the alpha men who steal their hearts.

Summer's Lease

A Winter's Tale

Absent in the Spring

By Virtue Fall

THE LOVE IN LONDON SERIES

Three books about strong and sassy women finding love in the big city.

Coming Down

Broken Chords

Canada Square

STANDALONE

Fix You

An epic romance that spans the decades. Breathtaking and angsty and all the things in between.

If you'd like to get an email when I release a new book, please sign up here:

CARRIE ELKS' NEWSLETTER

ACKNOWLEDGMENTS

Huge thanks to Ash, Ella, Olly and Plato the dog for putting up with terrible dinners, a distinct lack of cleanliness and my generally ignoring them while the writing gets done.

I have an amazing team working with me to produce these books. Rose David editing, Proofreading by Mich, Kirsty at the Pretty Little Design Company, not to mention Marian Girling — beta reader extraordinaire. Thanks to you all for being so damn amazing!

Amanda Walker - thank you for being an amazing PA and support. You rock!

My agents, Meire and Flavia at the Bookcase agency - thank you for ALWAYS believing in me.

I owe a huge debt of gratitude to my ARC team, my Facebook group (the water cooler - come join us!), my newsletter readers and EVERYBODY who supports me on social media.

Finally, to you, the reader. THANK YOU for picking up this book. I couldn't do this without you. You rock!

9 781916 516106